SIDEQUEST

In Realms Ungoogled

Frank J. Fleming

Frank J. Fleming
Visit my website at www.FrankJFleming.com

Printed in the United States of America

This edition published 2023 by NTM Publishing

First Published 2018 by Liberty Island

ISBN-10 0-9786832-6-9
ISBN-13 978-0-9786832-6-9

Other Novels by Frank J. Fleming

Superego
Superego: Fathom
Superego: Betrayal
Hellbender
Hellbender 2: Double Hockey Sticks

For the latest by Frank J. Fleming and to sign up for his Substack (which includes writing updates, short stories, and other fun content), go to:

FrankJFleming.com

To my silly sister Sarah, the most adventurous of the Fleming kids.

And to my mother, someone who fiercely protected our childhood, something I can only now appreciate as a parent myself.

CONTENTS

CHAPTER 1

Terrance Denby had always wondered about the unmarked road.

Between the second McDonald's and the third McDonald's he passed by on his way to work, there was a short section of undeveloped, forested area where he'd briefly lose sight of the modern world. It was a short respite, and halfway through, there was a right turn one could make that seemed to lead further into the woods. The turnoff was paved and modern-looking, but there was no sign marking it. In the thousands of times Terrance had taken this route, he'd often glanced at the right turn and briefly wondered where it led. The thought was always gone in seconds, though, and it only ever seemed a mild curiosity.

But one morning, Terrance had to slam on the brakes to avoid hitting a squirrel that had decided to sit in the middle of the road staring dumbly at the car. Stopped, Terrance found himself next to the right turn. He was a little early for work that day and decided, on a rare bit of whimsy, to go ahead and see where the unknown road led.

He made the right turn, and the road soon twisted and turned deeper into the forest. The trees seemed to rise even higher above him now, the sky completely concealed by a high canopy of leaves. Just as Terrance began to think that perhaps this would be better to explore on a day when he had more time, he noticed that the trees ended shortly ahead of him and so did the road, the asphalt fading into a patch of dirt near the edge of the forest. Terrance parked his Hyundai and climbed out.

He walked beyond the trees into a vast field of green grass and scattered wildflowers covering rolling hills. In the far distance loomed mountains more massive than he had ever seen. The sun seemed larger than normal in the clear blue sky, its heat enveloping Terrance like a warm blanket. Also in the sky he could make out what might be moons...but they were bigger than that. Other worlds, perhaps.

He walked further until he reached a stream of clear water. That's when he saw it: a palace of crystal floating high above the field. From it, a few winged figures descended. They looked like women clothed all in white, with wings like butterflies, but the wings were clear, as if they, too, were made of crystal. They were faeries, Terrance realized. Three of them floated down to Terrance until they hovered a few feet above his head. "You have come," said the blonde faerie who fluttered in front of him.

Terrance stared at her for a few moments, at her perfect silken features and eyes that seemed to peer right through him. Finally, he regained enough composure to speak. "Huh?"

"You came seeking," said the red-haired beauty floating to Terrance's left, "and you have found what you sought."

Terrance adjusted his glasses. "Oh, I was just curious where that road led. I didn't mean to get in the middle of anything."

"Your journey is about to begin," said a silver-haired faerie to Terrance's right, her voice soothing yet filled with importance.

"Oh no, I can't journey right now." Terrance checked the time on his smartphone, struggling to read the screen in the bright sun. "Yeah, I'm going to be late for work. I really need to get going. Nice meeting you all, though. Interesting place you have here."

The blonde one floated closer to Terrance, staring deeply into his eyes. The silence grew awkward, and Terrance became a bit self-conscious, checking his short, dark hair with his fingers and nervously adjusting his tie. Finally, the faerie slowly drifted away, keeping her eyes locked on Terrance's, and motioned to the ground. "Learn to use this, or you will perish."

On the green grass was a sword with a silver handle in an intricately detailed black leather sheath. Terrance carefully picked it up. "Um...this looks kind of expensive; are you sure...?" He looked up to see that the faeries were already returning to their palace. "Hey! What exactly is this about?" he called out. There was no response as the faeries disappeared into the floating crystal structure above him. Terrance looked back to the sword on the ground. He wasn't sure about taking it, but it felt wrong to leave it lying in the middle of the field. And he really had to be getting to work. So he picked up his new weapon and headed back to the car, wondering if there was a law against walking around with a sword in public.

* * *

"You going on a quest?" Lance asked, spying the sword leaning against the wall of Terrance's cubicle while smiling with his usual smarm that apparently some people found charming.

Terrance stopped his work on debugging a problem with a login page. "No, I just had a weird morning. I found a hidden...um...clearing, I guess, with faeries in it. And—"

"I don't think you're supposed to use that word."

Terrance raised an eyebrow. "Huh? Oh, no, I mean like women with butterfly wings."

"Little tiny women?"

"No, they were full-sized."

Lance nodded. "Were they attractive?"

"Well…they were kind of otherworldly. That wasn't really my focus."

Lance leaned in close. "Just answer the question."

"Yeah, they were pretty attractive. Anyway, the point is they came out of a floating crystal palace and gave me a sword and basically said, 'It's dangerous to go alone! Take this.'"

Lance looked at the sword again. "Did you have to pay for it?"

"No, they just tossed it on the ground in front of me and flew off. Have you ever heard of anything like that?"

Lance thought for a moment. "Nope. Have you tried Googling it?"

"No, not yet." Terrance picked up the sword by its sheath and felt the weight of it in his hands. "So, weird morning."

"Are we allowed to bring swords into the office?"

"I don't know." Terrance set the sword down. "Maybe I should have left it in the car."

"So do you think it's a magic sword? Like a magic faerie sword?"

Terrance threw up his hands. "Like I said: no idea."

"Think you're going to slay something with it?"

Terrance shook his head. "I wouldn't know what to slay."

"You ever slay anything before?"

"Just flies, with a flyswatter."

Lance looked more closely at the sword. "What kind of sword is it?"

Terrance shrugged. "I don't know. A *sword* sword. A long sword maybe."

Lance sipped his coffee. "A katana would be cooler."

"Well, obviously."

Karen, a gorgeous brunette from HR, stepped into the cubicle, holding a notepad. She was once again in a stylish and immaculate suit that made Terrance feel self-conscious in a way similar to how the faeries did. "Hey, guys, we have another empowerment ceremony coming up, with a potluck afterward. What can I put you two down for?"

"I don't know how to cook anything," Terrance said. "Can I just bring chips?"

"Yeah, sure." She wrote on her notepad. "And, hey, what's with the sword?"

"It's a magic faerie sword," Lance said. "Terrance is going on a quest."

She looked at the sword and then at Terrance. "That's kind of weird."

"I'm not going on a quest. The faeries just—"

"You probably shouldn't have a sword in the office."

Lance nodded. "That's what I told him."

Karen turned to Lance. "So what can you bring?"

"What do you need?"

"We could really use more main dishes, you know...not just chips."

"I make this really good chicken fried rice. You are going to love it."

"That sounds great." Karen smiled at him and wrote on her notepad. "See you later, and have fun questing, Terrance."

"I'm not questing!" Terrance shouted at her as she walked off. He looked at Lance, who was smiling. "You getting anywhere with her?" Terrance had a few times tried to make a pass at her, but she never even seemed to notice.

"The question, my boy, is whether she's getting anywhere with me."

A dark figure in a blue cloak approached them. It had black skin with a rocky texture, and slightly curled horns protruded from its skull. Its sharp teeth seemed almost too big for its mouth, and their edges were stained with blood. Yellow, snake-like eyes fixed on Terrance. "The login page."

"I'm...I'm working on it," Terrance said.

The demonic Darlor looked at the sword still leaning against Terrance's cubicle wall. "What is that?"

"It's a weird story..."

"I don't want it in the office."

"Oh, okay. Well, when I finish the fix on the login page—"

"Get rid of it now," Darlor hissed, and then he turned and left.

Terrance stood up from his chair and picked up the sword. He watched for a moment as Darlor disappeared back into his windowless office. "You ever notice how Darlor isn't human?" he asked Lance.

Lance thought for a moment. "He doesn't wear a tie."

"Excuse me?"

"Dress code is that we have to wear a tie, but the dress code only applies to people and Darlor never wears a tie. So it makes sense he's not human."

Terrance nodded, the sword feeling heavy in his hands. "He's like a demon or something."

Lance thought again. "Yeah, I guess that's what you could call him." He looked a moment at Terrance. "You have a point?"

Terrance stared out the office window down the aisle from his cubicle. A shadow passed over the world outside as something large flew in front of the sun. He felt a general sense of unease, but he couldn't figure out what it was about. Everything was normal. "No. No point."

CHAPTER 2

"The login is fixed and changes are checked in."

Pendergrass looked up from his computer at Terrance and nodded. He was head of the software division, but was probably much more comfortable coding than managing. "Good. I need you to start working on those bugs in the main algorithm."

Terrance frowned. "Not *that* stuff. It's like it was written before anyone invented coding standards."

Pendergrass brushed his thick mustache with his fingertips. "Yeah, I know. Usually I'd handle any problems with it, but I don't have time and we really need someone else familiar with that algorithm."

"Okay. I'll get on it. I just don't get how code works for decades and then suddenly breaks down." Terrance headed back to his cubicle—now missing the mysterious sword, which he had put in his car—and loaded up the main algorithm code. It was nearly inscrutable. It wasn't properly indented, the variable names were random nonsense like "rdlfdth" and "tprsnyrsl," and it was pretty much devoid of any comments clarifying the logic. Terrance wasn't sure who wrote it, but he hoped the person was no longer with the company.

After a long while of making no sense of anything, he finally spotted a commented line. It sat by itself, separated from the rest of the code by a couple of blank lines. It read: *It consumes us from the inside, eating our blood and guts until all that is left is a shell that looks like a man.*

Terrance stared at the screen for a few moments. Then he appended "unhelpful" to the end of the comment and signed it with his initials.

He jumped as something touched his shoulder.

"Calm down, buddy," Lance said. "We're going to Landing after work."

"Isn't that place kind of trendy?"

Lance laughed. "You say that like it's a bad thing."

"I just don't fit in with trendy."

"Oh, there's nothing to worry about; you're awkward everywhere."

Terrance shifted in his seat. "Well, tonight I kind of wanted to—"

"You don't have any plans. You're coming. And guess what: a very lovely lady is going to be waiting for you there."

"You're setting me up?"

Lance smiled. "Yes I am. You can thank me later. Or now. I'm not in a big rush."

"Last time you set me up"—Terrance thought about the woman, both beautiful and repulsive at the same time—"I think she was a succubus."

"And what's that?"

"She wanted to sleep with me to eat my soul."

"All I heard is she wanted to sleep with you," Lance said. "Are souls even a real thing?"

"I don't know, but she obviously wanted to do something unpleasant and unhealthy to me. Gave me the creeps. Plus, all she wanted to talk about was this HBO show, *Girls*. Never seen it."

"Well, this one is a winner, and know how I know? See, she's Karen's friend, and Karen took a lot of convincing—a *lot*—to let me set you up with her. So, once again, remember to thank me at some point."

"What's Karen's problem with me?"

Lance shrugged. "She doesn't have a problem with you. She just thinks you're kinda weird. Remember this morning how you were going on and on about your faerie sword?"

"I wasn't going on and on about it! And it's in my car now, so it won't be brought up again."

"Good. Don't bring it in the bar."

Karen walked up to them and asked Lance, "Did you tell him not to be weird?"

"I'm not going to be weird," Terrance insisted.

"You better not. Shannon is a very busy woman—too busy to meet people—so I said I'd set her up with someone. And...you're the only someone I came up with so far."

Terrance rolled his eyes. "Well, poor Shannon."

"Maybe she'll like you; I don't know," Karen said. "I'm just afraid she'll see you and think I didn't even try. I don't expect you to be great; just be passable. So no, 'Hey, look at this sword the faeries gave me!'"

"I was not the one bringing it up!"

Karen rolled her eyes. "I'm already regretting this."

"Karen, I'll do my best to make sure your friend doesn't hate you from how horrible I am."

"See, Terrance is a team player," Lance said. "He's only a little weird. Some women like guys who are quirky."

Terrance sighed. "Why don't you guys discuss how weird I am elsewhere and let me get back to my code?"

"Fine. Do your nerd stuff," Karen said, and left.

"So tonight, bring your A game," Lance said to Terrance. "And maybe you should watch *Girls*. A lot of people like that show."

"I'm not watching *Girls*. I don't care if it will make succubi like me."

As Lance walked away, Terrance took one last look over the code and noticed a short, useless statement at the bottom:

world = death;

Where did those variables even come from? He thought about deleting the line, but decided the safest thing was to just leave it.

* * *

"Here, take your glasses off. They make you look like a dork." Lance pulled Terrance's glasses off his face and put them in his front pocket.

"They're perfectly fine glasses." Not stylish or anything, but unobtrusive.

"Hey, I work in marketing for a company that does inventory management," Lance said. "It's my job to make boring things look interesting."

Terrance had checked himself in the mirror at the restroom at work before heading over. His hair had been a little messy, and he'd done what he could with water and his hand. It wasn't like Lance's perfect hair. It seemed like Lance used some sort of product in it and maybe had highlights or something. Terrance was just happy when he remembered to get a haircut before things got too disorderly.

They went inside Landing. For a moment, Terrance thought there was a power outage and the place was using emergency lighting. "I really prefer the bar near our apartments. I can barely see in here."

"That will work to your advantage," Lance said. "You'll have a chance to charm her with your personality before your face scares her off."

"Oh. Ha. I guess your advantage would be a noisy bar where—"

"Finish that quip later." Lance strode toward a female figure that Terrance soon made out to be Karen. The bar was large and was filled with a few dozen people. Terrance was curious about who he was going to be set up with, and scanned the crowd for hopeful prospects—but again had trouble seeing much.

Then he thought he saw something move on the ceiling.

"Hey, space cadet," Karen said. "I'd like you to meet Shannon."

Out of the darkness of the bar stepped an ominous figure. It had full armor of black steel, a black sword at its hip, and a helmet that looked like the head of a demon. But behind the helmet's wide-open mouth was a really cute face. "Hey, you must be Terrance," Shannon said.

Terrance gripped the offered gauntlet and shook her hand. He was a little intimidated by the sight of her, but tried to keep his focus on the sweet, smiling face. "Nice...um...getup you have going there."

She blushed a little. "I didn't have time to change out of my work clothes."

"Neither did I." He pointed to his white dress shirt and blue tie.

"You could probably take the tie off now."

"Yeah"—he loosened the tie and pulled it over his head—"and you could probably take the helmet off."

"Fair enough, but you keep a watch out and make sure no one sneaks up behind me and bonks me on the head." She pulled off the helmet and then undid her ponytail, shaking loose her blonde hair. Getting a really good look at her face, Terrance felt the need to eventually thank Lance.

"So here we are holding our tie and helmet. We feel better?" he asked.

"No, it's kind of inconvenient."

Terrance glanced around and realized he was standing alone with Shannon. "So they just left us?"

"I guess so. Um...so what do we do now? I've never been set up before. I guess we kind of talk and see if we're"—she motioned her hands together—"compatible."

"It's my understanding that's how it works. Want to go sit at the bar?" He held up his tie. "We can set our stuff down there."

"Good idea. We'll get some of that social lubricant." She made a drinking motion.

They went over to the bar and took two stools. Shannon put her demon helmet on the countertop and whispered to herself, "Don't forget it. Don't forget it."

"So...um...what is it that you do?"

"Oh, I'm a Sister of Torment. We're a group of women who serve the Darkness. That's sort of a...well, it's tough to explain."

"So you like the job?"

"Yeah, it's pretty neat. I'm like a...police officer slash soldier slash executioner."

Terrance managed a smile, though he was a bit uneasy. "So you go around lopping off the heads of bad people?"

"Well, I don't know if they're bad; I don't like to judge. But, you know, we keep an order to things. It's an important job—hard work but fulfilling. And it's a fun group I work with."

"Good...good. It's good to like the people you work with. Anything about the job you don't like?"

She thought for a moment. "Well, being fully dedicated to the Darkness, we have to remain virgins."

Terrance shifted uncomfortably in his seat. "Oh...that's..."

Shannon burst out laughing. "I'm just kidding. Sorry, I joke when I'm nervous."

"I'm making you nervous?"

"Oh no...no...you're fine. So what do you do, Ter? People call you 'Ter'?"

"Yeah, sometimes."

"How about 'Ance'? Can I call you 'Ance'?"

"I won't physically stop you. Anyway, I'm a computer programmer. I work on web applications—sort of the logic in web pages so that they...do stuff."

"So like when I buy something on a website, you make sure it properly handles the credit card and all that?"

"Yeah, that's basically it. I do some of the web pages, but I also work on the back-end stuff."

"That sounds dirty."

Terrance blushed. "I just mean the logic away from the web pages—back on servers somewhere."

"So you're pretty smart."

"Oh yeah, a genius. If it weren't for Einsteins like me, you'd click buttons on web pages and nothing would happen."

"So what kind of web applications do you do?"

Terrance couldn't tell if she was being polite or was actually interested. "Oh...nothing too interesting. It's for inventory management. Still, my company demands that we dedicate ourselves to the job and remain virgins as well."

"Doesn't that just happen naturally from being a computer nerd?"

"Ouch."

She laughed again. "Burn! I got you! You don't mind if I kid you, Ance?"

"No. That was a good one." She had an infectious laugh, and he loved her smile. His eyes moved briefly from her face, though, to notice a red stain on her arm. "You got a little something there."

She looked at the armor. "Oh. Whoops. Well, this thing cleans easy. So, do you like your job?"

"Yeah. I like tracking down problems to fix them. Debugging is a bit like being a detective."

"Like Batman."

He chuckled. "Yeah, exactly. Just like Batman. In fact, that's probably an easier way to describe my job in the future: 'I'm basically Batman.'"

"And you work with Karen?"

"She's in human resources, so I don't really work directly with her."

Shannon leaned in close to Terrance. Her hair smelled of sour apple. She whispered, "Good. She's kind of a bitch."

"Then you should lop her head off," Terrance whispered back.

Shannon laughed. "If I started cutting off people's heads for that, I'd wear out my axe."

Terrance chuckled, and then his smile slowly faded. "You...have an axe for that?"

"What can I get you?" the bartender interrupted.

Terrance turned to Shannon "What would you like, milady?"

"I will have a cosmopolitan."

"And I will have a Guinness," Terrance said.

"Ooh, manly drink," Shannon said as the bartender went to get their order.

Terrance nodded. "I usually wait until a few dates in and I'm more comfortable with a woman before I drink appletinis in front of her."

"I can pay for my own drinks, by the way. I'm a liberated woman."

Terrance nodded. "I can see that, but it's still my treat."

"Well, sexism is never going to end as long as it equals free booze."

They laughed and sat silently staring at each other for a few moments. "I think we need to ask each other more questions," Shannon said. "Again, I'm not really familiar with how this works."

"Well...uh..." Terrance thought for a second, but only one thing popped into his head. "Do you watch *Girls*?"

"No, I don't have much time for TV and don't watch much of the current stuff. Lately, though, I've been watching *Farscape* on Netflix."

"Really?"

"You've heard of it?"

Terrance nodded. "Yeah, I watched it on the SciFi channel back when they still spelled 'sci-fi' correctly. It's an underappreciated show."

"Well, don't spoil it. I'm only in the second season. With all the Jim Henson muppet aliens, I keep hoping the Pigs in Space make a cameo."

"They're actually part of a big arc in the fourth season."

Shannon went wide-eyed. "Really?"

Terrance laughed. "No."

"Oh! Now you're teasing me." She hit him seemingly lightly on the chest, but it almost knocked him off his stool. "Dangerous thing."

"Yeah, I'll be careful." He resisted the urge to rub where she'd hit him. He tried to think of another question to ask, and he kept thinking of more queries about her job...though they seemed to have moved past that topic.

The bartender delivered their drinks, and Terrance quickly took a swig of his. Shannon sipped her cocktail demurely. "So what do you do for fun, Ance?"

"Well..." He tried to think of something more interesting to say than "video games," but was at the moment failing.

"Uh-oh. You're a serial killer, and you're trying to think of a cover story!"

"And you'd think I'd have a few other interests than that, but serial killing uses up pretty much all of my free time. No, I play video games; I was just trying to think of a better answer than that."

Shannon glared at him. "A *male* in his twenties who plays *video games*?!" She turned to look around, shouting weakly, "Help! I'm with a freak!"

"So you play any video games, Nin, or do you just spend your time working on your stand-up?"

"'Nin'? Oh, I see what you did there. Well, I once tried some Call of Duty online, but I got sick of twelve-year-olds calling me a fag."

"And they're just so good at that game. You can't beat the homophobic twelve-year-olds. So, what do you do for fun? Also a serial killer?"

"No, that would be too much like my day job. I...well, I don't know if it counts as doing something, but I have a cat. Her name is Amidala."

"You named her from the *Star Wars* prequels?"

Her eyes brightened. "Yeah! I loved those! And that Jar Jar Binks was hilarious. I really don't know why they didn't use him more in episodes two and three."

Terrance sat up from his stool. "Oh, geez, look at the time. I have to get going."

Shannon laughed. "I'm not fooling you anymore, am I? You're onto me. I just liked the sound of the name; those movies were a travesty."

He sat back down. "I can put up with so much from a pretty woman, but not hating Jar Jar Binks is a bridge too far."

"Oh, you think I'm pretty." She batted her eyes.

"You really pull off that dark armor."

"Thanks. I feel a little self-conscious hanging around in it." No one seemed to be paying attention to her, though; it was only Terrance who felt it was a bit odd. Which seemed a good enough reason not to worry about it.

* * *

They chatted for hours about movies and old TV shows and other light topics. Terrance could tell he was a bit smitten with her; she wasn't only gorgeous, she was also witty and sweet. It was just that she apparently had a job where...

He shook the thought from his head. He figured he was making a big deal out of nothing, and he didn't want to ruin this.

Shannon looked around. "So Karen and Lance totally ditched us."

"It appears that way."

"I bet they're somewhere right now doing naked things."

"If they are, Lance will tell me in the morning."

"That reminds me." Shannon pulled out her cellphone from a leather pouch on her armor and checked the time. "Oh, I need to get going. I have to get up early tomorrow for the ole jobby job."

"Oh...well...it was really nice talking to you. Would you like to do this again? I haven't run out of all my opinions on popular science fiction."

She smiled. "Sure."

Score! "How about this weekend?"

"I'm busy all this weekend. My job is awful; I'm sorry. Um...I have time tomorrow night, if that wouldn't be too much of me too soon."

"Yeah, we can get dinner somewhere and maybe figure things out from there."

"Ooh. Adventurous. I like it. Just give me time to change." She motioned to her armor.

"Yeah, it will be nice to get you out of that." He blushed. "That came off a little too forward."

Shannon giggled. "I know what all the guys think: Does she actually fill that breastplate?" She thumped her metal chest. "Hey, if it's okay, I'm going to tell Karen you took me to your place and ravaged me."

Terrance nodded. "It's a believable story."

She stood up. "It was really nice meeting you. I was a little nervous about this—I just assumed Karen would set me up with a real douche."

"Glad to defy expectations, then." He took one last long look at her face. She was gorgeous; he could hardly believe his luck.

Out of the corner of his eye, he saw something move. He looked up at the ceiling, and there was something there staring back at him. He couldn't make it out except for the yellow eyes locked onto him.

"What is it?" Shannon turned and looked behind her.

"There's something on the ceiling staring at me," Terrance said, not breaking eye contact with it.

Shannon glanced at the creature. "Yeah, those things will do that." She looked back at him. "I have to get going. I have your phone number, so we'll meet up tomorrow."

He broke eye contact with the creature. "Yeah, looking forward to it."

Terrance watched as the armored figure of Shannon walked off, then he looked again at the dark creature on the ceiling. None of it was unusual, so why was he so bothered by it?

CHAPTER 3

Terrance couldn't believe his luck. Shannon was so beautiful and fun, and he actually had seemed to hit it off with her. So why was something in the back of his brain nagging at him?

He grabbed some Taco Bell on the way back to his apartment, and settled on his couch. He was about to turn on the TV to check what he had on his DVR when he saw the sword leaning against a wall near his small kitchen. He walked over and picked it up by the sheath. Things had been weird ever since he'd been given the sword that morning. Or they weren't weird so much as he was just agitated by things. Things that had never bothered him before.

For instance, he had been aware of the Sisters of Torment and had seen that type of people around, and what they did had never been an issue for him. But now he thought about it and something about them seemed…evil?

He saw movement by the window. Startled, he dropped the sword. It hit the fake hardwood floor with a loud clatter. As always with such a noise, it was answered by a couple of thumps from below. He was in a ground-floor apartment, so he never did know exactly what it was below him that didn't like noise. It was another odd thing that Terrance had been used to, but that was now suddenly disturbing him.

There was something at the window staring back at him. A small thing. He picked up the sword and crept closer until he had a good view of it. It had beady, black soulless eyes that seemed to conceal unfathomable secrets. And a fluffy tail.

A squirrel.

"Are you the squirrel I nearly ran over this morning?" Terrance asked. "You tricked me into going into that place, and now something is wrong with me. What's going on here?"

The squirrel watched him a few moments longer, and then jumped down from the window and scurried off.

"We're enemies, you and I! Next time I'll run you down!" Terrance shouted, causing the thing below him to make more thumps through the floor. He stared out the window at the darkness for a few moments. There was the light of the 7-Eleven nearby, but further in the distance was the glow of a volcano that was constantly spewing lava. He had always seen large things flying near it. This had never been of any interest to him, but now the thought came to mind that it was a place of great foreboding.

He shook the ideas from his head and placed the sword in the coat closet. He wanted to eat his Taco Bell before it got cold, because reheating it in the microwave always made the sour cream taste funny.

* * *

The next morning, Terrance was running too far behind schedule to even glance at the path leading into the wooded area on his way to work. He got to the office, rode the elevator to the tenth floor, settled into his cubicle, and prepared for a normal day...except, of course, for his date that night.

Lance soon appeared. "So how did things go with you and Shannon?"

Terrance smiled. "I'll be seeing her again tonight."

Lance hit him in the shoulder. "Good job! I knew she'd be a fit for you, because I had heard Karen describe her as 'kind of a dork.'"

"Yeah...it's great you'd hear that and think immediately of me."

"By the way, sorry to ditch you, but I decided Karen and I had other business we needed to attend to...if you know what I mean."

"You went for ice cream?"

"Whipped cream was involved."

Terrance looked back to his computer. "I'm going to exit the conversation now. But thanks for setting me up with Shannon. She's...great." The little thought at the back of his head started needling him again. "What do you know about her job, though?"

"Nothing. You're doing something wrong if you're tangling with those people."

"It's just...eh, never mind."

Karen walked over to them. "Hey, Terrance, did gnomes give you an axe this morning?"

"No, no mystical creatures gave me weaponry today, but thanks for asking."

"Oh, and I got an email from Shannon. Subject line, 'Ance in my pants.' She says that last night she went to your place and you showed her 'ecstasy hitherto unknown.'"

Terrance thought a moment. "Really? She used the word 'hitherto'?"

"Good job, Ter," Lance said.

"She also said she's seeing you again tonight. I have trouble believing either thing."

"Karen, I'm unbelievably awesome, and one day you're going to have to accept that fact."

"And in your awesomeness, did you bring the chips for the potluck?"

"Oh...I forgot that." Terrance looked at Karen with pleading eyes. "Don't tell Shannon about this. She won't want to date some chip-forgetting loser."

Karen sighed. "I'm guessing Shannon finds you hilarious. Later." She turned to Lance and smiled before walking off.

"So you like her?" Terrance asked.

"What's not to like?"

A meeting reminder appeared on Terrance's computer screen. "The empowerment ceremony is starting soon." Terrance shuddered; he didn't know why. He just hated meetings.

* * *

Terrance headed to the usual place for the ceremony: the subbasement of the office building. It was a large cavern lit by flickering torch light that cast moving shadows off everyone in attendance—mainly bored coworkers standing around. Terrance found a spot next to Lance. "What's this all about again?"

Lance shrugged. "Usual motivation nonsense. Plus I think it's to appease what lies beneath."

Ahead of them was a raised area made of stone on which a few robed figures stood, their faces hidden behind hoods. They stood around a large pit out of which echoed inhuman sounds.

"And what lives in that pit?" Terrance asked.

"I'm not sure it has a name. You've been through one of these before."

"Yeah...I guess I never really paid attention."

"Who does?" Lance pulled out his smartphone.

Terrance could hear a woman screaming. Up on the stage, more hooded figures led out a petite young woman clothed in white. She tried to fight against her captors, screaming, "Don't do this! Let me go!" Tears streamed down her cheeks.

"Um...that woman seems in trouble," Terrance said to Lance.

Lance was busy checking Twitter on his phone. "Yeah, not everyone is into these things."

The woman looked at the crowd below the stage. "Someone help me! Please! Someone stop this!"

Terrance did hope someone would help her, but he looked around the crowd and it was a mix of people watching dispassionately and bored people who weren't even paying attention. As the woman looked in his general direction with doe-like, pleading eyes, Terrance shuddered as a realization came to him: he was someone.

"Um...hey..." Terrance said weakly as he made his way to the stage. "Hey, guys!"

He got the attention of one of the hooded figures, who looked down at Terrance with a shadowed face and hissed.

The woman spotted him, staring at him with desperate eyes through her matted brown hair. "Stop them!" Her hands were bound, and the hooded figures kept pushing her toward the pit.

"Um...maybe we should..." Terrance started to say, but noticed none of the hooded figures were paying attention to him. "Hey!" Impulsively, Terrance climbed onstage. He immediately regretted it, as he could hear grumblings from the previously bored attendees who were now paying attention to him. He thought about climbing back down, but he had already gone this far. "I don't think..." he said softly, but fought the embarrassment and then said louder, "Something is wrong here!"

Now one of the hooded figures paid attention and drew a sword, pointing it at Terrance. "You're interfering!"

"Yeah, it's just..."

Long, dark tentacles arose from the pit as the inhuman cries grew louder, their deep rumblings vibrating the whole cavern. A mouth emerged—no face, just a mouth large enough to swallow a human whole and filled with long, sharp, yellow teeth.

"I didn't mean to get in the middle of this"—Terrance slowly inched toward the woman—"but it just seems—"

The woman burst from her captors and threw herself at the hooded figure holding a sword. They tumbled to the floor, but soon the woman was standing again, now holding the sword. She no longer seemed small and pathetic, but she appeared so bursting with strength that Terrance took a step back at the sight of her. Another of the hooded figures charged her, and she ran the sword through him. The unnamed beast roared and reached a tentacle toward her, but she chucked the sword into its open mouth. It screamed so loudly that the place shook as if there were an earthquake, and Terrance lost his footing and fell off the stage.

Dazed, he saw the woman in white pushing her way through the crowd toward the cavern's exit, taking one last glance at him with her large, fierce eyes—he found himself both frightened by and drawn to them. And then she was gone.

Terrance noticed a number of people staring at him, and standing directly above him was Lance, who looked at him quizzically. "Well, that was embarrassing."

CHAPTER 4

Darlor's office lacked a desk or windows. It simply had a throne upon which Darlor sat, staring down at Terrance with red eyes while Terrance was situated in an uncomfortable chair with a cloth seat. Next to Darlor's throne was a small table that held a laptop and a mug with the company logo on it.

"Explain yourself!" Darlor hissed, his sharp white teeth stained with flecks of crimson.

Terrance sunk in his chair, his eyes not meeting Darlor's and going to the rough carpet at his feet. "Um...I just thought something seemed off with what was going on, so I was just checking on things and..." He shrugged. "Whoops."

"The unnamed thing that resides beneath is enraged. Do you understand what that means for us?"

"Uh...not really."

"Then know this at least: You should not have interfered."

"I get that now. Um...so who was that woman?" He regretted the question the moment it left his mouth.

Darlor rose from his throne. "That is not the issue!"

"Yeah...sorry. I'm...having an off day, I guess."

"People were offended by your actions."

"I didn't mean to offend anyone."

"There could be legal repercussions for the company."

"Oh...I didn't know that. I'm really sorry." But really sorry for what? Terrance knew he was supposed to have done something wrong; it just didn't feel wrong to try and help that woman.

Darlor slowly sat back down, his red eyes probing Terrance's face. "You are a good programmer, Mr. Denby."

"Thank you, sir."

"You've done well here, and I'd like to think this was a one-time lapse of judgment."

"I'm sure it was. I don't know what came over me. I'll...be more considerate in the future." Terrance thought about what he was saying. He was promising to stand idly by while he saw horrible things going on. And he was promising it to a demon. *All of this is normal*, he tried to tell himself. *You're the only one freaking out.*

Other than that screaming woman, he thought in response.

"I'll be keeping an eye on you," Darlor said. "Any further incidents like this will not be tolerated. Are we clear?"

"Yes, sir."

"Then we are done here for now. I would like for you to write a letter of apology to the unnamed thing that resides below."

"I'll do that right away." He just wasn't sure how to address it.

Terrance left Darlor's office. As he headed back to his cube, he did his best to ignore the fact that most of his coworkers were staring at him. He tried to suppress the embarrassment, but he found that beyond the embarrassment was anger.

Get your head together, Ter. He sat down in his cubicle. He planned to write the apology letter quickly and then get lost in a programming assignment. No moral dilemmas there.

Then he noticed his empty coffee mug. He wasn't going to figure out how best to apologize to the unnamed terror beneath them without coffee.

Terrance headed to the break room, trying once again not to make eye contact with anyone he passed. Inside, Karen was setting up the potluck.

"No!" she shouted. "First you didn't bring the chips you promised and then you ruined the empowerment ceremony. You don't get to be a part of the potluck."

"Sorry. I'm just...getting coffee."

"What is wrong with you anyway? Do you understand how angering the thing below can affect bonuses?"

A small crowd had gathered to watch Terrance be chastised. "I just thought something was wrong there."

"Really?" Karen shouted. "Everyone else seemed to think everything was fine, but *you* thought there was something wrong?"

"It just that woman was screaming and—"

"What does that have to do with anything?"

"Well...doesn't it just seem a little wrong for a screaming woman to be fed to a horrible creature?" Terrance looked around the crowd for support. They just stared at him with confusion.

"Wrong how?" Karen demanded.

"I..." Terrance realized how pointless this was. "Never mind. I'm going to go write the unnamed creature a letter of apology, so hopefully everyone can just forget this whole thing."

He poured himself some coffee, careful to leave a little bit so he didn't feel the need to make another pot, and quickly left the break room. When he got back to his cubicle, his phone beeped that he had a text from Shannon. "Call me after you're done being Batman. I'm looking forward to a bold, exciting evening of excitement." Terrance smiled. Hopefully it wouldn't be a completely awful day.

He typed a reply. "It will be the most memorable night of your life, Catwoman. Thousands of years from now, people will sings songs about it. Probably dinner and a movie or something."

"You okay?" Lance asked, appearing behind Terrance.

"You ever work?"

"Checking on the well-being of coworkers is part of work. So what happened with you?"

Terrance took a deep breath. "Everything just seems...wrong."

"Haven't you felt that way ever since *Firefly* was cancelled?"

"I'm serious. I'm noticing things now. Things that never bothered me before and now...I dunno."

Lance thoughtfully considered Terrance's words for a moment. "Sounds like you need to get laid."

"Thanks, Lance. That's helpful advice."

"And I have more. Make sure when you see Shannon again tonight you don't bring up how you freaked out like a mental case today."

"I did not 'freak out like a mental case.' I just...you know what? I'm past it. And I'm definitely not bringing it up again."

"Cool. I'm sure you'll bring your game tonight. Probably a video game, but maybe that will work with her." Lance patted Terrance on the back and left.

Terrance took a sip of coffee and opened a new Word document to begin his letter of apology. He didn't remember seeing eyes on the creature he was apologizing to, though, and he wondered if it could even read a letter.

* * *

Terrance sat in the lobby of Toshiro's steakhouse, a quiet place just outside the main restaurant area, and glanced at his watch. A thought briefly went through his head that Karen had told Shannon what had happened today and now she wasn't going to show up.

Someone grabbed him from behind and quickly pulled him to his feet. "Gotcha, sucker!"

He was released and turned to see Shannon smiling at him. She wore jeans and a cute red top, which would seem to make quite a difference in mood from the dark armor, but her bright face dominated whatever she wore. "Yeah, you got me. You win...whatever game it is we're playing."

"I'm working on my stealth; I'm hoping to eventually get a promotion." She looked Terrance over. He wore what he thought was his best polo shirt to try to make a good impression, but it seemed woefully inadequate. He also had put gel in his hair and now felt really self-conscious about it. "Glasses? I don't remember you having glasses before." Shannon narrowed her eyes. "I don't date nerds."

"Glasses don't mean you're a nerd," Terrance responded. "You can be stupid and have bad vision."

Shannon nodded. "I see you wore a watch," she said. "A device strapped to you that performs only one function; how quaint. So why wear it? Are you too lazy to pull your phone out of your pocket to check the time?"

"It's my lucky watch."

"Needing luck, you think?" She narrowed her eyes again. "Or hoping to 'get lucky'? This is just a first date, you know. What sort of girl do you think I am?"

"Have I offended you with my watch-wearing?"

"No, just keeping my eye on you." She smiled. "Nice watch, by the way. Looks gold."

Terrance nodded. "That's what it's supposed to look like." He noticed a streak of red in Shannon's blonde hair. "I like your highlights."

Shannon looked surprised. "My what?" She touched her hair. "Oh! Come on!" She frowned. "Guess who forgot her helmet at the bar last night." She pointed two thumbs at herself. "This gal!"

"So that's..."

"Yeah, and worst of all, it's faerie blood; I have no idea what it will do to my hair."

"You killed faeries?"

"Let's drop this. We're just going to have to pretend it's not there"—she pointed to the stain in her hair—"for this night to work." Her face was quite red.

Terrance felt a heady mix of emotions. Shock and horror were part of it, and he was filled with questions about what she knew about faeries. But the most prominent emotion was sympathy, as Shannon looked hugely embarrassed. He'd already had a hard enough day, so Terrance decided to focus on being charming, because Shannon was sweet and funny and her occupation seemed of little concern to anyone else.

"You look great, by the way. Not that the armor was bad, but I like you this way."

She smiled, and they headed into the restaurant, which smelled of cooked steak and spices, and was filled with the rhythmic sound of chopping. Chefs stood at various large, flat grills, putting on a show as they prepared the food. The room was dimly lit, and Terrance found himself looking toward the ceiling to see if anything was there, which he'd never felt the need to do before. There was nothing there, and the maître d' led them to their seats at the end of a table where three other couples were already seated. Shannon clapped her hands. "This is going to be fun! I've never been to one of these before. All the places I've eaten, the cooks hide in back so they don't get bothered by the likes of us."

"Well, this time we'll get to scrutinize and criticize everything he does." Terrance picked up a menu. "And we will feast like samurai." He was hoping she'd like it; it was hard to be adventurous with restaurants.

"I'm going to get sake. Want to share?" Shannon asked. "It seems like a good idea to turn rice into liquor. And, it's fun to say. Sake! Sake!"

"Order whatever you like." Terrance folded his arms and sat up straight. "I make big programmer money."

"You're quite impressive. So did you have a good day of detective work?"

Terrance's smile faded. "Little off today. Got yelled at by the boss."

"What happened?"

He briefly thought of the horrible creature and the woman screaming for help. "Nothing worth bringing up again."

"So everything is fine?"

Terrance once again took in his pretty date. "Everything is great."

The waiter came to take their order. Being that it was a Japanese steak house, they decided to get the steak.

"So, nice email you sent Karen," Terrance said, hoping to head off any further inquiries about his day.

She blushed. "When I thought of the subject line, I couldn't help it. I like puns."

"They are the highest form of humor…right after cream pies to the face. So how do you know Karen?"

"We used to be lovers."

Terrance stared at her for a moment. Finally, she smiled. "Don't know if I'm joking or not, do you?"

"You like throwing people off, huh?"

"I keep an air of mystery about myself." She turned away demurely, and Terrance caught another glimpse of the faerie blood in her hair.

He wanted to ask more questions about the faeries and why people would be killing them, but that would bring attention to her hair again. *Just forget it for now*, he told himself. *Don't screw this up.*

The chef working at their table put a brown patty on each of their plates. "What's this?" Shannon demanded of Terrance.

"It's a chicken liver patty."

Shannon glared at the chef. "And what possibly made him think I'd want something like that?"

"It comes with every meal. You might as well try it." Terrance took a bite of his.

Shannon took a careful bite. "It tastes…like a patty made from the liver of chickens. Just as I feared."

"Well, you have to eat the whole thing or they'll make you cut off your pinkie finger."

She scrunched her nose at him. "So this is an authentic Yakuza Japanese steak house?"

"I did want to impress."

"They can try and take my finger, but I am a master of the miniature bo staff." Shannon wielded a single chopstick menacingly.

Terrance chuckled and ran through his list of tips for being a good date. An important one: show interest in things she's said. He tried to think of what she'd said that he could ask questions about, but the main things that came to mind were related to killing faeries, and he'd already determined it was best to wait on that. But he recalled something else. "You said you're working on a promotion? What would that be?"

"Oh, well there are a couple of career paths in the Sisters of Torment. Currently, I'm a Dark Maiden, which is on the lower level of those who serve the Darkness." She thought for a moment. "Let's say it's like a video game, and I'm a regular enemy from the fourth or fifth level...but not like a level boss. The promotion I'm looking for would make me a Night Mistress, known for stealth and speed. You know, quick, deadly, and able to sneak up on you...like a ninja. They're more like a subbosses...or at least regular enemies from the final level."

Terrance took a moment to take that in. "Do you think it's kind of odd that you compare your job to the bad guys in a video game?"

Shannon seemed taken aback. "It's just an analogy."

"Oh, I didn't mean anything by it, it's just—"

Shannon turned away from him and looked at the chef. "Chop! Chop!" she chanted as the chef rapidly cut a piece of meat.

"I don't think we have to cheer him on," Terrance said.

"We better show we're interested or he'll spit in our food."

"That would be hard with eight people watching him."

"Well, he's obviously very skilled. Plus, I don't really trust these other people." She pointed at the middle-aged couple seated nearest them, who were trying to ignore her.

"Don't point. They don't like that."

"Who doesn't like that?"

"People. People don't like that."

Shannon stuck out her tongue at him. "Like you know much about people, Mr. Programmer."

"What I mainly know about people is that they're always trying to figure exactly what input will break my programs, and they're very skilled at it. I don't have to do much exception-handling when programming for monkeys."

"Exception-handling—sounds important. So what are promotions in your field? You go from regular programmer to super programmer?"

Terrance shrugged. "Something like that. Or you go into management. You can only get so high in a company doing actual useful work. I've been thinking about going back to college for an MBA, but...well, I like programming. Just seems like eventually I'll need to think about other things."

"You should do what you like," Shannon said. "You can't just let society push you around. Stand up to the man!"

"And you like what you do?"

"Yes, it's very challenging. There's a big undercurrent to society that I don't think everyone is quite aware of. Like I don't think everyone knows to be cautious of faeries." Shannon pointed to her hair.

"Are they dangerous?" Terrance quickly blurted out. He didn't want to seem too interested, but he was afraid to miss the window to ask about them when they were topic-appropriate.

"Not physically dangerous. When I killed one today, all she did was wave her hands and say"—Shannon imitated a snooty tone—"'You ought not to do this!'"

Shannon giggled, but Terrance just stared at her, not sure how to react. "I guess you had to have been there," Shannon said. "Anyway, the problem with faeries is that they're wily—they're not always easy to hunt down. And the main danger is how they get in people's heads."

"What do you mean?" Terrance asked, trying to sound like he was only making casual conversation.

"Well, people just get all crazy when they come into contact with faeries. It's hard to describe...they just kind of lose touch with reality."

"What happens then?"

The waiter arrived with their sake. "*Namaste*," Shannon said to him.

"Wrong nationality."

Shannon poured warm sake into one of the small cups. "My first instinct was '*guten Tag*,' but that didn't seem right either."

"'Thank you' in Japanese is easy to remember because it rhymes with 'Mr. Roboto.'" Terrance poured himself some sake. "Um...so you were describing what happens to people who talk with faeries."

Shannon sipped her drink. "Most get over it. They eventually just go back to normal."

"But some don't?"

"Yeah...some don't." Shannon now looked a little uncomfortable. "When that happens, well, let's just say they become our problem."

Terrance wanted to ask more, but he could see this wasn't a line of questioning that was endearing him to Shannon. He took a big gulp of his sake. "Sounds like they should have PSAs about faeries."

"I know! I guess they just don't want people worrying about that sort of thing. It's the concern of those who share in the power of the Darkness. We protect people from things like that so you can all just worry about important things...like that exceptional handling."

"Exception-handling."

Shannon shook her head. "I'm pretty sure it's the other one."

The chef finished cooking their steaks and served them on plates with rice. Terrance eagerly dug into his food, but soon noticed that Shannon was struggling with her chopsticks. "You don't actually have to use those, you know."

"If I give up, I'll be a failure and it will follow me throughout my life. Plus, it ensures that I eat my meal daintily. I don't know if you've ever been a woman, but we have to worry about that sort of thing on a date."

"Well, good luck with that. I'll keep a close watch and get back to you later on whether the speed at which you're eating is a turnoff."

She carefully picked up a piece of steak and slowly put it in her mouth. "I'm not sure I like you, Ance." Her smile told a different story.

Terrance realized he was becoming even more taken by her than he'd been the first night they met, but a voice in the back of his head told him, *She's an evil warrior who serves a demonic power.* He was pretty sure that was just the faerie-induced craziness talking, though.

CHAPTER 5

"So what now, Ancey-boy?"

Terrance and Shannon headed out of the restaurant, arm in arm. "I'm not okay with you calling me that."

"Fine. So what now, Mr. Denby?"

"I was thinking we would go to one of those moving-picture shows all the kids are talking about."

"So dinner and a movie. How bohemian."

Terrance shrugged. "It's a first date. I'm not going to reinvent the wheel."

"Yeah, but there's a Michael Bay film playing right now. I don't like his movies."

"We can go to another film."

Shannon shook her head. "No. We'd be trying to concentrate on our movie, but I wouldn't be able to focus because I'd know that on the next screen over was a cinematic travesty with lots of explosions and Nickelback blaring."

"Kind of a snob, huh?"

"I am what I am. So what else you got?"

"Well, if not a movie, we could"—Terrance thought for a moment—"go bowling?"

Shannon raised an eyebrow. "You like bowling."

"Not really. It's just all I could think of."

"You've been on dates before, right? Or do I need to turn on tutorial mode for this one?"

Terrance considered it for a moment. "Is that an option?"

"You really this clueless?"

"No...it's just that a movie seems like a good first date. We'd learn a lot about each other by whether we make fun of the same things. If you don't want to go to the theater, maybe we can rent a movie."

Shannon narrowed her eyes. "And watch it...where?"

Terrance realized he hadn't considered the implications of his suggestion. "Um...well...my place is nearby." He frantically tried to remember what condition he'd left it in. Were there clothes strewn about? Dirty dishes on the counter? Visible Pokémon paraphernalia?

Shannon nodded. "I see what's going on here. First you're all, 'I never even dated a girl before. What is boobies?' to disarm me, and now you're trying to get me alone at your place. You're pretty smooth, and kinda sneaky."

"Hey, I was happy with the movie theater, *and* I have dated girls before."

"Real life or in a video game?"

"Both." Terrance gave her a sly smile. "And I am *very* smooth."

Shannon studied his face. "Okay. I guess I'm going to see the Batcave. So we'll go to a video store and pick out a movie?"

"What is it, the 1950s? We'll rent one through the internet."

Shannon nodded. "Oh yes. The sooner to get me alone in your lair."

Terrance followed Shannon to her car, a silver Prius. "A hybrid, huh?"

"They've been doing a green push at work. They actually help pay for a hybrid."

"Would have thought you guys just rode scary winged lizards or something."

"Those aren't for personal use."

Terrance laughed. Shannon stared at him. "What's so funny?"

"Oh...nothing." He smiled. "I guess you'll need my address."

* * *

Shannon took a few steps into Terrance's apartment. "Wow, I like the *nothing* you've done with the place."

"Uh...yeah." He did leave pretty much all the walls bare. His apartment was a place to eat, sleep, and play video games, and he never did quite understand decorating. "People worked hard on painting the walls white, and I didn't want to detract from that."

Shannon strolled toward Terrance's black leather couch, which faced his 47-inch TV. She dropped onto it and pushed her chest out provocatively. "So, you've got me alone at your place, now what are—" Something caught her attention. "Ooh! Mario Kart! We're playing that."

Terrance hadn't thought to suggest playing video games as a date option, but he was fine with that. "Okay, but I warn you I'm very good. I'm the master of the power slide." He started up the game and sat down next to Shannon.

"Bring it, Ancey-boy!" Shannon shouted as she gripped a controller.

"I thought we already discussed that attempt of a nickname, Shan...something bad."

"Yeah, I think *that* will stick. By the way, I get to be Yoshi."

"Fine with me." He navigated to the character-select screen and chose Luigi.

"Hmm." Shannon looked Terrance over.

"What?"

"Luigi is an interesting choice. Why would one associate oneself with Mario's lesser-known, younger brother? Seems to have a deeper psychological meaning."

Terrance raised an eyebrow. "You thinking I'm a serial killer again?"

"I haven't dismissed the possibility."

"I just think he doesn't get enough credit. He takes on all the goombas and Koopas too, but he doesn't even get the girl in the end. He's selfless. And why do you like Yoshi so much? What does *that* mean?"

"Yoshi is a dinosaur," Shannon calmly explained. "Dinosaurs are cool. There is no deeper psychological meaning behind choosing Yoshi."

"Yeah, I guess you're right."

"So what are we playing for?"

Terrance shrugged his shoulders. "I didn't know we were going to play for anything. I thought it was going to be a friendly game with some minor gloating. I might have even thought of being a gentleman and going easy on you."

Shannon leaned in close to Terrance, her lips nearly touching his ear, and whispered, "How about you win, and I go rough on you."

Blood rushed to his face and other places. "Okay."

* * *

"WE ARE NOT LOSING TO PRINCESS PEACH!!!" Shannon screamed.

There were loud thumps from below.

"What was that?" Shannon asked, not taking her eyes off the screen.

"Just something that lives below that doesn't like loud noises," Terrance said while trying to keep control on a tight turn. "Ignore it."

Instead of the game being a competition between Terrance and Shannon, the computer-controlled Princess Peach ended up being quite the competitor, leaving them in a near three-way tie in the final race. Shannon had ended the battle between the two of them, because now there was a new imperative: Princess Peach must fail.

"Gah! I missed the item box!" Shannon yelled.

"I got one." Terrance watched as it rotated through the possible items. "Come on, red shell..." It settled on a green shell. "No! A green shell!"

The red shell wouldn't have automatically locked onto their enemy, but the green shell meant Terrance would have to carefully aim it right at her. He considered waiting for a straightaway but realized they were almost to the finish line on the last lap, so as Peach rounded a turn ahead of him, he guessed where she was going and fired the green shell ahead of her. It slid dead on into the side of Peach's kart, spinning her out, and Luigi and Yoshi sped past her to the finish line to first and second place.

Terrance dropped his controller to the ground and stood up from the couch. "I am the greatest!"

He turned to look at Shannon and realized that she was standing right next to him. She grabbed Terrance by the shirt and kissed him. He pulled her close and kissed her back. Soon she was pulling off his shirt, and he was a little taken aback but decided to unbutton her blouse and push it off her shoulders. Then she started to push down his pants, which Terrance wasn't quite ready for, but he went with the flow and began to do the same to her jeans, which was more awkward than he expected, especially while still kissing her. They toppled over, which caused the thing beneath his apartment to bang angrily under the floor, but neither of them minded it.

They completely missed the Mario Kart awards ceremony.

CHAPTER 6

The sword. Terrance's mind kept returning to the weapon in his coat closet. *What if she finds the sword?*

"I know what you're thinking right now." Shannon lay next to Terrance, not looking at him. "You're thinking what a slut I am."

They had started out on the floor, but Terrance couldn't stop wondering when he'd last vacuumed, so as casually as possible, he'd moved the event to his bedroom. He had actually washed the sheets in the last month and was a lot less self-conscious there, which was good because he really wanted to concentrate on the beautiful woman throwing herself at him. And he definitely should have been concentrating on that now naked woman lying beside him, but once again his thoughts were straying, this time to the stupid sword the faeries had chucked at him.

"No, I was not thinking that," Terrance said, though he was caught off-guard by her coming at him like she had. He'd never attracted women so strongly before; he was always a bit of an acquired taste, it seemed.

"I don't know what came over me. I just felt we kind of had a connection and...well, it was so cool how you sniped Princess Peach with that green shell. I hate her so much."

"Most people do. I don't know what it is about her."

Shannon turned to look at Terrance. "I like you, Ance. You seem like a nice guy."

"I like you, too, Shannon. You're fun."

"Oh, yeah." She winked at him. "Bet you're going to tell all the guys how *fun* I am."

"No, I don't mean that. I mean...that was good. But before that."

She nodded. "Cool. Anyway, I don't want to take things too fast. I had a bad breakup recently. Maybe I needed a longer cooling-down period first. I shouldn't be jumping into bed with someone like this."

"I'm sorry I didn't...um...object."

"I can't expect a guy to do that."

It actually had occurred Terrance to say something—not just about the dirty carpet—but he'd been afraid of coming off as wimpy. "Still, if a mistake was made, I participated. And I was the one who suggested we come to my place."

Shannon sighed. "Wish I could blame the sake. Am I talking too much? Am I weirding you out? We were having fun before; now I think I'm just being mental."

"No, you're not being mental. We're just trying to figure out where we are, which is understandable."

"Your watch!" Shannon exclaimed. "You wore a lucky watch! We'll blame that."

Terrance glanced at the watch still on his wrist. "It was more of a helped-me-with-finals lucky watch. I didn't know it had this power."

"Well, you should have been more careful before unleashing it on an unsuspecting woman."

"Okay. I'm sorry."

Shannon nodded. "Apology accepted. So where do we go from here?"

"Well...um...I was thinking we could have another date if you're up for it."

She looked at Terrance and smiled. "I would like that very much." She frowned a little. "Except I work this weekend. I work a lot of weekends."

"Well, that gives me more time to think of date activities other than dinner and a movie. So far—just spitballing—I'm thinking lunch and a play."

She giggled. "I'm lucky I found you. I've had a rough time lately, and it's just so great to finally meet a nice guy."

"Rough time how?"

"Well..." She curled the blankets around her. "There was that breakup, but you don't want to hear about that. It was a few weeks ago and best left in the past. And then I got some bad news today."

He put his hand on her shoulder. "What?"

"It's a work thing. This person we captured...she escaped. She was about to be brought to one of the ancient unknowns, and then some idiot interfered and she escaped."

Terrance froze. "When did this happen?"

Shannon seemed not to have noticed Terrance's change of attitude. "Today."

"Oh." Terrance recalled the doe-eyed young woman, her desperate screams, her violent escape, and the intense gaze she briefly held with him. "Was she dangerous?"

"Very much."

"Like...faerie dangerous?"

Shannon frowned. "No. Big-time dangerous. When we brought her down, she slew two of my friends."

"Killed them?"

"Yes. She beheaded Erin and sliced Jess in half, from head to toe."

Terrance turned white and stared at Shannon in horror. "Oh dear...that must have been horrible."

Shannon seemed a little confused by the reaction, then smiled a little and waved her hand as if to brush away the concerns. "Oh, it sounds worse than it was. Anyway, the point is, she's out there and extremely dangerous. I don't want to throw around the word 'terrorist,' but all someone like her wants is to kill and destroy."

"And that's why she was being fed to...that thing?"

"Huh? The ancient unknown? Have you seen one before? They got one where you work?"

"Yeah."

"Well...that's complicated to explain. This is probably like you talking advanced coding stuff to me." She laughed. "Look at me going on a big work tangent right after we...were intimate. I'm not making this romantic at all."

"No, I want to know about your work." Or maybe he didn't, because it seemed like a big complication to what should have been a clearly good thing: gaining the affections of a smart, beautiful woman. "It seems kind of...dangerous."

"Meh." She leaned over and put her head on his shoulder while playfully touching his chest. "But it's cute that you're worried about me."

Terrance kissed her, as it seemed the thing to do, and they spent a few moments looking into each other's eyes. "You're very beautiful."

"And you're handsome."

Terrance didn't think he was anywhere near as handsome as she was beautiful, but he took the compliment. "So the ruling is that we'll go on dating as normal, as if this didn't happen."

"Yeah, well, I want this to work out, so I didn't want to rush things, but I've been so needy lately and now I'm just talking and talking and pretty sure I'm making things worse with that and please stop me."

Terrance put his finger to her lips. "Overthinking things and being neurotic is more my thing. We'll just regroup next date and not worry about this."

"We'll pretend we haven't already seen each other naked."

"Yep. I'm just going to go back to *imagining* what you look like naked while you talk."

Shannon nodded. "Okay, from here on, we'll take things slower and get to know each other." She thought for a moment. "Is it okay if I change my Facebook status, or is that too fast?"

"I don't even think we're Facebook friends yet."

"Yeah, we should probably do that first." She frowned a little. "So I'm not scaring you off with how crazy and needy I am?"

"No. You're not crazy. You're not needy. And you're definitely not scaring me off," Terrance said just as Shannon turned to fetch her underwear off the floor, giving him another glimpse of the bloodstain in her hair. And a part of him *was* scared. Terrified, even. But with a naked woman next to him, fear certainly wasn't his dominant feeling.

* * *

Lance's advice that Terrance just needed to get laid to relieve his worry about the world had seemed rather crude, but the next day all his previous worries about "odd" things like demons and whatnot seemed rather trivial compared to the fact that he pretty much had a girlfriend, a rather attractive and fun one at that. Still, he took a different route to work so as not to even pass by the unmarked road in the woods. Terrance had a good thing going, and he didn't want to ruin it with any more foolish musings, such as about what had led to his embarrassment at the work function the previous day. He was still rather worried about Shannon finding out that he was the one who had allowed the dangerous, doe-eyed girl to escape, and he really didn't want to give any more ammunition to the idea that he was some sort of weirdo.

So high was Terrance from his success with Shannon that he nearly forgot to get himself some coffee as soon as he got to work. He settled into his cubicle, hoping to avoid his coworkers and give them more time to forget his outburst from the other day, but Karen soon approached him. "I saw that Shannon changed her Facebook status. She says she's in a relationship with you."

Terrance leaned back in his office chair and sipped his coffee. "We're not Facebook friends, are we?"

"I don't need updates on what video games you're playing. Anyway, don't take advantage of her."

"I post video game updates to Twitter. And I wouldn't take advantage of her. I'm a nice guy." Did he take advantage of her? What had happened last night wasn't even his idea. "We just clicked, you know."

"Just be careful. She's a bit vulnerable after Chet."

"Chet?"

"Her previous boyfriend."

"Oh, she mentioned something about him." Terrance wasn't sure how curious he should be. He didn't want to violate Shannon's privacy, but he did want to know what he was up against. "Who was he?"

"A coworker of hers."

Terrance tried to imagine what that meant. "What happened with him?"

Karen hesitated a moment. "He was a jerk. He cheated on her. It's good she's not with him anymore, but I'm not really sure you're a step up."

"*I'm* not going to cheat on her."

"Probably only because there's such a small likelihood of you attracting two different women at the same time."

Terrance gave her a teasing frown. "You know, you're not a nice person. That's why you can't attract a nice guy like me, only jerks like Lance. You should probably learn more about being a good person from your friend Shannon."

"Shannon is a nutcase."

"Better than being mean. How are you friends with her anyway?" He paused for a moment, eyeing Karen carefully. "Shannon said you were lovers."

Her expression was unreadable. "Is that what she said?"

"Approximately. I don't have the transcript."

Karen sighed. "We were roommates in college. And we did briefly explore our sexuality together."

Terrance's imagination took a stab at that one. "Really?"

"No! Just slow down with Shannon, okay? You're probably just the rebound guy anyway."

Terrance hadn't considered that possibility. "We're moving at the appropriate speed," he lied.

"And try not to be a freak around her like you were here yesterday."

"I wasn't a freak, I just..." He briefly thought about the empowerment ceremony, and for some reason it caused anger to slowly swell within him. So he dropped the thought. "Please don't tell her about that." Having accidentally facilitated the escape of the woman who had killed Shannon's friends seemed like a big secret to keep, but he really hadn't done anything other than speak up a bit. If she was really dangerous, the whole incident seemed more like a security failure.

Karen stared at Terrance quietly for a few moments. "I'll just hold on to it as a little ammunition in case I decide I don't want her with you anymore."

Karen walked off. "If you were lovers, I wasn't going to judge!" Terrance shouted at her. After she was gone, he finally checked his email. A couple of juicy bugs had been sent his way. One user was causing a crash whenever he went to the accounts page. Terrance couldn't think of an obvious solution to it off the top of his head, which meant he'd have to puzzle it out. There was nothing he liked more than to spend his workday on a good puzzle. He started by checking the database to see if the user had any malformed data.

"So how'd the date go?"

Terrance spun around in his chair and glared at Lance. He hated being interrupted in the middle of a thought; it always made him angry. He calmed himself, though, as the anger seemed silly. "Really good. We're hitting it off. By the way, I don't like your girlfriend. She's mean."

"Karen? I don't know if she's my 'girlfriend.' We're just dating."

"Oh...well, Shannon is my girlfriend now. She changed her Facebook status."

Lance shrugged. "Seems like you two are moving kind of fast."

"Really? Is that fast?"

Lance nodded. "When was the last time you had a girlfriend?"

It took a moment for Terrance to recall. "A while ago."

"Well...guess you should cling to whoever you can get, then."

"I really like her. I'm not scared of moving fast. Just sucks that I won't get to see her again until next week, as apparently she works weekends a lot." Her work seemed a point of contention in a number of ways, though Terrance didn't want it to be. "Her job sounds kind of dangerous. She talked about a coworker of hers getting beheaded. Just seems kind of weird to be in a job where people get beheaded."

"Lots of people have weird jobs. You sit there at a computer and type at it and make it do stuff. That seems weird to me."

Terrance had trouble not taking that personally. "Everyone should know at least a little coding in this day and age. Computers are in everything, and it's good to know how they work."

"Nah, better system is to just let the dorks worry about it." He chuckled. "So, what did you end up doing with that sword of yours? Ever find out what it was for?"

Even the thought of the sword back in the closet in his apartment was a weight on him. "I don't know what it's for. Not really even sure I should have it. You know, I think those faeries did something to me; that's why I was all...weird the other day."

Lance nodded. "Blame your weird behavior on faeries; that's an excuse that will work once or twice."

"Do you think faeries could be dangerous?"

Lance shrugged. "They do seem like something not to mess around with, unless...how attractive did you say they were, again?"

They certainly didn't seem evil when he thought of them, but perhaps that was the effect they had on people. Then he thought of Shannon, and it seemed an easy choice. "I think I'm going to chuck that sword."

"Might get a couple bucks for it on eBay."

Terrance shook his head. "Just seems like something to be rid of. Things are going well, and I don't need weirdness."

"All right. Well, good luck on the sword-chucking."

Lance walked off and Terrance's phone beeped. It was a text from Shannon that read, *I can't wait the whole weekend to see you again. Think I can meet you for a brief lunch tomorrow.* The text included a picture that appeared to be a close-up of Shannon's mouth, in which she was gritting her teeth. He couldn't help but chuckle for some reason.

That would be the greatest thing in the history of everything, Terrance typed out, and then added a close-up photo of his nose.

He noticed an ominous figure out of the corner of his eye, but it was just the demon Darlor, his supervisor, heading by Terrance's cube with his cloak billowing after him. Nothing weird.

CHAPTER 7

The next few weeks were a whirlwind for Terrance. He enjoyed every moment he spent with Shannon. Every activity he did with her was fun, whether hanging at a coffee shop or wandering around the mall (something he usually had little use for, thanks to online shopping). They could talk about nothing for hours, cracking each other up constantly. Plus, he'd never known that vegging out in front of the TV could be so fulfilling; he'd just glance every so often at the beautiful woman snuggled next to him and feel like the luckiest human on the planet. And it was certainly the most passionate relationship Terrance had ever had; he could barely keep his hands off of her most of the time, and she was all over him every chance they got.

All the weirdness Terrance had recently noticed started to fade into the background again. Things were becoming normal again, even better than normal, because now he had Shannon. The only problem was her job. It still disturbed him whenever he caught brief mentions of it, but he learned not to pry, so as not to worry himself. Shannon was perfect, and if no one else seemed worried about her work, he didn't see why he should ruin everything by obsessing about it. Still, the hours for her job were unusual, leaving Terrance to himself many nights, especially on weekends. Shannon would text, email, and call when she could, but Terrance still had plenty of time alone, and that's when he'd think too much and start to worry about the odd things he had been noticing, wondering if they meant anything. Who *was* that woman they'd wanted to feed to the beast? And why was there a giant beast under an office building?

Because of all those questions that stirred in his head when he was alone, Terrance began to dread the time he was without her—except this weekend.

"The new Legendary Quest is out today," Terrance told Lance on Friday morning while sitting in his cubicle. "We're talking hundreds of hours of gameplay exploring a big, open world with countless side quests. It's supposed to be everything the previous games in the series were, plus much more advanced graphics, physics, and an even larger world."

Lance nodded. "All I heard was, 'I'm a dork. I'm a dork. I'm a dork dork dork. Duhhh.'"

Terrance frowned. "I didn't say, 'Duh.'"

"Well, if you decide you might not want to be pathetic, I'm going to a club with Karen tonight, if you want to come along."

"What in the world would I do at a club when I have girlfriend and she isn't with me?" He never found anything to do there under any circumstances. Clubs were always so loud, one could barely talk, and dancing—well, he could not dance like no one was watching.

"You can work on your game and try to pick up some women—and there will be no pressure, since you already have a girlfriend."

Terrance considered it for a moment. "There's a certain logic to that...while at the same time, it's a monumentally bad idea."

"So I guess you're just going to play a video game all weekend, then? Sounds kind of pathetic."

"More so before I had a girlfriend."

"I just can't imagine playing video games that much. Was never that into them."

Terrance looked at Lance with confusion. "How can you be from my generation and not be into video games? What did you do as a kid? Play sports like some caveman child?"

"Yeah, you hold on to that Shannon. I'm not sure you're capable of meeting another woman."

"Oh, ha ha." Terrance turned to check on some important data on his computer screen, then yelled in shock. Something was wrong. Very wrong.

"What?" Lance tried to get a look at the screen.

"Legendary Quest...it was supposed to have shipped already so I'd get it on release day! It hasn't shipped!"

"Well then, you'll get it later."

"You don't understand! That was my weekend! I was going to play it all weekend!" He had been looking forward to this for months, having preordered it before he met Shannon and before the faerie craziness. There was nothing better than a great new video game and a whole weekend to play it—except maybe having a girlfriend. But she wasn't going to be around, so what did Terrance have to look forward to other than playing his new game? "Hopefully I can find a store with it in stock. It's a very popular release; it might sell out."

"Lots of other nerds like you out there?"

"And it's not available for digital download for some insane—possibly malicious—reason," Terrance explained to the uncomprehending Lance. "I have to get a physical copy, or no game." Terrance thought for a second frantically. "Maybe I can get out at lunch and pick it up at Best Buy—except I have that stupid lunch meeting. Hopefully some store will still have it in stock after work."

Lance took a sip of his coffee. "Definitely call me after and tell me how it worked out, because this sounds really important."

Terrance was already busily checking online to see if stores nearby had it in inventory and could hold a copy. He was determined to save his weekend.

* * *

Terrance did his best to keep his mind on work for the rest of the day, and then checked a few stores for the game on his way home. He even went to a Kmart—he couldn't recall the last time he'd been in one of those. Every store he stopped at was sold out. So he went home, pulled up a list online of stores nearby, and began calling them to check if his game was in stock—something he hadn't done since he was a kid. It seemed so low-tech and inefficient, but it was the only option remaining if he wanted that game for his weekend.

His efforts were fruitless until he finally reached a Walmart in Demon's Peak, an area Terrance hadn't even heard of before.

"Is this the electronics department?"

There was an oddly long pause. Then a creaky voice answered, "Yes."

"Do you have Legendary Quest in stock?"

Another long pause. Terrance's heart nearly stopped with anticipation, and the voice finally answered, "Yes."

Terrance could feel a squeal coming on but forced it down, as that definitely wasn't acceptable. "Can you hold it for me?"

"We don't do that. If you wish to have it, then you must come and get it."

"Okay. I'll be right there." Terrance hung up and quickly checked Google Maps for the route to the Demon's Peak Walmart. The directions led up into the mountains a short way out of town, then stopped a couple of miles from his destination. He pulled up the satellite image of the area, and it looked like the road terminated in an area of trees and snow, never making it all the way to the Walmart. It was odd, but Terrance cared only that they had his game.

He went to the closet to pull out his best winter coat, gloves, and a hat. Inside, sticking up from behind a backpack, he saw the hilt of the sword. He had decided a while ago to chuck the thing, as he worried about how Shannon would react if she ever saw it. But in all the excitement with her, he had mostly forgotten about it. He stared at the hilt for a while, then finally reached out and grabbed it. He figured he might as well bring it along; after all, he was on a quest.

CHAPTER 8

When Terrance hadn't seen another building—or even another car—for ten minutes, he started to question the wisdom of heading to the Demon's Peak Walmart. But with his girlfriend working and no new video game to play, what else did he have to do?

As he followed the twists and turns up the mountain roads, snowflakes began appearing on his windshield, slowly at first and then at a greater frequency, until he had the windshield wipers on maximum speed and the whole world began to disappear in the whiteness. Soon, all he could see was the snow and a few glimpses of the road lines reflecting his headlights. He began to wonder if he had headed out to his death in his little Hyundai Accent, but then the road came to an abrupt end at an impassable snow bank. Unsure what to do next, he noticed some lights to the right and drove toward them. There, barely visible through the snow, was a 7-Eleven.

Terrance parked his car and got out, zipping his coat up tight. He pulled the sheathed sword from the backseat and strapped it to his back. Peering through the blizzard in the direction of his destination, he could faintly make out a path through a densely forested area. He considered his options for a moment, then headed into the 7-Eleven.

The inside was nice and clean. This surprised Terrance for such an out-of-the-way place, but he figured it probably didn't get very much foot traffic. Behind the counter stood a clerk with a mangy gray beard and a face lined by decades of hardship. Terrance waved hello and went to the coffeepots, where he filled a 20-ounce cup with the darkest roast they had. He carefully sealed a lid onto it, slipped on a paper sleeve, and walked to the counter.

"What are you doing here?" the clerk demanded. "There's nothing but death out here."

Terrance was a little confused. "And a Walmart, right?"

"Aye, and a Walmart. You'll head out on foot from here, through the Grim Forest."

"There's some sort of trail, right?"

The man chuckled a little, ending it with a cough. "Getting lost will not be your biggest worry." He carefully looked Terrance over. "You brought a sword?"

"Oh. Sorry. Is that allowed in here?"

"I care not, but do you think it will protect you from what's out there?"

Terrance shrugged. "I don't know; I just thought I'd bring it. What's in the forest?"

The clerk smiled. "Trees. So what brings you here?"

"It's the only Walmart with the video game I want in stock."

"And that's worth the danger?"

"Well...IGN gave it a 9.7."

"I don't know what that means."

"IGN is a game site and—"

"Nor do I care. It will be a dollar twenty-nine for the coffee."

Terrance pulled out a debit card. He felt silly using it for such a small purchase, but keeping cash on hand seemed so inconvenient. When he finished the transaction, he headed back outside. He stood there for a while looking down the path, holding the coffee near his lips but not drinking, as it still seemed too hot. Then he remembered the video review of Legendary Quest, and all he could think about was how much he wanted to spend the weekend playing that game. Thus he ventured forth.

There was little to see down the path besides the snow falling down on him and the tall pines towering above him. He took a few sips of coffee while looking around. A couple of times, he thought he saw movement in the darkness beyond the trees. Then he heard a noise, a small sound, growing louder and louder.

It was his phone. He'd always set it to make a regular phone-ring sound, since he found anything else confusing, but out of whimsy he'd set it to play "The Imperial March"—one of his favorite songs—whenever Shannon called. He took off a glove and fished the phone out of his pocket, fumbling to swipe the screen correctly. "Hello?"

"Hey, Ance. I miss you."

"I miss you, too." Though he expected to miss her less if he got his video game. "I can't believe you're gone the whole weekend working."

"Yeah, well, it's really imperative we get to this little village."

"You need to defend them against something?"

There was a brief pause on her end. "Not exactly. So what are you up to?"

"There was this big video game release this weekend—"

"The new Legendary Quest, right?"

"Yeah, exactly." She *got* him. "I had preordered it, but it didn't get shipped for some reason. It was sold out everywhere, but this one Walmart at Demon's Peak has it. Except the roads don't make it all the way there, so I'm having to hike through a blizzard on foot to get to it. That's pretty weird, right? Why would a Walmart be so out of the way?"

"I don't know. I have no idea how they decide where to put Walmarts. Be careful, though."

"I will. The guy at the 7-Eleven was talking about how this forest is dangerous or something, but I think he was just trying to scare me. Plus I have—" He was about to mention his faerie sword but caught himself. "I'm prepared."

"I'm sure you are. Especially if you run into a software bug."

"Yeah. Maybe the whole problem with the forest is a malformed SQL query."

There was another pause. "I don't know what that is."

"It's a programming thing."

"I like it when you talk dirty to me. Still, I need to get off the phone; we have some prep work to do tonight. I'll talk to you soon. Can't wait to see you again."

"And I can't wait to see you. Try to stay safe."

"I will, but there's not really anything to worry about; the villagers are defenseless. Later, Ance."

"Bye," Terrance said, still trying to process that last statement. He decided to let it go.

He looked about him, but it was hard to see much through the trees, most of which were nothing but faint shadows. Then he thought he saw movement.

He immediately stopped and looked again: nothing but the tall shadows of trees. But one of the shadows drew closer.

He couldn't tell if it was the trees that were moving or some creature as large as them, as there was too little visibility to make anything out clearly. Either way, it was a little scary. Or a lot scary. Especially since whatever it was appeared to be moving toward him.

Terrance backed away as he began to hear the loud thud of footsteps from the massive thing heading his direction. He snapped out of the fear long enough to try to think of an action, and remembered the sword strapped to his back. He reached over his shoulder with his right hand to grip the handle, and unsheathed it.

Or tried to. He couldn't actually reach his arm high enough to pull the sword all the way out of its sheath. He thought he had seen plenty of people with swords strapped to their backs in movies and video games, and he didn't remember any of them running into this trouble. He awkwardly tried to bend forward to give himself more leverage, and ended up falling over into the snow. The creature continued toward him, now only yards away.

Then it stopped, and so did the snow. Terrance could still barely make out the creature among the trees where it stood, but it appeared to be looking skyward. Suddenly, it turned and hurried away, shaking the ground with quick, heavy footsteps.

Terrance looked up as well, but all he could see was darkness. A *moving* darkness. Something massive was flying above him, temporarily blocking out the snow. Then the snow started again as all that was above him was the giant flying creature's tail, which slithered after it in the sky like a huge, spiky anaconda.

After the flying creature was completely out of view, Terrance continued to stare at the sky for a few moments, with dread. He finally forced himself to his feet and ran down the trail. Soon he saw something glowing blue ahead of him.

The Walmart sign.

As he crossed the empty parking lot, he noticed a sign on a light post saying the area around the Walmart was monitored by security cameras. He hoped the creatures in the forest cared about that sort of thing, and headed for the entrance at a more reserved pace.

The glass doors parted for him as he approached, and inside was a smiling, elderly man in a blue smock. "Welcome to Walmart."

Terrance smiled and nodded. "This one is kind of out of the way."

The old man shrugged. Terrance continued into the store and noticed there were very few fellow shoppers—which wasn't that surprising for a store hidden on a treacherous mountain. Even with everyday low prices. He scanned the area until he spotted a wall covered in flat-screen TVs marking the electronics section. He quickly headed in that direction, and as he got near he looked for the video games. Finally, in a special display only a few yards ahead, he saw it: one last copy of Legendary Quest.

Someone stepped between him and his game. It was a young woman in a white cloak with a hood, inspecting a set of steak knives she was holding. She then looked up at Terrance with a stare of recognition. It was the doe-eyed girl.

They locked eyes on each other. A number of emotions ripped through Terrance. Fear was one, for despite how small and innocent the girl looked, Shannon had described her as quite deadly—and he had even caught a glimpse of her in action himself. Excitement was another emotion...though he couldn't quite comprehend why. He wanted to talk to this woman. She knew something he needed to know.

The last emotion was dread, because she was between Terrance and the last copy of Legendary Quest, which anyone could grab at any moment. He really wished he had snatched the copy, *then* run into her.

"You," the woman finally said, moving toward Terrance. She brushed aside one of the dark strands of hair that poked out from under her hood. "You were there. You tried to stop them."

"Well...it was more that I was just trying to get clarification about what was going on."

"Your eyes were open. You saw what was going on." There was a sharp edge to her voice.

"Yeah...it's just that everyone else seemed to think—"

"You bear a sword," she interrupted, looking over Terrance's shoulder at the sword strapped to his back.

"Oh. Yeah. Well, this Walmart is really out of the way. Do you know it's really hard to draw a sword when it's strapped on your back?"

"It's meant to go at the hip." She pulled back her cloak, revealing two short blades sheathed at her hips, over her jeans.

There didn't seem to be anything threatening about the woman's movements, but Terrance was growing more nervous. Still, he decided to risk mentioning one thing, to possibly see what she knew. "Anyway, faeries gave me this sword about a month ago."

She now stared at Terrance more intensely. "Faeries gave it to you?"

"Yeah, in some weird meadow I stumbled upon." "Meadow" didn't seem to be the right word as he remembered the vast mountains that stretched into the distance.

"They *gave* you the sword?"

"Yeah...I'm not sure what for."

She was quiet for a few seconds, looking Terrance over. "Who are you?"

"I'm Terrance Denby. I design web applications." He wondered right away whether he should have given her his last name.

She was quiet again.

"You know on websites how you click a button and it will process—"

"I know what web applications are."

Terrance nodded, and they continued staring quietly at each other, the woman so intensely that it made Terrance very uncomfortable. "Um...and you are?"

"Talia. You don't need to know my last name. Or my occupation."

"Okay...um...so how did you end up...um...about to be fed to some underground beast thing?"

She smiled. The smile did not make Terrance feel more comfortable. "A good question, Denby. To answer simply, there are things very wrong in this world...as you may have noticed. Many ignore these things. They turn a blind eye to the evil even as it consumes them. But some fight. I fight."

"Fight how?"

"Odd question from a man with a sword strapped to his back."

Terrance was fascinated and wanted to ask more, but then he remembered Shannon's warnings. "I heard that maybe faeries do...something to us. And that's why I'm suddenly starting to...get weirded out by things that are actually quite normal."

She took another step toward Terrance, getting right into his face. "So you think if it weren't for the faeries, you would have considered it a normal thing, me being torn apart by a hideous beast while others watched? Is that a *normal* thing, Denby?"

"No...it's just no one else..."

She stepped back. "Fools. Fools all waiting around until they fall into the maws of oblivion. So what are you doing here?"

It took Terrance a moment to remember: the game! He tried to peer past Talia toward it. "Well, this was the only store that had this video game I wanted and—"

"A video game!" she spat. "You've begun to realize things beyond this mere existence, and you want to deaden your senses with a video game?"

Terrance had never understood why everyone always had to hate on video games. They're *fun*. "Well...you apparently have realized the same things and you're getting steak knives."

She looked offended. "Have you tried cutting meat with a butter knife? Steak knives are not for mere pleasure! This is a hard store to get to—I probably would not have ventured here had I not had a unicorn to ride for the journey. Thus, with the difficulty of the destination, I thought perhaps you came here with purpose. But you don't have purpose, do you, Denby?"

He was getting a little tired of her accusations. "I don't know *what's* going on, okay? I don't know why there are faeries handing out swords. Or why I'm suddenly noticing all these things that I've always known about but that now seem completely insane—like my boss is a demon and there is something living under my ground-floor apartment and there was this popular series where the vampires sparkled."

"I liked those books," Talia said.

Terrance decided to ignore that. "And what is *this* place? Why is there a Walmart on top of a mountain? Why do you have to go through a dangerous forest to get here? And why was there some creature the size of a whale flying overhead?!"

She smiled again, seeming to enjoy his frustration. "The large flying thing is Malcus. I think he is after me." She looked proud. "As for everything else, think of it this way. Have you ever had a dream during which you realized it was a dream? Suddenly your mind is awake and you finally realize the ridiculousness of the situation you're in—that you can fly, that monsters are chasing you, that you somehow got to school without your pants—when previously your mind was in a fog and you just accepted it all.

"That's where you are, Denby. Your mind is awake. And you have a choice: Do you try to wake from the dream? Do you continue to tear at the foundation of the absurd situation you are in? Do you continue noticing what you ignored before? Do you continue exploring the places you had always overlooked? Do you begin to remember who you really are? Or do you grab your video game and pretend all is normal? Do you try to put your mind back to sleep and accept the dream as real? Believe me, even though it's not real, there are things in it that can destroy you."

For a moment, Terrance actually considered not getting the video game. But only for a moment. It had gotten *really* good reviews. "And if I continue...being 'awake'...what then?"

"Then things begin. I'll warn you, though: when you are not asleep like the others—when your eyes are open—the Hollow Ones may take notice of you."

"The Hollow Ones?"

"The Dark Enforcers. The Sisters of Torment."

Shannon? "I need to avoid them?"

"They are men and women who devote themselves to the darkness that traps us. They will fight for it without mercy, and they are quite powerful. You'll know them when you see them, and if you see them, run."

"I'll...take that under advisement."

"I'm not sure about you. But if..."

He noticed a teenager behind Talia, approaching the electronics section. Without thinking, Terrance stepped around Talia to try to finally grab his game, but he was too late and the teenager got to it first. Terrance turned around in defeat, and Talia was nowhere to be seen. So no game, and many more questions to be answered. Terrance sensed it was going to be a long weekend.

He headed to the grocery area to grab some beer.

CHAPTER 9

Terrance trudged into his apartment, dropping the beer and a Wendy's takeout bag on the coffee table. He tried to pull off his coat, but the sword that was still strapped around him prevented that. He undid the strap and tossed it to the tiled entryway floor, where it landed with a metallic clamor.

There were loud thumps from below in response.

That was it. "Shut up!" Terrance yelled as he stomped on the floor. "I'm on the ground floor! You shouldn't be there, whatever you are!"

The responding thumps were so strong that the apartment shook. He decided he wasn't in the mood for a contest and pulled off his coat, tossing it over the back of the couch. He was about to plop down and finally relax, but decided he shouldn't leave the sword sitting out. He walked over and picked it up to put it inside the coat closet, leaning it against a wall. Then he noticed something.

There was an outline in the carpet on the closet floor. Terrance moved a never-used tennis racket and a backpack out of the way, and saw what looked like a square trapdoor. He did remember seeing it when he'd moved in and assuming it was the entrance to a crawlspace, never giving it a second thought.

There was a handle in the center of the trapdoor, and Terrance used it to carefully lift off the cover. Below was not just a few feet down ending in concrete and debris; instead, there was a narrow tunnel with a ladder that went so far down, it disappeared into darkness. But at the very bottom of the tunnel—more than a hundred feet below—there shone a light.

Terrance stared at the faraway light for a moment. Finally, he yelled, "Hello!"

There was the usual loud thump from below in response, although this time it echoed up the tunnel.

Terrance remembered what Talia had said about noticing what he had once ignored and exploring the new places he had always overlooked. But he was already tired from the day. And his spicy chicken sandwich was getting cold.

* * *

Terrance had trouble sleeping that night. There were too many thoughts dancing around in his head. Talia had warned that his sweet, funny Shannon was dangerous...and this wasn't easily dismissed. On the other hand, Shannon had said Talia was quite dangerous and had even killed her friends, and there *was* something quite creepy about Talia. Then there was the tunnel beneath his apartment and whatever lived down there that didn't like Terrance making noise. And that stupid faerie sword he didn't know what to do with.

Finally, there were Talia's words about noticing things being wrong in this world, noticing things beyond "mere existence." He couldn't shake the feeling that something important was going on that he couldn't quite grasp. If there *were* really important things going on that he was beginning to become cognizant of, what did this mean for him?

He really wished he had that video game to take his mind off of everything. Instead, he found himself wide awake at 7 a.m. on a Saturday. Not sleeping in on a Saturday was unimaginable to him, but he just couldn't lie in bed anymore. He needed to do something. So he did what he always did when he found himself up early for some reason on a Saturday: go get McDonald's for breakfast.

Terrance threw on jeans, an ironic T-shirt, and a jacket, and headed out the door. He went through the nearest McDonald's drive-thru for a bacon, egg, and cheese biscuit, an Egg McMuffin, three hash browns, and coffee. He didn't feel like heading back home, though. There was nothing there to do—just all his old video games he was bored of, and the strange tunnel deep beneath his apartment that he still didn't feel like dealing with. So he drove, not sure where he was going—though soon it became apparent.

He slowed down as he came to the unmarked road in the forested area and turned onto it. He followed the road until it ended, then parked the car. He grabbed his bag of food and his coffee, and walked through the forest into the clearing.

It was as he remembered it: fields of green stretching out in a way that made them seem infinite, yet he could see where they ended at a vast mountain range in the distance. What lay beyond that, he couldn't fathom. In the blue sky, he could see the outlines of worlds hovering above him.

What he couldn't see, though, was the floating crystal palace. Since he wasn't in a rush today, Terrance thought maybe he could have a longer conversation with the faeries about the whole sword thing, but they apparently weren't there anymore. It was a *floating* palace, after all, so it was feasible that it had moved.

Terrance decided to explore a little bit as he waited for his coffee to cool enough to be drinkable. He headed through a field of wildflowers, dodging past a couple of large butterflies, then hopped over a small brook. A shadow passed over him, and he looked up to see a huge bird flying far overhead. Or maybe it wasn't a bird; he thought he could make out four legs.

He ignored it for now and headed up a hill to get a better view of things. He could see a single small tree at the top of the hill, which seemed like a nice spot to sit and eat his breakfast. When he reached the top, though, he could see that the land sloped far down below him. In the far distance, to his left, he could see water—perhaps a sea or a large lake. To his right, he could see a large forest that appeared to stretch out endlessly. Straight ahead were those mountains that seemed impossibly far away and impossibly large.

Terrance went over the map of the area in his head and realized he should be staring at the back of a Home Depot in this spot. This place seemed to exist outside of the regular world, which felt like something he should be concerned about. Using the shade of the tree, Terrance looked at his smartphone, but there was no cell signal, which was really odd since he had Verizon.

He sat down and leaned against the tree trunk, then pulled out his Egg McMuffin and ate it while staring at the mountains in the distance. He felt like he was on the cusp of something that he couldn't quite articulate, and he was a bit scared about it.

He ate his breakfast, trying to peer past those mountains, filled with a sort of wonder he couldn't completely understand. As he finished his last hash brown, he decided he was doing nothing but making himself crazy. Monday night, he'd be seeing Shannon again, and he wanted his head in the real world for that. He liked her—there was no question about that—and if she said Talia was dangerous and crazy, then he probably should just listen to his girlfriend.

He picked up the McDonald's bag, which was now filled with trash, and continued sipping his coffee as he turned to head back to the car. There was nothing he needed to ask the faeries. He was done with all of this.

Then he saw something in the grass ahead, staring at him. A squirrel.

Terrance locked his eyes with its beady black ones. "You're that same squirrel, aren't you?"

It did not answer, its expression as inscrutable as that of any other squirrel.

"You got me here in the first place, and since then you've been following me. Why?"

Again, the squirrel did not answer, only staring at Terrance with its dark eyes. Or staring beyond him. Something about that stare creeped him out.

"You're going to give me answers!" Terrance yelled, but the squirrel stood its ground. Terrance set his trash and coffee cup on the ground. "Know what I'm thinking? I'm between you and the only tree for at least a hundred yards. And while I know you things can scurry pretty fast, I don't think you can move faster than a human in a straight-out run."

The squirrel finally reacted, moving closer to the ground as if getting ready for a burst of speed. Terrance darted for it, and it ran away. But true to his supposition, he quickly began to catch up and was soon within a foot of being able to bend down and grab it.

It suddenly turned, stood still, and bared its teeth.

Startled, Terrance redirected his momentum to the side of the squirrel and quickly lost his footing, tumbling down the slope of the hill. He tried to stop his roll, but there was nothing to grab on to. He ended up tumbling right off a cliff and falling a pretty scary distance into some bushes.

He shook the dizziness from his head and stood up, adjusting his askew glasses. Nothing seemed broken. Ahead of him were much taller cliffs that he was glad he hadn't fallen from, with a waterfall pouring down the center of them. The cliffs surrounded a large clearing of grass, at the center of which was a tall, shiny tower. A skyscraper. A very modern-looking one, with nothing but reflective glass visible on the outside.

Terrance looked behind him and realized it would be a bit of a trek to get around the cliff to be able to go back up the hill. He turned back to the skyscraper that stood alone in the field. It was curious, and he had nothing but time on his hands today, so he decided to check it out.

As he got near, it looked to be at least forty stories high. There was an automated revolving door, through which he entered the fancy marble lobby. The only slightly odd thing was that the ceiling seemed lower than he would have expected for a building this size. Ahead of him was a desk about half the height of a normal reception desk, but no one was sitting behind it.

"Can I help you?"

Terrance turned to see that standing near him was a little man with pointed ears, wearing a green cap. He was the size of a small child, but his facial features made him look middle-aged.

"Oh, I'm just looking. I was in the area, and I was curious what this place was."

"It's an office building," the little man answered.

Terrance looked around. There were flat-screen monitors showing off the products being worked on in the building, such as magic dust, enchanted cloaks, and cookies. "So, are you a gnome?"

"An elf."

"I thought elves were tall."

"Why would you think that?"

Terrance thought for a moment. "The *Lord of the Rings* movies."

"Well, it's not true. May I ask why you're in the area?"

"Oh, I was looking for a floating crystal palace with faeries in it."

The elf narrowed his eyes suspiciously. "What for?"

"They gave me a sword the other day, and I just wanted a better explanation of why."

"You have the sword with you?"

"No, I left it at home. If I brought it to you guys, would you be able to tell me anything about it?"

The elf shook his head. "We don't deal with weaponry. Are you a warrior?"

Terrance shook his head. "No. I'm a computer programmer who works primarily on web applications."

"So what are you doing here, looking for faeries?"

"It's just...um..." Terrance thought about it. "I just want some answers, I guess."

"To what?"

"Well, I've just noticed a lot of weird stuff lately—things that don't seem right."

"That's not a question. Can I offer you some advice?"

The elf seemed sincere, so Terrance nodded. "Sure."

"Let's be logical about this." Terrance found it hilarious that someone with pointy ears was talking about being logical, but he let it go. "As you said, you're not a warrior, but the faeries like to interfere in things, and that leads to only one outcome: conflict."

"Interfere in what?"

"Things," the elf repeated. "Things over which blood is constantly shed. The point is, you're not carrying your sword. That tells me you don't want to use it. You're not a warrior, but the path you're going down will only lead to a fight. Are you looking for a battle?"

Terrance shook his head.

"So stop worrying about this. You explored. You found an office building in a hidden field. You looked inside, and it's just an office building. Nothing interesting."

"It's just..."

"Nothing interesting. Do you want to get killed over things like this?"

"No." Now he was more worried. "Are people going to kill me?"

"They just might. And you don't look prepared to defend yourself. Now, why don't you scamper back to where you came from."

The elf stood there with an odd smile on his face, and Terrance turned and left the building. This whole area seemed weird—magical even—but he didn't know what he expected to find here. He didn't know what was so important to look for. And he didn't see the point in talking to the faeries again when he already knew he wanted to be done with all this nonsense and put his focus back on his life, his job, and his girlfriend, who was cute and sweet and therefore ridiculous to think of as evil.

The blue sky had turned gray, and the occasional raindrop landed on Terrance's head as he found his way back up the hill. He fetched his garbage and coffee cup, which were still by the tree, and headed back to his car. When he got to the trees at the edge of the clearing, he looked at his cellphone and saw he had a signal again. He checked his email and found a message from Shannon, telling him she was having lots of fun with her friends in the small village but she really missed him. He was about to reply when he felt a presence nearby.

Terrance looked up to see a large figure standing near his car. He was wearing dark armor, and his face was completely concealed by a horned helmet. Between his size and the horns, he stood nearly twice Terrance's height. Strapped to his back was a massive battle-axe, the head of which looked to be about the size of Terrance's torso. If this were a video game, Terrance would have felt like he'd just walked into a boss battle.

"Terrance, I presume," the man announced in a booming voice.

"We know each other?" It seemed a dumb question; Terrance was pretty sure he would have remembered this guy.

"I know of you. What are you doing here?"

"Had the morning free, felt like finding a nice spot to eat some McDonald's." He held up the trash-filled bag. "Why?"

"Odd place to seek out." It sounded like an accusation.

Terrance thought he knew what this guy was: a dark enforcer, another of the Hollow Ones that Talia had warned him about. But he had the sinking feeling he also knew exactly *who* this was. "So who are you?"

"I am a servant of the Darkness, and I smite its enemies. They call me Chet."

Shannon's ex. Terrance was already pretty certain he was a huge jerk. "Well, Chet, I have things to do," he lied, "so I need to get going."

"Guns don't kill people. People with mustaches kill people."

For a moment, Terrance was confused. Then he realized Chet was reading the T-shirt Terrance had thrown on that morning.

"I notice you don't have a mustache," Chet said.

"Do you?"

Chet was silent for a moment, then said, "I have an axe."

"Well, you have fun with that." Terrance took out his keys and unlocked the car.

"I'll be watching you," Chet said as Terrance got into the driver's seat.

"That's creepy." Terrance pulled the door closed, started the car, and got out of there as quickly as a four-cylinder would allow.

CHAPTER 10

Terrance wasn't sure what to do with himself the rest of the weekend. He watched a couple of shows on Netflix and putzed around the internet. He checked if there were any games on Steam that he hadn't played and that he felt like buying and downloading, but his spirit was too broken from not having Legendary Quest. A couple of times, he thought about checking out that strange tunnel beneath his apartment, but decided he'd had more than his share of nonsense this weekend already. He was bored and frustrated, the only highlight of the weekend being the occasional text or email from Shannon.

Sunday evening, there was a knock at his door. It was Lance. He lived in the apartment above Terrance, which was the main reason they were friends, since they didn't really share any interests and were nothing alike. "You busy with your game, or do you want to go get some drinks?" Lance asked.

"I wasn't able to get my game."

"Then I bet you definitely want a drink. Come on."

It was raining hard, so Terrance grabbed an umbrella. They headed over to Tappers, a small bar within walking distance of their building, and ordered a pitcher of beer. Terrance had a number of things he wanted to talk about, and after they settled at a table with their drinks, he decided to start with the subject he thought Lance would consider most relevant. "I ran into Shannon's ex. Actually, I think he was following me."

"He's stalking you?"

"Looks like it."

Lance scanned the faces around the darkened bar. "Did he seem dangerous?"

"He's giant and has an axe."

Lance took a sip of his beer. "Might need to pop him one to get him to back off."

"I'd have to get him to take his helmet off first." Plus, Terrance wasn't sure he could reach that high. "Hey, did you know there's a tunnel under our apartments?"

"A tunnel?"

"Well, you know how sometimes in my apartment, something beneath knocks on the floor because I'm making noise?"

"Yeah."

"But I'm on the ground floor."

Lance thought about it while sipping his beer. "I guess it's something beneath the earth that doesn't like noise."

"Yeah, well, I opened what I thought would be an entrance to a crawlspace in a closet and found this tunnel that leads deep down below the building...and I could see light down there. What in the world do you think it is?"

Lance shrugged. "Storage?"

"I feel like it's something big. Like it's something I should check out."

"So, if you're left alone for the weekend and don't have a video game to play, you get weird and obsessive."

"It's not just that. When I went to this Walmart to find my game—which was weirdly on some mountain and surrounded by monsters or something—I ran into that woman, the one from the empowerment ceremony at work who got away."

"Oh yeah; you got weird and obsessive that day, too, and made a big scene."

Terrance ignored him. "Her name is Talia, and she talked as if there was some big conflict going on. I got the same vibe from an elf I talked to in an office building in a hidden meadow."

Lance looked confused. "Why are you going into random office buildings?"

"Because it was all alone in a secret meadow!" Terrance noticed that some people were now looking at him, so he lowered his voice. "It seemed important. I dunno. It just seems like there are weird, important things going on all around me and no one seems to care."

Lance nodded. "So is everything all right between you and Shannon?"

"Yeah, she's great, it's just..." Terrance took a deep breath. "I'm really starting to wonder if she's...evil. I think this weekend she went to slaughter a defenseless village. And Talia warned me about her kind; called them the Hollow Ones, whatever that means. What do you do if you think your girlfriend is evil? Do you confront her about it? I mean, I really like her, but it just doesn't seem like I should let that go."

Lance was quiet in contemplation for a few moments. "Here's what we're going to do. Over there are some hot college girls."

Terrance looked across the bar to where two attractive young things sat talking to each other.

"We're going to go hit on them," Lance said.

"I have a girlfriend."

"So this will be just for fun. All we're going to do is get their numbers. It will be a confidence-booster so you'll have less trouble satisfying Shannon in bed."

Terrance turned red. "That's not the problem."

"I'm getting a vibe that it is. So come on. Just follow my lead." Lance got up, and Terrance followed. He wasn't sure how far he was going to take this hitting-on-other-women business, but he knew better than to argue with Lance. As he got near the girls' table, he noticed a pale man in the corner, with what looked to be an unconscious woman in his arms. The man was looking greedily at her, then bared his teeth—which included fangs.

Terrance grabbed Lance's arm. "Is that a vampire over there?"

Lance reluctantly took his eyes off the prize and looked over to the corner. "I dunno. Maybe. Why?"

"He's preying on that woman. Shouldn't someone do something?"

"It's not really our business. Now don't get distracted; I need your head in the game here."

But Terrance was still staring over at the vampire, who now opened his mouth, preparing to bite into the woman's neck.

"Hey!" Terrance yelled, walking toward the fiend.

The vampire dropped the woman to the ground and stood up. He was taller than Terrance, muscular, and had a fierce gaze from his gray eyes. Plus, he was a vampire, which Terrance just realized was really scary. "What's your problem?"

Now shaking a bit, Terrance weakly said, "You were about to bite that woman."

The woman slowly lifted herself up, shaking the daze from her head. She took one frightened look at the vampire and ran for the exit.

"Wait!" the vampire yelled after her, but she bolted out the door. The vampire turned toward Terrance and glared at him.

"See," Terrance said, "she didn't want—"

The vampire struck Terrance with his open palm, knocking Terrance backward across the room and into a table. Terrance ached all over, and struggled to get to his feet. Lance helped him up and announced to the bar, "Sorry, my friend has had too much to drink; I'm going to take him home."

The vampire still looked angry, but stayed back as Lance led Terrance to the exit. Terrance then noticed something moving on the ceiling. Once again, there was something dark up there, and from the glint of its eyes, Terrance could tell it was staring at him. He stared back, until Lance yanked him out the door.

"Don't get us banned from our local bar," Lance said while the rain poured on them.

"He was a vampire! Someone had to do something!"

"And you did something: you looked like an ass and then got the crap beat out of you. You happy?"

His pride was hurt—along with his body—but he didn't feel that bad about it. "It just seems like people shouldn't ignore things like that."

"You're going crazy again. I'm going to go back in and grab our umbrellas; you stay out here and try not to be a weirdo for five seconds."

Lance ran back into the bar, and Terrance noticed a light in the distance—the glow of the volcano by the fortress far outside of town. There was a streak of lightning behind it, which silhouetted something large flying near the volcano. He was pretty sure it was the thing he saw fly over in the forest. Malcus. He shuddered at the thought.

* * *

Terrance poured a can of Campbell's Chunky Soup into a bowl—chicken corn chowder—and stuck it in the microwave. While waiting for his dinner to heat up, he went to the window and looked out toward the fortress. There was something great and evil out there...but he wasn't sure if that concerned him. He'd nearly gotten himself killed confronting a vampire, so why was he worrying about even greater threats he could do nothing about? He was a computer programmer; if something needed to be done about evil, then that seemed like someone else's job.

He looked over at the closet that contained the sword and the entrance to the tunnel beneath his apartment. He had a strange feeling that maybe there were answers down there. Answers to what questions, he had no idea.

He turned back to the window and noticed something on the grass outside: a squirrel sitting in the rain, staring at him. "What do you want?" Terrance yelled at it through the glass. "I don't know what your problem is, but I'm going to get you and wring your little squirrel neck!"

The squirrel just sat there, as Terrance realized that he was screaming at a rodent; maybe he was just going crazy.

There was a knock at the front door.

Terrance slowly walked over and opened it. He was startled to see a dark, armored figure standing there in the rain. He suddenly realized it was Shannon.

She stepped inside, pulling off her helmet and shaking out her blonde hair. "I missed you."

"I missed you, too." *If you're going to fight evil, then what are you going to do with her?* he thought, but the idea was soon lost in her pretty face and sweet smile. They embraced and kissed, and his worries melted away.

The microwave beeped.

Shannon pulled back. "Am I interrupting something?"

"Yes, you are...and thank you for that." He kissed her again and she pulled his shirt up and off of him. He tried to figure out how to get her out of her armor, but it was even more complicated than a bra strap.

CHAPTER 11

"Grah! Noise! No noise!" Shannon had her head buried in her pillow and was hitting Terrance in the face with her palm.

Terrance rolled over and turned off the clock-radio alarm. He looked back at Shannon. "You're sleeping in, I gather?"

"Murh," she grumbled. She apparently had the day off, but it was a usual Monday for Terrance.

He took a shower, and after he got out and brushed his teeth, Shannon was no longer in bed. He got dressed and headed to the kitchen, where he found Shannon wearing one of his T-shirts and making coffee.

She poured Terrance a mug. "It's our one-month anniversary today. We're, like, totally serious."

"Eh," Terrance answered as he took the coffee. He stepped over a piece of Shannon's armor still lying in the living room as he headed to the couch.

She sat down next to him and looked at him with a faux-serious face. "You have to make a huge deal out of this, because it was a month with *me*—the greatest woman you have ever met. Probably the greatest woman in all of existence. If you don't make a big deal, I'll find someone else. Easily."

"I made plans."

"What? You'd better tell me; I know how to torture information out of people."

Terrance wasn't sure from her tone whether that was a joke. "I'll tell you later." He took a big swallow of his coffee.

"So how was your weekend, by the way? Was Legendary Quest fun?"

"I wasn't able to get a copy."

She frowned. "I'm sorry. It must have been a torturous weekend without me. What did you do?"

Terrance wasn't sure how much he should tell her. He felt like he was keeping a lot of secrets from her, and as he'd learned from watching sitcoms, that could eventually lead to wacky situations. He decided to tell her at least one thing, now. "I just kinda hung around. I ran into someone, though. Chet."

Shannon's face tensed with anger. "What? What did he say to you?"

"That he's going to be watching me or something. He's kind of creepy."

"He is. I don't know why I was with him for so long. And I don't want him bothering me or you."

"You want me to beat him up?"

Shannon nodded. "Yes."

"Okay, cool. I was already planning on beating him up, but I was just wondering how severely. I'm going to go with a 'thorough' beating."

"Seriously, though, just avoid him if you see him again."

"Is he dangerous?" That seemed a silly question about a giant armored man with an axe.

"No, just an idiot and a jerk."

"So I don't need to worry about...the axe."

Shannon scoffed. "No, don't be silly. That's just for...people who need an axing, you know?"

"Not really. Who?"

"Not people like you. Don't worry about it. But do avoid Chet, and tell me if you see him again."

"Deal. So did you have a good weekend?" He regretted the question when he asked it; nothing good would come from prying about her job.

"It was work. But me and the girls, we had fun."

She didn't elaborate on what she'd had fun doing, and Terrance had the will to not inquire further. "Cool."

"So anything else happen with you this weekend other than stupid Chet?"

He carefully considered what else to tell her, and then decided to venture one thing. "I got punched by a vampire."

Shannon looked confused. "Why?"

He was about to give her the very reasonable answer, "Because I kept him from biting a woman," but stopped himself, as he somehow knew that would be a contentious answer. "I asked if he sparkled."

"Were you drunk?"

"I was hanging out with Lance." That seemed like an answer to the question.

"I don't like Lance. I don't think he treats Karen very well; he seems like kind of a jerk."

"I won't argue against that too vehemently." Terrance finished his coffee. "I'd better get going."

"And I need to stop by my place and check on Amidala."

"She'll probably still be a dumb, overweight cat, but maybe you'll get lucky."

She playfully hit him on the back of the head. "You're a jerk too. So when do I find out about my super-fantastic one-month anniversary surprise?"

"I never said it was super-fantastic."

She stared at him wide-eyed with comically over-the-top intensity. "Well, it better be, because as I said, I can just find someone else who will appreciate me enough to give me a super-fantastic one-month anniversary surprise. I'm pretty hot."

"I need to work on making you more insecure; I can't have you always lording your hotness over me." He pointed at her head. "Your hair is kind of weird."

She came at him with a series of playful slaps. "I haven't had a chance to work on it yet! Shut up!"

They kissed. "I'll see you later, Ance. Go do your Batman stuff."

"Okay, Catwoman. And I promise you'll like your surprise." He took one last look at her pretty, smiling face, thinking how much he had lucked out, and then he stepped over another piece of armor as he headed out the door.

* * *

Terrance was not at all sure Shannon would like his surprise. He thought maybe it was a great idea, but also feared it was really stupid and that Shannon would think he was an idiot.

He worried a bit about it during his workday, and all the weird things from the weekend faded away as concerns. It had all seemed so important at the time, but he had a girlfriend and real problems to worry about, not some silly made-up conflict over good and evil that the crazy-seeming Talia had ranted about.

The head of software, Pendergrass, had sent Terrance a list of bugs to look into, and soon Terrance found himself in the midst of a debugging sweet spot, where all of the world's concerns disappeared as his mind was fully devoted to puzzling out some esoteric coding problem. He eventually had to get up to get some more coffee, though, and in the break room he saw Karen fetching an apple. She glanced at him but didn't say hi. Terrance was going to ignore her, too, but he thought of something—a real concern he did want to know more about.

"I ran into Shannon's ex over the weekend," he told her as he poured his coffee.

Karen had a very immediate and brief reaction that almost looked like fear, but it quickly faded away. "You feel threatened by him?"

"No. He seems like a huge jerk."

"He is. I've told Shannon she needs to get further away from him...maybe even change jobs."

"Do you think she might do that?" Terrance blurted out. No matter how hard he tried to convince himself otherwise, Shannon's job was a big issue to him, and her leaving it would be a load off his mind.

"I don't think so. She's always going on about how great and important it is."

"How did she end up as one of the Sisters of Torment anyway?"

Karen took a bite of her apple and thought for a moment. "She was kind of bouncing around trying to figure out what she wanted to do after college, and...well, she met Chet. After they started dating, she kind of got enamored with, you know, those people. Whatever it is they do."

Now Terrance liked Chet even less. "So what do you think of...those people?"

Karen shrugged. "They're okay...I guess. They seem important."

"Did you think of joining them?"

"Briefly. Shannon tried to talk me into it."

"Why didn't you?"

Karen looked a little perturbed by the question. "I just decided not to. I hear you got beaten up at a bar last night."

"I got struck once," Terrance said. "Seems like you need to get hit multiple times for it to qualify as 'beaten up.'"

"Well, you don't want to even get struck once by Chet, so make sure you avoid him." Karen left the break room.

Terrance thought about fighting Chet. He had taken some Tae Kwon Do as a kid, but it didn't seem like that would be adequate.

* * *

"I'm warning you: expectations are high."

"Well, it's nothing too big," Terrance said as he drove Shannon to the surprise. "I thought it would be something different to try, but I might be wrong."

"Don't try to backtrack now," Shannon said melodramatically as she narrowed her eyes at him. "You told me this morning you had a surprise, and I've been anticipating it all day. My expectations are so high that a surprise I normally would have loved will seem awful and stupid, and I will hate you for it."

"Did you get me a surprise?"

"Don't try and change the subject! Plus, I am your surprise. I'm the awesomest, most beautiful girlfriend ever, and it's insulting that you want anything more from me. Now there are even more expectations for your surprise, because it has to make up for the insult as well."

Terrance pulled into the parking lot of a gas station. "I've changed my mind; we're not going. You're too high-maintenance. I'm going to find a girlfriend who isn't set at nightmare difficulty."

"No, I'll be good!" Shannon pleaded while cracking up. "Take me to the surprise! You're the best boyfriend ever, and I should be nicer to you even though I won't be!"

"Okay. Best behavior." Terrance got back on the road and drove a bit longer until he went into the parking lot of the Family Speedway. "Here it is: go-kart racing."

Shannon's expression was neutral for a few moments as she looked the place over. Then she shot her arms in the air, punching the roof of Terrance's Hyundai. "Awesome!"

"Since on our first date we played Mario Kart, I was thinking maybe we could try some actual kart racing."

"Foster a pure kart-based relationship."

"That would be the ultimate goal."

Shannon smiled. "So can we throw turtle shells at each other?"

"No, I checked the FAQ on their website. They don't allow that. So does this sound fun?"

"No, not fun." She looked at Terrance with her game face plus a smile. "This is competition, and you're going down!"

* * *

It seemed to Terrance that go-kart racing would lose a lot of its appeal when one had a driver's license and could drive actual cars, but it was still extremely fun. Plus, the actual driving experience gave him a big advantage over the little kids. In the race they were in, it was quickly down to him and Shannon. They were neck-and-neck and constantly fighting for the inside lane on turns. A couple of times, Shannon nudged him, but he kept control and the lead. He was one turn away from finishing the last lap when he suddenly noticed a figure in the crowd watching them. A woman in white. Talia.

Shannon slammed into him as he was distracted, and this time he spun out and ran into the guardrails. By the time he righted himself, two more karts had passed him, and he ended in fourth.

"I'm the greatest racer ever!" Shannon yelled as she pulled off her helmet.

Terrance scanned the crowd but couldn't find Talia.

Shannon slapped his helmet. "Hey, space cadet. I beat you. You're supposed to be vowing vengeance."

Terrance pointed a finger to Shannon's face. "You spun me out. I will have my revenge, woman." They both laughed and headed off the tracks. As Terrance took off his helmet, he kept looking for Talia but couldn't see her. He started to wonder if he'd imagined her; it seemed like he had been seeing a lot of weird stuff lately.

"You all right?" Shannon asked.

"I...thought I saw a ghost."

Shannon nodded. "I assume the famous phantom of the go-karts, which is totally a thing and not something I just made up right now."

"And his appearance invalidates race results. So I guess we'll have to rematch."

"That is a very well-known rule about the phantom. So, new race." Shannon put back on her helmet. "And I will destroy you!"

"A date is supposed to bring us closer together, so I'm starting to wonder if a competitive date is a bad idea."

"Your face is a bad idea!"

Terrance laughed. "Fine. Just let me use the restroom, and then you can spend five minutes staring at the back of my go-kart."

"Okay, but don't sneak out of a window in there to avoid a whupping!"

Terrance headed into the nearby restroom, which was empty, so he had his pick of urinals. He chose the one furthest from the door and unzipped.

"Psst. In here."

Terrance turned his head to see Talia peering out of one of the stalls. He immediately zipped back up. "What are you doing in here?"

"Just wanted to talk. Join me."

"I'm not getting in a bathroom stall with you."

"Then get in the one touching this one. Hurry, Denby. Before we're seen."

"Seen by who?" Terrance asked as he went into the stall next to Talia's and shut and locked the door.

"Whom. Seen by *whom*."

He sat on the toilet. He reminded himself he'd need to wash these jeans. "Just answer the question."

"Perhaps you've noticed that there are those who want me ripped to pieces. I don't fear them, but I always exercise caution. Who is the girl with you?"

It was Terrance's understanding that Shannon and Talia had fought before, but apparently Talia hadn't recognized her out of her armor. "My girlfriend."

"Lovely thing." Sounded more like an insult the way Talia said it. "Let me guess: you fornicate with her in an attempt to forget the world—forget what you've seen and what you know. You cover yourself in the filth of this world so you forget all that is beyond this mere sliver of existence."

"That's...kind of personal. And inappropriate. I really have to get going." He also still needed to pee.

"You tried to stand up to the Darkness the other day. You fought a vampire—a creature of malevolence."

"Are you following me?"

"I looked you up, saw how you waste your days."

He worried that she'd seen Shannon arrive at his apartment in her Sisters of Torment getup, but he assumed Talia would have brought that up if she had. "Why are you spying on me?"

"A better question: Why didn't you have your sword? You have the means to truly fight evil, yet you shy away. Why won't you embrace what you are, Denby?"

"I'm a computer programmer who designs web applications; I don't really think fighting evil is my thing. I mean...shouldn't that be a police matter or something?"

She laughed. "You don't understand anything. Your eyes are open, but you're still not ready to see." She handed him a piece of paper under the stall barrier. Terrance accepted it and took a look. Written on it was, *Meeting of the Infinite. 6 p.m. Thur. Beyond the Hobby Lobby.*

"What's this?" Terrance asked.

"There are others like me. If you want to learn—if you want to truly understand—then come."

He wasn't quite sure he wanted to be in a room full of others like Talia. "I'll think about it."

"There will be snacks."

"Well, I guess I'll see if I'm hungry that evening."

"You will come. You can try to pretend that you can live your life normally, but you won't be happy. You'll be like Tantalus, but instead of the things you truly desire being out of your reach, you'll just never even try to grasp them. The best you'll do is attempt to smother all the thoughts of grander things in the embrace of your whore."

Terrance rolled his eyes. "So I'm guessing my girlfriend isn't invited."

"If you think she is ready to see, then you can bring her. If not, then we have no use for her and neither should you."

"It's getting pretty serious between us. We've dated a month and—"

"We're done here."

"Well, I have to pee, so can you leave?"

"I'll leave after you."

Terrance sighed, put the invitation in his pocket, and left the stall. He went to a urinal, but it took him a while to start, knowing that Talia was in a stall behind him and perhaps watching. As the stream finally began, Talia uttered, "You have a destiny, Denby."

"Yeah, I'm getting that. Thanks." He quickly finished, ran some water over his hands, and hurried out of the restroom.

"You fall in?" Shannon demanded. She was leaning against a wall just outside the restroom. "I was about ready to recruit a search party to send in after you."

"I had business to attend to."

"'Business,' eh. Just took you a while to muster the courage to take me on again." She smiled at him mischievously. He loved her smile, but his enjoyment of his girlfriend was undercut by how many secrets he was keeping from her. It gave him a sense of dread, but he wasn't sure what to do about it. Coming out and telling her everything was an option, but then Shannon and her people would probably do something nasty about Talia and her people—and he couldn't convince himself to support that.

Shannon's expression became more serious. "Are you sure nothing is the matter?"

Terrance smiled. "I'm just still getting over the trauma from that last race." He kissed her and hoped that was enough to forget his worries, but he knew he was now in the middle of something. And it was unlikely to end well.

CHAPTER 12

The next night, they relaxed at Terrance's place. They tended to hang out there since Shannon lived in the evil-looking fortress up on the mountain, which was kind of out of the way (and very ominous), and frankly Terrance wasn't in much of a rush to get near it. Of course, he had never told Shannon this; it was just another secret he was keeping from her. The secrets were becoming a huge weight on his mind, to the point that they began to ruin his time with Shannon. He wanted to unload some of these burdens, but everything seemed like a minefield. For instance, he thought about telling her about the tunnel under his apartment, but then maybe she'd want a look and his sword was in the closet and he was *really* afraid of her finding out about that for some reason. If he wanted to continue his relationship with her, he'd have to get rid of it.

If. There was no "if" to it, he thought as he looked at the lovely woman sitting next to him on the couch. He enjoyed every moment he was around her, and he certainly would enjoy his time around her even more if he got rid of the anxiety he had about a number of issues. That's what he had to address. All he had to do was settle his mind about a few things and all would be well.

"Thanks for watching *Farscape* with me." Shannon snuggled up next to Terrance as the music played during the end credits of another episode, and rested her head on his shoulder. "You really don't mind even though you've seen them before?"

"No, I enjoy it." It all seemed so simple: he just had to forget about Talia and his sword. And then he'd have to convince himself that the things he thought were awful weren't really so awful. After meeting Talia in person, it was more understandable that someone would want to feed her to a horrible monster. But the gathering she had told him about promised more answers. And what she'd said about fighting evil—a little part of Terrance perked up at that idea.

Then again, apparently part of the evil he would be fighting was Shannon. He looked at her, cuddling against him. There was nothing even slightly evil about her. Her hair smelled nice.

"Are you excited about Lacey's birthday party on Friday?" Shannon asked, a touch of sarcasm in her voice.

"Oh, yeah, on pins and needles." He was dreading it. First off, he was never good at parties where he didn't know anyone, and he was terrible at starting up conversations with strangers. Second, Lacey was one of Shannon's coworkers, and he was a bit scared of being surrounded by people from Shannon's job; he just hoped they'd be in normal clothes and not demony-looking armor. Third, the party was going to be at the evil-looking fortress, the one Malcus and other ominous things were always flying around, and Terrance shuddered at the thought of even getting near it.

"My friends from work are cool; you'll like them," Shannon assured him. "Just don't show weakness, because they hone in on any perceived weakness."

Terrance shuddered. "Like what do you mean? Will they—"

"I'm kidding!" Shannon chuckled. "You look like a scared puppy. You're going to have fun on Friday." She kissed him on the cheek. "And sorry I have to work the next two nights."

"You work a lot of nights."

"Well, it's just more intimidating a lot of times to attack at night."

"So...what are you attacking?"

"I dunno. I'm not really at the high level with the planning. They just kinda throw us into places—but usually it's pretty obvious what to do."

Stop asking questions! yelled a little voice in Terrance's head, but he was determined this time to try to understand. "I just never really got what the point of your organization is. Is it associated with the government?"

Shannon giggled. "No. This is stuff beyond government matters."

"Beyond?"

"Yeah, they don't get involved with these things. It's above them." She sat up and looked at Terrance. "Why are we talking about boring work stuff?"

"I don't find this boring. I want to understand this."

"Well, you can't; that's the thing." She looked deep in thought for a moment, trying to come up with the right words. "You know how science explains, like, everything?"

"Yeah."

"We're concerned with the stuff it doesn't explain—the things that shouldn't *be*, really. We're trying to keep this universe together, basically, because there are things trying to tear it apart. People, even."

That certainly didn't make what she did sound too bad. But it didn't quell all his concerns. "You know how the other day I had a run-in with a vampire? That seems like one of the things that falls outside of the...um...normal realm. Do you handle things like that?"

Shannon hesitated a bit, seeming to work quite hard on forming her answer. "As part of the...um...let's just say 'cracks' in this universe...some things may seem bad when they really aren't."

"And other things like faeries may seem good when they aren't?"

She nodded. "Exactly."

"So there are cracks in the universe?" Terrance asked. "That seems like an important thing everyone should be worried about."

Shannon shrugged. "There's not anything most people can do."

"Are scientists looking into it?"

"No. As I said, these are matters beyond science, and scientists only care about things within science."

That seemed to sort of make sense while also being completely ridiculous.

"Why are you asking so many questions about this anyway?" Shannon asked with a smile, but Terrance could sense a little tension.

"It's your job. I just want to understand it."

She smiled. "That's sweet. I want to understand your job, too, but it sounds boring and nerdy."

Terrance chuckled, but his humor quickly faded as the one question he really wanted to ask lingered in his mind. "So, in your job, do you ever worry that what you're doing is wrong?"

Shannon quickly sat up and faced him. "What do you mean?"

"It's just you seem to be killing lots of things...and raiding villages...and I guess sometimes harming people, and doesn't that maybe seem a little...um...bad to you?"

Her expression tensed, squeezing out all the sweetness that was usually in her face. "Why would it be wrong? I explained to you what we're doing and why." Her voice kept rising, anger building behind it. "Why in the world would you think any of that is wrong?"

This was exactly what Terrance feared. He knew he was on a precipice: another step forward and things would fall apart. So he backed away. "Well, you sometimes get blood splattered on you; that seems like a health risk."

"Oh," Shannon said, nervously laughing and then becoming visibly relieved. "No, that's nothing to worry about." She snuggled up against Terrance again. "But it's cute that you're worried."

"I just wouldn't want something to happen to you." He ran his hand through her hair. "Then I wouldn't get to go to this fun birthday party I'm super-duper excited about."

She giggled. "It won't be bad." She turned to face him. "But don't ask my coworkers a lot of questions like you've been asking me, okay?"

"Of course not."

His eyes went briefly to the coat closet, where there was a faerie sword and a tunnel deep into the ground. If he wanted answers, he could try to find them. But he dreaded what he'd discover.

CHAPTER 13

Terrance sat in his living room the next evening, staring at his coat closet. He so wished he had a copy of Legendary Quest to take his mind off things, but it was still sold out. Tomorrow was the meeting Talia had told him about, the meeting of people perhaps trying to destroy the world, as Shannon described it. He really wanted to accept Shannon's description of things—it would make life so much easier. Talia and whoever else she was with were bad and to be avoided. All the weird stuff Terrance noticed simply had to be ignored, and then he could enjoy Shannon's company with no reservations and everything would go back to normal for him.

But for some reason he couldn't accept that, no matter how much he wanted to. He needed to find more answers first. He needed to explore the places he'd previously ignored, as Talia had told him to.

Terrance got up, went outside, and climbed the stairs to the apartment above him. He knocked on the door, and Lance answered. "What?"

"I'm going to explore that tunnel under my apartment."

Lance looked confused. "Why?"

"To find out what's there."

"What do you expect to find?"

"I don't know. I guess I'll see."

Lance was silent for a moment. "You really don't know what to do with yourself when your girlfriend isn't around, do you?"

"I guess not. So...want to come?"

"Why would I want to come?"

"Well...it's a little creepy. Plus down there is whatever has been pounding on my floor. I thought maybe the buddy system would be a good idea."

"Yeah, I don't think so, dude. I just don't get the point."

"You sure? Who knows what we'll find? Might be interesting. Last time I was exploring, I found an office building alone in a field with an elf in it."

"That sounds stupid, so no, I don't think so. If you're scared, do you have a gun or something you can take with you?"

"Well, I have a Glock .40 caliber my dad gave me, but I never got a concealed-carry permit. I've meant to, but it's kind of a hassle because I have to take a class and then get fingerprints taken and get a form notarized. Anyway, I don't know if a tunnel under my apartment counts as my property or not, so I should probably have the permit if I were going to take the gun. So you're sure you're not coming?"

"Yes. If you're bored, why don't we just go to Tappers?"

Terrance shook his head. "No, I need to find out what's down there."

"No you don't. You're descending into weirdness, Terr."

Terrance shrugged. "I guess that's just who I am."

He headed back to his apartment and prepared for his descent. He got his Maglite and strapped his Leatherman tool in a sheath on his belt. He opened the coat closet and stared down at the entrance outlined in the floor. He looked at the faerie sword leaning against a wall next to it. He decided that if he wasn't taking his gun, he would take the sword. He strapped it to his back again; even though it was hard to reach, it seemed like it would be easier to descend a ladder that way than if it were at his hip.

So he was ready. He moved the backpack and other things out of the way and lifted up the trapdoor. He stared down the hole for a moment. The ladder descended far out of view. He couldn't tell how far down, just that there was a light at the bottom. He took a deep breath, eased himself onto the ladder, and began to descend.

It took a while. He eventually became afraid of looking down, not quite sure how high up he was. The whole passageway was quite narrow. Terrance had never been claustrophobic, but he also hadn't spent minutes in a nearly endless passageway of such a small size. A couple of times, he thought about heading back up, but by that time, it would already have been a long climb, and he was hoping that getting to the bottom would be quicker. Eventually he saw the ground, and finally, for the last few yards, the passageway opened up into a brightly lit cavern nearly the size of his apartment. The light was coming from glowing, pinkish crystals embedded all about the cavern.

Terrance set his feet onto the rocky ground and slowly walked over to one of the crystals. It was larger than his hand and warm to the touch. He pulled out his phone and snapped a picture.

He looked around the cavern and saw a tunnel just big enough for a man to fit through. It had no crystals in it and was quite dark, but he could see light spilling in from the other end. Terrance took his Maglite in hand—more for security than for light—and slowly headed into the tunnel. Again, it made him a little claustrophobic, but after he turned a corner he could see the light coming from another room. He upped his pace and came to the exit of the tunnel.

The room was enormous—a cavern so large, a football stadium could fit inside with room to spare. The ceiling appeared to be hundreds of feet above him and the walls were covered in the glowing crystals. Ahead was a vast underground lake, and at the far end he could barely see what looked like a temple built into the rock face. He stared in awe for a few moments, then took another picture with his phone. It was one of those things that were hard to portray on a two-dimensional image; it looked flat on his phone's display compared to the vast grandeur he saw with his own eyes.

Terrance approached the lake. The water was clear, and crystals illuminated it from below. He could see fish swimming in it, and then something much larger headed his way. He backed up as it suddenly emerged above the surface.

"Hi!" It was a young woman, holding her upper body out of the water. She wore nothing but a big smile, her dark hair covering her bare chest.

Terrance forced his eyes to hers. "Hey. You...uh, live here?"

"I hang out here a lot. Technically I live in the ocean."

"Are you a mermaid?"

"Yep!" She ducked her body back into the water and lifted her blue fish tail above the surface. It was scaly like a fish, but had horizontal flukes like an aquatic mammal tail. Terrance decided to ignore the incongruity.

"Are you the one I keep bothering down here with the noise from my apartment?" Terrance asked.

"No, I never hear you. Are you noisy?"

"I don't think so...but I'm bothering someone down here."

The mermaid shrugged. "Anyway, I'm Jenna. It's nice to meet you. Are you a warrior?" She pointed to the sword on Terrance's back.

"No. My name is Terrance, and I'm a computer programmer who works on web applications."

"Ooh! That sounds fun!"

It didn't sound like she was mocking him. "It is, actually. Once you gain an understanding of programming, it can be quite engrossing."

"Neat! So what are you doing down here?"

"Well...um...just exploring, I guess. I've started to notice things..."

"Like what things?"

Terrance looked at the temple beyond the underground lake, but it was hard to see much detail. "I don't know exactly; things seem to be going on that I hadn't noticed before...maybe like a war. Have you heard of the Infinite?"

"Nope."

"Do you know anything about faeries?"

"I know they don't like swimming. You think a war is going on?"

"Well, I know of soldiers on one side, and I may be meeting some from the other side. Some sort of good-versus-evil battle...though I'm not sure who is who."

"Sorry, don't know about that. I stick to the water, and things are peaceful here."

Terrance chuckled. "Well, of course; you have Aquaman protecting you."

Jenna's smiled disappeared. "Are you making fun of Aquaman?"

Terrance hesitated. "It's just—you know—a lot of people do. His superpower is talking to fish."

"He *commands* fish; he doesn't talk to them." She began to look angry, but then seemed to calm herself. "You know, in his original comics in the early 1940s, he fought the Nazis."

"Then I thank him for his fictional service to my country."

"He's a good superhero; I think more people need to give him a chance instead of making fun of him."

"Okay...I'll check out his comics."

She smiled again. "If you give me your email, I can send you a list of the good series to look into. Hey, if you think about it, being a programmer, you're kind of like Aquaman—but instead of commanding fish, you command computers."

Terrance carefully hid how insulted he was to be compared to Aquaman. "Actually, I've had my job compared more to Batman in the past."

Jenna grimaced. "Who would want to be like Batman? He doesn't even have superpowers."

Terrance wasn't going to dignify that with a response. "So what exactly is going on down here?"

Jenna's smile faded again, but now her expression was serious without looking angry. "Do you want to know the secrets of this cavern?"

"Um...I guess. It *is* under my apartment, and something down here keeps hitting my floor from below when I make noise."

"Then come into the water with me; I'll show you everything."

Terrance considered the half-naked lady—or, more accurately, the completely naked half lady. "I wasn't really planning on getting wet. And I have my phone..."

"You can leave it on shore. No one will steal it."

Terrance fidgeted with his hands. "Um...here's the thing. I have a girlfriend, so I don't really think I should be swimming with a naked woman."

She giggled. "My bottom half is fish; nothing is going to happen."

"Yeah...I see the logic there. Still, I don't think I want to go swimming right now; maybe some other time."

Jenna frowned. "But there is so much you need to—" She quickly turned to look behind her. "Oh no." She turned back to Terrance. "An evil thing comes; hide."

"Huh?"

Jenna did not respond; she simply disappeared into the water. Terrance noticed something very large—almost like a whale—moving in the water toward him. He backed away, and the creature surfaced with a splash, sticking its broad head above the water. It was dark green and scaly, with large yellow eyes and a wide mouth big enough to swallow Terrance whole, filled with sharp-looking teeth. Terrance had put some distance between himself and the water's edge, desperately hoping that the thing was unable to go on land.

It spoke. "Do not listen to the mermaid; it lies." Its voice was deep and raspy, like a frog's croak.

Terrance ran through his mind what Jenna had said, to figure out what had possibly been a lie, but she mainly had talked about how Aquaman was actually a decent superhero—and he already suspected the truth about that. "She said she was going to show me the secrets of this area."

"She would lead you to your doom," the thing said. "If you wish to learn, follow me."

"Get in the water with you?"

"You can ride my back." It surfaced some more, and now its scaly back, perhaps thirty feet long, stuck out of the water.

Terrance took a careful look at the scary-looking creature and its mouth full of teeth. He didn't want to get in the water with it, either, but this was less of a moral quandary. "I was just coming down here to get a look at the place; I really need to be heading back."

"That is your choice, but I have lived here for a long, long time. If you wish to know its secrets, then I can show you."

"I'll keep that in mind...um...you wouldn't happen to be the one who doesn't like the noise from my apartment?"

"No, I do not hear you up there. What you wake with your noise is something far more ancient than even I."

"What?"

"I can only show you."

Again, Terrance looked at the creature's teeth and decided he really wasn't that curious, after all. "Well, I'm just going to watch some TV and get to bed, as I have to work tomorrow. Nice meeting you, though."

"We shall meet again." The creature sank back down until it was once again just a huge shadow beneath the surface of the water, then it floated away.

Terrance took one last look at the vast cavern and its underground lake. He really didn't know what to make of it, but he decided to worry about it another time, as he really did have work tomorrow. And there was a very long ladder-climb ahead of him.

CHAPTER 14

"So there's a cavern under our apartments, and I found a mermaid there."

Lance poured himself a cup of coffee from the pot in the break room. "Was she hot?"

"Yeah, pretty much. She also wasn't wearing...anything."

"No seashell bra?"

Terrance shook his head. "I guess that's a Disney thing. It would probably be uncomfortable."

"Never worn a bra; wouldn't know. If you'd said there would be hot mermaids, I probably would have gone exploring with you."

"Well, I didn't know what I'd find. That's why you explore."

"And what happened?" Lance asked.

"What do you mean, what happened?"

"With you and the mermaid?"

"Well...we argued about comic books."

Lance sipped his coffee. "You really know what to do with a naked woman, Terr."

Terrance ignored that. "She got scared away by this other creature in the underground lake. A big, scaly thing, large as a whale but reptilian."

"A dinosaur?"

Terrance scoffed. "Yes, Lance, I discovered a dinosaur—a creature thought to be extinct for 65 million years—and came to work the next day like everything was normal. It was just some monster or something."

Lance sipped his coffee. "The naked mermaid sounds more interesting."

"So, have you heard of the Infinite?"

"Nope. Who are they?"

"I don't know; that's why I was asking." Their meeting was tonight, and he still hadn't decided whether he was going.

The dark figure of Darlor approached, the lights of the break room seeming to dim in his presence. "Mr. Denby, are you working on the bugs in the legacy algorithm code?"

"Yeah, I've had to get a little help from Pendergrass, because the stuff is really old and confusing, but I'm making progress."

"Good. See it done without delay." Darlor gave a slight smile, revealing his sharp teeth flecked with red, then turned and left.

Terrance looked at Lance. "Why does it always seem like his teeth are bloody?"

"Maybe it's what he eats."

"What's he eat?"

Lance thought about it. "When we went to Chili's a few weeks ago, he got a live deer."

"They have that at Chili's?"

"It's not on the menu; you have to ask for it."

"Well, I better get to work." Terrance grabbed his coffee and headed to his cubicle. As he sat down, his cellphone rang. It was Shannon.

"Hey, lover, am I interrupting?" she said in a sultry voice.

"Of course; I'm a very busy, important man."

"Well, I just wanted to say I miss you."

"I miss you, too."

"I really hate my stupid work schedule. One day I'll get a promotion and it won't be like this anymore. A Night Mistress is more of a lone assassin, so I'd have more control over the mission times and parameters."

"That sounds great!" Terrance said, thinking he sounded pretty convincing.

"So what have you been up to without me?"

"Just sitting around being alone and sad." It was a joke, so it wasn't really lying.

"Aww. Well, we'll have fun tomorrow. Can't wait for you to meet some of my friends from work."

Dread slithered through him, but he pushed it away. "That should be fun. I really miss you."

"Me too. You're a great boyfriend; I hope you know that."

"I try." He felt like a horribly deceitful boyfriend.

"Well, I have to get going. I just wanted to touch base so I wasn't some super-absentee girlfriend."

"Your time away makes you more mysterious. If I saw you more, you'd probably quickly become annoying and boring."

"Lies! Remind me when I get back that I must smack you for your lies."

She could hit surprisingly hard. "I'll write it down."

"Bye, Ance."

"Bye."

He set down the phone and once again contemplated whether or not he should meet with Talia's group. What did he hope to learn from them? It was like he was searching for something, and he was hoping they could finally tell him what.

Terrance set the idea aside and went back to his programming. He pulled up the old, horribly formatted main algorithm code. It was so complex-looking and inscrutable that it was hard to imagine it didn't have thousands of problems. He noticed a comment in the code, one of the very few in it. It read, *It watches. And it waits. As you fall apart.* One of these days, Terrance figured he'd need to hunt down who wrote this code and give him a piece of his mind, but for now he was happy to just lose himself in fixing it.

* * *

Terrance parked his car and looked at the handwritten note. *Beyond the Hobby Lobby.* In front of him was a strip mall with a building labeled *Hobby Lobby* with a block-lettered orange sign. He wasn't sure what hobbies it catered to, but he suspected video gaming wasn't one of them.

He got out of his car and looked at the sheathed sword lying on the rear seat. That was what he was here to get answers about—or at least one of the things he wanted answers about. He picked up the sword and attached the scabbard to his belt. It was an odd weight at his hip, and his left hand went down to the hilt to hold it still. He had a strange sense of peace as he touched the sword at his side.

He looked around for where the "beyond" of the Hobby Lobby would be, and noticed a really thin alleyway between it and the pizza joint next door. He paused to reassess what he was doing there. What was he committing himself to by talking to these people? He told himself he'd just find out if they were all nutty, and if so, then he could dismiss them and move on. After that, he'd at least have some peace of mind.

He headed down the narrow alleyway. It was just wide enough for him to pass through, and was surprisingly long. As he reached the end of it, he thought he heard waves. When he finally exited the alleyway, he found himself on a clifftop hundreds of feet high, overlooking the ocean. A portion of the clifftop jutted further over the ocean and on it sat an ancient-looking castle that had become worn with age. Terrance hadn't thought there were any old castles in North America...but then again, this whole area didn't make any geographic sense. He was starting to come to the realization that nothing was ever going to completely make sense to him again.

For a moment, he stared out over the ocean. The sun was beginning to set, and its red light emphasized a large, mountainous island far in the distance. It was hard to see much detail, yet a desire to get to it boiled somewhere deep inside him. He shook away the notion and headed for the castle.

A large wooden double door was the entrance. One of the doors was ajar, and a piece of white paper was taped to the other, with a message written on it with a Sharpie: *MEETING OF THE INFINITE INSIDE.*

Terrance stepped through the open door and into a large stone entryway. Ahead, he saw an African American woman who appeared to be lighting torches along the wall with a box of matches. She turned and smiled as soon as she saw him. "You must be Terrance. Talia told us about you." She was wearing a simple blue dress, though at her hip was a sword. She walked over to Terrance and extended her hand. "I'm Vivian." She had a kind face that instantly put Terrance at ease.

He shook her hand and took another look around. The walls had mostly crumbled, but he saw a few doors, one with a piece of paper and an arrow taped next to it. "I'm just here to...um...maybe learn a little. I'm not really sure what's going on, especially ever since I was given this." He tapped the sword at his side.

She patted him on the shoulder. "We've all been there. We'll tell you what we know, and maybe you'll even have some things to tell us. If you want to head to the meeting room, there are cupcakes and lemonade if you're hungry. My husband, Curtis, also brought coffee."

"Okay, thanks." He chuckled a bit. "I was a little afraid you would all be like Talia."

"Oh." She hesitated a moment. "Yes, Talia is...special. She has an intensity to her, doesn't she? She's very sweet, she just has...um...a lot of enthusiasm and her own unique way about her. We're very grateful for what she contributes."

Contributes to what? he wanted to ask, but he assumed they'd answer that at the meeting. He headed for the meeting room. Inside were a whiteboard on a wall and a number of folding chairs arranged in a circle. The room was lit by a single bulb on the ceiling with a dangling metal-link cord to turn it on and off—though it was hard to imagine that this old castle was wired for electricity.

A folding table held cupcakes, a pitcher of lemonade, and a coffee carafe, and next to it stood an African American man, who looked at Terrance with a friendly smile. He wore slacks and a red sweater, which contrasted with the sword at his belt. He was tall but not a big man, and despite the weapon, he was yet another person who didn't look like a warrior. "Hi, I'm Curtis."

They shook hands. "I'm Terrance."

"It's great you're here. Why don't you grab some food if you're hungry, and take a seat," Curtis said. "Hopefully we'll have some answers for whatever questions you need to ask."

"And hopefully we don't scare him off," said another man, laughing. Terrance turned to see an older man with a graying beard seated in one of the chairs. He wore an old jacket that looked military and also had a sword at his hip. "I'm Randolph, by the way."

"Nice to meet you." Terrance took a cupcake and a napkin and poured himself a coffee. He never refused free coffee when offered. "I'm just hoping you guys can tell me something about my sword. Were you given yours by faeries, too?"

"You saw faeries?" asked a little girl. She was in the corner with some toys and coloring books and an even younger little boy. They looked to be about seven and five years old, respectively. "Did you see their palace? It's neat. I want to go up in it!"

"Yeah, I saw the palace," Terrance told her, "when they gave me the sword."

Curtis chuckled. "Faeries are an interesting thing. And don't worry, Terrance, we'll talk about all this when everyone arrives. We're all still learning here. These are my children, by the way, Grace and Daniel."

"Hi," he said to them. Grace smiled and waved at him, but Daniel kept playing with a toy truck.

Terrance took a seat, and soon a young couple who appeared to be about his age entered, two attractive people who looked like they must have been the stereotypical star quarterback/head cheerleader couple in high school. "Hey, bro, name's Travis and this is Erica," the man said with a big, friendly smile as he extended his hand.

Terrance shook it, and it was a more forceful handshake than he was expecting. "Terrance."

"Ready to get out there and destroy evil?"

"Well...uhh..."

"Don't push him," Erica chided Travis. She turned to Terrance and put her hand on his shoulder as if she were calming a child. "I bet this is all new and scary for you, but we'll help you through it. We've all been there ourselves."

Behind them, a middle-aged woman in scrubs walked in. "New guy!" she exclaimed upon seeing Terrance. "I'm Joyce."

"Terrance. So, are you a doctor?"

She straightened her scrubs. "Nope. Just a fashion statement. All the kids are wearing scrubs these days; haven't you seen it? I bet you're wondering what we're up to here, but it's nothing *too* weird, I assure you. Live sacrifices are scary the first time, but you get used to them."

Terrance went pale. "Wait, what are we—"

Curtis shook his head. "Don't listen to Joyce about anything."

A Hispanic man in a nice suit with a neatly trimmed goatee entered next. "I'm Donald."

"Terrance."

"Good to have you here," Donald said as he took a seat. Terrance found it refreshing to meet someone who wasn't talkative.

Next to arrive was a dark-haired teenage girl in glasses, dressed more like a woman in her forties except for her backpack. "Hi, I'm Felicia."

"Terrance. Um...aren't you kind of young for this?" Not that Terrance was quite sure what "this" was, but everyone in the group did have swords.

"I don't think anyone is really ready for it," she said sheepishly.

"The forces of the Darkness don't spare you on account of age," Randolph said. "I certainly don't get a senior discount."

The last to arrive was Talia, still dressed in her white cloak, head concealed in her hood. She walked in cautiously and immediately locked her eyes on Terrance. "You came. You didn't bring your 'girlfriend'?"

"I wasn't sure this would be her thing."

"Hopefully, she'll come around," Travis said. "Just to give you a heads-up, bro, it's definitely going to be an issue in the relationship. Erica was part of the Infinite before me, and I was all like, 'Why is she so crazy?' Eventually, I opened my eyes and wised up, though. So, just be patient with your girlfriend, and hopefully things will work out."

Terrance nodded. "We'll see." His girlfriend was definitely what he didn't want to be focusing on right now.

"If things don't work out," Talia said, "then you're better off without her." She cautiously approached the cupcake table, then turned to Vivian and asked, "Are they safe?"

"They're gluten-free."

Talia nodded and took a cupcake. She didn't take a seat like the others, but instead found an empty corner of the room to stand in.

"I guess that's all of us," said Curtis, who was now seated in the circle. "Why don't we start off by explaining things to Terrance, who I'm sure has a lot of questions."

They all looked at Terrance. He felt a bit on the spot, but everyone seemed pretty friendly and he wasn't too nervous...yet. "Um...for starters, who exactly are you all?"

"To put it simply," Curtis said, "we're warriors who fight evil."

Terrance looked around the group again. Only the older man, Randolph, looked even slightly threatening (well, Terrance *was* a little afraid of Talia). They all looked as out of place as he did carrying a sword. "And how does that work?"

"Well, a while ago you saw what they were going to do to Talia, and you intervened," Vivian said. "That's what we do."

"I didn't really do much. She saved herself."

"I'm sure she did," Curtis said with a slight chuckle. "But the point is, you took notice of what was going on. Most people just ignore the evil; we fight it."

Terrance had so many questions, it was hard to figure out where to start. "So where does this 'evil' come from?"

"Let's try an overview to help you understand." Curtis stood up and walked to the whiteboard on the wall. He picked up a blue marker and made one small dot on the board. "This is the known universe. This is the limited reality we can comprehend—everything we see and know of this world. This is all that science can quantify. The universe, planets, stars, whatnot." He drew a large circle encompassing most of the board, dwarfing the little dot. "This is the broader reality, in which our universe is but a tiny speck. It's probably not even really bound.

"Now, there are beings that are not just of this limited reality," he pointed to the dot, "but of the whole, true reality. The *infinite* reality." He looked at the group around him. "We are those beings."

Terrance took another look at the rather unremarkable group. "You're powerful multidimensional beings?" He started to wonder if he should begin planning an exit strategy.

"Be careful how you look at us," Joyce, the probable doctor, said. "We can shoot lasers out of our eyes." The group laughed.

"We can't shoot lasers—or do anything special," Curtis said. "It doesn't work that way."

"It would be awesome if it did," said Travis.

"But you're saying you're not of this world...right?" Terrance asked, being cautious with how incredulous his tone was.

"Not just us," Curtis said. "You too. All people, in fact."

Terrance mulled that over. "So everyone in the world is a transdimensional alien?"

"We're not aliens," Talia said. Her expression wasn't amused like the others. "The analogy is prisoners. We're prisoners. And this small sliver of the true reality is our prison."

"Imprisoned by who?" Terrance asked.

"Whom," Talia corrected.

"However you say it," Curtis said, "that is quite the question. There is a single being—or perhaps we should say entity—that is behind all of this. It has somehow constrained us to this world and filled it with evil things—the Darkness—to keep us in line. And it does this to feed off of us."

Terrance shuddered from some unfathomable fear. "It eats us?"

"Not like that." Curtis went back to his chair. "I think of it more like a leech—a parasite. It drains us while we let it."

"*The world is a vampire*," Joyce sang. "But we aim to be more than rats in a cage."

"Yes, it's complacency that this thing wants," Curtis continued. "It will only consume us if we let it. We are nearly infinite beings, but when we limit ourselves to this finite world, the rest of our body atrophies and is vulnerable to the Adversary."

"That's what you call him?" Terrance asked.

"We don't know enough about him to call him anything else."

"This all sounds pretty crazy, doesn't it?" Erica said, Travis holding her hand and nodding.

"Just a bit, yeah," Terrance answered. Somehow, though, it didn't feel so crazy that he could easily dismiss it. "Do you have any evidence for all of this?"

"You've seen all the strange things in this world—the things that don't belong," Talia said. "The magical creatures, the demons. You know in your gut that something is wrong, and that is why you're here."

Terrance nodded, and it was true that something seemed wrong in this world. Still, the ideas that something was awry and that this was a group of crazy people weren't exactly mutually exclusive. "But is there any, like, scientific study of this?"

"The magical things—the things you understand not to belong—these are things of other worlds. Science is only concerned with the things of this world," Curtis said. "It ignores the magical things."

"So scientists see these demons and such, and ignore them?" Terrance asked.

"Basically."

"That doesn't make any sense."

"Maybe not," Curtis answered, "but there is a lot people don't see—don't want to see—when their eyes are closed."

"So how do you guys know about all this?" Terrance asked.

"Let's call it prophecy," Curtis said. "Some of it is passed on from others like us. Some of it is gathered from the more benevolent creatures from beyond this world, like the faeries—though they're not often very straightforward."

"Just want to smack them sometimes, actually," Randolph said.

"Though that's probably bad luck or something," Joyce said.

"We also find information hidden in ancient texts," Curtis continued. "Old poems and stories long forgotten. And it's not that we search them out—we just seem to happen upon them. But it's only bits of information we find, pieces of a whole. It's taken time to put this all together."

"And who hid this information?" Terrance asked.

Curtis smiled. "We're not sure. We believe there is something opposed to the Adversary and trying to help us, but we know little about it. The faeries, for instance, seem to work to guide us in some ways and protect us from the full power of the Adversary, but to what end and who sent them, we do not know."

"As for why important info is scattered in ancient texts," Vivian said, "our best guess is that this makes it hard for the Adversary to know of it. He controls much of this world, so it takes a lot of effort to hide things from him. He has eyes everywhere, as I'm sure you've begun to realize."

Terrance shuddered as he thought of the little eyes glinting at him in the darkness.

"In the end, though," Curtis said, "we are really just confirming what we know in our hearts to be true. Our true selves know these things well, but that is who we've lost touch with. That's why you're here: you know something is wrong, and you want to do something about it."

Terrance looked down at the sword at his side. "And these swords?"

"The evil is from beyond this world," Randolph said, standing and unsheathing his sword to let it gleam in the light. "We need weapons from beyond this world to fight them."

"And that's what you people do?" Terrance said. "You fight the evil things? And you expect to eventually defeat the Adversary?"

Curtis said. "We have to. Or we're stuck here forever."

"So are you saying that saving the world is up to you few?" Terrance asked.

"There are groups like us all around the world, and others that are local," Curtis said. "We try to keep in contact and share what we know. But we keep individual groups small, as the Adversary has many allies, and the larger we get, the more likely he is to bear down upon us."

"Everyone who wants to live must fight," Talia said. "We help each other when we can, but at the end of the day the only one who can save you is yourself. No one is coming to rescue us from the Darkness; it's up to us all."

"But the Adversary seems much more powerful than"—Terrance took another look at the group who would look more in place in line at the DMV than fighting a powerful enemy—"well, you guys."

Curtis smiled. "That it seems. This world may appear giant and all-encompassing, but it is small in the scheme of things. That we know. And our true selves are more powerful than the Adversary. It's hard to tell, but he's weakened over time. The more in the world that seems out of place, the more he is losing control. The more the walls of his prison are breaking."

"Yeah...I don't think, geographically speaking, that there is supposed to be an ocean here," Terrance pointed out.

"And we're not sure the Adversary's minions were always so obvious," Vivian said, "but it's hard to know. Our memories are another thing of this world. The Adversary can alter them, too. He does whatever is necessary to keep us complacent and locked in this world."

Terrance was starting to weigh the idea of leaving again. "If he can alter our brains, then this sounds like kind of a pointless battle."

"There are greater parts of us that are beyond his control," Curtis said. "That's what we have to rely on, even as he controls all else. The fact is, the Adversary wants us to believe this sliver of the true reality is all there is, but we believe that the fact that things that don't fit with it are appearing—things from worlds beyond—means that his grip on us is weakening."

"But aren't you saying he can just alter the world again to hide the magical things better, and our memories of them, so we won't even know?" Terrance asked.

Curtis nodded. "Perhaps, but he is not like us. His power is finite. The important thing is that we fight him and his minions. That we don't let him drain us to nothing while nourishing himself."

Strangely, a small part of Terrance found that he wanted to believe this, but a larger part thought it was all made-up and really stupid. "So, how exactly do you fight?"

"When we see evil, we confront and destroy it," Talia said.

"But can't it kill us back?"

Curtis looked somber. "It can. Just our forms here, though. As for the greater part of us...we're not exactly sure what happens while the Adversary keeps his prison together."

"So death is death, basically." As it usually was.

"It's nothing to fear compared to the Adversary feeding on us and destroying us forever," Talia said. "That's what happens if you don't fight."

Terrance laughed. "So, no choice really."

"There are always choices," Curtis said. "There may be only one good choice, but there are always other options, and people often take them. For instance, you may have seen some of those we call the Hollow Ones: the Dark Enforcers and the Sisters of Torment. Like much of the Adversary's evil, most people pay little attention to these groups, but I assume you have begun to notice them."

"Yeah," Terrance said, trying not to sound too definitive.

"They are people who have also realized how things are not right in this world," Curtis continued, "but they have instead sided with the Adversary. They are very powerful in this universe. But they've given up their true selves to the Darkness— they are hollow inside. And they're more numerous than we are."

Terrance tried to think of Shannon as a force of evil. Even when picturing her in her dark armor, it didn't quite jibe in his head. "And you fight them?"

"They fight for the Adversary more zealously than anyone else," Curtis said. "All their power—all that they are—is in him."

"Eventually we will take the fight to them," Talia announced. "You've seen their fortress near the volcanoes to the north. We plan to attack it."

Terrance remembered how Shannon had called these people dangerous. "What would that accomplish?"

"We believe their fortress blocks a pathway to the Adversary," Curtis said.

"Why do you believe that?"

Curtis grinned. "Prophecy."

"What happens when you actually get to the Adversary?"

Curtis took a deep breath. "That, we'll have to find out."

"And it's so simple, too," Joyce chuckled. "We just have to fight the Adversary's army and slay the giant demon dragon. Easy-peasy."

"Demon dragon?" Terrance asked.

"Malcus," Talia said. "I think you remember him."

Terrance shuddered, thinking of the huge thing that had flown over as he passed through the forest on the way to Walmart.

"Malcus is a challenge, but his presence means we are making progress," Curtis said. "The Adversary likes to keep any battle with those who oppose him subtle and in the background, so as not to draw attention, but Malcus's deployment has been a rather aggressive move."

"Being chased by a giant dragon means we're winning," Joyce said with a laugh, though the laugh seemed a bit nervous.

"Actually, the primary purpose of this meeting," Curtis said, "is to further plan our assault on the fortress and discuss what we've found. There is a center of evil there, and we need to eventually tackle it, then see what lies beyond it."

"So, as I understand it," Terrance said, "you few are planning to fight an army of people loyal to the Adversary—"

"Demons," Talia said. "We fight demons...though some of them look like people."

Terrance nodded as he rose to his feet. This group was actively plotting to kill his girlfriend—or to be killed by her. "Okay. So you few are going to fight and...slay them all..."

"There are others," Curtis said. "As I've said, we keep our groups small to avoid the Adversary's notice, but when the assault happens, many of us will join together. Also, as you've seen from the faeries, we have allies from beyond this realm. We are not completely alone. But it is on us to take the initiative."

"Okay," Terrance slowly began heading for the door. "Well, this was interesting...but I don't really think I'm going to be of much help. I don't even know how to use a sword."

"You hit who you don't like with the sharp parts," Randolph laughed.

Terrance chuckled nervously. He again noticed the two children who had been sitting quietly in the corner working on coloring books. It made him kind of sad, as he didn't think things were going to end well for this group. "Anyway, thanks for the cupcake, but I have to get—"

"Coward!" Talia suddenly yelled at him.

She was angry, but the others looked a little surprised by her outburst. Vivian turned to her. "That's not necessary."

"It's true," Talia said. "He can see the evil. He saw what they tried to do to me. He knows something has to be done. And he's fleeing." She looked back at Terrance, her eyes tearing right through him. "He's a coward."

Terrance nervously played with the sheathed sword at his side. "I just don't know about all this and am not really ready to take sides in a war..."

"You're taking a side." Talia approached him until she was right up in his face. "You either confront the evil or you decide to ignore it and let it happen until you eventually join it yourself. If you're not ready to man up and fight for what you know is right, then get out of here, you little coward."

Curtis pushed his way between Talia and Terrance. "That's enough," he told Talia, then turned to Terrance and forced a smile. "This was probably a lot to absorb at once. Why don't you think it over some?" He took out a business card and handed it to Terrance. It said *Dayton Auto Repair*, and a cellphone number was handwritten on it. "You can call or email me later if you have more questions."

This seemed like an easy exit, so Terrance took it, with one last glance at Talia's hateful glare before leaving the room and the castle.

Outside, the sun was setting over the ocean, leaving an orange streak on the water before it and a red glow in the clouds around it. The distant island and its mountains were now just silhouettes. He was again absorbed in the feeling that something was out there, something important.

He shook himself back to reality—reality being that he was standing near an old castle on a cliff overlooking an ocean that geographically shouldn't be there. He so badly wanted to ignore all of this, but he knew nothing could ever really be normal again, because his eyes were open to how *not* normal the whole world was. But the idea of running around hacking away at beasts and enemy knights was unthinkable. And then there was Shannon, whom the Infinite were basically plotting to kill. Didn't he have to tell her about them? What would she and her people do to them?

He wished he hadn't come. He thought he wanted answers, but the more he knew, the more difficult things became.

"Hey."

Terrance turned and saw the Hispanic man in a suit who'd been at the meeting, whose name he had already forgotten. He appeared to be only a bit older than Terrance. "Oh, hi. Just about to head out."

"Those places you see in the distance"—the man pointed toward the island—"you can never reach those. Not from this world, at least."

"What are they?"

He shrugged. "The best way our brain can represent some larger truth in this world, I guess."

Terrance chuckled. "Nothing makes any sense."

"Not from where we stand, at least. Anyway, I'm pretty new at this, too. It's all weird and overwhelming, and kind of silly at times. What I recommend is that you try carrying your sword with you and use it when you need to. That's how you find out who you are, and that's what this is all about: finding out who we really are."

Terrance nodded and headed back toward the alleyway to get away from the place that shouldn't exist, and to his car. As he hurried off, he noticed a figure in white watching him from the castle's entrance. Talia. Her glare was still full of anger. He was a bit scared of her. He was scared of a number of things. And he wasn't sure carrying the sword was going to help with that.

CHAPTER 15

He saw her smile, and for a moment everything seemed like it would be all right again.

Terrance had spent Friday feeling like he was carrying around a heavy stone, like there was a constant weight threatening to crush him at any moment. He had considered the advice of the guy whose name he'd forgotten, but knew that carrying around his sword would cause a conflict with Shannon. He was pretty sure he didn't want that. And even if the Infinite had some point in their ramblings, he was quite sure he didn't want to be involved in some all-out assault on Shannon and her friends.

So it seemed that he had made his choice. He thought that would have lifted his burden, but everything still weighed on him, until he saw Shannon and her smile again. He kissed her, and a voice inside told him, *Everything is fine. Everything is good. You're silly to worry.*

She had come to his apartment to pick him up for her friend's birthday party and was in normal, cute clothes, not her dark armor. After the kiss, she pressed herself against him and put her head on his shoulder. "Was being apart from me everlasting torment?"

"You'll find a big pile of whiskey bottles next to the couch, as I had to drown my sorrows in drink."

"Aww...that's so sweet. Just remember to recycle the bottles. You ready to go?"

"Let me check." He looked down. "Yep. Got pants on. Ready to leave the house."

Shannon put a finger under his chin and gently tilted his head up so they were eye to eye, her expression mock serious. "You have to be your best today, as I'm showing you off to my friends. You need to be awesome and make them jealous and hate their own stupid boyfriends."

Terrance scoffed. "I doubt anyone there is going to be able to stand up to my mad programming skills. Their boyfriends will probably be doctors and Army Rangers and dumb things like that."

"Seriously, though, my friends are really fun, and we're going to have a great time. All right, Batman, to the Shannonmobile!"

They got into her Prius and headed off on their journey. "This is a weirdly quiet car," Terrance said.

"It's a hybrid! Every time I drive it, I'm helping to save the environment."
"I don't think it works that way."
"The faster I drive it, the more trees grow!"

Terrance chuckled, but through the windshield, he saw their destination in the distance. The dark fortress on a mountaintop, lit by the fires of nearby volcanoes. Large, winged things flying around it. He shuddered, though it seemed silly. He was just going to a birthday party.

* * *

The fortress loomed over them. Even close up, it was so dark that it seemed like a silhouette. It had spires that soared hundreds of feet into the air. The things flying about were vaguely lizard-like and thankfully seemed to take no note of the people below. Terrance wondered if he might see Malcus fly by, and shuddered at the thought.

Their destination was actually a few hundred yards from the fortress: ruins that rested on the lip of a volcano, partially lit by the glow of the orange magma bubbling down below. The ruins themselves were jagged structures made of black rock, casting odd shadows over the land around them. Terrance got an odd feeling from the place, as though something ancient and evil had once resided inside, or perhaps its ghost still did. Echoing from within the ruins were the sounds of "Gangnam Style."

Shannon's friend Lacey had apparently commandeered the ruins for her party. Colorful strands of paper decorated the ominous jagged pillars, and the whole structure came alive in the strobe lights.

"What is this place?" Terrance asked Shannon as they approached.

"Just a spot near the fortress that we use a lot for gatherings," she said. "I hate that this place is so far from town. Everyone wants a dark fortress where their enemies are tormented, but no one wants it in their backyard."

Terrance nodded and looked at the fortress again. Curtis had mentioned its blocking the path to the Adversary, but all he could see beyond it was darkness and the flying lizard things.

"We'll crash at my place tonight," Shannon said, pointing to the fortress, where her apartment apparently was. "Just watch out for Amidala; she likes to claw in the middle of the night."

"Cats are so lovely." Terrance had the odd thought that if he fell asleep in the ominous fortress, something would eat his soul.

"Hey, guys!" someone called out. Terrance turned to see Lance heading toward them with Karen at his side. "Well, ain't this a crazy place?"

Karen took in the surroundings with an expression of disgust. "Why would you have a party here?"

"Because of the volcanoes, it's warm all year round," Shannon said.

"Isn't being so close to volcanoes dangerous?" Karen asked.

Shannon shrugged.

"I think it's cool." Lance put his hand on Terrance's shoulder. "The only thing dangerous here is Terr. He's always crazy at parties."

"Yep, that's me," Terrance said dryly. "Never left a party on my own volition; always had to have the cops drag me away."

"The cops don't come up here," Shannon said. "It's not really in their jurisdiction."

"Oh," Terrance answered, trying to figure out what that meant.

"Come on." Shannon pulled Terrance forward. "I want to introduce you to my friends."

"Don't let them steal Terrance away from you," Karen said behind them, chuckling.

In the ruins were numerous young men and women drinking and chatting. Terrance wondered how many of them would be called the Hollow Ones by the Infinite; everyone looked pretty normal. There were a lot of hot girls, though. If there was an entity trying to get people to look past evil in the world, having lots of hot girls on its side was probably helpful.

He glanced at Shannon again, and she smiled back at him. He had the thought that maybe that was what Shannon was: a temptress sent to draw him into the grasp of the evil Adversary. It seemed silly, though. His attraction to her wasn't based solely on looks; she was a fun person to be around, someone he felt he could actually relate to.

Yet he was always second-guessing his relationship with her. He thought perhaps it was normal to have jitters when your girlfriend was so great that you wanted to make sure you held on to her.

"Happy birthday, Lacey!" Shannon called out as they approached a platinum-blonde woman in a skimpy outfit. Lacey's flawless appearance almost made Terrance wonder if she was an actress he had seen before. She regarded Shannon with a slight smile but didn't make even that small effort for Terrance. Flanking Lacey were three other gorgeous women, all wearing outfits emphasizing the lovely curves of their bodies. Terrance made a note to be careful where his eyes focused, especially since he was standing next to his girlfriend. The other women all smiled at Terrance, but the smiles didn't seem friendly. The warning about the Hollow Ones being dangerous came back to his mind.

"Hey, Shana-nana," Lacey answered. "I like birthdays. I like having a day when everyone recognizes how great I am, though I'd prefer it more than once a year. So is this the guy you told me about? Tully or something?"

"It's Terrance," Terrance said.

Lacey shook her head. "No, that wasn't it. I must be thinking of another guy."

Shannon fake-laughed. "You are so droll." She looked at Terrance. "Anyway, this is my friend from work, Lacey. She's...how should I explain her? She's like if you took the concept of 'being a bitch' and put it into human form."

Lacey nodded. "Yeah, that's about right."

"And this is Elissa." Shannon pointed to a redhead next to Lacey, who continued to smile at him in a way that was somewhere between sexy and creepy. "This is Vicky." She was a raven-haired beauty who gazed at Terrance with bored indifference. "And this is Amber." The brunette smiled at him, but there was something almost threatening about it. "They're all slutty and really dumb. I can't overemphasize both those aspects."

"One more drink and I'll probably be throwing myself all over him," Elissa said. She downed the contents of her red Solo cup. "Uh-oh."

"Well, it's nice to meet you all," Terrance said, though he was trying to decide whether that statement was true.

"It's great to meet us," Lacey said. "And as Shannon's friends and fellow women-at-arms, it's our job to carefully approve anyone she dates."

Amber approached him and casually felt the material of his polo shirt. "And we like to be very thorough."

"Be nice to him," Shannon warned.

"This is us being nice," Lacey said. She looked at Terrance with a smile, but her eyes were filled with menace. "So what do you do, Terrance?"

"I design web applications."

"Explain further."

"Well, if you've ever used a web page that did something—like when you click the submit button on an order—I write the code behind it that allows—" He was interrupted by Vicky's loud yawn.

Lacey gave Shannon a thumbs-up. "He seems like a *safe* choice."

"This isn't being nice," Shannon said.

"Nice is boring." Lacey carefully looked Terrance up and down. "Now spin around and give us a good look at you."

"Yeah...I'm not going to do that."

"DO IT!" Lacey barked, her voice and face so intense that Terrance almost reached for the sword he didn't have on him.

Terrance quickly turned around in place.

Lacey nodded. "He's easily intimidated. That's good. So, girls, what do you think?"

"He's kinda cute from certain angles," Elissa said.

"With a couple drinks in me, I'd do him," Amber said.

"I want to know more about his sexual prowess," Vicky said. "Shannon, tell us everything. Don't leave anything out."

"Guys, come on." Shannon was starting to look angry.

"You tell us these things all the time," Lacey said. "Now you're just telling us in front of him. We're helping you have a more honest and open relationship."

Shannon sighed. "Fine. As I told you before, Terrance's biggest problem is—"

Terrance's could feel himself going flush, and his brain was in denial that this was happening. Then he saw they were all laughing, Shannon included.

"That was fun." Lacey wiped a tear from her eye. "I've never seen anyone turn that red before. Shannon, apologize to your boyfriend for subjecting him to us."

Shannon turned to Terrance and smiled. "I'm sorry; that was kind of mean. It's just me and my friends—well, we've been through a lot and kind of have a crazy sense of humor. And part of that is we like to haze each other's boyfriends when we first meet them."

"You learn a lot about someone when they're under stress," Elissa said. "But I assure you, there's nothing to be scared of with any of us."

"We're all actually nice people," Amber added, smiling in a much friendlier manner than any of them had so far.

"We're just a bit wacky," Vicky said.

Shannon's face turned more serious. "I didn't make you mad, did I?"

Terrance wiped the sweat from his forehead and smiled weakly. "No." He turned to Lacey. "So did I pass this test or whatever it was?"

Lacey gave him a thumbs-up. "You did all right. And Shannon has told us a lot about you; you seem like a nice guy. Which is good."

"But if you break her heart," Vicky stated, smile fading, "we'll literally rip you apart."

Terrance got the feeling that Vicky was using "literally" correctly.

"Hey girls!" called a singsongy voice. Terrance turned to see a demon headed their way. Once again he tensed, but was unable to do anything but stand there.

The demon had a voluptuous female form, her skin an almost golden yellow. Terrance could see quite a lot of her skin, as she wore a black cloak—more like a cape—and little else. Her eyes were blood-red, as was her long hair. Her lips, though, were black, and parted in a smile to reveal a set of fangs. Terrance was horrified by her, but also a little aroused. He found himself fighting the urge to run both from her and to her.

"I'm really enjoying this party," the beast said in an extremely cheery voice. "Is this iPod music that's playing?"

Vicky rolled her eyes. Elissa answered, "Yes, this is music from an iPod."

"It's amazing how much music they get on those," the demon said. "I don't know how they get the record that small."

"I don't think that's how it works," Lacey said. "Anyway, Shannon is introducing us to her new boyfriend, and you know how we are with fresh meat."

The creature locked her eyes on Terrance, curling her smile even more. "Oh."

"Terrance, this is my boss, Despina," Shannon said.

Terrance looked at her and nodded, trying not to keep his gaze on her for too long. But then Despina walked right up to him, sauntering past the point of violating Terrance's personal space. She had a sweet smell that was at first alluring but then sicklier, like the sweeteners that give lab animals cancer. "It's nice to meet you, Terrance," she said, her red eyes just inches from his. "What do you do?"

"I...uh...design web applications."

Despina raised a red eyebrow. "Is that like a thing with the...um..."

"Internet," Shannon offered.

Despina giggled. "Sorry, I'm just not good with technology. I had enough trouble trying to use one of those electronic typewriters, and then they put a TV on them and it was...well, just too much for me, you know."

"Yeah...computers are complicated," Terrance said, trying to break away from those red eyes staring at him.

"Well, Shannon is a great girl," Despina said. "These ladies here are my stars. They are fearless and ruthless and hack our enemies apart with a real love for the work."

"It's nice to enjoy what you do," Amber said.

Terrance nodded, his brain not working well enough to lend him words in a coherent order at the moment.

"It was nice meeting you, Terrance. Now I'm going to go make myself one of those fruity alcohol drinks." She walked off, and Terrance had to force himself to stop staring at her as she left.

Lacey chuckled. "Not a party without the boss around."

"Despina is nice; she's just a little annoying sometimes," Shannon said. "She tells the cheesiest jokes. I think it's just the way her generation is."

"Her generation?" Terrance asked, barely hearing himself over the pounding of his heart.

Shannon shrugged. "I think she's, like, thousands of years old."

"By the way," Lacey said, smiling apologetically, "Chet's here."

It was just what Terrance needed: more excitement. He began scanning the crowd, but realized he had no idea what Chet looked like out of armor.

Shannon glared at Lacey. "What? Why'd you invite him?"

"It just seemed it would be making too big a deal to tell him not to come. And I was hoping when he saw you with your new boyfriend, he'd get that it's all over."

"You really got my back, Lacey!" Shannon shouted.

Lacey waved her hand in the air. "I'm sure Terrance can handle Chet if he does anything. Terrance is like...smart or something...I assume."

Terrance was already feeling completely worn-out simply from meeting Shannon's friends and her boss, and he didn't feel like he could handle much more. He kept looking for whoever might be Chet, but didn't see anyone definitive. He did see some pale-skinned, eyeless creature in armor, though. "I think I could use a drink."

"Why don't you go fetch one," Shannon said. "I actually need to talk to Lacey alone for a minute."

Terrance nodded and headed toward a keg. He felt like he could use a moment alone, but he also felt more exposed without Shannon at his side. Most of the people around looked normal, but there was also something abnormal about everything here. He couldn't quite place his finger on it, but just felt generally disturbed. It seemed like a problem alcohol might solve.

He poured himself some beer from the keg and took a sip. No one seemed to be paying him any attention, which was Terrance's comfortable norm for parties. He noticed some movement out of the corner of his eye, and looked up to see one of those dark things up on a pillar, hiding in the shadows and watching him with shining eyes. He felt a chill, but he stared back defiantly and made a gun shape with his hand, firing it at the creature. It reacted slightly, turning its head just a little bit and tensing its body as if preparing to pounce.

Then he saw something rush toward him. Something small.

"Squirrel!" Terrance shouted as he tripped over his own feet trying to dodge the creature, falling against a nearby table and spilling his beer on the stone floor, which would have been upsetting if it weren't Coors Light.

He couldn't see the squirrel anymore and started to pick himself back up, but noticed something under the table: a little man. An elf, to be precise. He appeared to be the same one Terrance had met in that office building. He looked at Terrance, put a finger to his lips, and jumped down a hole.

Terrance had the urge to scream, the craziness overwhelming him, but he suppressed the feeling and got back to his feet. He found Karen standing next to him. "Life is just one weird, awkward adventure for you, isn't it?"

He always thought about telling Karen off, but since she was dating his best friend and was a coworker, that would probably cause more problems than the momentary relief would be worth. Instead, he changed the subject. "Shannon's ex-boyfriend is apparently at this party. Do you know what he looks like? I've only seen him in his armor."

"Just think of the word 'douchebag' and try to put a face to it."

He tried that, but all he could think of was Lance. "Hey, where's Lance?"

"Somewhere around here having fun."

"And you're not?"

She shrugged. "At least I'm not sweaty and nervous-looking."

"Maybe you'd have more fun if you were a nicer person."

She sipped her drink. "That doesn't seem worth trying."

Behind Karen, Terrance noticed another pale, eyeless face. Noseless, too—just two nostrils. And a mouthful of sharp, yellow teeth.

"What are you staring at?" Karen asked.

"Oh...there's some sort of demon soldier at this party."

"There are lots of weird people here." Karen looked behind her, then started to walk away. "I think I've talked to you enough; I'm going to mingle elsewhere."

The thing was facing Terrance—not that Terrance was sure it could see him, but he made sure to direct his attention elsewhere. He was never comfortable at parties, but he seemed to have reached his nadir this time. He headed back to where Shannon had been, but all he found there now was Lance talking to Shannon's friend Amber. He couldn't hear what they were saying, but as he got near, Amber smiled at Lance and walked off.

Lance turned and saw Terrance. "Hey, I have to say, Shannon has a lot of attractive friends."

"Aren't you dating Karen?"

"Well...yeah. But it's not super-serious."

"Does she know that?"

"You worry too much, dude."

Terrance looked around the crowd. "I have reason to worry. Shannon's ex-boyfriend is here, and he seemed kind of psycho when I last met him."

"What's he look like?"

"I don't know. I've only seen him in big, scary armor."

"Like that?" Lance pointed to a figure across the room in a horned helmet. Chet. He was looking right at Terrance, walking toward him.

"Dammit." He turned to Lance. "If something happens, will you back me up?"

Lance glanced at the approaching figure. "Against him? I'll give you moral support."

"Terrance!" Chet called to him, his booming voice loud and clear over the din of the party.

"What?" Terrance stood his ground. "I don't think we have anything to talk about."

Chet came right up to Terrance, looming over him. "I disagree, little man. I am wary of you."

Terrance felt he should have been a little more scared—especially because of the giant axe strapped to Chet's back—but with all the weirdness going on, he was happy to have someone to lash out at. "Well, wary away, buddy, but leave me and Shannon alone."

Chet leaned in close and whispered. "You are nothing, and she will be mine to enjoy again."

Now Terrance really wished he had his sword. He was so enraged that his first instinct was to punch Chet, but he knew that was a bad idea because of the armor, so instead he struck Chet's helmet with an open palm. Chet barely budged, but returned the favor with much more force to Terrance's head, sending him backward into a folding table, knocking it over. Terrance was dizzy and his face felt wet. He tried to get up, but Chet was on top of him, pressing him down and whispering, "I know about you, little man. I know your secrets. This is only the beginning."

Shannon screamed obscenities, rushing to Terrance's side as Chet stood up. "Get away from us, you psycho!" Shannon yelled.

Chet chuckled and turned to leave. "It's not me you should worry about."

CHAPTER 16

Frightening, snake-like eyes stared at Terrance, yellow with vertical black slits in the middle. There was something disturbing and unnatural about them that chilled him to his very soul. Sure, in his memory, cats always had eyes like that, but it was yet another one of those things that, for some reason, Terrance now thought just weren't right. Like demon soldiers wandering around a party. A vast cavern under one's apartment. One's girlfriend having an ex who always walked around in armor, carrying a huge axe.

"Just lie still." Shannon doted on him, dabbing his face with a wet cloth. She frowned. "I'm so sorry this happened."

Terrance was having a bit of trouble getting comfortable, as he was currently inside the evil-looking fortress next to the volcano. It was Shannon's apartment, though, so the walls of black stone were decorated with posters of kittens, and pink curtains decorated the window overlooking the volcano and the large flying creatures above it. And silently staring at him was an overweight tabby cat named Amidala—though Garfield seemed like the better pop culture reference, if Garfield could still be considered "pop" culture.

Terrance was lying on Shannon's soft bed while she sat next to him, watching him carefully. Standing near them was Lacey, looking embarrassed. "This is all my fault," she said. "I should have just told Chet not to come."

"It's okay," Terrance said. "I'm okay."

"I just feel awful," Lacey continued. "We teased you, and then you get hit by Chet. I really want to make it up to you." Lacey started to unzip the back of her dress. "Here, let's have a three-way."

"Not funny, Lace!" Shannon shouted. "You're making him all red again."

"Sorry. Sorry." Lacey looked at Terrance, her expression more serious. "You're a good guy, Terrance. I appreciate how you stood up for Shannon. Next time we see each other, hopefully it will be in much friendlier circumstances." Lacey turned and left, her dress still partially unzipped.

Terrance lay back on the bed and took a deep breath. "You have some interesting coworkers."

"Me and the girls, we are something," Shannon said. "But sorry you even had to see Chet."

"That one is a real piece of work."

"Yeah, I feel stupid for ever having anything to do with him. You didn't need to try to fight him, though."

"I didn't like how he talked about you. I definitely don't like him near you." He was worried about Shannon's safety around someone like Chet, but that wasn't all of it. He wondered how much there was to Chet's claims about knowing his "secrets."

"I avoid him most of the time, but I can't always do that because of...the job."

"Maybe...get a different job."

Shannon laughed. "Over him? No. I love this job. And you should see me and the other girls in action together." Shannon hesitated a moment. "Well, I guess you probably shouldn't see that, but anyway, we're really good at what we do."

He remembered how Shannon had told him that Talia had slain a couple of her coworkers. "Do you often lose your friends in this line of work, though?"

She lay down on the bed and snuggled up next to him. "That's nothing to worry about."

"I don't understand how that's nothing to worry about."

"Then just trust me." She kissed Terrance on the forehead. "What I'm worried about is you getting into fights. You really fought Chet over my honor?"

He really had. He certainly had never done anything like that before, but when Chet had referred to Shannon as a possession, Terrance's anger made him forget all his fear and other concerns. She was beautiful and sweet, and he wanted nothing more than to protect her from jerks like Chet and every other evil in the world. A realization came to him, and with trepidation he voiced it: "I love you."

The pause before Shannon reacted felt like an eternity, but then she smiled as happy tears welled up in her eyes. "I love you, too!"

They kissed, the moment only somewhat spoiled by Terrance's cut lip making it slightly painful.

After the kiss, they continued to lie on the bed together, looking into each other's eyes. "I have a man who loves me and fights for my honor." Shannon giggled. "Well, you're very brave. Like Batman."

"Batman would have lasted longer than one punch."

"Yeah, well Batman probably couldn't code web applications, so you're even."

Terrance thought about that; his guess was that Batman was a pretty good programmer, but he decided not to dispute the assertion.

"Anyway"—Shannon frowned—"because I love you, please don't do something dangerous like that again. If you ever run into Chet, just ignore him."

"Seems like someone should do something about him before he hurts anyone."

Shannon shook her head. "He only hit you because you hit him. He's never going to start anything or do any real harm...unless it's against one of those terrorist people."

"Terrorist people?"

"Yeah, the ones I told you about before, the ones trying to destroy this world. I believe they call themselves the Infinite."

That's who he'd assumed she meant. The moral choice of having to pick a side in some supposed fight between good and evil had been tearing Terrance apart, but now that he realized he loved Shannon, things seemed clearer. There was so little he understood lately, but now he had one thing to hold on to: he and Shannon loved each other and needed to be together. The other details would have to be figured out around that. He wanted to believe her, about her people fighting on the side of good and preserving the world, but if he decided her side was evil, then he'd have to save her from it somehow. It was as simple as that. "So what does this fortress guard?" Terrance asked.

"What do you mean?"

He sat up in the bed and looked out a window at the things flying outside. "It's just, well, a fortress. Up on a mountain. I thought maybe there would be something behind it that it was guarding."

Shannon sat up, too, and shrugged. "I don't know; that's above my pay grade." She leaned her head on Terrance's shoulder, her soft, blonde, sour-apple-scented hair rubbing against his chin. "Probably something important but not worth worrying about."

He put his hand around her waist and held her close. There was so much he still had to decide, but he was determined to figure it out.

The building shook with a high-pitched roar. Terrance pulled Shannon closer and looked out the window to see something flying just outside, massive and covered in spikes.

Shannon giggled. "That's just Malcus. Don't worry about him."

Terrance couldn't avert his eyes from the terrible creature until it was out of view. "What is it?"

"A demon dragon—a combination of a demon and a dragon. He was sent here to help with stuff."

"Sent here by who?"

"I don't know. The higher-ups."

"Who are they?"

"Again, I don't know. Wow, you sure ask a lot of questions about my work. You make me feel bad that I never ask many questions about your job."

"My job is stupid and boring." Terrance once more looked around the dark, stone room deep within the ominous fortress, decorated with girlish sensibilities. This was wrong, and he couldn't convince himself otherwise.

"I guess what I do may seem interesting, but it's all pretty routine," Shannon said.

"A demon dragon is routine?"

"Whatever gets the job done."

"And that job is?"

"To protect this world." She gently caressed Terrance's cheek. "And everything we care about. Now, I think we have better things to talk about." She kissed him, and Terrance tried to lose himself in the moment, but it was hard with the soreness, the overwhelming sense of evil in this place, and the cat watching them.

* * *

Terrance needed to pee. It was the middle of the night, and Shannon was sleeping soundly next to him. He watched her lying there peacefully, feeling once again how lucky he was—other than that he had apparently stumbled into some giant world conflict involving her. And his need to pee didn't make him feel too lucky, as Shannon's little apartment in the fortress didn't have its own bathroom and he'd have to wander down the dark hallways of the creepy, evil-looking place to find the men's room.

There was no other option, so Terrance got up, pulled on his pants and shirt, and looked out the window. He didn't see Malcus...not that he was likely to run into the giant monster on the way to the bathroom. He glanced down again at sweet Shannon. This was insane; he had to get her away from all of this somehow.

He headed out of her apartment, into the hallway. It was long and very dimly lit, the only light coming from the glowing eyes of demons' heads carved into the walls. Terrance slowly crept down the hallway, looking carefully at each of the demon faces to make sure they weren't actually moving. He definitely preferred it when he and Shannon crashed at his apartment.

He eventually reached a wooden door labeled *MEN* and slowly pushed it open. Inside, it was pitch-black. He groped against the stone wall until he found a switch. He flipped it, and a couple of fluorescent bulbs hummed to life. It was a normal-looking bathroom, other than the black stone that made up the walls, ceiling, and floor, and Terrance quickly made his way to a urinal. After completing his business, he went to wash his hands, but it was one of those annoying faucets that you push down and the water runs only for a few seconds. With some effort, he got his hands washed. When he glanced back up at the mirror, he thought he saw a face behind him.

The lights went off. Terrance spun around, looking through the darkness in terror. Then he saw the shine of eyes from the ceiling. One of those dark things that he had seen in many other places was up there, staring at him. "Hey." With effort,

Terrance got some control over his trembling. "I'm just going to head out of here, okay?"

Suddenly, there was another pair of eyes on the ceiling next to the first, then another. And then another and another. He looked down to find that they were standing next to him on the floor, too. They were all around him, moving toward him. He was about to cry out but something grabbed him from behind and clasped a cold hand over his mouth. Then they were all on him.

CHAPTER 17

Terrance found himself on a hard, smooth floor. He must have blacked out, but he was now in a place that was well-lit. He was on his back, staring up toward the ceiling...but he couldn't see it. The building he was in seemed to go up and up forever. The heating bills for the place must be enormous. He got to his feet and looked around. It was a very large room with a marble floor, lit quite brightly, though Terrance couldn't make out any light sources, and above him was the infinite ceiling. It was like he was in a completely hollowed-out skyscraper.

Near one wall was a throne on a platform, and on it sat a cloaked figure. "Hello, Terrance," the figure called out in a friendly voice.

"Um...hey." Terrance approached the man. "Where am I?"

The figure rose from his throne and descended the stairs of the platform. "You are nowhere, really."

Terrance finally got a good look at the figure: he was dressed in a red hooded robe, black gloves, and a golden mask for a face that stared out with black eyes and a frozen, stoic expression. It creeped Terrance out more than a little. "So, who are you?"

"This we will discuss. But first..." He made a sweeping motion with his arm, pointing to the side. "Coffee and doughnuts."

Terrance looked in the direction of the gesture, and saw an elegant oak table holding a box of doughnuts and a cardboard container of coffee. He didn't really feel hungry or thirsty, but when he noticed the doughnuts were Krispy Kreme and the coffee was Starbucks, it was difficult to refuse. "Oh, thanks."

"You may sit if you wish to be more comfortable," the masked figure said.

There was a maroon easy chair next to the table. Terrance loaded one of the elegant china plates on the table with three doughnuts—a cream-filled, a jelly-filled, and a plain glazed—and poured himself a cup of coffee, then took a seat in the chair. All the while, the figure stood nearby, watching silently through his frozen, golden mask. "Thanks for the doughnuts," Terrance said. "So, what's going on here? Am I in trouble?"

"No, we are just going to talk. Oh..." The figure walked to a cabinet, opened it, and leaned over it. Terrance could only see his back, but when the figure stood up and turned back to Terrance, he was wearing a new mask. It was golden like the first, but featured a large, grotesque smile, as though it was the death mask of someone who had died from the Joker's laughing gas. "Hopefully this face appears friendlier."

Terrance had found the first one much less creepy. "Are the masks necessary?"

"I have no corporeal form."

Terrance nodded, as he guessed that made sense. "So who are you?"

"Think of me as like the one called Drakpor."

"I don't know who that is."

The masked figure was silent for a moment. "Sorry, I must have gotten confused; I thought that was a pretty common reference from your universe. What's the name of the planet you're from?"

"Um...Earth."

The figure nodded. "Okay, I remember which universe now. Think of me as like the Wizard of Oz...the unseen man behind the curtain, manipulating things."

"So should I call you Mr. Wizard or something?"

"I am often referred to as 'The Caretaker' in your realm, when referred to at all, for I am the caretaker of your universe and many others."

Terrance wondered if this was the Adversary that the Infinite had told him about. "Have I done something wrong?"

"Again"—the Caretaker pointed at his freakish smile—"this is a friendly discussion. I like to keep close watch over the inhabitants of my universes and to personally get involved when necessary. I always have time for my people, because I live in a realm beyond time."

"That's nice." Terrance finished his jelly-filled doughnut, still feeling like he was in trouble. "Do you always abduct them with those dark, creepy things that watch everybody?"

"Those are merely my most direct way of keeping tabs on your world; don't worry about them. Anyway, I've been watching you and I've become a little concerned. Keeping a universe in working order is no small task, but there are those who work against us, and their actions could lead to the destruction of your universe and perhaps others. I know you talked to a group that calls themselves the Infinite."

Terrance was pretty certain now that he was in trouble. "Yeah...I just talked to them to see if they could help me figure out all this weird stuff I started noticing."

"Understandable. As the realms become unstable, more 'weird stuff' occurs. Much of that can be scary to those who don't understand it, and I can understand why some may feel the need to lash out. But those people are pushing this world to destruction."

Terrance sipped his coffee, which was still very hot. "They say we're infinite beings and that something has trapped us in this world and is feeding off of us. They call that something the Adversary."

"And I think you're aware that that is nonsense. Do you feel like an infinite being? Do you feel like you're being sucked dry?"

"I just feel confused lately."

"And I can tell you which path will lead to further confusion. You can join with the Infinite and play around with faeries and other creatures trying to undermine your world, making things ever more strange as reality is chipped away because of your interference. Or you can give up that foolishness and focus on the real world. You have quite a nice girlfriend; why would you threaten that?"

Dread crept into Terrance. "You're not going to tell her about this, are you?"

"I operate at a very high level; I don't normally chitchat with the foot soldiers trying to protect your world. But do you think you can flirt with those trying to destroy her and she won't eventually find out? At some point, you have to choose: do you like your life and job and romance, or do you want the pointless conflict and destruction of the Infinite?"

Terrance looked again around the giant room and at the strange masked figure, trying to wrap his brain around what was happening, but it was too far out of his norm to classify. "So this is all because you saw me going down a bad path and you wanted to help?"

"I am the caretaker of your world." The Caretaker floated over to Terrance and patted him on the shoulder with a gloved hand; Terrance could barely feel it. "I am concerned with all of the beings under my benevolence. I don't want my worlds torn apart. I am trying to explain things to you so that you can make the right choice and we can all be happy."

"And if someone doesn't choose the right path?"

The Caretaker was silent for a few moments, then finally said, "I am a being that exists out of your space and time, and yet, as you saw, I control things that watch you at all times and I have armies and soldiers and other things that serve me—I think you've seen Malcus. Is there any point to my making an outright threat?"

Terrance tilted his head back to try once again to see the ceiling of the room. It seemed to go on forever until the walls converged at a single point. "I see what you mean. So there's not much of a choice, then. You're saying if I join with the Infinite, one way or another it's destruction?"

"Yes. Of you...or perhaps the whole world. Reality is a much more precarious thing than many realize. I assume you've taken a physics class; thus, you must understand how complex the universe is. That's why it requires those like me to keep order."

"And what of the evil things I see?"

"What makes you call things evil?"

"Well...they're just obviously wrong. Like a screaming woman being fed to a horrific monster."

"Then tell me, if it's so obviously wrong, why were you the only one reacting?"

He had a point. But it was a point that disturbed Terrance rather than reassured him. "So I should just ignore those things?"

"Yes. And I assure you, after you do it enough times, you'll stop seeing them completely, and all this craziness will go away."

It was a lovely thought—things back to normal. He could hardly remember normal. "You know, I didn't ask for any of this. The faeries gave me that sword and...I don't know what happened."

"Yes, you just stumbled into this. And I'm telling you how to stumble out. You could have a good life—a great life—but you need to make better choices. Are we clear?"

He was clear, but Terrance simply didn't trust the noncorporeal being with the frozen smile. "So you're telling me this for my benefit?"

"There is no need for conflict here. We have a nice universe, and we all need to work together to preserve it. If some try to fracture things or give aid to the creatures trying to chip away at the edges of your reality, it will be quite agonizing for all involved."

The Caretaker spoke in a very plain manner, and Terrance couldn't quite figure whether he meant what he said as a threat. "This troubles you?"

"Well, no harm would ever come to me whether your universe collapses or not, but I'd be heartbroken to see its destruction."

"You give this talk to lots of people?"

"Only when I see it's needed, and when I think it may help. Any other questions, Terrance Denby?"

Terrance took a few bites of the cream doughnut while he thought about it. "How'd you get this position as caretaker?"

"It's difficult to explain. Suffice it to say, it is my job to ensure the safety of your universe along with numerous others. Anything else?"

"You seem pretty powerful. Why not just take out all the people causing trouble?"

"It's more complicated than that. Plus, violence never solves anything."

"You have armored knights and a demon dragon serving you; you seem quite prepared for violence." He tried to phrase it nicely to avoid being too accusatory; he was somewhat afraid of this being.

The Caretaker was silent at first, then said, "Violence *by itself* never solves anything. Any more questions?"

Terrance thought for a bit. "Do you have an email address if I think of questions later?"

"I'm afraid not."

"Really? How can you not have email in this day and age?"

"I exist outside of time and space. This makes internet connections...complicated."

Terrance nodded. That did make sense.

"Well, it seems we're done. I hope this has been informative, and I hope you choose a path that allows you to lead a long and happy life. I will now return you to your girlfriend."

Suddenly, the room began to dim until Terrance was in darkness. Around him, he began to see the shining eyes of the dark watchers. "Oh, come on!"

* * *

When Terrance woke up, he panicked at first but quickly realized everything was back to normal: he was lying in a bed with a sleeping Shannon, inside her apartment in an evil fortress next to a volcano.

Terrance rolled over and put his arm around Shannon, reflecting on how "normal" seemed to have left him permanently.

CHAPTER 18

Terrance stared at the sword inside his coat closet. He had a choice to make.

After the evening when Terrance had told Shannon that he loved her and was later abducted by an entity from beyond space and time, he had spent the day hanging out with Shannon and forgetting everything. They went to the park, and when that got boring, they went to a movie. Then they went back to his place and made out, and then they played video games. She was the perfect woman, and Terrance was done with the sword of Damocles figuratively hanging over his head and literally sitting in his coat closet.

So he had a choice to make, but it was actually quite simple. He loved Shannon. Those people calling themselves the Infinite seemed a bit crazy, and a powerful being had basically threatened him. He was just a programmer of web applications, not someone waiting to take on the universe and all the terrors within it.

So he was chucking the sword.

Shannon's work schedule had once again left him alone on a Sunday evening, so he determined it was time to finally follow through with his decision and be done with the nonsense once and for all. The only question was how to get rid of the sword. He remembered that there was a giant canyon behind his apartment complex, which seemed like a good place to dump it. At first he thought it was weird that he knew there was a giant canyon behind his apartment complex that he never paid much attention to, but then he told himself that it was this kind of weirdness that he was trying to move past, so he just needed to chuck the sword and stop overthinking things.

Terrance grabbed the sword and headed outside. It was dusk, and the streetlights had turned on. He liked that it was dark, because this didn't seem like something to do in the full light of the sun. He could see a few people out, but no one paid him attention; he didn't really know anyone in the apartment complex other than Lance. The complex was made up of a large number of quadruplexes, and most of the residents seemed to keep to themselves. He walked past the clubhouse, which he never used, and the pool, which he also never used, as he headed to the rear of the complex, where there was a hole in the fence he had used numerous times as a shortcut to pick up dinner from a nearby Pizza Hut.

"Stop!"

It was a small voice that had cried out, the voice of a child. Terrance headed toward the source. In an alleyway between two buildings were a pair of children, a boy and a girl who both looked about ten years old and who were backing away from a figure, perhaps eight feet tall, that was slowly approaching with a large, claw-like hand outstretched toward them.

"Go away!" the girl cried.

Terrance looked around. He could see other people milling about, but no one seemed to hear the crying children. A car drove between Terrance and the tall creature, the driver paying no attention to it. This was what the Caretaker had told him about: he just had to ignore things like this and soon he'd be like everyone else again and not even notice them anymore.

Terrance watched as the dark creature crept toward the children, its claw-hand extended toward them. He saw the fear in their eyes. He noticed his hand had wrapped around the grip of his sword. *What are you about to do?* he asked himself. The thing looked terrifying to Terrance and would probably rip him apart if challenged. If he did fight it, he would apparently be angering forces larger than he could comprehend, forces that could crush him and destroy everything he loved. To do anything other than turn and walk away was to throw away his own life. As he looked at the evil thing and the frightened faces of the helpless children, he realized with sadness that he had no choice.

He drew the sword. Its silver blade sparkled in the dim rays of the streetlights. It was well-balanced and felt right in his hand. And beyond that, it felt...familiar.

It wasn't like the movies, as drawing the sword made very little sound. The creature still hadn't noticed him and was hovering over the terrified children. "Hey!" Terrance called out, his voice small. The children cried out in fear once more, and soon Terrance's anger began replacing his fear. "HEY!" he shouted as he crossed the street toward the monster.

It stopped and slowly turned its head to look at him. He couldn't see the face under the hood, but he could see the faint glint of two eyes. "Who are you?" it hissed.

"I'm a software engineer." Terrance kept the tip of his sword pointed at the eyes, which hovered further above him the closer he got. "And you're going to leave those kids alone or there will be trouble."

It backed away from the kids. Its gait was inhuman; Terrance thought he could see the movement of multiple legs under its cloak. "I wasn't going to hurt them."

"Damn straight you're not!" Terrance circled around the creature, putting himself between it and the children. "Get out of here!" he yelled over his shoulder at the children.

They scrambled to their feet and ran. The creature growled. "You are interfering in things you don't understand." As it talked, Terrance could see light reflecting off needle-like teeth.

Terrance took a couple of steps back, his sword still pointed up at the creature's eyes. "I understand enough to know I need to interfere."

The creature made a strange clicking sound. Laughter, perhaps. "I will teach you otherwise."

Terrance reassessed the situation. He was standing alone against a monster that was a couple of heads taller than him and had giant claws. He felt the weight of the sword in his hand, which gave him some reassurance, and he remembered what the Infinite had said about how he was far more powerful than anything he saw in this world. He stood up straight and relaxed his grip on the sword a bit. "If you want a fight—"

A claw shot out at Terrance, knocking him to the ground and sending the sword flying out of his hand. He rolled over on the grass, trying to see where it had gone, but as soon as he spotted it, the monster scuttled between him and the sword on its tarantula-like legs. "How much have you bled before?" the thing asked. "I'm hoping this will be a new experience for you."

Terrance realized that, all in all, things were going about as well as would be expected for someone who had never wielded an actual sword before. He scampered to his feet, but the thing pounced on him, pinning him to the ground on his back. One cold claw held down Terrance's head as the monster leaned in, putting its face near his. All Terrance could see were empty, black eyes and teeth like tiny, thin blades. "I'm glad you intervened," it said, a tongue whipping around behind its teeth. "This is going to be fun."

The creature stood up and backed away from Terrance. "I'll give you a choice." It pointed to Terrance's sword, which lay in the grass. They were now a perfect triangle, the points being Terrance, the creature, and the sword. Terrance slowly got to his feet, and the monster said, "You can choose to continue trying to fight me or to run away."

"I'm not giving you the same choice," called another voice. Talia, in her white cloak, stepped forward out of the growing darkness, toward the creature.

It did its clicking laugh again. "Fine, I shall—"

There was a quick flash of steel as Talia sliced off one of its claws. Her second blade stabbed straight through the thing's head. With a yank, the blade came up and outward, and the giant body of the beast collapsed in a heap. Blue flames started emanating from the body, consuming it.

Terrance walked over and picked up his sword as he watched the body of the creature disintegrate in flame and ash. "What was that?"

The flames died down, and now where the creature had lain, all that was visible was grass. "Nothing," Talia answered.

"Were you spying on me again?"

She returned her blades to the sheaths under her cloak. "I happened to be in the area and thought I'd take a look to see if you've decided to stop being useless."

Terrance wiped his brow and tried to catch his breath. "Well...thanks."

"Just doing my duty. Have you decided to do yours?"

"I don't think I'm very good at it." He headed back across the street and picked up the scabbard he'd left there, returning his sword into it.

Talia followed him, hovering nearby. "You learn by doing."

"Seems more like I'll get my head ripped off by doing."

"So what? We're so much more than our forms here. To have our bodies ripped apart is less than a pinprick to our whole."

Terrance rubbed his neck. "It seems like a big deal."

Talia stood in front of him and stared at him intensely. "So, what, then? Next time you're just going to stand by while children scream for help because you're too scared?"

Terrance looked around. He didn't see the children; they must have fled as instructed. "Speaking of, do you think those kids will be fine?"

"For now," Talia answered. "Hopefully there will continue to be people like us in the future; there are many threats in this world."

Terrance stared at his sword. At times, it was a reassuring weight in his hand. But mostly it felt like a burden. "Let's go to my apartment; we can talk there."

Terrance walked back to his apartment, Talia following but never coming too close to him. When he got inside, Terrance dropped his sword to the floor, which earned some thumps from the thing below. He ignored it and plopped down onto the couch, then noticed that Talia was still standing outside the doorway. "What are you? A vampire?"

Talia looked around Terrance's apartment carefully. "Excuse me?"

"You can't go into a place unless invited?"

"I didn't know that rule applied to vampires."

"It does; just not to the sparkly ones. You want to come in and close the door?"

Talia still hesitated. "I don't know about going into a strange man's apartment."

"You're the strange one; I assure you, I'm much more scared of you."

Talia stepped inside and closed the door, but she didn't move any further. "Was there something you wanted to ask me about?"

"I'm pretty sure I do; we just fought some big monster thing..." Terrance shook his head. "I'm just trying to get my thoughts together. So, other people don't notice that? They don't notice kids screaming for help?"

"Is it that unusual?"

He thought of the kids crying for help, and there was something vaguely familiar about it. It made him shudder. "So we live in a completely messed-up world, huh?"

"There are awful things out there, and great things. We destroy the evil for the sake of the good. Simple enough. Are you finally ready to do what must be done and shed your pathetic self so you may take part in the fight?"

Terrance thought of the thing on top of him, holding him down with its claws. It could have easily killed him if it hadn't decided to play with him first. "I don't feel like an infinite being. I feel like a small thing being crushed by larger forces."

"Then you need to change your perspective. Stop believing the pathetic schlub I see before me is all you are, or it will be all you are. Or less."

Pathetic schlub. Now Terrance was self-conscious on top of the general fear. "And if I do decide to join with the Infinite, how do I start? Do I just sort of patrol the streets looking for evil to fight"—he chuckled to himself—"like Batman?"

"That's part of it. You can consider me Batwoman. That's a thing, right?"

Terrance nodded. "Yep. Has bright red hair. Is a lesbian."

Talia paused, then said, "That doesn't describe me."

Terrance had been so ready to toss his sword, and then a monster had nearly killed him when he tried to wield it, so he was surprised to find he was still considering joining the Infinite. But he knew it wasn't a choice to take lightly. "I think I met the Adversary."

Talia looked surprised. "Really?"

"I've seen these things that hide in the dark and watch us. They ganged up and grabbed me. And then I was in some giant room with him. He wore a mask and said he wasn't corporeal."

Talia nodded. "Good. If he's come after you, that means he's scared of you. You may not be as useless as you seem."

"It doesn't seem like a good thing." A touch of panic seeped into Terrance's voice. "He appears capable of coming after me at any time and—"

There was a knock at the door. Talia jumped away from it, her hands going to the blades under her cloak. Terrance quickly rose from the couch and picked up his sword as he crept toward the door. "Who is it?"

"It's me, Terr," Lance answered. "Come on; I know you're not busy."

Terrance cracked open the door and looked out. "Actually, I am kind of busy right now."

Lance narrowed his eyes. "What are you hiding?" He suddenly shoved the door open, knocking Terrance back. Startled, Talia drew a sword. Lance looked her over with a befuddled expression. "Terr, are you having an affair?"

"I told you." Talia kept her sword pointed at Lance. "If a woman enters a man's apartment alone, people are going to assume things."

"You didn't tell me that, and put your sword away." Terrance looked at Lance. "I'm not having an affair. I'm just in an odd situation."

Lance watched as Talia sheathed her weapon. "Odd how?" He looked at the sword Terrance was holding. "Faerie-sword odd?"

"It involves that."

"Yeah, well I don't care about that sort of thing," Lance said. "Anyway, I wanted to tell you that Karen and I broke up."

Talia scowled. "We were talking about matters of great import. You seem like a useless person, and we don't care about your silly romances."

Lance stared at Talia, then switched his gaze to Terrance. "Who is she again?"

"Oh...um...this is Talia. Talia, this is my friend Lance."

The two stared at each other for a few seconds. "Do I know you from somewhere?" Lance asked.

"Um...you remember that empowerment ceremony at work?" Terrance said. "You know how they were going to feed a woman to that creature, but she got away? This is her."

Lance nodded. "Yeah, you looked like an ass that day, Terr."

Talia's expression toward Lance turned even more intense, to the point that Terrance was a little afraid she was going to draw her sword again. "So you were one of those just standing there and watching...witnessing an evil and being complicit in your inaction?"

Lance looked at Talia, uncomprehending, then turned back to Terrance. "Want to go get a drink? You can bring the crazy chick you're not having an affair with."

"I don't ravage my mind with alcohol," Talia said.

Lance took another glance at Talia. "Yeah, she seems like loads of fun. So come on."

* * *

"Please don't bring up Shannon's occupation in front of Talia. She doesn't know about it, and it would be kind of a sore point." Terrance said as he and Lance waited at the bar for their drinks. "Also, please don't mention Talia to Shannon."

"What do you have going on, dude?"

"It's just there's like two sides fighting over this world, with monsters and faeries and all-seeing powerful forces, and I'm kinda caught in the middle right now."

Lance nodded. "You have really stupid problems. So are you carrying around that sword permanently now?"

Terrance looked down at the scabbard on his belt and shrugged. "I don't know."

They picked up their drinks—two beers and an iced tea—and brought them back to the table where Talia was waiting. She looked at them suspiciously. "What were you talking about over there? Were you plotting against me?"

Lance smiled and sat next to her in the booth. "I was just asking if you're single."

"Denby doesn't know enough about me to answer that question," Talia answered sharply. She turned to Terrance. "So this one you met that you believe to be the Adversary, what did he say to you?"

"Who are we talking about?" Lance asked.

"This...um...force behind trapping us in this"—Terrance looked at Talia—"what do you call it?"

"Sliver."

"Sliver of reality. And he's responsible for the evil creatures here and is somehow feeding off of us."

Lance nodded. "Okay. Let's talk about my problem. So Karen and I broke up."

"I'm sorry to hear that," Terrance said.

Talia frowned. "This is not of any importance."

"Yeah, well things just weren't really working out. I mean, she's kind of stuck up, you know? Not an anything-goes free spirit like Sunshine here." Lance motioned to Talia.

"So you broke up with her?"

"Yeah...didn't go so well. Things were said."

Terrance sighed. "You know we still have to work with her. This is why you have to be careful with office romances. She already doesn't seem to like me for some reason, and now she's probably going to hate me for being associated with you."

"Yeah, something about you just puts her off."

"I don't get that. Everyone likes me. I'm easygoing."

"I don't like you," Talia said.

"Anyway." Lance folded his hands. "So what do you think of Shannon's friend Amber?"

Terrance rolled his eyes. "Is that what this is about? You've decided to go after Karen's friend instead?"

"Karen is friends with Shannon. And she kind of knows Lacey. She's not friends with Amber. So if Amber asks about me..."

"Don't tell her the truth about what a horrible human being you are."

Lance nodded. "Yep."

"Do you see what's going on here?" Talia once again stared intensely at Terrance. It made him pretty uncomfortable. "You're being drawn into the pointless dalliance of this empty husk that sits next to me."

Lance sipped his beer. "Is she hitting on me?"

Talia ignored Lance and kept her gaze on Terrance. "You have a purpose...a duty. You can drift through this meaningless existence while you waste away to nothing, or you can fight. What is your choice?"

Terrance thought about that brief moment when he had first drawn his sword and everything had seemed to fall into place. He then thought about how easily he had gotten pummeled immediately after. "It's not that simple. It looks to me like you're talking about a life of being hunted by forces I don't even understand." He looked up and saw on the ceiling one of the dark things staring down at him. He lowered his voice. "He's even watching us now."

Talia stood up and drew one of her swords. The creature quickly scrambled away along the ceiling. Talia looked back to Terrance. "Don't fear them. Make them fear you. Or just sit there and whine like a frightened child. Your choice."

Lance leaned toward Terrance. "Man, I'm going to have to drink a lot more before I get the courage to hit on your friend here."

Talia looked at him. "I have no interest in you unless you're also ready to fight and not just feed our enemy with your own soul."

"I totally would, but I don't have a faerie sword."

"The swords don't come from faeries." Talia looked back to Terrance, pulled a pen and paper out of her cloak pocket, and handed them to him. "You left our meeting the other day before we could get your email address. We of the Infinite have a Google Group we use to keep in touch."

Terrance sighed and wrote down his personal email address and handed back the pen and paper. "I'm not committing yet to any large-scale war."

Talia motioned for Lance to get out of her way so she could leave the booth. "There are no sidelines. Both of you will one day take a side in this war. The only question is which side. I'll leave you to your drinking." With that, she left the bar.

"So we're clear on Amber?" Lance asked.

"Yeah, sure." Terrance looked down at his sheathed sword and felt the grip. It both excited and frightened him.

"And I really wouldn't cheat on Shannon with that girl if I were you."

"I'm not cheating on Shannon! But don't tell her about any of this." Joining the opposite side of a war, against his girlfriend, seemed potentially worse than cheating. "Giant forces beyond my understanding are trying to crush me."

Lance nodded. "Yeah, we all feel that way sometimes."

Terrance looked up to find that one of the dark creatures had returned and was staring at him. He put his hand on his sword grip and stood up threateningly, but the creature didn't move. Terrance sighed and sat back down, finishing off the rest of his beer in a few gulps before heading back to the bar to get something stronger.

CHAPTER 19

Terrance thought he saw an elf in the break room. The little guy had disappeared into a cabinet when Terrance turned on the lights. Whatever he had been doing in there, it wasn't making coffee, so Terrance started making a pot, since elf sightings were a bit much to deal with when you hadn't had enough coffee.

While it was brewing, he went back to his desk to check his email. His work email was a bunch of boring company announcements that he didn't need to pay any attention to, so he went to Gmail to check his personal account. He saw a number of messages from the Infinite's Google Group, discussing various things. The number of people in the Google Group seemed to be much larger than those he had personally met. One thread was on sightings of evil creatures and their subsequent slaying by the members. Vampires, demons, and goblins had been seen and ended by the various men and women of the Infinite. Another thread was on dealing with the Hollow Ones. This thread was less cavalier, with many fleeing the conflict instead. And there was a thread on Malcus but it was only about sightings, as no one seemed to have yet tried to confront him. At the end was a mention of an attack on a gathering of one group of the Infinite. Apparently, Malcus's fire breath had burnt off the side of a mountain, turning rock to ash. Two were dead. The email listed the names of a man and a woman, though they weren't anyone Terrance knew. He wondered what it meant when an "infinite being" was killed in this world. He suspected it was no different than when anything else was killed.

Terrance also saw another email, this one from Shannon. Subject: *Here's my face.* The contents were just a close-up picture of Shannon's face, with her doing an over-the-top, comical smile as though she'd just had her name called on *The Price Is Right*. It made him smile. He replied, *It is good to see your face.*

A new thread from the Infinite appeared, this one with a list of meetings, though the locations were only vaguely referred to. He saw one meeting listed that would be headed by Curtis and Vivian Dayton at the "usual place" that evening. Terrance thought a while about whether he should go, and decided that this was the sort of thinking that required coffee.

He had brought his sword today, but had left it in his car, as he didn't want any conflict with his boss, who was apparently an evil demon. He thought once again about holding the unsheathed sword and confronting the creature the previous night. During that moment, he had felt so righteous...and then he got smacked around like a kitten fighting a gorilla. The fact was that he wasn't a warrior. But somewhere inside, he sort of wanted to be one.

Terrance didn't see an elf in the break room this time, but instead something scarier: Karen. She was pouring herself some coffee as Terrance cautiously approached the pot with his mug. She turned around and looked at him, her expression perfectly neutral. Terrance wasn't sure what to say to someone his friend had just broken up with, so he settled on, "I think I saw an elf in here earlier."

Karen's expression was no longer neutral. It was now taking a firm stance on the pro side of Terrance suddenly bursting into flames. "Don't pull me into your weirdness, freak."

"What exactly did I do?"

"I'll tell you," Karen said, stepping forward right into Terrance's face, but she bumped him with her mug, which then spilled its contents right onto Terrance's crotch.

The sound he made was not very manly.

* * *

"Sorry, dude."

Terrance sat in his cubicle, his coat tied around his waist to hide the stain that was still drying. He had considered driving home to get new pants, but it was a long two-way trip and he just didn't feel like it. He looked up at Lance, who was standing at his cubicle entrance. "Why is she angry at me? You're the one she should hate."

"She just doesn't seem to like you. More so since you've been hitting it off with Shannon."

"I don't like her either, but I'm guessing I can come up with more concrete reasons to explain that. Can't believe she did this."

"I thought it was an accident. Didn't she apologize?"

"She handed me paper towels and walked off," Terrance fumed. "That's not an apology. And this happened because she was being hostile. I should report this to HR."

"She is HR."

Terrance shifted uncomfortably in his seat. "I mean to whoever her boss is in HR...I don't really know the hierarchy."

"Know who does? Karen, since she's in HR. You could email her to ask who to complain to."

"This isn't funny!" Terrance shouted. "I mean...I can see how this could be funny and probably will be later on, but it is leagues from funny right now."

"What you should do is forbid Shannon from being friends with Karen anymore."

"I don't think I'm at the 'forbidding' phase in the relationship, or that that actually is a phase. It seems like a bad idea."

"No, girls like it when a guy takes charge. They love it when you forbid stuff."

Terrance nodded. "That sounds like really terrible advice. I don't know why I ever talk to you. In fact, being your friend apparently subjects me to splash damage."

"Maybe the reason Karen doesn't like you is because you whine too much."

Terrance turned back to his computer screen. "This isn't funny yet."

"Okay. I'll come back later and hopefully it will be then."

Lance sauntered off and Terrance checked his email again. There was a message from Talia with the subject line: *IMPORTANT.* The message read: *Meet me at the mall food court at noon. Be armed.* Terrance considered replying "no," but he didn't have lunch plans anyway.

* * *

Terrance stood next to his Hyundai for a few moments, staring at the sheathed sword in his hand. The scabbard and sword were both simple and practical things, yet he'd still feel pretty flamboyant walking around with them in a public place. He thought of the monster he'd seen the other night, threatening the two kids. *There are things out there that need the point of a sword in them*, he told himself. *And that will only happen if you have your sword with you.*

With only a little difficulty, he attached the scabbard to his belt over his left hip. He took a deep breath and turned to head toward the mall, but as he did, the scabbard slammed into his car. He inspected the spot where it had hit, and there was a tiny dent. "Dammit!"

He adjusted the scabbard so that it was more perpendicular to the ground, then headed for the mall. As he went inside, he passed a couple of people. He couldn't tell if they were staring at him and his sword, because he did his best to avoid any eye contact. When he reached the food court, it was crowded with the lunch-hour rush. That actually made him feel more comfortable, as with that many people, no one was paying attention to him. Now all he had to do was find Talia and figure out what she wanted him and his sword for. He hoped that whatever it was, there actually was time for lunch, since the food court had a Chick-fil-A.

He found an empty table and took a seat. He felt less exposed sitting—because people couldn't see his sword *or* the stain on his pants—and figured he could just wait there until he spotted Talia or she saw him. He noticed someone was watching him, though: a little boy at the next table over. The boy stared at Terrance's weapon with wide eyes. "Is that a sword?"

114

"Um...yeah," Terrance answered hesitantly, as he didn't think strangers were supposed to talk to children.

"What do you have it for?"

"Well...in case of monsters."

His eyes grew wider. "You've slain monsters?"

"Sorta. So...um...have you seen any around the mall?"

The boy shook his head. "I did see one at the park yesterday. I ran away from it."

"That was a good idea. If you see monsters, run away and tell your parents."

He frowned. "My mom won't listen to me when I do."

"Don't bother that man," the boy's mother said, and gave Terrance a suspicious glance.

Terrance turned away and looked back at the crowd in the food court, scanning for Talia. Everyone appeared to be absorbed in their own business, not worrying about monsters or evil or giant forces out to suck dry everyone's life force.

"We are born with our eyes open. The world teaches us to close them."

Terrance turned around and saw a figure in a white cloak was behind him at another table, facing the opposite direction. "Hey, what—"

"Don't look toward me," Talia said, still facing away. "Act like you're sunk in your own business. That is, act like yourself."

Terrance turned back to his empty table. "You can't ask for my help and be mean to me."

"Quit whining. This is serious. One of the Hollow Ones has been after me. I think it's time to show it we're not afraid."

Terrance wasn't quite certain he was not afraid. "A person is after you?"

"Don't think of it as a person. The Hollow Ones are much more cunning and much more dangerous than those with an outward demonic appearance. I'll need you to charge it from the front as a distraction, and I will sneak-attack from behind while it's engaged with you."

"We're just going to cut a person down in the middle of a crowded mall?" Terrance asked. "Are we going to fight off the police next?"

"It's not a police matter. They are unlikely to interfere. Do you understand?"

Terrance sighed. "I don't understand anything. Couldn't you have asked one of the other Infinite with more experience to help?"

"I'm trying to teach you to be a useful human being. So quit your caterwauling and just do this."

Terrance grimaced to no one. "Caterwauling?"

"The Hollow One is trying to be sneaky and isn't in its armor yet. It's wearing bedazzled jeans and a purple T-shirt with ponies on it."

"Sounds like a really dangerous person."

"Not a person. And I think it's wearing the T-shirt ironically. Anyway, get to it. When you see it, draw your sword and cut it down. If you're lucky, you may get a blow in before it gets its defenses up. If not, I'll finish it off. I've done this before; don't worry."

It was hard to catalogue all the different worries Terrance currently had. He finally turned around toward Talia. "I'm not really sure—" She was gone.

Terrance stood up and considered just leaving the mall. He wasn't sure what he had been expecting when he came to meet Talia, but it seemed like this was going to be a dangerous, awkward situation. The awkwardness was soon confirmed when a woman called out, "Is that you, Terrance?"

It was Shannon's friend from work, Amber, in a purple T-shirt with ponies on it. Terrance quickly turned sideways and stood near a pillar to hide his sword. "Hey, Amber."

"Hope you didn't mind us teasing you the other day," she said. "We really are nice people."

"I know." Panic began to take hold of Terrance's body. Sure, he was considering helping the Infinite, but there was no question in his mind about attacking one of his girlfriend's friends. He tried to subtly wave his hands outward to signal Talia to stop.

"Shannon's pretty smitten with you, so I hope you know any teasing is just because she likes you."

"Yeah, we tease each other constantly." He waved his hands more vigorously, not sure they were visible.

Amber took a confused glance at his hand motions. "Well, I probably should get going. I know it doesn't look like it, but I'm actually on duty right now. There's a dangerous person near here that I have to...take care of."

Terrance smiled and nodded as he tried to spot Talia's location. He had no indication that she had seen his signal, and as panic consumed him, he started saying, "Abort!" louder and louder until he was yelling it.

Amber stared at him wide-eyed. "Well, Shannon did say you have a wacky sense of humor. Hey, I have a question about your friend, Lance. Is he—"

A blade point shot out through Amber's chest, the look of shock frozen on her face. Talia was behind her, her hood now down revealing her dark hair in a ponytail and the grim determination in her eyes as she held the blade. Terrance was in complete horror and couldn't move or speak.

Surprisingly, someone who could move and speak was Amber, who grabbed the blade point fiercely with one hand and said, "You missed." She elbowed Talia with tremendous force, knocking her backward into a table.

Terrance stared at Amber, who stood with Talia's sword through her torso, as he backed away. Amber then spied the sword at his hip. "What is this?!" she demanded. With a scream, she yanked the sword out of herself and tossed it away. Fire then consumed her clothes, leaving her in black, form-fitting armor, and more fire arose in her hand. When it died down, she held a black sword.

Terrance finally gained enough composure to speak. "Why don't we take a moment and talk about this before there's any more violence?"

Amber smiled, a thin, wicked smile that sent a chill down Terrance's spine. "All I want to hear is your screams."

Talia charged her, now armed with only one sword. Amber quickly parried and kicked Talia, knocking her back again. Amber then leaped twelve feet into the air and all Terrance could do was stand there dumbly and watch, until he realized she was coming at him, sword blade swinging. He drew his own sword and held it defensively in front of himself, blocking her blow, though the force of it sent him staggering backward. Amber giggled. "I guess you're about to have a nasty breakup—your head and body, that is."

Terrance looked around. Some people had moved out of the way of the battle, but most weren't even paying attention to it. He saw a few kids watching, though.

Talia had retrieved her second sword and moved close to Terrance while Amber stayed back, waiting for them to make a move. "It's not a good idea to fight these things head-on," Talia said, "but we can do this if we work together."

Terrance very much did not want to fight Amber, but he could see from her expression that she was not of the same mind. "Come on, guys!" she said, laughing. "The power of teamwork! You can do this!" She touched her blade with a fingertip and it ignited in a blue flame.

"What the hell!" Terrance exclaimed, his sword shaking in his hand.

"We'll come at it from different angles." Talia moved away from Terrance. "Ready...charge!"

Talia rushed at Amber, but Terrance simply moved a little closer, not really sure what he was planning on doing. Talia unleashed a quick flurry of blows, but Amber, despite her armor, seemed to move even quicker, parrying each strike and pressing into Talia. It was all so quick, Terrance couldn't follow the fight, but finally Talia shrieked and staggered backward as Amber pressed in for the kill.

Before Terrance was fully aware what he was doing, he charged into the fray. He swung his sword at Amber, but she quickly turned and deflected the blow. She swung back at him, but he ducked under the attack and swung his sword upward. Amber blocked, and now they were pressing their swords against each other. Terrance pushed with all his might, but Amber was obviously stronger and he could see her flaming, black sword coming toward his face.

"Do you see the situation you're putting me in?" Amber said as she pushed against Terrance, her sword so close to him that a blue flame leaped from it and stung his cheek. "How do I break it to my friend I had to hack apart her boyfriend? It's going to break her heart—when I hand her yours."

With a quick shove, Terrance was knocked backward, and Amber turned to deflect a blow from Talia. Terrance lost his balance only a little and swung at Amber's unguarded side. She didn't block quickly enough, and the blow connected...with a loud, useless clang against her armor. Terrance didn't know what he'd expected it to do; why in the world would metal cut metal?

In a single motion, Amber kicked Talia back into a table while swinging her sword so forcefully it knocked the weapon out of Terrance's hand and caused him to stumble to the ground. Then Amber was standing over him, pointing her sword at his face. He was about to die, and the realization caused a strangely empty feeling in him. He forced his eyes away from the sword tip to look at Amber, who stared down at him with a wicked smile. "You fight like a little bitch." She reared back for the stab but was distracted by the sight of Terrance's pants. "Did you wet yourself?"

Talia was back, charging her, and as Amber turned to her opponent, Terrance wrapped his leg around hers, tripping her. As Amber stumbled, Talia's sword cut through her armor with ease. Amber cried out and fell to the ground. She tried to get her sword up, but Talia cut through her arm and the sword fell. Talia stabbed straight through Amber's chest, then yanked the sword upward, bisecting her head.

Terrance was back to being horrified, but quickly realized there was no blood. Instead, more blue flames erupted from the wounds until they consumed Amber's entire body. Within a few moments, it all disappeared as if she had never existed in the first place.

"They're not human?"

Talia sheathed her swords. There was a red stain on the shoulder of her white cloak. "No. I thought we explained that."

Terrance got to his feet and retrieved his sword from the floor. He thought of Shannon and wondered if she was an empty thing like her friend, but he couldn't believe it. "They feel real."

Talia looked at him with confusion. "You felt her up while we were fighting her?"

Terrance quickly got hold himself. "No."

Talia looked him over carefully. "Did you soil your pants?"

"No!" He sheathed his sword and stared despondently at the empty spot where Amber had been. Terrance had been playing two sides, but now it looked like that was coming to an end.

CHAPTER 20

I should be back this evening, read the email from Shannon. *I'll come straight to your place and we'll pick a romantic comedy to watch. And you'll watch it politely and pretend to like it. I've decided we're at the phase of our relationship where I start training you. Is that okay? (HINT: The correct answer to that question should be something like, 'Yes, my love; anything for you.')*

Terrance couldn't help but smile while thinking of Shannon...even though he had just helped kill her friend and he knew that was going to be a really awkward conversation. He just hoped it didn't come up tonight. Still, in his heart, he knew everything was about to come crashing down. He typed a response on his smartphone. *I would die a thousand deaths for you, but telling me not to make fun of a romcom is asking far too much.*

He was standing in the alleyway next to the Hobby Lobby. He had told work he was taking a personal day and wasn't coming back after lunch, then spent the afternoon in the Infinite's castle hideaway, waiting for them to show up. There was no cell service there, though, so he had to venture out every so often to check on things. Terrance was getting the impression that certain areas, such as the castle and the clearing where the faeries had given him his sword, existed outside of normal time and space, because, really, why would any place not have cell service these days?

He headed back to the castle. The sunlight spilled through the windows, and it was quiet and peaceful inside, the only sound the waves crashing against the rocks down below the cliff. He looked out a window across the ocean, staring at the island in the distance. It looked like a beautiful place of grass-covered mountains and quiet forests. He wished he were there, resting under the shade of a tree and forgetting everything.

He heard footsteps behind him and turned to see Talia, the first of the Infinite to arrive. After the mall, she had left for other business, though she wouldn't tell him what. She had apparently changed white cloaks, as the bloodstain was gone. "How's the arm?" he asked.

"It was just a scratch."

"You often get wounded in fights like those?"

She walked over to stand beside him, and glanced at him briefly. She then pulled her hood more around her face as she stared out the window. "You worry about the wrong things, Denby."

"I'm just trying to understand. I have a sword but no actual training for using one, and I'm supposed to be fighting skilled warriors who apparently have magical powers. I don't really get how I'm going to be able to do that."

Talia nodded. "Have you tried whining about it?" She looked at him, her eyes cold and fierce. "Oh, you did, and it didn't help."

Terrance walked away from her and leaned against a wall. "You're a real pleasure to talk to, you know that?"

Talia turned back to the window. "I'm just trying to snap you out of your sniveling little worldview. You have a small mind. You focus on small things. You took on one of the Hollow Ones today. It had strength and speed beyond that of mortal men, but after that fight you are standing and it is not."

Terrance thought about the fight, and how clueless and befuddled he had felt in it, his sword just something to put between himself and someone who wished to do him harm. He thought about how Talia had cut through Amber and there really was nothing inside. "All I did was fall down a lot. You were the one who tore Amb—"

He didn't catch himself quite quickly enough, as Talia was now glaring at him with accusing eyes. "You knew her name. I saw you talking before the battle; you two knew each other." She took a couple of steps toward him, her eyes locked on his. "What aren't you telling me?"

She was a small woman, but she scared the hell out of him. "I'm working some things out; don't rush me," he stammered. Without thinking, his hand went to the hilt of his sword.

She looked at the hand on his sword and stepped back. "What are you doing?"

"You're scaring me!" Terrance didn't take his hand off the sword.

Talia looked confused. "What do you think I'm going to do to you?"

"I don't know! Maybe hack me apart like you have others!"

Now Talia looked mad. "You think I'm a murderous psychopath or something?"

"I don't know what I think about anything anymore!"

"Well, you two make a cute couple." Terrance turned around to see Curtis entering the room along with his wife, Vivian, and their two kids, Grace and Daniel. Curtis was in mechanic overalls, while Vivian wore a modest green dress. They carried a couple of foil-covered trays—presumably the evening's snacks.

"He's hiding something!" Talia jabbed a finger in Terrance's direction. "He knew the Hollow One we fought!"

Curtis shrugged. "If he wants to tell us about it, he'll tell us about it."

Terrance released the hilt of his sword. "It's complicated."

Talia scowled at him. "It's only complicated when you know what you must do and don't want to do it."

Curtis set the trays down on a table. "Now that might be oversimplifying things."

"If you have something you need to get off your chest," Vivian said, "we're all here to support each other."

"What happened to your pants, mister?" asked Grace.

"Coffee spill." Terrance realized he really should have at least gone home and changed his pants before the meeting.

The girl seemed satisfied by the answer, and the two kids scampered off.

"So are you okay?" Vivian asked, her voice filled with genuine concern. "A Hollow One may have been a bit much for you to take on at this stage."

Talia rolled her eyes. "He did fine. He just needs to commit himself more, but something is holding him back."

Joyce walked in, wearing blue scrubs once again. "What's happening? We interrogating the new guy? Should I get a rubber hose?"

"Hey, he came back!" Randolph exclaimed at Terrance with a big smile as he followed Joyce in. The old man immediately took a seat. "I thought maybe Talia had scared you off for good."

"I don't scare people off," Talia said. "And if you'd checked your email, you'd have seen that he and I battled a Hollow One today. He seems to want to fight, but I can also tell he has other priorities."

"Let's just leave Terrance alone," Vivian said. "He'll talk about things when he is ready."

That's what Terrance was debating with himself: how much he was ready to tell them. He wanted to tell them about his situation with Shannon, but he was afraid their solution would be to immediately hunt her down and destroy her the way Talia had destroyed Amber. But thinking of the emptiness of Amber and the blue flames that had engulfed her, he wondered if there was any of Shannon left to save. *You know there is*, he told himself. *That's why you're in love with her.*

The rest of the group arrived—Felicia, once again with a backpack like this was an afterschool activity, the young couple Travis and Erica, and the mostly quiet man in a suit whose name Terrance had forgotten (Donald, and he vowed to remember it this time).

"So, I heard you fought a Hollow One," Travis said to Terrance. "You're really jumping right into this, bro."

"I think he knew her, though," Talia said.

Erica looked concerned. "Well, that has to be scary—someone you know being like that. Are you okay?"

"I didn't really know her," Terrance said. He wasn't a very good liar, but it was pretty much true; he'd met her only once.

"You have to be careful of the Hollow Ones," Curtis told him. "They can seem normal, but they are ruthless when provoked."

"So, any other associations you want to tell us about?" Joyce asked Terrance.

Terrance was just thinking of how to dodge that one when a voice boomed from outside, "Terrance Denby!"

Everyone reached down for their swords except for the children, who just looked confused, and Terrance, who sat frozen with a chill going down his spine.

"What have your secrets brought upon us?" Talia asked, her fierce eyes once again boring into Terrance.

"I don't..." Terrance stood up, looking at the faces of these people who perhaps he had put in danger by not being honest with them. "Maybe I should go check this out."

"We'll be right behind you, bro," Travis said as he and the others prepared to embark.

"I know you and your friends are in there, little man!" boomed the voice as Terrance marched outside, followed by the others.

There, near the rocky outcropping, was a large figure standing alone, which Terrance immediately recognized as Chet. "You know this guy?" Curtis asked.

"Sorta. Why don't I go talk to him?" Terrance said, then realized how much that prospect frightened him.

"Why don't we just hack him apart right now?" Talia suggested.

"Because it looks like a trap," Randolph said, stroking his beard.

It certainly does, Terrance thought, but found himself walking toward Chet anyway.

Chet stood with his arms folded, his large axe strapped to his back. His eyes, barely visible through the slits of the helmet, looked down at Terrance. "I think you're keeping some secrets from Shannon, aren't you, little man?"

"I guess you found me out." Terrance kept a tight grip on his sheathed sword. "You're outnumbered, so I don't know what you're expecting."

Chet lowered his voice. "And do these agents of chaos behind you know about your other associations? What are you planning here?"

He really didn't know what his plans were, and that was the problem. Obviously Shannon was going to find out about him soon, and most likely the Infinite would find out about the secrets he'd kept hidden from them. So he dodged the question. "What are *you* planning?"

"The same as always: for my axe to taste the blood of fools." Chet laughed.

Terrance drew his sword, pointed it at Chet, and said, "That won't be easy." It didn't sound as intimidating as he'd hoped.

Chet looked him over. "Did you pee your pants?"

"No! It's a cof—"

Chet kicked him in the chest, knocking Terrance backward onto the ground. He lifted up his head to see a few dozen large figures emerging from the rocky path behind Chet. They were eyeless soldiers in dark armor with pale skin and sharp little teeth.

Terrance scrambled to his feet and backed away from Chet to join the others, keeping his sword between himself and the enemy, for what little good it did. As the enemy advanced, the Infinite also had their swords drawn as they watched with steely faces—except for Curtis and Vivian's children, who stood behind and watched the scene unfold with great curiosity.

"What are those things?" Terrance asked.

"We call them 'cavefish,'" Curtis answered. "They're foot soldiers of the Darkness that we're seeing more and more of. They seem to have access to them in large numbers."

"And you brought them here," Talia growled.

"I...didn't know he was following me." Truthful, though Terrance still felt that he was being quite deceptive. He saw Grace and Daniel behind him and felt extra guilty, though they didn't look frightened and were simply interested in seeing what was going on. Terrance looked back at Chet and said, "If you have a problem with me, leave the others out of it." He tried to say it forcefully, but his voice faltered as he looked at Chet's horde.

"Oh, we deal with stuff like this all the time; don't worry about it," Randolph said, holding his sword relaxed by his side.

The cavefish assembled behind Chet, blocking off the Infinite from the only escape from the castle on the cliff. The creatures were brandishing their weapons and stomping their feet, ready to charge at any moment. But they stayed where they were.

"Why aren't they attacking yet?" Donald asked.

"We could ask him," Joyce answered. "Hey!" Joyce started to call out, and then stopped and looked at Terrance. "You know his name?"

Terrance was starting to get a little tired from holding up his sword. "Chet."

"Hey, Chet!" Joyce yelled. "Why aren't you attacking yet? Why not yet, Chet?"

Chet laughed. "I am simply biding my time. All I have to do is wait while you stand where you are, and you'll be dead."

"Like from starvation, or do you have something more immediate in mind?" Joyce responded.

"Patience," Chet said. "The end is coming."

Joyce looked at the others. "I guess we're in the middle of some trap or something."

Randolph shrugged. "That seems pretty obvious."

"Guys," Terrance said, "I'm really sorry I—"

"Could you stop whining!" Talia shouted. "I say we attack them. If they expect us to stand here and wait for the machinations, then we disappoint them."

"A rather blunt solution to this problem," Curtis said, "but I'm not sure what our other options are."

Felicia tensed, preparing to fight. "And I have a bad feeling about what we're waiting for."

The sky began to darken, the blue turning to gray. Erica looked up and then moved closer to Travis. "And I think I see it."

The others looked up. In the distance, a black dot in the sky was growing larger, and as it grew, so did Terrance's overwhelming sense of doom.

"Malcus," Curtis uttered, his face betraying his fear.

Chet started laughing, a huge, booming laugh that only added to the panic, as he stood still and watched.

"Maybe if we engage them in battle, it won't breathe fire on us," Travis suggested.

"I wouldn't count on it." Vivian sheathed her sword and took her daughter by the hand. The little girl was also watching the sky, but without the same amount of dread. "We have one way out of here fast."

Everyone groaned except for Terrance. "What are we doing?"

Curtis picked up his son. "Jumping into the water."

Terrance looked toward the cliffs around the castle. "The water down there?"

Chet's laughter seemed even louder, and Malcus was now close enough that instead of being just a black blob in the darkening sky, it was a horribly spiky black blob.

"We'll be fine," Curtis said, and then jumped over the cliff holding his son. Vivian followed, jumping hand in hand with her daughter.

"This isn't suicide?" Terrance asked, trading panicked glances between the cliff and the approaching demon dragon.

"Not if we're assuming we live." Joyce ran and jumped off the cliff.

"Stop them!" Chet roared, and the cavefish began to run toward them.

"Yeah, that's our cue," Travis said, and held close to Erica as they both took the plunge. Randolph, Donald, and Felicia quickly followed.

"Come on, idiot!" Talia yelled at Terrance, the two of them the only ones left.

Terrance sheathed his sword, took off his glasses and slid them into his pocket, and looked down the side of the cliff as he prepared to jump. The fall was farther than he'd thought. He looked back at the charging cavefish, who were almost on them, and then up at Malcus, now clearly visible as a massive black creature covered in spikes. Its red eyes seemed to be locked on Terrance. In its mouth something glowed, and he could tell it was about to incinerate him

Talia yanked on his arm and Terrance stumbled backward with her, off the cliff. As they fell, black flames erupted from Malcus's mouth, and the whole cliffside became covered in fire. Above them was nothing but the horrible, unnatural-looking flame, black at its center but tinged red at the edges. But the flame died down quickly, and the castle and much of the cliffside were gone.

Then he hit the water.

CHAPTER 21

From the height of the cliff, Terrance had expected that hitting the water would be like slamming into pavement, but the surprisingly warm water accepted him gently and gracefully, almost like a reassuring hug. When he opened his eyes, he was looking over an underwater valley hued in blue, with glowing creatures swimming throughout. Jellyfish hung about in the water like street lamps as fish of all sizes swam about. Terrance saw a long eel-like creature—longer than a bus—slithering beneath him. Something the size of a whale swam off to his side, but it had a tail like a fish and was dotted with glowing spots. From the size of the creatures, Terrance felt he should be afraid, but he wasn't and instead watched them with fascination. In the distance and further into the depths below, he saw a cluster of lights that looked like an underwater city. He was enthralled by the scene, temporarily forgetting his situation and how he had ended up in it, until a current suddenly yanked him backward.

Terrance turned to see that he was heading for the rocky cliff he had jumped from, but the water pulled him through an entrance below the cliff. He found himself tumbling through a large tunnel that was somehow lit, but he was moving too fast to see what produced the light. He remembered that he was underwater, which meant that breathing should become a concern at some point. He wasn't panicked for air yet—he didn't even feel like he was holding his breath—but he hoped his water ride would end soon and that it wasn't sending him further underwater.

The current finally threw Terrance out of the tunnel, and he felt himself float upward. When his head crested the surface, he took a deep breath of air just because it felt like he should. He quickly spotted the others swimming toward the shore, and followed them. They soon reached rocky land, and Terrance took a moment to sit and take in the surroundings. They were in a large cavern lit by hundreds of glowing crystals, and on one side of the underground lake was what looked like a temple. "I know where we are," Terrance said. "There's actually a ladder to my apartment near here."

"That's convenient," Donald said. His suit was dripping wet like everyone else's clothes. "You have any towels there?"

Terrance looked at the size of the group. "A few."

"Can we do that again, Mommy?" Daniel asked. Grace was busy looking at one of the glowing crystals with quiet fascination.

Terrance felt an intense guilt, watching Curtis and Vivian's children; his secret-keeping had almost gotten them incinerated along with the rest of the group. He walked over to Vivian. "I'm so sorry I put you all in danger like this. I had no idea that—"

"It's okay." She patted him on the shoulder. "These things happen."

Having escaped from a giant dragon into a massive underground cavern, Terrance was pretty sure these things did *not* happen, despite Vivian's assurance. "I got your whole castle burned away and—"

"It's really not a big deal." Erica looked over her wet clothing. "I'm just glad I left my purse in the car."

"Yeah, we've all made mistakes, bro," Travis said. "This whole thing is a big learning process for all of us."

"We're all in constant danger." Curtis knelt next to his son. "Especially children. You just have to learn to deal with it, not ignore it."

Terrance looked around the group. None of them looked angry at him. Except for Talia. "He's hiding something!" Talia shouted. "Why does he know so many of the Hollow Ones?"

Curtis stood up and walked over to Terrance. "If he's hiding something, he'll have to deal with it. And if he needs our help, he'll ask."

For a moment, Terrance considered telling them his situation. He did feel so alone in it, and it would be nice to have some help. And after what he'd put them through, it seemed like he owed them the truth.

"Hey, Terrance!"

Terrance turned around to see Jenna the mermaid, holding her top half above the surface of the water. "Oh, hey."

"I saw you in the water and was going to swim over to you, but you were with others and I didn't know if it was a party I wasn't invited to or something."

"No, we're just...um...fleeing mortal danger."

"Mommy, it's a mermaid!" Daniel said.

"Yes, it is," Vivian said, pulling him close. "And she's not...wearing a shirt."

"Nope. I don't own any," Jenna said. "They don't keep well in the water."

Talia glared at her. "You're indecent."

Jenna sunk lower into the water so that only her head was sticking up. "I'm sorry."

"Don't be mean to the mermaid, Talia," Randolph said.

"I don't trust her," Talia said.

Randolph rolled his eyes. "That's a surprise."

Felicia was trying to fix her hair. "Hey, someone mentioned something about towels."

"Oh yeah, there's a ladder over this way." Terrance started to lead them away.

"Nice meeting you all!" Jenna yelled, waving at them as they left.

With the long ladder climb, they all made their way up to the entrance to Terrance's apartment. He had to give the little trapdoor a big shove to knock away the stuff on top of it, then they came in one by one while Terrance tried to find all the towels he had.

"Will blankets work?" Terrance asked, bringing out a few spare ones.

Donald took one. "I'll give it a try."

The group was now dripping all over Terrance's apartment and furniture. He still felt pretty bad about the whole thing, but most of them looked a bit amused by the situation. Except, of course, Talia. "We need to find a way to take on Malcus," she said.

"That is true." Curtis dabbed himself with a towel. "I don't think the direct approach is going to work."

"I'd better call my mom soon." Felicia pulled out her cellphone, which was protected in a plastic Ziploc bag. "Of course, I don't think I want to tell her I'm dripping wet in a strange man's apartment."

"You put your phone in a plastic bag?" Terrance asked. He didn't even want to check on how his phone had fared.

Felicia laughed. "You do this a while, you learn to be prepared."

"Where are we, anyway?" Vivian asked while helping her daughter dry off.

"Tall Oaks apartments," Terrance answered.

"I'm near here," Randolph said. "I can give everyone a ride back to where you parked your cars."

"Man, I hope the cavefish didn't key them or something," Donald said.

"Again, guys, I know you say it's not a big deal," Terrance said, "but I'm sorry about how—"

The front door opened, and Terrance froze in abject horror. There stood Shannon, smiling at first, then looking more and more confused by the scene in front of her. Luckily, she was dressed in regular clothes, so the Infinite didn't regard her with suspicion (except Talia, but that was starting to seem like her normal manner when greeting anyone), but Shannon looked over the dripping-wet strangers, and the swords at their hips, with a blank expression for what seemed like hours. Finally, she looked at Terrance and smiled. It was disturbing, as it was her perfectly normal smile, not betraying anything. "You didn't mention having guests today."

Had he put them all in danger again? Terrance wasn't sure, but Shannon certainly didn't appear dangerous at the moment. "Yeah...it's a long story. Um...hey, everyone, this is my girlfriend, Shannon."

They all said hello, then Daniel walked up to her and said, "We went swimming in the ocean and saw a mermaid!"

"Wow! That sounds exciting!" Shannon looked at the group. "So...you all go swimming in the ocean with swords?"

"I don't know how much Terrance told you about us, but it's a little hard to explain," Curtis said. "Anyway, we had to quickly escape a demonic dragon...so, the ocean."

Shannon nodded. "I didn't even know we got dragons in these parts...or oceans. But, no, Terrance hasn't told me much about you. Boy, I'm just glad I didn't show up here wearing my work uniform."

Terrance's heart sank into his stomach, and he found himself frozen in place again.

"Your uniform?" Vivian asked.

"Yeah." Shannon slowly walked over to Terrance and stood beside him. "I'm a barista, and it always smells of coffee...which Ance just loves." She then whispered. "It makes him a bit amorous. If I had it on, he'd be all over me, which would be embarrassing in front of company." She put her arm around Terrance, then quickly pulled it away. "Ew. You're wet."

Talia moved nearer to Shannon but still kept her distance. "Do I know you?"

Shannon betrayed her smile just slightly while looking at Talia. "Do you enjoy high-quality, fair-trade coffee?"

"No. I drink Folgers."

"Then I don't think so."

"Well, I think we'll all get out of your hair now," Curtis said while heading for the door. "Thanks for the towels, Terrance."

"No problem. Sorry again about the whole...um"—he glanced cautiously at Shannon but realized there was nothing left to conceal—"castle getting burned away and jumping into the ocean."

"We all have days like those; don't worry about it," Curtis answered. "We can get a new meeting place. But if you have some personal matters to sort out, you'd better get working on those."

They all headed out, Randolph subtly motioning at Shannon when she wasn't looking and giving Terrance a thumbs-up. When they were all gone, Shannon closed the door and turned to Terrance, still smiling normally, which was creeping him out. They stared at each other silently for a while, Terrance having no idea what to say. Eventually, Shannon pointed to the couch, then sat down while Terrance adjusted the sword at his hip before taking a seat beside her. Shannon gently felt along the sword's scabbard with two fingers, and Terrance almost thought he could feel the blade stir. With the same two fingers, she touched Terrance on the cheek. "Sounds like you had quite a day."

"I...guess we need to talk."

Her smile finally faded. "About what?"

CHAPTER 22

"So—funny story—just before I met you, I sort of ran into these faeries who gave me a sword," Terrance said.

"And you never thought this was worth mentioning to me?" There was anger in Shannon's eyes, but it seemed like a low boil right now. Terrance made a mental note to step very carefully.

"I was embarrassed," Terrance explained. "I really like you...and I got the feeling this would be an issue. So, I just tried to figure things out about it by myself."

Shannon nodded. "So you've been secretly meeting with people who are plotting to kill me and my friends."

Terrance realized this was not the sort of issue where there was any way to step around it carefully. "I'm...it's just...this is all very confusing..."

"Well, I know what I understand!" Shannon shouted. "You said you love me, but apparently you don't trust me enough to talk to me!"

"Sorry, I guess I was just afraid of losing you over this. I didn't know how you'd react and—"

The anger in Shannon's eyes died, and she took Terrance's hand. "I love you, Terrance. I know all this stuff can be weird and confusing, but we're going to get through this together. Here's what we're going to do: we're going to go to Walmart and buy a shotgun. Then we're going to go throw this sword away, find the faeries who gave it to you, and blast them. Then you'll forget all about this."

Terrance stared at Shannon with incomprehension. "We're going to blast the faeries with shotguns?"

Shannon nodded. "It's their weakness."

Terrance was trying hard to stifle the urge to stare at her in horror. "Their weakness is getting killed with shotguns?"

Shannon grimaced. "It was kind of a joke, since everything's weakness is getting blasted with a shotgun. I guess you're not at the joking-about-blasting-faeries-with-shotguns stage yet. Seriously, though, didn't you mention before that you have a handgun? That will probably work just fine."

Terrance rubbed his temples. "I'm not murdering faeries."

"You don't have to. It just seems like the easiest way to get through this."

Terrance stared at her as she earnestly stared back at him. This next part he wanted to be very careful with, but he sensed there wasn't really a way to avoid a head-on collision here. "Don't you ever get the feeling that maybe your job is...not a good thing?"

Shannon tensed a bit. "No, we talked about this."

"We talked a little," Terrance said, "but as soon as I started questioning your job, you began to get angry. That's why I knew there was a problem discussing these things with you."

Shannon rolled her eyes. "Well, everyone gets angry if you imply they're evil or something."

"Not you," Terrance said, "but your job seems pretty evil."

Shannon looked confused. "How?"

Terrance stood up and paced as he tried to organize his thoughts on what about Shannon's job seemed evil, but it ended up being too much to put into a coherent order, so it just came spilling out. "First of all, there's your armor with the demony-looking helmet that seems pretty much designed to say, 'Hey! Look at me! I'm evil!' Then there's how your job seems to be mainly slaughtering defenseless things. And your headquarters is an ominous fortress on the side of a volcano."

Shannon looked a bit flustered. "We've talked before about how my job can seem—"

"And you serve the Darkness." Terrance had too much momentum now to stop. "What good thing has ever been referred to as 'the Darkness'? And what's your group called? The Sisters of Torment? Torment! And there are demons in your employ—oh, and that horrible demon dragon thing. There are vampires and other monsters, like this thing I saw threatening children the other day—and I can only assume it was under your group's protection. It's not just that the organization you work for is evil, it's that they don't even make the slightest effort to not appear evil."

Shannon stood up, starting to look angry again. "I explained this! We keep order in the world, and that can appear at times—"

"Oh, and I'm getting so tired of that!" Terrance interrupted. "'Throwing puppies in a woodchipper is part of some larger world order.' You know who justifies their evil activities with, 'I'm just keeping order!'? Every villain in every movie, ever!"

"Fine! I'm EVIL!" Shannon screamed, waving her arms around theatrically. "I do nothing but murder and spread misery. So why are you with such a horrible, evil person? Why did you never mention this before?"

"Well...I wanted to, but I really like you, and this relationship moved so fast and—"

"What's that mean?" Her expression was anger, but she also looked like she was on the verge of tears. "I knew it! You never respected me after I slept with you on our first date. Ever since then, I guess I've just been your evil slut girlfriend!"

"No, that's not—"

"Your friends the Infinite must love the tales of your evil slut girlfriend!"

The thing from below was pounding at all the noise now, not that Terrance much cared. "Well, obviously I hadn't told them about you."

"Of course you didn't tell them! You're embarrassed by your evil slut girlfriend! But I guess you've chosen sides with those idiots, so there is only one thing left." She stretched out her arms and thrust out her chest, a couple of tears now running down her face. "Come on! Pull out your sword and slay the evil! You'll feel so much better, I'm sure."

And, of course, Terrance couldn't even contemplate doing that. But the suggestion brought to mind what he saw when Talia had cut through Amber. "Are you human?"

"What?" She lowered her arms, looking confused.

"With how the Darkness has changed you—are you even human still?"

"Like in an 'If you prick me, do I not bleed?' sort of way?"

"I...guess."

Shannon shook her head. "Then no...not really. Is that what this is about? You know I'm not exactly human, so anything you do to me is okay?"

"No." Terrance put his head in his hands and gave himself a moment's pause, as if that time would allow him to finally get a handle on the myriad thoughts bouncing around inside his head. "But...don't you ever worry about what they've done to you—about what they've made you become?"

She hesitated. "Everyone has doubts at times. This is all a lot for any person to deal with."

"Karen told me it was Chet who got you into this," Terrance said. "Isn't that a bit of a red flag?"

"That's...that's not really the issue. Every organization is going to have jerks."

"And take away your humanity?"

"They've made me more than human. I know it can appear...bad...but it's a good thing. It's just hard for everyone to see it that way because of the...you know..."

"Evil stuff?"

"No!" Now Shannon looked frustrated. "I know it appears that way, but what is the other choice, really? Join those nitwits you've thrown in with? They say they're infinite beings, but I can tell you for a fact they bleed and die like anyone else!"

Terrance shuddered. "What a non-evil way of putting it."

"Hey! I don't enjoy this work...I mean, not always." She was silent for a moment, and Terrance could only imagine what she was thinking. Whatever it was, she shook the thought from her head. "Let's take a break. We're not going to sort all of this out right now."

"Sounds like a good idea." Terrance took a deep breath. "Sorry I haven't been forthcoming about everything."

"It's not stuff people usually want to deal with at all." Shannon walked over to Terrance. "So are you okay? Did you get hurt doing...whatever it was you were doing?"

"We were fleeing from Malcus and had to jump off a cliff into the water. I think I'm fine, though."

"You're shivering. You should get out of those wet clothes."

Terrance nodded, then unbuttoned and shrugged out of his dress shirt, then kicked off his shoes and pulled off the coffee-stained (and now soaking-wet) pants. All the while, Shannon was standing nearby, watching Terrance—now just in an undershirt and boxers—with an odd expression. He stopped and returned her stare, and she smiled a little. He leaned over and began to slip off her T-shirt.

She thrashed away from him when she realized what he was doing, accidentally ripping her shirt, which came off in Terrance's hands. She covered her bra with her arms. "What the hell are you doing?"

"Oh...I thought we were doing the make-up thing."

"We haven't made up! We're just pausing the fight for a few minutes!"

Terrance looked down at the torn shirt in his hands. "I guess I misread that. Sorry."

"You are such an idiot sometimes!" As Shannon reached over for her shirt, the door crashed open. She jumped back, looking ready for a fight, and similarly Terrance quickly ducked down and grabbed his sword and sheath from the floor. Lacey, Elissa, and Vicky, all in full armor, charged into the apartment with their swords drawn. They came to a halt and stared at the shirtless Shannon and pantsless Terrance.

"Hey, I think I know what this is about," Shannon said, "but I'm handling it."

Lacey sighed. "I'm not sure this is the sort of problem awkward dorky sex can solve...as useful a solution as that usually is."

Terrance started to reach down to grab his pants, but the three armored women brandished their swords menacingly as soon as he started to move.

"What's going on in here?" Lance asked, peering in through the busted doorway.

Shannon snatched up her torn T-shirt and tried to cover her chest with it. Terrance once again tried to reach for his pants, but Lacey and her compatriots took that as a threat, so he just kept still.

"Is something the matter?" Lance inquired, looking over the scene without much comprehension. He looked carefully at the faces of the three Sisters of Torment in their armor. "Is Amber around?"

"No," Vicky said. "Your friend here slew her."

Lance stared at Terrance in disbelief. "Dude! I told you I liked her!"

The look of betrayal was even greater from Shannon. "What? Were you going to mention this?"

"I was about to," Terrance said. "She attacked me! And it was Talia who slew her. I tried to stop the whole thing, but it got out of hand pretty quick. I'm really—really—sorry."

"Oh, he apologized," Lacey said. "I guess we can just go then."

"He should buy us ice cream first," Elissa said. "To really show he's sorry."

"Fancy stuff with toppings," Vicky added. "And I want a stuffed kitty."

"Well, there is a Cold Stone Creamery—" Terrance started to say, and then noticed that Shannon was shaking her head. "Oh...you're being sarcastic, aren't you?"

"You really won the boyfriend lottery with this one, Shana-nana," Lacey said. "Someone want to text Despina and tell her we found him and are about to do really mean things to him?"

Vicky shrugged. "A text message will just confuse her; she might think her phone has come alive and is talking to her."

Terrance tightly gripped the hilt of his sheathed sword. "What are you planning to do?"

Lacey smiled. "There will be more terror if it's a surprise."

Terrance turned to Shannon, who looked worried as she watched her friends approach Terrance. She said to Lacey, "Guys, can't we handle this off the books?"

Lacey had her eyes on Terrance like a predator approaching its prey. "Maybe if he cooperates, we can spare him some of the unpleasantness."

"So Terrance is in trouble or something?" Lance asked, gaining nobody's attention.

Shannon turned to Terrance. "Maybe it is best if you just give yourself up and we can get this over with."

Terrance glanced at the approaching Lacey and back at Shannon, and started to draw his sword as he backed away. "And what is going to happen to me?"

"Well, they'll..." Shannon started to say, but seemed pretty hesitant to fill in the rest.

Lacey now had a wicked smile. "Come on. Draw the sword. Let's make this fun."

"Lacey!" Shannon screamed. "Let's just hold off on this!"

As Lacey took another step forward, Terrance drew his sword, but found his arm grabbed by Shannon, who stripped the sword away. Lacey didn't stop her charge, though, raising her sword for a blow. Terrance stumbled to the ground trying to back away, shielding his face with his arms, as if that would stop the sharp steel. As

Lacey's sword came down, there was a flash of steel, and her sword hand separated from her arm and fell, still clutching the sword, to the floor at Terrance's side.

"WHAT THE HELL?!" Lacey screamed, grabbing her stub, which burned with a blue flame.

"I told you to wait!" Shannon yelled back, waving around Terrance's sword anxiously.

Elissa took a step toward her. "Shannon, you better—"

Shannon held out her left hand and a blue fireball flew from it, striking Elissa and knocking her into Vicky, and they both tumbled to the ground. Terrance had gotten back to his feet, and suddenly Shannon was yanking him toward the door.

"Should I—" Lance started to ask, but Shannon shoved him out of the way as she pulled Terrance out of the apartment and toward her car.

"Here, take this back," Shannon commanded, holding his sword out with distaste. She pulled her keys out of her pocket and threw some wary glances back at the apartment. She handed the keys to Terrance. "You drive; I may need to hold them off."

Terrance nodded, sheathed his sword, and quickly got into the driver's seat and started the car. "You can throw fireballs?"

"Yes, like an evil demon from Doom," she said, looking behind them.

Lacey, Vicky, and Elissa emerged from the apartment just as Terrance was backing the car out of the spot. "You will know torment unlike you could possibly imagine!" Lacey screamed as they sped off.

Terrance glanced carefully a couple of times at the rearview mirror. "Thanks," he muttered to Shannon.

"I just need time to think, you know." She took a deep breath. "And just because I'm on the run with you doesn't mean I don't feel really angry and betrayed by you."

"I understand, but—"

There was a thud, and the car shook as something large landed on its roof. A face descended over the windshield from above: a dark creature with two red eyes. It opened its shark-like mouth, revealing not just a jaw but an entire throat filled with hundreds of sharp teeth. Terrance immediately slammed on the brakes, and the creature flew forward but caught itself in the air, beating large, bat-like wings to stay aloft. It hovered in front of the car as the headlights reflected off of its dark body, which had six thin legs like those of an insect, and two claws like those of a scorpion.

"It's a chimera," Shannon said. "We sometimes ride them."

One of Terrance's hands was almost crushing the steering wheel, while the other was feeling the hilt of his sword. "Then maybe you can tell it not to eat us."

Shannon peeked her head out of the car window. "No, Mr. Cupcake. You shoo. Shoo!"

It considered Shannon's command for a moment, then looked back at Terrance, baring its teeth one more time before flying off. Terrance immediately pressed down on the gas to get further away from it. He took a deep breath. "Mr. Cupcake?"

"Yeah, I recognized him. Cute story behind that name...well, it's a little violent."

Terrance was panting, his heart racing. "Maybe save it for another time."

"I'm sorry I got you into this."

"Well, it's probably more my fault. I'm really, really sorry about what happened with Amber and not telling you about it. It's just with all that's—"

Shannon put her hand on his shoulder. "It's okay; these things happen. But in a relationship, we don't keep secrets. If you think your girlfriend is part of an inhuman evil, that's something that you can't just bottle up. That has to be brought out in the open and discussed so we can get through it. I've had things go poorly in the past, so I've read a lot of relationship books. Well, two."

Terrance kept a close eye on the rearview mirror to see if anyone was following. He also glanced nervously a couple of times at the sky. "I'm sorry. I didn't mean to be dishonest; it's just that everything has been very scary and confusing for me lately. This certainly isn't anything I'm used to dealing with."

"Which is why we'll work through it together," Shannon said. "I think now that we've confronted it, we can get through it and become stronger as a couple...unless we're hunted down or something."

"So how are you doing with this?"

She frowned. "I've never heard of one of the followers of the Darkness rebelling; I don't know what happens with that...I guess I'm kinda scared and confused, too."

Terrance stopped clutching his sword and instead put that hand on top of Shannon's. "It's going to be okay."

"Is it? I'm not really sure about things right now. I mean...now that I think about it, maybe there are a few things about the Darkness that are kind of evil. I used to love unicorns as a little girl, but now they attack me on sight. So there's some stuff I'm a little uncomfortable with, but it's not like there's any point in going up against them. So...I'm not sure where I'm going with this right now."

"Maybe it's not so desperate," Terrance said. "I mean, people do oppose the Darkness. Sounds like they have been for a long while."

Shannon shrugged. "I'm not sure they've ever accomplished anything, though. So where are we going?"

Terrance looked down the road. "I dunno...east? You got any ideas?"

CHAPTER 23

Karen looked at the two of them in disbelief—Shannon with no shirt and Terrance in an undershirt and boxers, holding his sheathed sword—and uttered, "Nope," before trying to slam her front door.

Shannon stuck her foot in the way. "Come on! We're being hunted down and we really need to borrow some clothes."

Karen rolled her eyes. "Fine. Come in."

Karen's home was meticulously neat and organized and stylishly painted and decorated to the point that Terrance felt like they might have been interrupting her from filming an HGTV show. Karen was in purple pajamas, and it looked like they had interrupted her from watching *The Bachelor*. Off the front room was a dark hallway, where Terrance thought he saw movement. He drew his sword and ran over to switch on the light, but whatever it was scampered away.

"Watch it with that thing!" Karen barked at him. "Don't cut my walls!"

Terrance ignored her and turned to Shannon. "I think I saw one of those dark watcher things."

"Of course," Shannon said. "They're everywhere. It's not like we can hide."

"Then what are our options?"

"I don't know! I'm following you! You're the one who is part of a group trying to take on the universe or some other nonsense!"

Karen sighed. "Are you guys just going to yell at each other all night? Because I don't want that here."

Shannon looked at Karen. "Do you think I'm evil?"

"What?"

"Like, my job and stuff—does it seem evil to you?"

Karen threw her hands in the air. "I don't know, and I don't care! What mess did you guys get yourselves into?"

Shannon pointed a finger at Terrance. "It turns out that Terrance—completely behind my back—has been part of an organization trying to destroy all servants of the Darkness." Shannon paused for a moment. "Yeah, I guess I can see how that sounds kind of evil."

"Break up with him, then," Karen said. "What do you want from me?"

"Well, Lacey, Elissa, and Vicky are after him because he helped slay Amber with the help of"—Shannon frowned—"Talia."

"Who is Talia?"

"Remember the empowerment ceremony?" Terrance asked. "Talia is the woman they were going to feed to the unnamed beast below our building."

Karen nodded. "Yeah, you really acted like a complete spaz that day."

Terrance sheathed his sword. "I saw something evil, and I tried to stand up and do something about it!"

"Behind my back!" Shannon shouted at him. "If you love someone, you don't sit around thinking how evil they are without saying anything!"

"I know that now, okay? I'm sorry."

Karen sighed loudly again. "If people are hunting you down, does that mean they're going to come here and mess up my place?"

"I'm sure Lacey would let us take it outside," Shannon said. "But if it's Chet—oh man, I bet Chet is after us right now."

"Your ex?" Karen looked angry. "You really have to get completely away from that guy."

"That's not easy!" Shannon said. "I'd have to quit my job...and I don't even know if that's possible."

Terrance rushed over to Shannon and gently held her. "Maybe it is possible. Maybe we can stand up against all of this, together." He smiled at her, and she smiled back. She was so beautiful...and her torso was currently naked except for her black bra. "Hey, Karen," Terrance said, keeping his back to her. "Do you maybe have some pants I could borrow?"

"Yeah, and I could use a shirt," Shannon said.

"Oh...and a belt to hold my sword," Terrance added. "And maybe shoes or something?"

"I'll see what I have," Karen grumbled and headed to a back room.

Terrance heard an odd meow. "What's that?"

"Oh. I got a text." Shannon pulled her phone from her pocket and read the screen, laughing.

"What is it?"

"It's Lacey. She says they have Lance and are going to start cutting pieces off of him if we don't turn ourselves in."

Terrance's eyes grew wide. "Oh man. What do we do?"

Shannon scoffed. "Oh, they're just bluffing...most likely."

"Well, you two have gotten yourselves in quite a mess."

Terrance and Shannon turned to see a little elf sitting on Karen's couch in stereotypical green elf clothing, smoking a pipe.

Shannon scowled at him. "What do you know, elf?"

"What I know isn't the question," the elf answered. "The question is, what will I tell you?"

"You're the elf I saw in that office building, aren't you?" Terrance said.

"I am."

"And I think I saw you at Lacey's birthday party."

He puffed his pipe. "Maybe you did."

Shannon stood next to Terrance and held his arm, as if holding him back from danger. "Don't trust him. You can't trust elves."

Terrance paused briefly to figure out how to put his question delicately. "Is that like how you think faeries are bad and dangerous?"

The elf chuckled. "Oh no. We really can't be trusted." He gave Terrance a wicked smile. "But you'll deal with me all the same."

There was a shriek. Karen was standing in the hallway, holding some clothes and staring at the elf. "What is that? And why is it smoking?"

"I'm an elf—my name is Beauregard—and I smoke because it is relaxing."

"You can't smoke in here!" Karen shouted.

Beauregard relaxed on the couch. "I smoke where I please. And wherever 'here' is, that is where I am pleased to smoke."

Karen dropped the clothes and picked up a magazine from an end table. She rolled it up and started to approach the elf, but Shannon grabbed her arm. "Don't. If you make him mad, he'll just come back here while you're sleeping and smoke all he wants. You really can't stop him."

"I'll also go through your underwear drawer and steal things," Beauregard added.

Karen growled and pointed at Shannon and Terrance. "You brought this on me!"

Beauregard puffed on his pipe. "It's true."

"Sorry, Karen; we'll get out of your hair soon." Shannon walked over and picked up the clothes. She handed a pair of pink sweatpants to Terrance.

"These are pink," Terrance said after observing their color, which was pink.

"I don't have men's clothes," Karen said. "Those will stretch to fit you. And here's a belt and some sandals."

The belt was decorative and girly—but not as girly as the pink sweatpants. With a bit of effort, Terrance pulled on the sweatpants, which came up just below his knee, while Shannon put on the plain white T-shirt. He strapped on the belt, which was so tight he barely got it around his waist, and attached his sword to it. He also slipped his feet into the sandals, which weren't comfortable but seemed like they'd do for now.

"You two look ready to hit the town," Karen said. "So why don't you do that? And take your elf."

"Do you know where we should go?" Terrance asked Beauregard.

Beauregard looked quite comfortable and not ready to go anywhere. "It depends on what you wish to do. If you wish to surrender to the allies of the Darkness, then I know many places you can go."

"I don't want to do that."

"Then you should be prepared for a fight. I'd start by slaying that one"—he pointed to Shannon—"before she wises up and turns on you."

"I'm not doing that!" Terrance shouted.

"And I'm not turning on him," Shannon said, sounding hurt.

"Yes you are," Beauregard said. "Let's not operate under the assumption that this thing between you two will end well."

"Well...what if"—Shannon twirled a lock of her hair around a finger as she thought long and hard about her next statement. "I want to cut ties with the Darkness?"

Terrance was overjoyed at the thought, but held himself back from reacting too strongly. "Are you sure that's what you want?"

"I think so." She looked at Terrance, sadness in her eyes. "I didn't consider myself evil—but maybe I just never thought about it very much. Maybe I didn't want to. I mean, just thinking of the things I've done...the people I've hurt. Maybe I am an evil monster."

"No, you're not." Terrance embraced her. "We'll get through this."

"No, you won't," Beauregard said.

"We will," Terrance said firmly. "How can she cut her ties with the Darkness?"

"If there is any bit of her left that is not fully owned by the Darkness, and she truly wants to give up her power, she would need to talk to the faeries."

"Okay. How do we find them?" Terrance asked.

Beauregard shrugged. "They don't like dealing with me, so I don't know. But I think I know who would." He took out a wallet—normal-sized, not elf-sized—and removed a business card, handing it to Terrance. It was a card for Curtis Dayton's auto repair shop with his personal cell number written on it—much like the one Curtis had given Terrance when they first met. Actually, it *was* the card Curtis had given him. Beauregard was holding his wallet.

"Hey!" Terrance snatched the wallet out of the elf's hands.

"I noticed you didn't have any cash in there," Beauregard said, "but it's customary to tip an elf when he gives you information."

"All you told me was to contact someone I already knew to contact about stuff like this."

"It's customary," Beauregard said firmly. "I put my card in your wallet. It has my email address on it; you can send a tip through PayPal."

Karen had settled in a chair across the room and was looking at them like they were an infestation problem. "So are you guys about done here?"

"If we aren't, are you going to dump coffee on us?" Terrance responded.

"I said I was sorry about that."

"No, you didn't actually."

"Well, you're friends with that jerk Lance, so I don't like you."

"You already didn't like me even when you liked Lance!"

Karen rolled her eyes. "So it stands to reason that I'd like you even less once I also didn't like Lance."

"Well, I'm having a very bad day, and Lance is being tortured by Shannon's coworkers, so I hope you're happy."

Karen raised an eyebrow. "Tortured?"

Shannon shook her head. "He's probably not being tortured." She looked at Terrance. "So, want to get going? We stay anyplace too long, Lacey and the others will probably catch up with us."

"Okay, let's go." Terrance took his sheathed sword in hand and checked to make sure his too-small pink sweatpants were on as properly as they could be. "Let's do this."

Terrance and Shannon headed for the door with Beauregard following. Shannon turned and said to Karen, "If Lacey comes by, tell her you didn't see us. And blast her with a shotgun if you have one; that might slow her down."

Karen growled. "I don't want more company tonight."

"Yeah, I know," Shannon said. "Anyway, thanks for the clothes, and sorry you're a bitch."

Karen got up to lock the door as they exited. "Sorry I let Lance talk me into setting you up with Terrance."

Out in the crisp night air, they stood near Shannon's Prius, the top now scratched from the chimera's landing on it. "So where are we going?" Shannon asked.

"I know this guy who leads one of the groups of the Infinite," Terrance said. "You sort of met him today. Beauregard seems to think he'll be able to help us find the faeries."

Shannon looked around at the sky. "Let's call him from the road."

"Okay." Terrance turned to Beauregard. "So, are you coming? 'Cause I don't think we have a booster seat for the car." Also, Terrance figured Shannon didn't want him smoking a pipe in there.

"No, I will depart from you now. Good luck. I hope everything doesn't turn out as disastrously as seems inevitable."

"Um...thanks."

Beauregard quickly strode away, disappearing behind some bushes between houses. Terrance and Shannon got into the Prius, Shannon started up the quiet engine, and they got moving. "You know where we're going?"

"Not yet. I'll need to borrow your phone to make a call." He watched her face for a moment, dimly lit by the streetlights passing by. "Are you ready for this?"

She nodded. "I thought I was fine with what I did—happy about it, even—but I wasn't always. I once was where you've been recently: starting to notice all these things and feeling horrified." She stared out the windshield, and Terrance got the notion she wasn't just looking at the road but instead at something far more distant. "It seemed impossible to fight against it, but I was convinced that if you just embraced the Darkness, all the fear went away. But other things went away too. Ever since then, I've felt...emptier."

"Hollow?"

She laughed, though she didn't smile. "That's what they call us, isn't it? The Hollow Ones. We gained so much power in the Darkness, I never really thought about us losing anything."

"They say we're infinite beings, so there must be something to us that's hard to destroy—even with all they've done to you. There has to be some way to find the real you and restore it."

"Maybe. But they'll be after us, and I have a better understanding than you do of exactly how vast they are."

"Are you ready to fight them?" Terrance asked.

She glanced at Terrance and smiled. "I thought that would be an impossible thing, but it seems less impossible when you're not alone." She looked back to the road. "I don't think the faeries are going to like me when we find them. And I wonder how hard they'll be to track down." She giggled. "This could be like a quest for the two of us. A fun couples' thing."

Terrance smiled. "That does sound fun." He was on the run from forces of a power he could hardly comprehend, but suddenly things were looking much brighter, as if a huge burden had been lifted. "I'll call Curtis now."

"I wonder how he'll react to working with a Hollow One," Shannon said. "Whatever happens, just promise you won't let them hack me to pieces."

CHAPTER 24

"Hey!" Terrance shouted as Curtis pressed his sword against Shannon's neck.

"Not so loud." Curtis kept his eyes on Shannon. "The kids are sleeping."

Vivian came into the living room and looked at the scene with confusion. "What's going on here?"

Shannon moved her eyes away from the sword point and smiled. "Hi, I'm Terrance's girlfriend, Shannon."

Vivian nodded. "Yes, we met earlier today."

"Yeah, but I wasn't exactly honest with you about what I do for a living. I don't work at a coffee shop. I'm actually one of those you call the"—she very slowly raised her hands to form air quotes so it wouldn't seem like a sudden movement—"Hollow Ones."

"Oh." Vivian said, her expression freezing for a moment before she looked over at Terrance. "Oh, I see. Yes, you did allude to some personal situation you were dealing with." She glanced at Terrance's pink sweatpants. "And you've been having lots of pants problems today."

"Yes, I have been."

"Anyway, I'm looking to cut ties with the Darkness and restore my old self," Shannon said. "Terrance thought maybe you could help."

"Sorry, I know I already caused a bunch of trouble and got your meeting place destroyed," Terrance said, "but can you help with this? An elf told us that maybe the faeries would know how to restore her."

Curtis kept his sword steady at Shannon's throat. "You can't trust elves."

Vivian stepped closer to Shannon. "You really want to end your ties to the Darkness and join the fight against them?"

"Yes," Shannon said firmly.

"Then we will do what we can to help." Vivian motioned to Curtis to lower his sword.

Curtis didn't move. "What if this is a trick?"

"What if it isn't?" Vivian answered.

Slowly, Curtis took the sword away from Shannon's neck and sheathed it. "We will do what we can to help. So, can I offer either of you a beverage?"

"Do you have coffee?" Terrance had a feeling this was going to be a long night.

"We'd better get moving again, quickly," Shannon said. "They have to still be after us. Chances are they'll soon find out where we are."

Curtis nodded. "Usually they wouldn't pursue so doggedly, but I think your involvement may change that. If the Adversary were to lose those he thought were already under his power, it could be devastating for him. We should expect heavy opposition."

Shannon looked pensive. "You think this can be done, though?"

"Our full selves are infinite," Curtis said. "I wouldn't expect them to be easily destroyed, even when surrendered to the Adversary. Still, there is no time to waste here. You are compromised while you are under the Adversary's power—in ways we can't fully understand. If you are ready to sever that tie, then we set out to do so tonight. We can't wait."

Terrance was really wishing he could have that coffee now; he wondered if things were too desperate for a Starbucks drive-thru. "You know how to find the faeries, then?"

"I do. The problem will be those who are pursuing us." Curtis turned to Vivian. "I guess you'll need to stay with the kids. Can you contact the others and tell them to meet us at Sentinel Forest?"

"Okay. Except I won't contact Felicia. She'll want to help, but she has school tomorrow."

The idea of getting a posse together was encouraging to Terrance...until he realized Talia would most likely be part of it. "Oh, and you don't need to bother Talia, either," he blurted out. "She has already done enough for me."

Curtis grabbed his coat from the closet. "She's perhaps our best warrior. We'll need her."

Shannon narrowed her eyes at Terrance. "And why don't you want me around her?"

"Because she's not exactly friendly."

"She's a bit blunt, but she can be counted on to do what's right," Vivian said.

Terrance looked at Vivian. "I didn't already put you at risk by coming here, did I?"

"Don't worry about me," Vivian said. "The forces of Darkness are not so foolish as to attack a mother in her home."

Curtis kissed Vivian. "I'll be back in not too long."

"Be safe."

Curtis smiled. "Safety is evil defeated."

* * *

They headed out of town to an area Terrance was unfamiliar with. First they passed by farmland, then took a dirt road that led them between some grass-covered hills. On the other side was a forest with some of the tallest trees Terrance had ever seen. After they parked, they got out and wandered into the forest, Terrance marveling the whole time at what was above him. The trees were all evenly spaced, as if on a grid, with about ten yards between each one. On the ground around them were mainly grass and a few scattered plants—it was almost like the whole area was landscaped. The trunks of the trees were only about two feet wide, yet they stretched up so far into the night sky that Terrance couldn't make out their tops. And they seemed to have only a sparse amount of leaves, such that the full moon easily shone down into the forest, bathing the whole area in a blue light. Floating around the trees were what looked like lightning bugs, but bigger.

Shannon stood next to Terrance and looked up at the moon. "What an odd color."

"What do you mean?"

"The moon is usually more of a blood-red color when I go out to do stuff at night."

Terrance thought maybe she was joking, but she betrayed no smile as she stared up at the moon with a somewhat sad expression. Terrance held her close and kissed her cheek.

Curtis leaned against a tree. "The others should be here soon."

They noticed the silhouette of a figure approaching through the forest. Terrance put his hand to his sword but could soon see it was Randolph, who looked at Shannon as he approached. "Why are the cute ones always evil?"

"I'll still be cute when this is over," Shannon said. "At least I hope so."

Randolph stared at her with an expression that seemed friendly enough, though something seemed to lie beneath the surface. He then looked at Terrance and chuckled while stroking his beard. "Well, don't you bring us all sorts of trouble?"

"We're all in the same boat here," Curtis said. "Just trying to figure things out."

They noticed two more figures approaching. Travis and Erica. They waved hello, then gazed at Shannon uneasily until Erica finally said, "It's funny because I was just telling Travis we should see if Terrance and Shannon wanted to do a couples' thing."

Travis didn't smile. He looked at Curtis. "You think it's possible to help her out of her current situation?"

"I assume all things are possible," Curtis answered.

Soon another figure appeared. With the spacing of the trees, it seemed impossible for them to be snuck up on in this forest. This time it was Joyce, finally in civilian clothes—a brown jacket and jeans—and not scrubs. She had a broad smile on her face. "Taking one of the Adversary's minions directly to the faeries they've been trying to destroy—I can imagine a myriad of ways this can go right." She

146

looked at Shannon. "You sure you want to join the good side? We have to deal with this crap constantly."

"Happy warriors," Curtis said.

Joyce laughed. "Practically bursting with happiness. Which reminds me"—she looked around—"is Princess Sunshine here yet?"

Curtis shook his head. "And is Donald coming?"

Travis shook his head. "No, couldn't get in contact with him."

"He's probably sleeping," Joyce said. "Like a sane person."

Curtis glanced at Terrance and Shannon. "Talia should be here soon, and then we'll get going."

Randolph chuckled. "I bet she's going to love this. Are we sure she's not going to just run in here and behead Shannon?"

Joyce shrugged. "That would get us to bed quicker."

Terrance had actually been more than a little worried that that was exactly what Talia was going to try. Shannon didn't look afraid, though, just very serious. Erica patted her gently on the back. "Talia won't behead you." She hesitated a moment and then added more quietly, "She probably won't be very nice, though."

"Nice doesn't help the situation," came a voice, though they looked around and saw no one. Finally, Terrance looked up and saw Talia above them, perched in the branches of a tree.

"How'd you get up there?" Joyce asked. On all the trees, the nearest branches looked to be at least ten yards off the ground.

"A better question is, *why* are you up there?" Randolph said.

In the moonlight, Talia was barely more than a silhouette above them because of her white cloak. "One doesn't just walk right into a trap in the way the enemy is expecting."

"No trap," Shannon said, "but if you want to stay up in that tree, I'm cool with it."

Even at this distance, Terrance could hear Talia grumble. She leapt from the tree, plummeting to the ground and landing on her feet in front of Shannon with a tremendous thud. "That looked like it hurt," Terrance said.

Talia ignored him and walked right up close to Shannon until their faces were only inches apart. "So are we to believe there is some penitence rattling around in this empty husk?"

Shannon was visibly exerting a great amount of restraint. "I know you don't have any reason to believe me..."

Talia laughed and turned to Terrance. "Out of curiosity, did you meet her before or after you obtained your sword?"

Terrance's left hand rested on his sword's hilt. "Well...just after."

Talia brought her gaze back to Shannon. "That's interesting timing."

More anger was creeping into Shannon's face. "I didn't start dating Terrance as some ploy."

Talia kept her eyes locked on Shannon's. "I know we can't expect Terrance to think things through, since we know what member of his body she's leading him around by, but I hope the rest of you see the obvious here. They've never been able to gain access to the faeries' palace themselves, but if she is somehow able to convince us to willingly give her help..."

"We are all on guard," Curtis said, "but if Shannon is being truthful with us and it's possible for those owned by the Darkness to break their bonds, then finding that out is worth the risks."

"I disagree." Talia stood still in front of Shannon, her arms crossed and her hands hovering near where her swords were under her cloak. "She made her choice, and as we know these things, there is no humanity in her left to save."

"That's not true!" Terrance shouted, pushing Talia back so that he could step between her and Shannon. "If you don't believe that, you don't need to be here."

"I know she's engendered some loyalty in you through the sexual favors she's performed," Talia told him, "but I would not get too attached to such a thing. You're just going to get yourself hurt...in more ways than one."

"You don't know what you're talking about." Terrance stood beside Shannon, though he noticed she now had one hand curled into a fist.

Curtis stepped between the two groups, facing Talia. "You've said your piece. So will you help?"

"I certainly won't abandon you to whatever trap she has planned."

"Is everyone else okay with this?" Curtis asked the group. "Expect a fight ahead...especially if Shannon is sincere. My guess is the servants of the Darkness will be after us in full force to prevent one of their own from being restored to her true self."

"We're ready," Travis and Erica said in unison.

"I'm for helping the pretty young thing," Randolph said.

"And I'm too tired to think rationally enough to say no," Joyce said.

"Then we better get moving." Curtis took a cautious glance at the bits of sky they could see between the leafy canopy above them.

"Where are we going?" Terrance asked.

"The edge of the world. Now let's go."

CHAPTER 25

"The edge of the world is within walking distance?" Terrance asked as they wandered through the Sentinel Forest.

Curtis kept the lead. "Yep, it's not too far from here."

"Hey, I thought I saw something!" Travis exclaimed, looking off through the trees.

"That was just my unicorn, Cloppers," Talia said. "He keeps his distance because he doesn't like crowds." She glanced at Shannon. "Or certain types of people."

"They say pets resemble their owners," Joyce said.

"You can't own a unicorn," Talia responded. "You can only gain its trust."

"So, while we're walking," Erica said, "can we ask some questions of our new friend here?"

Shannon kept close to Terrance, almost pressing up against him. "You can ask me questions if I get to ask some, too."

"She is going to probe us for weaknesses." Talia kept up the rear.

Shannon laughed. "You are aware we already know all about you people? We know that your group and others are planning an attack on our fortress. We also know who you all are and where you all live. If the forces of the Darkness wanted to come after you in the middle of the night while you were sleeping, they could."

"Thanks," Joyce said. "That squashed a bit of my desire to go home and sleep in my bed."

"Why don't they do it?" Terrance asked.

Shannon shrugged. "I guess they think it would draw too much attention. We'd much rather let things fizzle away than have to strike them down abruptly."

"The harder they come down on us, the more they are losing," Talia said, "and the more they risk inadvertently opening the eyes of others to their evil. And when that happens, they really lose."

"Something like that, I guess," Shannon said.

Talia stared intensely at Shannon and Terrance. "Are we really to believe that you didn't know about Terrance?"

"I didn't!" Shannon insisted. "That doesn't mean that others weren't aware."

Terrance looked at Talia. "I told you about how I met that guy who called himself the Caretaker. He knew…though he said he kept it to himself."

"The Caretaker is that weird guy with the mask, right?" Randolph asked.

Terrance raised an eyebrow. "You've seen him, too?"

"He seems to take a personal interest in those who try to fight being trapped in this world," Travis said. "He is a little creepy, to say the least."

"And very powerful," Shannon said. Terrance could see a bit of fear in her face, and he put his arm around her. "And no, he didn't tell me about Terrance. We rarely hear from him ourselves."

"Anyway, I hadn't gotten to my question yet," Erica continued. "What does lie beyond the dark fortress?"

"The Caretaker's realm," Shannon answered.

"What do you know of it?" Curtis asked.

"Not much. The Caretaker likes his privacy. I believe he has some sort of tower there."

Terrance remembered looking up and not even being able to spot the ceiling. "I've seen the inside of it."

"Then one day we will find out what that thing has to say to us when we fight our way past your fortress and face him with weapons in hand," Talia said.

Shannon seemed to ponder that for a moment. "I expect consequences from such an action...to say the least. What exactly do you expect to gain from confronting him?"

"He has trapped us in this sliver of reality and feeds upon all those inside it," Curtis said. "We are merely looking for a way to free ourselves."

"And you don't fear what he'll do?"

Curtis stopped and looked at Shannon. "When one understands what he truly is—how powerful he is and how much of him exists beyond this world—there is nothing to fear."

Talia came nearer, staring pointedly at Shannon. "Of course, having given herself to the Darkness, we don't know how much of her is left."

Shannon ignored her and looked at Curtis. "How do you know these things?"

Curtis continued leading them through the forest. "Your people don't know how we get our information?"

"We know faeries never seem to give straight answers and you can't trust elves," Shannon said. "I'm not sure who else you might consult. You seem to gets bits and pieces of information from somewhere."

"Now she does kind of seem like she's probing us for something she doesn't know," Joyce said.

"It's not to report back on you," Shannon said quickly. "It's just...if I'm to join you, I need to understand...what is understood."

"We find small bits of information here and there, and we have to piece them together," Curtis explained. "The things we are most certain of—the things we really know—come from inside ourselves. It is not the rational mind that knows these things; it's the part of us beyond this world that comprehends these truths."

Shannon frowned. "I don't really follow."

"You have the explanation of the world from the followers of the Darkness, and I'm sure their arguments are quite compelling," Curtis said. "And yet here you are. Some part of you still saw the truth. That's what you have to listen to."

"Unless this is all a ploy," Talia said. "And there is really no human part of her left to appeal to."

Shannon grimaced at Talia words, but Terrance saw more sadness than anger in her face. He, though, now had plenty of anger. He stopped and spun around to face Talia. "I've had enough of you! You didn't have to come! We get that you don't like her and you think she's an evil monster, so just shut up; we don't need to hear it anymore. She already had to fight her own friends to save me, but it's like you're trying to push her away. And if you think I won't punch a woman, just keep it up!"

Talia looked shocked for a moment, but then her face changed to a scowl. "No, I don't think you'll punch a woman."

Terrance thought about it for a moment and realized she was probably right.

"She's got you in her thrall," Talia said, "and you're going to be the one hurt the most when—"

"He's right; enough," Curtis said.

"But—"

"We'll see the truth of the matter soon enough," Curtis said. "So your opinions aren't needed, Talia. Just your courage and your help."

Talia took one last look at Shannon and then stared briefly at Terrance before facing Curtis. "All right; I apologize. I will be prepared but will hold my tongue."

"Come on; we're almost there." Curtis led the way again.

They continued, all quiet now, until Joyce finally broke the silence. "So, Randolph, how's that sports team you like?"

"It's not football season."

"Fascinating."

Shannon whispered to Terrance, "Thanks for sticking up for me."

"I know this has to be hard for you."

She simply nodded.

Ahead, Terrance could now see light at the edge of the forest. As they approached, it became so bright that it seemed like a sunrise, but Terrance checked his phone to see that it was nearing midnight. Finally, the forest ended, and ahead was a field that appeared to end abruptly at the light. At the edge of the field was a wooden shack and what looked like an old sailing ship. As they got closer, Terrance could see that it was a cliff they were approaching, and the light was coming from beneath it. The rest of the party headed for the wooden shack, but Terrance moved ahead of them, curious about what was on the other side of the cliff. When he looked down, he did see blue, but not the blue of water as the nearby ship implied. Instead, it was blue sky and clouds beneath him, and nothing else. The light was coming from the sun, but not from the sky above; instead, it came from a sky below. Terrance looked up and saw the blackness dotted with the stars of night that were still out, then he looked back down at the clouds and blue sky below. He backed away from the cliff's edge, a little worried of what it meant to fall off it into the sky.

"Edge of the world."

Terrance turned to see Randolph behind him. "I thought the world was round."

Randolph nodded. "Yep. They have photos from space and everything."

"So what's this?"

Randolph smiled. "Its edge."

Terrance took one last glance at the sun below him, but whether above or beneath, you weren't supposed to stare at it. He saw that Shannon was standing next to him, also staring down into the blue. "We are where man is not meant to be."

"Is that what they told you?"

She nodded. "By wandering off the main path like this, reality and the world start to break down."

"Are you still worried about that?"

She took Terrance's hand and smiled at him. "I guess I'm still figuring out what's worth holding together."

They headed toward the ship, an old wooden vessel like in a pirate movie. It was then that Terrance saw that it was beyond the edge of the cliff, resting on a cloud somehow. "Are we going to ride on that thing?"

"Don't worry; this ship is sturdy," Travis said.

Terrance looked over the vast ocean of clouds lit from below. "What happens if you fall off?"

Travis frowned. "I don't know, bro; haven't known anyone to fall off."

The door to the wooden shed opened, and out stepped a brown bear. Terrance's hand went to his sword, but the bear stopped before them and stood up. It was wearing a red vest, and Terrance thought for a moment that maybe it was a circus bear. He wasn't sure why a circus bear lived out in a shack next to a flying ship, but the whole situation already didn't make much sense.

And then the bear spoke. "How many?"

"There's eight of us," Curtis said.

The bear looked them over. "And where are you going?"

"We need to get to the faerie palace."

The bear nodded. "I can get you there. One silver piece per passenger. I also accept credit or debit."

Shannon pulled a debit card out of her pocket. "I can pay, since this is all about me."

"All right." The bear took the card in his paw and went back into the shed to swipe it.

Terrance turned to Curtis. "Why is a bear the captain?"

Curtis shrugged. "Who would you imagine would pilot a cloud ship?"

The bear returned and handed Shannon back her card. "We can go ahead and board." He led them to a wooden ramp that was the entrance to the ship. As Terrance crossed the ramp, he paused to look over the edge and saw that there was nothing but blue sky beneath him. It made him a little queasy.

Joyce slapped him on the back. "Scared of heights, champ? Technically, if we're not over anything, you can't measure height, so there's nothing to be scared of. And that's what you have: a lot of nothing below you. To be scared of."

Terrance laughed weakly, then quickly got onto the ship. It did rock and sway like a normal ship, which was much more disturbing, considering that they were on nothing.

"We're possibly being pursued," Curtis told the bear.

"Evasive maneuvers as needed are part of the package," the bear said. He went to the front of the ship and turned to face the whole group. "Hello, I am Captain Swaggerty. You can call me Captain or Swaggerty. Do not call me Cap or Swag unless you can fly home yourself. There's a blue bin behind you. I'm going to need each of you to take a life jacket out of it and demonstrate that you know how to put one on in the case of an emergency."

They opened the bin, and each person took out an orange life jacket and began putting it on. "Will these help us if we fall out of the ship?" Terrance asked.

"I can't imagine how they would," Swaggerty answered. "But this is technically a ship, so by regulations I must provide life jackets and make sure all passengers know how to use them."

"Is this on right?" Erica asked as she tightened a strap on hers.

"I have no idea," Swaggerty said. "Now please put them back into the bin. As part of your voyage, if you're over twenty-one, you can have three beers from the fridge below deck. If you're under twenty-one, you get only one beer. I don't have food, because I don't want to have to deal with allergens or any of that crap."

"Beer has gluten in it, which is an allergen," Talia said, hanging back at the rear of the group, as usual.

"If you're allergic to beer, don't drink beer." Swaggerty looked them over one more time. "Before we get going, do you know that one of your group is a minion of the Darkness?"

"Yes, we know," Curtis said.

Swaggerty nodded. "If you didn't, we could have had a mystery cruise figuring out who. Instead, the entertainment will be me, being a tour guide. I'll mainly be pointing out clouds. We ready to go?"

Terrance was staring at Swaggerty. "How do you talk?"

Swaggerty looked back at Terrance with his dark bear eyes. "Using a tongue and a larynx."

"But I mean, why do you talk? Is that like a magic vest or something?"

"I got it at Target."

"And what happens if we fall out of the ship?"

"Nothing good," Swaggerty said. "Now, the first three dumb questions are free, but I start charging after that."

"We'd better get going," Curtis said.

"All right then." Swaggerty untied the ropes holding the ship to the dock. "Everyone prepare to depart." Swaggerty pulled some ropes and unfurled the sails. The ship lurched forward, gliding over nothingness. Terrance clung tightly to the side and glanced over the railing. He could see a cloud below being cut up in the ship's wake, and beneath that, the blue skies and the sun. He feared for a second that if he fell out, he might plummet into the sun, though he realized that was ridiculous, since the sun was millions of miles away.

Terrance felt a hand on his shoulder and turned to see Shannon. "You okay?" she asked.

"This is really weird...right?"

Shannon nodded. "As I said, we're far off the path, where men aren't supposed to be."

"Aren't supposed to be, according to who?"

Shannon shrugged. "Those who want to be in charge, I guess. But screw them, right?" She leaned over the side and took a look. "Pretty day below." She looked up. "Pretty night above."

There seemed to be a number of scientifically implausible things about seeing both day and night at the same time. It was just weirding Terrance out. "So are you ready for...whatever this ends up being?"

She continued staring out over the skies. "Something's missing...I think I've felt it for a while. And I want it back."

"You two: keep an eye out," Talia shouted at them as she climbed a rope ladder up to a small crow's nest. "We are putting ourselves at risk for your sakes, so at least be useful."

"I don't trust her," Shannon muttered.

Terrance looked around for threats in the night sky above and the blue sky below, but saw nothing more than stars and clouds. "She's unpleasant but not untrustworthy."

"Nonetheless, keep your distance from her."

"I'm going to go get my three beers," Randolph announced. "And Talia's three beers as well, since she's not going to drink them."

"Stay lucid!" Talia shouted down from the crow's nest.

"Too late in the day for that." Randolph headed below deck.

Terrance didn't want beer; he wanted a nap. And he wanted to not be wearing pink pants on a ship floating on nothing—with an attack presumably imminent. He headed over to Curtis, who was talking to Erica and Travis. "So what exactly do we do if they attack?"

"I'm not sure. I guess we'll figure that out when it happens," Curtis answered.

"I have a bow," Erica said, pointing to the black case strapped to her back.

Terrance was shocked. "We can bring other weapons? Why didn't we bring guns?"

"No, it's like a special bow," Erica said. "I got it on a mystic quest."

Travis nodded. "I remember when you disappeared all day for that."

"Yeah, I was just doing some research for class and ran into an old poem," Erica explained. "It looked like nothing significant, yet somehow I had this feeling it was addressed to me and was talking about this cave I knew of nearby. I went ahead and checked it out and...well...it's kind of personal what happened. But afterward, I had this bow in addition to my sword, and it has been quite handy."

"So, we can get other weapons?" Terrance said. "Does anyone ever get a gun or anything?"

Curtis shrugged. "I don't know; I'm not sure how it works. You like guns?"

"It just seems like a better weapon choice when facing supernatural beings more powerful than ourselves," Terrance said.

"We'll fight with what we're given, and we'll do fine," Curtis assured him.

Shannon's hand went near the hilt of Terrance's sword. "I'm sure you're quite good with that anyway."

Terrance shook his head. "I know you hit the enemy with the sharp point. I feel like I need some training."

"You learn by doing, bro," Travis said. "You jump in there swinging your sword enough, it becomes second nature."

Terrance nodded, but that was what he was afraid of. If the ship were attacked, he felt extremely ill-prepared—and tired on top of that. At least the rest of the Infinite seemed confident, but he wished he had more of that himself, for Shannon's sake. He looked to the skies, fearing that he'd see something move in them, but above was just the blackness of space, punctuated by the stars and the moon. Terrance didn't know too much about constellations, but it did seem that the star pattern wasn't very familiar.

He had wandered a bit while looking up at the dark half of the sky, and realized he was now standing next to Swaggerty, who was relaxing near the front of the ship. He did just look like a normal bear, in a vest, standing on his hind legs, with a hint of intelligence in his eyes, but Terrance wasn't sure how well he could manage the ship with bear paws.

Terrance realized he was staring at Swaggerty, who was staring back. "Um...nice vest," Terrance blurted out, feeling like something needed to be said.

"Ridiculous pants."

Terrance adjusted the tight-fitting pink sweatpants and headed to the side of the ship to look over it again. There were no clouds above, only below. And the very disconcerting sun hovering down there among them.

"I think you're taking this too seriously," Joanna said with a Budweiser in her hand.

"This is all just crazy." Terrance took a step back from the ship's side, as it was making him uneasy again. "And I know I'm putting everyone at risk. It seems rather serious."

"We're on a ship driven by a bear, floating through clouds." Joyce sipped her beer. "Not a single serious thing about this."

"The forces of the Darkness could descend on us at any moment and kill us all."

Joyce laughed. "Again, you're taking this way too seriously. Just take a look out there." She pointed to the skies. "What do you see?"

"I really don't get how we can have night and day—"

"Tell me what you *see*, jackass. Not what you think."

Terrance looked out over the skies, the clouds and blue below stretching out as far as his eyes could see. He wondered what lay beyond his sight. It couldn't possibly go on forever—perhaps the edge of another world would be out there if they traveled far enough. Then he saw Shannon a few yards away, also looking over the edge with a small smile on her face, lit from the sun below. She was so beautiful, and for a moment the sense of dread left him.

"They're coming!" Talia screamed from above. "Prepare for battle!"

"Crap." Joyce quickly finished the rest of her beer and tossed the can over the side of the ship, into the nothingness.

Terrance turned to look behind the ship. It was hard to see against the night part of the sky, but there were dark things coming their way. And under the clouds was a shadow moving toward them, a shadow of something much, much bigger.

CHAPTER 26

"Prepare for evasive maneuvers!"

Terrance tore his eyes away from the approaching menace to look at Swaggerty. "How do we do that?"

"You hold on," Swaggerty said. "And that answer cost you five dollars."

Terrance darted over to Shannon and grabbed the railing next to her, which she also clung tightly to. She looked up at him and smiled weakly. "I'm sorry about all this."

He watched the chimeras approaching them, and chuckled. "Hey, it happens."

Suddenly, it was like the floor dropped out from beneath them. The night sky above was lost as they fell into the clouds below. Terrance could make out the shadow of Malcus's massive body above them, and from it erupted dark flames, tearing through the nearest cloud and pelting them with raindrops. The ship tilted to one side, and the demon dragon flew out of view again.

"I probably can keep ahead of the big guy," Swaggerty called out, "but I'm guessing the chimera riders will catch up, so keep ready." The big bear stood calmly at the helm of the ship and looked unaffected by the recent turbulence.

Erica dropped her long black case onto the ground and pulled out her bow, anchoring herself by putting a leg through a rope that ran along the side of the railing. Above, Terrance could see three chimeras with riders nearby. Erica let loose an arrow, and it struck one of the chimeras in the neck, sending it and its rider falling away.

"Down!" Shannon shouted. Terrance spun around to see her hand glowing with a dark power. She made a throwing motion, and a fireball flew from her hand toward one of the riders. The rider adjusted to dodge it, and ended up falling behind the ship as it changed course again. The third chimera landed on the ship's deck, and its armored rider hopped off. He was a Dark Enforcer, and for a second Terrance thought it was Chet, but its helmet and physical size were different. Travis, Joyce, and Curtis drew their swords and charged the Dark Enforcer, so Terrance drew his sword and attempted to do the same. The ship quickly changed course, though, and Terrance lost his footing and tumbled along the deck until he crashed into a mast. He looked toward the Dark Enforcer to see him deflect an attack from Travis, then knock Joyce into Curtis. Suddenly, Talia slammed into him from above, piercing him with two swords.

There was a high-pitched shriek, and out of the corner of his eye, Terrance saw something coming at him. He barely had time to duck before the large claw of a chimera sliced through the air where his head had been. It landed next to him, and Terrance tried to hold himself steady on his feet as he pointed his sword at it. It bared its sharp teeth and raised its head high on its long neck. It snapped at him, and Terrance quickly dodged away, swinging in a panic and accidentally connecting with the mast, the impact causing him to lose his balance and trip. The chimera was poised over him, then lunged down, mouth agape. Terrance held up his sword to try to block its mouth, but it kept coming, its head hitting the sword and then rolling off to Terrance's side. Terrance slowly realized that the head had separated from the body. Randolph stood over him and offered a hand. Terrance took it and was pulled to his feet.

"I get one of your beers for that," Randolph said as he looked around for more threats.

Terrance watched as Talia and Curtis knocked the Dark Enforcer over the side of the ship, and for a moment there was peace. But then the whole ship lurched, and Terrance barely held his footing against the mast. Over on the port side (or the starboard; Terrance wasn't really clear on nautical terms), he could see the massive, spiked body of Malcus flying near them. The ship dropped again, and Terrance clung to a rope on the mast for dear life. The clouds parted, and now there was nothing but clear blue on all sides, with a thick, dark layer of clouds above. Against the blue, Terrance spotted more dark figures.

"Prepare for more attacks!" Curtis shouted.

Terrance watched as Erica pulled back to aim another arrow and Shannon prepped another fireball, but he wasn't sure what to do himself but brandish his sword in one hand and hold tight to a rope with the other. The ship leaned to the side, then ascended back into the cloud layer, Erica and Shannon firing at pursuers as it disappeared into cover again. Soon, though, amidst the fog of the clouds, the large, dark figures of the chimeras began landing on the ship. When the ship rose out of the cloud, Terrance could see four dark warriors on the deck. Curtis, Talia, Joyce, Randolph, and Travis all charged them, and Terrance followed along, running toward one near him, which looked the smallest. It was a Sister of Torment, and she came at Terrance with a quick series of blows that put him immediately on the defense. Joyce attacked as well, and the warrior had to ignore Terrance temporarily to parry those blows. Terrance moved around her and attacked from a different angle, which the warrior easily blocked. Joyce used the opening to impale her opponent through the chest. The warrior fell away, consumed by a dark fire within.

Terrance looked around at the rest of the fighting and saw that everyone else on the ship, except for Swaggerty, was engaged in hand-to-hand combat with the enemy. Joyce patted him on the back. "Good job, there."

"I don't think I'm very good at this."

"Bah. Half the sword fight is just showing up. The other half is not getting impaled. You're two for two so far."

Terrance watched as Talia beheaded a warrior. "How's this battle looking?" he asked Joyce.

Five more chimeras landed on the ship, and armored foes dismounted. "Like we're not going to survive it." Joyce smiled. "So, pretty usual. I guess they really want to stop you and your girlfriend. Oh well." She charged the nearest warrior. Terrance glanced around to find someone to fight, but a large Dark Enforcer attacked him first, swinging a mace at him. He jumped out of the way, stumbling and rolling along the deck floor. He quickly got back to his feet to see a sword swinging his way. He blocked the blow, but the warrior elbowed him in the gut, sending him to the floor again. The ship tilted up at the same time, and Terrance found himself sliding toward the rear of the ship (or aft, as he for some reason remembered it was supposed to be called). He slammed into a wall near the entrance to the captain's cabin and used that to brace himself as he got back to his feet. It was then that he saw the giant, horned figure carrying an axe. Chet.

Terrance gathered up his courage and pointed his sword at Chet. "You're a big jerk, and I'm sick of you!" Terrance shouted and immediately realized how stupid and childish that sounded, not at all as intimidating as he'd hoped. Chet laughed and swung his axe downward, and Terrance dodged to one side as it splintered the deck. He realized that with Chet's axe giving him a reach at least twice as long as his own, he had absolutely no idea how he was supposed to fight him. Terrance briefly considered charging Chet and trying to get too close to him for him to properly use his axe, but the thought was interrupted by a horizontal swing that forced Terrance to throw himself to the ground to duck under it, while emitting a most unmanly yelp.

"Leave him alone, Chet!" Shannon yelled. She was still in her T-shirt and jeans, but she seemed to have summoned a dark flaming sword into her hand.

Chet laughed again. "Or what?"

Shannon growled and charged, but Chet backhanded her, sending her flying. Terrance yelled out angrily—an animal-like noise that was fiercer than his other utterings, though still pretty idiotic-sounding—as he got back up and ran at Chet, preparing a fierce sword swing. He actually seemed to have surprised Chet a little, but Chet quickly swung his axe, the flat of the blade hitting Terrance in the head. Dazed, Terrance stumbled backward, lurching into the railing and toppling over it.

He was falling. As far as he knew, he'd fall forever. But just as he had that thought, he slammed into something. He felt around under himself, and it was rock-hard and quite bumpy. He sat up, and saw his sword next to him. He picked it up and tried to get to his feet, but he felt the ground move beneath him and he stumbled back down. He was in a cloud, so it was difficult to see in the fog, but he could make out large black objects rising up and falling to either side of him. Giant wings. He was on Malcus. And though it was a nice little respite from the battle, it overall did not seem like a very safe place to be.

Malcus lurched upward, and Terrance found himself rolling down the dragon's back. Soon, he was in freefall again, but stopped suddenly once again as something clasped his shoulders. He looked up and realized a chimera had its claw around him.

"Don't worry; it's me!" Shannon shouted down from atop the beast.

Terrance gave her a weak thumbs-up as his feet dangled over the nothingness below him. He then saw something approaching from behind. "Look out!"

Shannon turned but not quickly enough, as a Sister of Torment on a chimera flew toward her, swinging a sword. Shannon tried to bring her own sword up in defense, but the cut went right through her arm, severing it from her body. The chimera holding Terrance spun off to the side and quickly lost its grip on him, but the fall was once again brief, as he soon landed on another hard surface. This one was smooth and gray, but he didn't spend long trying to figure out what it was and instead got to his feet, brandishing the sword he had somehow kept a grip on. Shannon was lying near him, clutching the nub that remained of her arm. Before he could try to comfort her, someone landed near him. A Sister of Torment. Lacey. And she was no longer missing a hand. "Oh, the sword says he's ready to fight, and the pink pants say he fears nothing."

Terrance tried to look fierce. "You don't want to mess with me!"

Lacey pointed her flaming sword at Terrance. "But I'm so looking forward to seeing you bleed a little." Two more chimeras landed near her, and Elissa and Vicky dismounted, also pointing swords at him.

I'm going to die very badly, Terrance's mind yelped as he slowly backed away and stood over Shannon. "She's done with you people. Let this go, or it will not end well."

The three Sisters of Torment laughed. "Oh, he is cute," Lacey said. "He's like a little puppy. Now be a good boy and turn around so Chet can punch you in the face."

"Huh?" Terrance said as he quickly spun around, just in time to get an armored fist slammed into his face.

CHAPTER 27

Terrance was dizzy and his face ached. He was vaguely aware that someone was dragging him. Soon after, he was thrown down on rough-carpeted ground. There were voices around him yelling, and an odd, constant hum in the background. He kind of just wanted to go to sleep, but he remembered that the situation was urgent, so he couldn't do that yet. He slowly sat up as he felt his sore face, which was sticky from his own blood. When he looked to his left, he saw Shannon, who appeared extremely worried. "It will be all right," he told her. He had no idea if that was true, as he was still trying to remember what was going on.

"What the hell, Shannon?!" Lacey shouted. "I mean really, what the hell?!" She was standing over them, still in armor, her long blonde hair looking quite immaculate for having just been inside a helmet. Elissa and Vicky stood next to her, looking down on them with disdainful expressions, as though Terrance and Shannon were racists or something. He could see his sheathed sword in Vicky's hand. All around were light-colored walls on which hung inoffensive art, like one might find in a hotel.

"I'm not sure that what we do is right," Shannon answered. She was clutching her arm...or what was left of it.

"Don't tell me you're listening to those morons!" Lacey yelled. "And it's all because of this?" She pointed at Terrance. "This pathetic excuse for a boyfriend?"

Terrance tried to get to his feet. "Why don't you—"

Lacey charged at him, and Shannon tried to intervene but Lacey backhanded her, hard. Terrance quickly reached out to hold Shannon, and noticed that where Lacey had slammed her face, there was no bruise. And he caught a glimpse of the wound on her severed arm. There was no blood where the bottom half of her arm was missing, just darkness at the wound with little bits of flame emanating from the edges.

Vicky chuckled. "So what was the plan, Shannon? Plead with the faeries until they filled you back up with goo and red stuff?"

"Oh, yes; then she'd be an infinite being like her boyfriend," Elissa said. "So, Terrance Terrington, do you feel like a being of infinite power right now?"

Terrance was aching. He was dizzy. He was tired. He was scared. He felt small. But when he saw that Shannon was almost in tears, the main thing he felt was anger. "All I know is I don't want to be a part of you people."

"What a brave little man," said a deep voice behind Terrance, followed by a laugh. Terrance turned to see Chet and his giant axe, towering over him. He shuddered but tried to keep his face defiant. He realized he had no idea what these people were ultimately going to do to him and Shannon.

"Are you enjoying this?" Shannon asked angrily.

"Certainly not," Chet said in a dull, flat tone. "After we parted ways, I wished you the best. It pains me to see you this low."

Lacey laughed. "Chet's probably too nice to tell you, but the reason he strayed was that you bored him. And did you ever consider that if your plan actually works and you go back to your old self, maybe Terrance will lose interest in you, too?"

Terrance wasn't sure what they meant, but he saw the worried look on Shannon's face and it broke his heart. He let go of her and stood up. "I'm getting sick and tired—"

A shove from Chet sent him back to the ground. "No one cares what you think, little man."

Elissa smiled. "But I do find his squeak of righteousness endlessly amusing."

"Things are getting a little too heated here," said another voice. Despina sauntered into the room, once again wearing what looked like a black cape and little else covering her gold-skinned body. She grabbed Terrance's arm and helped him to his feet, her claws digging into his skin. Once he was standing, she smiled at him with her sharp teeth and brushed him lightly on the cheek with a fingertip. She looked at Shannon. "Someone cut off your arm?"

"I did, and it was rather satisfying." Lacey flexed her hand that had been recently severed. "I think we should leave it that way."

"Maybe give her a hook instead," Vicky suggested.

"And an eye patch and a parrot," Elissa added. "We'll call her Shannon the Pirate and make her walk the plank."

"Let's be nice," Despina said as she gazed at Shannon. "Hold out your arm, dear."

Shannon held out the stub, and Despina touched it. Immediately, dark flames erupted from the wound. When they died down, Shannon's arm was as good as new.

Terrance looked around the room again. Out a round window he could see the sky, and he had the sense they were moving. "Where are we?"

Despina moved closer, nearly pressing against him, her sickeningly sweet smell causing Terrance to almost lose his train of thought. "You are in our flying fortress."

He listened to the hum permeating the room, and an odd thought popped into his head. "Are we in a blimp?"

"It's a rigid, lighter-than-air vehicle."

"A Zeppelin," Lacey explained.

"It's very modern," Despina said. "It has wireless communication and GPS. And it is filled with either hydrogen or helium."

"That's neat." The mere presence of Despina was strangely panic-inducing for Terrance, but he tried to focus. "What happened to everyone else—my friends on the ship?"

Despina shrugged. "They were inconsequential to us. We kept them occupied while we spirited you away. It's of no concern what's happened to them since."

Terrance wondered if they would be coming to rescue him and Shannon, but he wasn't sure they would know where to find them or how heavily guarded the "flying fortress" was. And he didn't know what they'd be saving them from. "What happens to us?"

"Yes," Lacey said. "What are we doing with the traitor and the twit?" Her hand went to the sword at her hip. "I think it will help Terrance grasp the reality of the situation if we make him bleed."

"Oh, let's be nice, Lacey; he and Shannon just made some mistakes." She reached up and ran her hand through Shannon's hair. "We all have."

Shannon's expression was somehow both intense and neutral. He could tell there was a lot going on in her head and he wanted to reassure her, but surrounded by the enemy, he wasn't sure he could fake assurance. "Has this happened before?" Shannon asked.

"People get silly ideas all the time, but nothing ever comes of them," Despina said. "I don't want to downplay this—it was of great interest to the Caretaker himself—but let's not act like it's the end of the world. Now, why don't we all just relax for a bit and think things over. We like you, Shannon, and we want you to be happy. Terrance seems nice, too, and there's no reason for him to be in all this craziness." She looked at him. "I bet you're tired. Would you like some rest?"

Terrance had the notion that maybe he should act tough, but he ended up nodding anyway.

"So let's get you some rest—but just a short talk first." Despina turned to Shannon. "Is it all right if I borrow your boyfriend briefly?"

Shannon looked quite unsure of that prospect, but Despina didn't wait for an answer. She grabbed Terrance by the wrist and started leading him away. "Watch dear Shannon but treat her nicely," Despina said over her shoulder as they headed down a hallway. They soon came to what looked like a suite, sparsely decorated with a queen-sized bed and a small couch. Despina shut the door behind them. "Sit. Get comfortable."

Terrance sat, but he did not get comfortable. He was alone in a room with a half-naked she-demon and had no idea what was coming.

"Do you want something to drink?" Despina asked. "I have Ovaltine. Do you like that?"

"I haven't drunk that since I was a kid."

"Oh. What do people your age usually drink? Mead?"

Terrance saw the small bar in a corner of the room and realized he really could use a drink. "It looks like you have Johnnie Walker. I'll have some of that."

"Oh yes. Scotch whisky. That's a pretty popular new thing." She filled a red coffee mug with scotch and handed it to Terrance, then sat down. The couch was so small that she was right up against him, and she stared quietly into his eyes with an expression like there was a secret shared between them.

"Wha...what are we doing here?" Terrance asked. "You just want to talk?"

"Yes, we're just going to talk." She leaned over and pressed her lips to Terrance's ear and whispered, "Unless you want to do other things." She leaned back and smiled at him.

Terrance took a big gulp from his mug of scotch. "Talk is...is fine. I already talked to the Caretaker, though, so I think I know all you have to tell me."

She placed her hand on Terrance's inner thigh and tightened her grip, her long black fingernails digging into him through the soft material of the pink sweatpants. She smiled, baring her sharp canines. "But I am so much more pleasant to talk to."

Terrance wanted to get up and run. He wanted to grab Despina and...do things to her. His mind wasn't focusing, so he took another drink and tried to think of something to say. "Am I in trouble?"

Despina laughed. "So you do the computer programming languages?"

"Yeah."

"Do you enjoy that?" She leaned into Terrance, overpowering him with her sickly sweet smell.

"Um...yeah. It's good work."

"You've ventured quite far away from that, though. Quite far away from everything."

"Well, I'm just trying to understand..."

"More than that." Her long fingernails traced Terrance's cheek. "You've taken arms against vast, powerful forces and ventured to places apart from your world. Places you know you shouldn't be. It sounds exciting, but tell me: right now, do you want to be out in the great unknown, adventuring, or back in your bed?"

Terrance felt so tired he could barely think. When he could think, all his thoughts were focused on how he didn't know what lay ahead for him. "Bed."

"So why are you here, Terrance Denby?"

"I...I'm just trying to do what's right."

Despina giggled. "And in this realm of things so far beyond anything you've ever known or understand, how are you supposed to know what is right?"

Between the sleepiness and the big gulps of scotch, Terrance couldn't come up with an answer.

Despina looked more serious. "You are putting everything you have at risk on foolish notions that you don't even understand. Anytime you want, you could be back at your computer language programming job and spending the evenings with your lovely girlfriend, or you can continue down this path you're on now and lose everything. And to what end?"

It seemed like a good question. The Infinite had told him that he was a being of great power and that the forces of the Darkness would slowly eat him away if he didn't fight back, but before he was given his sword, he used to think everything was fine. And now that he had fought back, he felt worse than ever.

Despina pressed closer to him. "We are very powerful. You can rail against us, tempting us to destroy you to preserve the order of this realm, but that is not what we want. We want to work with you. This power we have—vast and in control of everything—can instead be for your benefit. You just have to allow it." She came in so close that she was now on top of him, her body rubbing against his. The mug fell out of his hands, spilling the remainder of the scotch onto the carpet. Despina put her cheek against his, lightly pressed her lips to his ear, and whispered, "The only thing standing between you and everything you've ever wanted is a little voice in your head telling you that you shouldn't have it. Ignore the voice. Take what you want."

Terrance put his hands on her naked shoulders. Her skin was smooth and warm. He was so tired and scared, and he could barely keep his thoughts together. It was a nice thought that he could just choose to end this all—choose to make things go back as they were. And there was nothing he had to do. In fact, that's what they wanted him to do: nothing. When he saw evil, he must ignore it. When he heard cries of terror, he had to stand back. When he saw what they had made Shannon become, he had to let it be. That was the price for all they offered.

He pushed Despina away by her shoulders. "You don't have anything I want."

Seeing her expression, Terrance thought maybe he hadn't put that delicately enough. She grabbed him by his neck and picked him up with tremendous strength, slamming him into a nearby wall and pinning him there. Terrance tried to pull her hand away, but it was immovable. "We gave you a chance," Despina growled. "If you want things to be difficult, then we will make it so."

Terrance struggled against her grip. The pressure was mainly on his chin, which left him just enough room to breathe. "So what now? Are you going to feed me to some monster like you once were going to do to Talia?"

Despina laughed. "You don't understand a thing. The point of that monster was not that it was going to rip her apart to bloody pieces—though that was nice, too. The point was to break her. And that's what we're going to do to you, Terrance

Denby. We're going to destroy all that you have and all that you are. Everything you love, you're going to witness it crumble apart. You haven't even begun to know pain and loss, and when you are but a shattered husk of your former self, you're going to come crawling to us, begging forgiveness. And then do you know what we'll do?" She let go of him, and he fell to the floor and immediately began rubbing his sore neck. Despina smiled down on him. "We'll welcome you with open arms. You're looking at a lot of pain in your future, but it will stop whenever you ask for it to."

Terrance stared up at her. He felt he should offer some retort, but he was frightened and weary and all that came to mind was, "Are we done here?"

"For now." Despina picked up a pair of jeans from a dresser and tossed them to Terrance. "And here are some trousers. You look ridiculous."

CHAPTER 28

"What did you do with Shannon?"

Lacey had him by one arm and Elissa by the other as they led him down a hallway. "She got back with Chet," Lacey said. "They're in a passionate lovemaking session."

They opened a door to a small, windowless room that contained only a bed, and tossed him inside. "You're kind of a jerk, you know that?" he said to Lacey.

"Your words wound me." She slammed the door shut.

Terrance changed into the jeans Despina had given him (hoping they weren't some sort of evil pants) and sat on the bed, plotting what his next move should be. He knew he had to find Shannon and figure out what they were doing to her for her betrayal, but he felt so ill-equipped to take on anyone here—assuming he could find a way out of this room. On top of it all, he was almost too tired to think. The bed looked surprisingly comfortable, so he lay down for a moment to gather his thoughts. The hum that permeated the Zeppelin was actually kind of peaceful, and the slight sway of the room was relaxing.

Terrance was awakened by an alarm blaring. He realized he must have fallen asleep, but it seemed something was now happening, judging by the screech of the alarm, the yelling, and even one voice he heard call out, "Something's happening!"

The door to the room burst open as someone kicked it in. It was Shannon. The white T-shirt she'd borrowed from Karen was slightly torn, but otherwise she looked fine. Terrance ran to embrace her. "Are you okay?"

"I'm fine; I was able to get free in the commotion. I think your friends are back and attacking; from my previous experience with them, they like doing that sort of thing." She smiled at him. "How are you?"

Terrance smiled back. "I just want us to get out of here." He kissed her. "I love you."

She held him close. "I love you, too." After a couple of moments, she released him and handed him his sword in its sheath. "I found this."

Terrance hadn't been very useful with his sword, but it still felt better to have it. "Any idea how to get out of here?" he asked.

"Follow me." She led him into the hallway and quickly to a stairway before anyone could see them. They went down it into a large hangar with dozens of chimeras milling about. Terrance reached for his sword.

Shannon put her hand on his arm. "It's okay. Just be calm and I'll get us a ride out of here." Her face brightened. "Mr. Cupcake!" Terrance followed her gaze to one of the dark beasts that looked no different than the rest and no less ready to eat him. "Go get on him and I'll open the hangar door," Shannon instructed as she headed for a panel.

Terrance slowly approached Mr. Cupcake, watching the other beasts, who all seemed to be watching him back. *I bet they can smell fear*, he thought. *Evil things can smell fear. No, wait—dogs can smell fear, and they're good, I'm pretty sure.* He stared into Mr. Cupcake's red eyes, with their slit black pupils. *Yeah, he can smell fear.*

The hangar door began opening. Shannon ran back toward Mr. Cupcake. "Come on!" She jumped on the weird hairy back without a moment's hesitation, taking her place on the saddle. Terrance followed more cautiously as Mr. Cupcake followed him with those red eyes. He moved between two of its thin insect legs and tried to climb up the side. Its hair was much thicker and coarser than any hair he had seen on an animal before, and for some reason it made him think of a tarantula, which made him shudder. Yet he fought through the disgust and climbed up onto the large back of the beast, settling right up behind Shannon, as that seemed safest. The chimera skittered toward the open hangar on its six legs, then Terrance heard something behind them.

"Stop!" Lacey cried as she sprinted to catch them. With a dive, she grabbed Mr. Cupcake's alligator-like tail just before it jumped out of the hangar. Terrance turned ahead to see that he was staring into nothing but stars below. The skies had now flipped; there was the sun and the blue of day above and the star-studded black nothingness of night below. For some reason, falling into the black eternity was an even more frightening thought than falling into the infinite blue of day.

And falling was a good possibility, as Lacey was now standing on the chimera behind him, flaming sword in hand. Terrance uneasily turned around, stood up, and said, "I got this. Just try and keep him flying level." Shannon nodded, and Terrance stared at Lacey's cold, determined face and the sword in her hand, and realized that "I got this" was a really stupid thing to say and much better would have been, "She's going to kill me! Please help!"

Terrance pointed his sword at Lacey, too afraid to move, since he didn't feel that he had very sure footing on the back of a flying chimera. Lacey smiled at him. "I'm going to make this as traumatic an experience as possible for both of you."

"You're mean," Terrance rejoined, and finally found the courage to strike at her. She easily deflected the blow, but Terrance persisted, pressing another immediately. It was a quick series of blows that Lacey seemed to fend off without much difficulty, but suddenly the movement of the chimera caused her to stumble. Terrance saw an opening and swung with all his might into Lacey's unguarded torso. She cried as dark fire erupted from the wound and she fell back, and Terrance came at her again with a strong downward blow. Lacey was too slow to block, and the sword sliced through her head. And then she was nothing but flames falling away into the night sky below.

Terrance could hardly believe it: he had defeated an enemy all by himself. Maybe he was finally becoming the warrior against evil that he felt he should be. He returned to his seat behind Shannon, but realized that he shouldn't brag to her. "Sorry, I know she was a friend of yours."

Shannon shrugged. "It's been happening." She got Mr. Cupcake to quickly climb. Terrance glanced behind them to see the Zeppelin they had left. It was enormous, almost like a flying city, and around it he could see flying figures that definitely weren't the chimeras. Below him, he saw the frightening drop of the black nothingness of space, but he spotted the full moon almost directly underneath, and for some reason it was a little less frightening to know that if he fell, he might land on the solid moon.

They passed up through the clouds, and soon Terrance saw the blue sky and the warm, welcoming sun above them. This made him feel much better as long as he didn't concentrate on the clouds and darkness below. "I really can't wait to get back over solid land," he told Shannon.

"This stuff is much more dangerous over solid land."

A creature emerged from the clouds below. It had the head and wings of a giant eagle, but appeared to have the body of a mammal. On it sat Randolph, who waved happily at them. He moved the griffin closer as it and Mr. Cupcake kept a wary eye on each other. "So you guys got out by yourself? Great!" he called to them. "I really didn't want to have to try to go into that thing to get you."

"Bad childhood memories of the Hindenburg disaster?" Terrance called back.

"Oh. Ha. Well, good to see you have a sense of humor. Wasn't sure what they were doing to you in there." He looked them over. "They gave you pants."

"Where are we going?" Shannon asked.

"Just follow—"

Another chimera broke through the clouds and charged at them, Randolph's griffin barely dodging the swing of an axe by the chimera's rider. The chimera continued up toward them, one of its scorpion-like claws grabbing onto Mr. Cupcake. Terrance turned to see that he was face-to-face with Chet. "Did you really think you could run? Now you'll—"

Anger flared in Terrance upon the sight of Chet, and perhaps it was that, combined with feeling cocky from his first real victory in battle, that caused him to immediately embark on a really stupid course of action: leaping from his chimera onto Chet's with sword in hand. Terrance bowled into him, his sword piercing Chet's torso as they collided, and the two of them fell off the chimera and tumbled into the blackness below. Chet tried to wrap one of his gauntleted hands around Terrance's neck, but Terrance kicked him away, freeing his sword from Chet's chest and sending Terrance falling solo, away from the Dark Enforcer.

Terrance slammed into something, bringing his fall to an abrupt stop. He felt he had done a lot of slamming into things lately, and hoped it wouldn't have any permanent repercussions. But none of his bones seemed broken and he was able to get to his feet, picking up his sword that was still lying beside him. He looked around and saw that he was back on Swaggerty's boat, with Swaggerty himself at the helm. "This counts as another trip, so I get paid again," the bear informed him.

"Do I get three more dumb questions?"

"No, that was a one-time thing. That one just cost you five bucks."

Terrance peered over the side of the boat. He could see the black of night and numerous stars, and he couldn't help but smile thinking of Chet tumbling into that.

A number of griffins began landing on deck, carrying Curtis, Talia, and Joyce. Travis and Erica were on another griffin together, Erica behind Travis with bow in hand. Finally, Randolph landed, with Shannon. She jumped off and rushed to embrace Terrance. "Don't do things like that!"

He squeezed her tightly and smiled. "I was just really tired of that guy."

"Mr. Cupcake flew away," she told him, as if that was something he cared about—which he only vaguely did.

The rest had all dismounted their griffins. "Sorry to take so long," Curtis said, "but we had to borrow some griffins to come after you."

Joyce chuckled. "There's not a griffin rental for miles around here."

"So what did they do to you?" Talia demanded, looking only at Terrance.

"Threatened me and stuff. Said they'd destroy everything I care about, which sounded pretty scary, but I also got the impression that it was pretty boilerplate for them. And a she-demon tried to seduce me, which was weird." He looked at Shannon safe beside him and thought of his recent victories in battle. "But I'm doing good now."

"And how are you?" Erica asked Shannon.

"I'm fine. They just tried to tell me how much I was giving up by defying them— that sort of thing."

Talia went to the edge of the ship to look out for enemies. "Their power is illusion, and their promises are worthless."

"They're definitely still after us." Curtis looked at Swaggerty. "How far are we?"

"We'll be there soon."

"Hey, how come he gets to ask a question?" Terrance said.

"Because it wasn't a stupid one," Swaggerty answered. "Five bucks."

"Malcus!" Talia shouted. "He approaches!"

Once again Terrance could see a giant dark mass coming at them through the clouds. He grabbed Shannon around the waist with one hand and a rope on the railing with the other as the ship shot upward, tilting back. They soon emerged through the top of the cloud layer, and ahead, Terrance could see it: the floating palace of crystal, glinting like a jewel in the sunlight. A terrible screeching roar made Terrance look behind, and there emerged Malcus, his awfulness now fully visible in the light. He was larger than the whole ship, and covered in black, jagged scales and spikes, none of which reflected the sunlight. The only thing that glinted in the light was his eyes—six of them, two large ones under four smaller ones. As he stared at Malcus, all of Terrance's happiness and feelings of security disappeared, and the only thing left was a feeling of doom.

Malcus opened his mouth, but it wasn't a regular jaw. Instead, the bottom part of his face split apart on a vertical seam. These side-opening jaws were filled with black teeth, and between them was a long pink tongue sticking out through a throat that was covered in more teeth. Something glowed down the throat, and Terrance realized Malcus was about to breathe flame onto them. He looked at Swaggerty, but the bear was concentrating on keeping a steady course. He turned back to Malcus just as the black flames spewed forth from its mouth, directly at Terrance and the ship. All he could think to do was to hold Shannon tightly and close his eyes as the end came.

After a couple of seconds passed without his obliteration, he opened his eyes to see that there was a pink glow between the ship and Malcus, as if there was some barrier shielding them from the demon dragon. The massive creature stayed on the other side, roaring at them, but seemingly unable to attack.

"And this completes our trip," Swaggerty announced. Terrance turned to see that they were pulling up to a crystal dock that extended from the palace.

Terrance took another look at the nightmare flying near them. "It can't attack us here?"

"The power of the faeries holds it back," Curtis said. "The barrier they make is the only thing we know of that its flames can't destroy."

Malcus roared once more, then dove under the clouds into the darkness of night below and was soon out of sight. Terrance let himself heave a sigh of relief.

Shannon was staring at the palace, whose spires soared hundreds of feet above them. The translucent crystal it was composed of made it seem like you could see inside, yet the interior was a mystery that enthralled Terrance. "I guess this is it," Shannon said. "Do we just enter?"

"They will let us in," Curtis answered.

"I still don't trust you." Talia approached Shannon. "You try anything here, you don't know how quickly I will end you."

Shannon rolled her eyes. "Thanks for the warning."

From out of windows high up on the palace, faeries floated down toward them. There were a dozen of them, hovering gently in the air as they fluttered their thin wings. One came close and looked down at Shannon. "We know you."

"Yeah." Shannon scratched the back of her head. "Sorry. I'm here to change myself back...if you'd help."

"You may enter," the faerie said. At the end of the crystal dock, a door parted, creating an entrance into the palace.

"Do we just wait out here?" Curtis asked.

Another faerie floated above them. "You will stay."

"That is not a good idea," Talia told the faerie. "These things are treacherous. You should have someone watch her—defend you if needed."

A faerie glided down toward Terrance. "Terrance Denby, you will go with her."

"Okay." Terrance took Shannon's hand and smiled at her, but she looked apprehensive.

"Good luck. Hopefully this will work," Joyce said to both of them, though somehow it seemed directed more at Terrance.

"We'll see you soon," Travis called out.

"Everything will work out. You'll see," Erica added.

"I hope this succeeds," Talia said, "but lop her head off if she tries anything. That's the surest way to kill her."

Randolph touched Shannon on the shoulder, his face strangely serious. "Shannon, you're a pretty girl, but I can't wait to see you when you are whole again."

She smiled at him, and then she and Terrance stepped off the ship onto the dock. Through the crystal beneath his feet, he could see the clouds moving below. It seemed like something that should be scary, but it was strangely reassuring now. Terrance kept a tight grip on Shannon's hand as they headed inside the palace. It was brighter inside than out, the crystal of the walls somehow amplifying the sunlight that poured through, bathing them in a warm white light. They were in a hallway with perfectly curved walls that seemed molded from the crystal. Ahead, Terrance could see a bright purple light. He heard a sound, and turned to see the entrance close behind them.

Terrance looked at Shannon. "Are you ready for this?"

She chuckled. "I'm a bit nervous. I'm not sure what this will do."

Terrance kissed her. "I don't know what lies ahead for us, but I...know what's right, I guess. We certainly need to get you away from those people, from that darkness."

She rested her head on his shoulder. "I love you, Ance."

"I love you, too."

Hand in hand, they headed down the hallway toward the purple light and emerged into a large, open room with a purple flame burning in a pit at the center. Positioned around the flame were four red crystals that glowed dimly in comparison with the fire. Above, the light of the sun was an almost-blinding white glow as it was amplified by the crystal walls. From out of the light, a shape emerged, a faerie, who descended to the ground before them, her white robe fluttering behind her. She was an otherworldly beauty bathed in white light, her hair shining as if made from strands of gold. "You are here," she pronounced.

They stood in silence for a few moments. Terrance glanced at Shannon and saw that she looked quite nervous, so he spoke. "We're here so that you can help Shannon."

The faerie turned her eyes to Shannon. "Shannon Anders, what is it that you require help with?"

"I...I want to be restored. Restored to what I was before I swore myself to the Darkness."

"Why do you want that?" the faerie asked.

Shannon hesitated, then said, "I don't feel...right, as I am."

"Perhaps this is true," the faerie said. "Well, Shannon Anders, there is but one thing we can do for you in this situation: we can kill you."

"What?" Terrance exclaimed.

Shannon looked confused and a little angry. "Are you threatening me?"

"It is not a threat," the faerie said. "We will only do it with your permission."

"Why would I want that?" Shannon demanded.

"Because what you are needs to be destroyed," the faerie answered.

"But can't you change her back to human?" Terrance asked. "Make her what she was before?"

"That is beyond our power," the faerie said matter-of-factly. "All we can do is end what she is now." She turned to Shannon. "Is that what you want?"

Shannon stared back at the faerie, her anger slowly fading.

"Please," Terrance pleaded. "There has to be something else you can do."

The faerie did not look at Terrance, but kept her eyes on Shannon. "We are wasting our time here, are we not? Do what you came here to do."

"What do you mean?" Terrance asked. He looked at Shannon, and she stared down at the floor with a sullen expression. When she looked up again, her face contained no emotion. And into her hand she summoned her sword, which she plunged through the faerie's chest.

CHAPTER 29

The faerie's body slumped to the ground, and blood spread out over the crystal floor. Terrance watched in silent horror for a moment, then Shannon finally turned to him and said, "There has been a change of plans."

"What?"

"We tried things your way; now we're going to try things my way." With a swipe of her sword, Shannon shattered one of the four large red gems surrounding the purple flame.

"Your way? What are you doing?" It occurred to Terrance that he needed to stop her. His sword was at his side, but the thought of drawing it against Shannon was as horrifying as what he was witnessing. Instead, he stepped in front of her and her sword. "Let's talk this through."

"We will." Shannon shoved Terrance out of her way with massive strength, then shattered a second of the red gems. "That should be enough to weaken the barrier. We don't want to bring this place crashing down...yet."

Terrance saw other faeries float in above, staring down with unreadable expressions at their fallen colleague and Shannon's destruction. But they did not do anything to stop Shannon, and Terrance somehow knew that they were incapable of doing anything. He looked at them with a wordless apology and turned to Shannon. "I thought you were going to leave the Darkness!" he shouted. "I thought you were going to restore yourself! Were you just using me?"

"No! Not at all!" Shannon walked over and put her hand—the one without the sword—on Terrance's shoulder. "Well...not initially. I really just didn't want Lacey to hurt you, that was all. And when we ran off and you started talking about me leaving the Darkness, I thought it would at least be useful to know what the options are and what the Infinite are like. But when we were captured and brought to the flying fortress, I kinda told them this was all just my plan to get to the faeries and their palace." She motioned toward the two shattered crystals and waved sarcastically at the faeries who floated above, watching. "And it was actually a pretty good plan...even if it wasn't my original intention."

"But we fought our way out of the blimp!"

"Yeah, that was staged."

"They threw the fight?" It did give Terrance an uneasy explanation of why he suddenly seemed to have gained competency in swordplay. "But I killed Lacey..."

Shannon hesitated a moment. "'Kill' is a strong word."

"Excuse me?"

"Let's just say this: what I've learned from hanging out with your friends—the Infinite—is that they don't know a damn thing. I mean, they have absolutely no clue what they're up against. They cobble together a few half-ideas from bits of ancient text and use that to try to take on forces with power their little brains can't even begin to make sense of. It's so pointless. I mean really, Ance, what do you know about all of this other than some vague platitudes about you being an 'infinite being'?"

Terrance thought for a moment, and the answer came easily. "That what you're a part of is wrong, and someone has to fight it."

Shannon rolled her eyes. "Yeah, I get that it sometimes seems that way, but you don't know enough to judge any of that. I mean, I did think for a time that all of this was awful, and you got me thinking that way again, but it's just that we have small minds, and big things are scary. The Darkness is huge and powerful—so big, and beyond normal people, you aren't even supposed to know about it." She patted his cheek. "And that's what you need to go back to. You're going to forget all of this, and everything will be nice and safe and happy. And it will all be good again, because we love each other."

The white light faded for a moment as a dark shadow passed overhead. A few of the faeries gasped. "What's that?" Terrance uttered.

"Your friends are dangerous and spread nothing but misery with their interference—people are happy until the Infinite get their nonsense inside people's heads. Along with these faeries, they have to be stopped. Just stay with me, and you'll be fine."

With barely a thought, Terrance drew his sword and ran back to the entrance of the palace. They had risked their lives to help him—to help Shannon—and he had led them into a trap. When he reached the crystal doors, they were open again. The cloud ship was still at the dock, but on its deck all he could see was the dark armor of the minions of the Darkness. A melee was going on, but since he couldn't see any of the Infinite through the enemy, it didn't look like it was going well. He noticed three griffins with riders flying about, but they were far outnumbered by the chimeras that also blotted the sky. Swaggerty stood at the helm of the ship watching the battle with what looked like annoyance—though it was hard to discern a bear's expression.

For a few breaths, Terrance stood frozen on the crystal dock, unsure of what to do. It all looked hopeless. Then he was yanked from behind while a hand stripped him of his sword. He fell to the dock and turned to see Shannon standing over him, holding his sword. She was still in her jeans and the T-shirt she'd borrowed from

Karen, but somehow there was something darker about her now. "Let it go," she assured him, but there was no warmth in her voice. "It's all going to be okay; just don't do anything stupid." With that, she chucked his sword over the side of the dock, and Terrance watched as it disappeared into a cloud, falling now into the infinite black starscape that lay below.

A giant form rose from the dark: Malcus. Two of the griffins with riders immediately dodged away, but one kept course directly for the beast. Terrance recognized the rider as Randolph, who held back his sword in preparation for a swing against the gigantic beast. But Malcus parted its terrible jaw, and from its throat came dark fire, which enveloped both griffin and rider. When the fire disappeared, Randolph and his steed were gone, as if they had never existed.

Terrance watched in stunned silence as the rest of the scene unfolded. The other two griffins with riders were soon overwhelmed by the chimeras and were forced to land on the ship, where what once was an active battle had now gone eerily still. Shannon strode past Terrance toward the ship, her face an impassive mask. The dark soldiers on the ship parted, and Terrance could see the rest of the Infinite looking bruised and bloodied, with their hands up and their weapons on the ground. Erica and Travis were being pulled off their griffin, which lay slain on the ship's deck.

Curtis stood tall as Shannon approached, clutching a bloody wound on his face. "You're making a foolish choice."

They were covered in shadows for a moment as Malcus again passed overhead. "Foolishness is standing against powers you can't even fathom. You saw what happened to the old man; we are done playing around with you idiots. And now the faeries' palace is ours, and when we destroy it and the faeries inside, its protection of all who oppose us will also disappear."

Terrance finally moved himself to action, running up behind Shannon. "You don't have to do this," he said, but when he looked at the rest of the dark soldiers watching him, and at the swords they were pointing at the Infinite, he realized what a weak protestation that was.

Shannon's dispassionate mask melted away for a moment as she touched Terrance's chin and smiled. "Just stay back; everything is going to be fine." The menacing look returned as she turned back toward the Infinite. "I hope you all understand that you're defeated."

Talia stared back with defiance. "With every action, you march closer to your own destruction, but you cannot defeat us."

One of the soldiers removed her helmet. It was Amber. "Remember me from the mall?" She put her sword to Talia's cheek. "Did you think you accomplished anything by striking me down? We're immortal, you stupid twits."

"Immortal?" Terrance asked, looking Shannon over. She looked so much like a normal woman—albeit one holding a sword—but there was something unsettling about her that he couldn't quite place his finger on.

"Yes, it's...complicated," Shannon told him. "It's not a fact we like to flaunt, and it is apparently yet another important detail about how the universe works that these people you are following are completely ignorant of." Judging by their expressions— shocked with a hint of despair—this was news to the Infinite. Shannon turned to address them. "You can't win; I hope you finally get that. You're just silly, ignorant fools fighting things you don't even understand."

"I know you want to believe that," Curtis said, the resolve returning to his eyes.

Amber approached him. "You can win tiny battles from time to time, but we'll always come back." She put her sword to his cheek. "If we kill you, though, that's it."

Talia started laughing. "You fools think you're immortal? The power of the Darkness may appear vast, but it is not infinite. We may slay you a million times and you may come back each time, but one day you will cease to be because of the doomed path you follow."

Amber turned her attention to Talia, aiming the point of her sword between Talia's eyes. "I think we may need to kill another one to get the message through."

Talia looked unperturbed. "You have no power over my existence, silly thing." In a blink, Talia was on the ground snatching up her swords and then rising with them and slicing through Amber, who disappeared in blue flame. Talia stabbed another soldier through the head before several of them descended on her at once. The other Infinite tried to make a move, but soldiers tackled them, held them to the ground, and beat them. Without thinking, Terrance ran to help, reaching for a sword that wasn't there.

Talia cut down soldier after soldier, but Shannon approached her at a slow, unconcerned pace. Talia turned to face her foe. "Come on, betrayer. You're nothing to me."

It was such a quick strike that all Terrance saw was the spray of red that erupted from Talia's torso. She stared at Shannon in disbelief, then smiled slightly before toppling backward over the ship's railing, into the blackness below.

"Now what are you going to do, little man?" growled a voice behind Terrance. He turned to see Chet standing there, holding his axe. It was a good question. He couldn't run. He had no weapon to fight with, and the rest of the Infinite were being pounded into submission, so there was no one to help him. He looked at Shannon standing there in her white shirt stained with blood, and she smiled at him as if everything was right in the world. He turned back to Chet, who was now chuckling. Anger flared up in Terrance and he leapt at Chet and tried to wrest the axe away, but his actions were as useless as ever, and a simple backhand from Chet sent Terrance stumbling backward. Terrance hit the side railing of the ship and began to tumble over it, and the thought passed through his mind that he should have struggled to grab on to something, but his will was gone. Instead, he fell limply into the stars and darkness below, at least now putting some distance between himself and his own failure.

CHAPTER 30

The scenery kept changing from black to blue as Terrance tumbled through the air. Would he fall forever? He didn't know. It was like a bad dream. All of it was. But it wasn't so much that he wanted to wake up as that he wanted to go back to sleep.

He tried to steady himself to get an idea of where he was falling, but that only caused him to spin faster through the air, to the point that he couldn't tell what he was looking at. He was getting dizzy and decided to close his eyes for a moment and hope that somehow the world would sort itself out.

But the world seemed to have trouble with that, and he felt himself being jerked in different directions as if gravity couldn't decide which way to pull him. This went on for a few seconds until finally he shot forward in one direction for a while until a jolt went through his entire body as he slammed into something hard. For a moment he was nothing but pain, and then he was at rest, lying on his back on an unknown surface. He slowly opened his eyes to stare up at a clear blue sky. He wondered where he was, but to find out, he'd have to lift his head, and he was pretty sure a fall like that should have broken every bone in his body. Then again, he wasn't sure how far he'd fallen or in which direction. He eventually decided to try moving his head, and though it ached a little, it seemed fine. Looking around, he saw that he was in a grassy field, which he soon recognized: the clearing in which he'd first been given his sword.

Terrance decided to get up, and all his limbs seemed to be working, though they were a bit stiff. When he fell out of the ship, he'd really thought that he was going to die, but he was too heartbroken to celebrate the mixed blessing of still being alive.

Something glinted in the sun. Terrance wandered toward it to find his sword stuck into the ground. He pulled it out and returned it to its sheath. It didn't make him feel safer to have it back, though; it was just added weight. A thought struck him, and he looked around for Talia's body, but saw nothing but the grass and flowers of the field. He hoped she had gone to a better place, along with Randolph.

There was a deafening crash and the earth shook so violently that Terrance fell to the ground. He spun around to see that the crystal palace had crashed into the earth about fifty yards behind him. It was barely recognizable—just a mass of giant, broken pieces of crystal sticking out of the ground. A shadow passed overhead and he looked up to see the jagged form of Malcus crossing the sky. He shuddered a bit as he watched the beast fly off toward the distant mountains, but there was anger mixed with the fear.

Terrance surveyed the shattered palace for a few moments more, and thinking of nothing else to do, he headed out of the clearing and back to the road.

With no phone, his only option seemed to be to walk home. It was a depressingly long walk in the not-very-comfortable sandals he had borrowed from Karen, giving him plenty of time to think about his failures. Of course there were the Infinite, who were captured or dead because of the mission they'd taken on for him. He realized he'd have to tell Vivian about how her husband had been captured; he wasn't sure whom to tell about the others. And he wasn't sure what to do now about Shannon. When he thought of her, what popped into his head was the image of her coldly cutting Talia down. He couldn't be with her anymore; he was certain of that. Despite her assertions, there were certain things he could not overlook, things he would never be okay with. But were Shannon and he enemies now? Terrance felt the hilt of his sword; it seemed so useless to him. He wasn't a warrior, and if he pretended to be one, the only thing that seemed to be in his future was a fate like that of Randolph and Talia.

After trudging for what seemed like hours, Terrance finally made it all the way to his apartment. He noticed that his car was parked in front of his building. He didn't think anything of it at first, but then remembered he'd last left it at the Hobby Lobby near the Infinite's meeting place. Terrance put one hand on his sword and slowly entered the broken front door of his apartment.

"Hey there, buddy." It was Beauregard, sitting on the couch, smoking his pipe.

Terrance relaxed his hand on the sword and shut the door behind him. "What are you doing here?"

"I figured you'd have a tough day, so I thought I'd help out a little. I brought your car back."

"Thanks." Terrance tossed his sheathed sword onto the floor and headed for the fridge. The thing below pounded a couple of times, but Terrance couldn't bring himself to care.

"I drank all your beer, though."

"Dammit!" Terrance walked to the couch and plopped down opposite the elf.

"So...I told you this would end horribly," Beauregard said.

"Yeah, but you also told me that I couldn't trust you."

Beauregard nodded. "Yeah, I was lying about that. We elves can be tricky at times, but lying is such a simplistic way to trick people. Kind of beneath me, really."

Terrance looked at the elf. He felt that he should be angry, but he was too tired. "So you knew this was going to happen?"

"I figured something like this was the most likely result."

"Are you happy about it?"

"I wouldn't worry about my feelings. Do you understand how grave things are, now that the crystal palace has been destroyed?"

Terrance slouched in his seat. "I don't understand anything about anything."

"The Adversary will have its minions move much more directly against those who oppose it. Are you ready for that?"

"No!" Terrance yelled. "Not even slightly! I'm not a warrior!"

Beauregard chuckled. "Aren't you an infinite being of some sort?"

"Are you mocking me?"

The elf nodded. "Of course. Anyway, I tried to advise you before to leave all of this alone. You didn't listen."

"It's hard to ignore all the evil stuff out there."

"People do it all the time."

"And...it's too late now. I got some of the Infinite captured. Others...killed."

"Not your problem."

Terrance took a deep breath. "I need to at least get in contact with Vivian Dayton and tell her that her husband and the others were captured. And that Randolph and Talia were..." He couldn't bring himself to complete the sentence; all he could do was watch their deaths over and over again in his mind.

"And once you tell Vivian this, what are you going to do? Storm their hideout—perhaps fight Shannon one-on-one—and rescue those still alive?"

Terrance glared at the elf. "What's your game? What do you want out of all of this?"

Beauregard puffed at his pipe. "If I answered that, why would you believe me?"

Terrance thought about it. "I don't like you smoking in here."

"When an elf smokes, it makes everyone around him healthier."

Terrance looked at the elf and his mischievous grin. "I think you're making that up."

Beauregard shrugged. "Maybe I do like lying."

"The Imperial March" started playing. Terrance stared at his phone without moving.

"You going to answer that?" Beauregard asked.

"It's Shannon. I don't know what I want to say to her yet."

"If you don't want to fight her, you might as well embrace her. She's a lovely thing when she's not all murdery, isn't she?"

Terrance rubbed his temples. "Those are the only two choices? Fight her or join her?"

"Well...we could just forget all of this. You could stay away from the Infinite and from Shannon and her ilk."

"Just ignore it all?"

"The Infinite are in a hopeless battle, as you've seen, and the forces of the Darkness are too evil for you, so you could just go back to work tomorrow and forget everything."

It was the most attractive option Terrance could think of. When he'd tried to go back to normal before, he'd continued dating Shannon, which made all the weirdness difficult to ignore. Maybe if he stopped seeing her, he could forget it all. "I still need to tell the remainder of the Infinite what happened."

"I can tell them," Beauregard said. "You are now absolved from all of this." Beauregard waved his hand around as if casting a spell on Terrance. "There, you are back to normal."

"You're still here."

"Well...there is one thing you need to do if you want to be done with this." Beauregard pointed to the sword at Terrance's hip.

Terrance felt the hilt of his sword. "There is so much evil out there."

"And *you're* going to fight it?"

Terrance thought of the blood-splattered Shannon smiling at him. Something deep within him ached at the memory. "I tried to, but I was useless...less than useless. Everyone is worse off because of me."

"Maybe because it's nonsense," Beauregard suggested. "This whole idea that you, Terrance Denby, computer programmer, are supposed to be taking on vast, universe-manipulating powers."

"If I give up, then it's destruction."

"Because of the Adversary?" Beauregard asked.

Terrance nodded. "Yeah...that Caretaker guy I met, I guess."

"That could be more nonsense, but I'll tell you what isn't: if you stand up against him, you will be killed. So really, it's possible destruction—if the Infinite aren't full of crap—versus certain destruction."

Terrance considered that for a moment. "Whose side are you on, anyway?"

Beauregard smiled. "If I claimed one or the other, you wouldn't believe me."

Terrance thought of those who'd been captured. Of Randolph burnt to nothing. Of Talia being cut down. Of Shannon orchestrating it all with a smile on her face. "I want out of this. I want normal again. No sword. No evil to fight. No Shannon."

"Then let's go toss the sword," Beauregard said. "When it's gone for good, the choice is made and no more worrying about it."

Terrance stared at the sheathed sword. "Last time I was about to do that, I found kids being threatened and I stopped to help. Of course, I didn't get my head ripped off only because Talia came to help me. That's not going to happen again."

"It's a noble thing to want to help," Beauregard said. "But you're...you. You're just going to get killed, for little purpose."

Terrance stood up. "Okay. Let's go."

"Right behind you," Beauregard said, following Terrance out of the apartment.

This time, no conflict stopped Terrance as he walked through the apartment complex and went through the fence. After hiking a little longer, he saw the ground before him drop off in the direction of the setting sun. Soon he reached the edge of the canyon that lay beyond the apartments. It was about a hundred yards wide and stretched beyond sight in either direction. He crept to the edge and peered over. The bottom of the canyon was so far down, he saw nothing but blackness. Or maybe not just blackness—he thought he saw stars twinkling down there.

"Is this a bottomless pit?" Terrance asked.

Beauregard puffed at his pipe. "Just another weird thing that you no longer want to deal with."

Terrance detached the sheathed sword from his belt and held it out in front of himself. "I just wanted to help."

"Good intentions. Road-paving. Hell. That sort of thing," Beauregard said. "The question is: do you want to die?"

"No one does." He remembered the faerie's offer to Shannon, to kill her. Who would accept that? "But what if I am an infinite being? Then I can't die."

Beauregard chuckled. "Then you especially don't need the sword. But do you really believe that?"

Terrance felt weak and useless. That was the truth of it. He dangled his sword over the edge. "I feel like a coward, just leaving it all behind—especially my friends who were captured."

"There are plenty of fools in the Infinite who are used to that sort of thing," Beauregard said. "I'm sure they'll launch some sort of rescue mission, but would you be of any help in that?"

Terrance played the failure over and over in his head. Especially the spray of blood as Shannon cut into Talia, and Talia's body falling limply into nothingness. He'd spoken up that first time he'd seen her in peril, but ultimately it was all for naught. "I can't help anyone." With that, he let the sword slip from his fingers, and it tumbled down into the canyon until it disappeared into the blackness below. An odd thought leapt into his mind, to jump in after it, but he was through with foolish notions. "So I guess that's it."

There was no answer. Terrance turned around and saw that Beauregard was gone. His world was becoming more normal already. There was no happiness there, though, only the hope that the pain he was feeling would soon fade.

CHAPTER 31

Terrance had turned off his phone. He turned it back on the next morning and found that Shannon had called a few more times throughout the night. He was hoping that by now she might just assume he was dead, making the whole breakup easier. He felt like a coward for not handling it more directly, but he already felt that his cowardice had been well-established by letting Beauregard handle giving the bad news. And by tossing his sword. Terrance's hand reflexively went to his hip but found nothing. Cowardice, in the face of odds he couldn't hope to take on, felt justified at least.

He was set for his drive to work, hoping to achieve that more-normal day that he longed for, but he started noticing things along the way. He kept seeing those eyeless cavefish in groups of about a half-dozen, out in the open, moving between buildings, such as one group descending on a Burger King as he drove by. He saw chimeras flying overhead, and occasionally he saw the Hollow Ones with the cavefish, moving toward some purpose, though he couldn't tell what as he watched at red stoplights.

He saw more of the forces of the Darkness as he got nearer downtown. The regular people on the sidewalks seemed to be making an effort to avoid them, rather than just ignoring them as if their presence were normal. Something was going on, but Terrance determined it wasn't his concern, because what exactly could he do about it anyhow?

In the parking garage, some of the dark things with the shining eyes were crawling around on the ceiling, watching him. He did his best to ignore them as he headed into his office building.

He had been gone a day and a half, so there was a lot of email to catch up on when he sat down in his cubicle. It was mainly a number of error notices on the system and an email from Pendergrass wondering where he was with the main algorithm code. He quickly checked his personal email, which included one from Shannon with the subject line *Are you okay?* He didn't click on it; he felt he still had to give himself some time to figure out what he was going to do. And coffee. He needed coffee.

He headed for the break room. When he got back to his desk, Lance was waiting there. Terrance rarely ran into him on his way out of their apartments, as Lance always got in a little later. "Hey, what's going on?" Lance asked. "Last I saw, you were running off with Shannon, and then I didn't see you for a day."

Terrance sighed and sat back down at his desk. "I don't really want to talk about it. We got a text from Lacey threatening to hurt you—but she didn't do anything to you, right?"

Lance chuckled. "I wouldn't mind her doing stuff to me. So, um...you okay?"

"Yeah, I'm fine." At least that's what he wanted to be. "I don't think it's working out with me and Shannon, though."

"Oh, well, sorry to hear that. Um...so, do you have any idea what's going on today?"

Terrance raised an eyebrow. "With what?"

Lance looked a bit uncomfortable. "There's...you know...people like Shannon and her coworkers out and about everywhere doing...something."

"I don't know anything about it. I'm trying to stay out of that sort of thing, now. It's been a big mess anytime I've tried to get involved."

"You don't think it concerns us?"

Terrance slumped in his chair. "Just ignore it, and we'll be fine. I think that's how it works."

Lance looked down the row of cubes, toward the window. "Okay. So you're not running out there with your faerie sword?"

Terrance thought of how the crystal palace had shattered as it collided with the ground. "No. I got rid of it."

Lance nodded. "Oh, okay. Well, sorry about Shannon." He walked off.

Terrance was just beginning to contemplate getting to work on the algorithm code when Karen appeared. "We need to talk," she said, and motioned for him to follow.

Terrance sighed. "Okay." He followed her to the stairwell, which gave them a little more privacy. "I kinda lost your sweatpants," Terrance told her. "I left them in a room on a Zeppelin somewhere past the edge of the world." He doubted there was an appropriate lost and found he could call.

"I don't care about that." Karen had her usual sour expression that Terrance was never quite sure was directed at him or at life in general. "Shannon called me and said she can't get in contact with you and she's worried something has happened to you. Why haven't you called her back?"

Terrance shrugged. "I was...getting to it."

"Are you breaking up with her? What happened with you two? I thought you were helping her quit her job or something?"

"That didn't work out. Instead, she"—Terrance thought again of Randolph's being burnt to nothing in the dragon fire, and of the spray of blood when Shannon sliced through Talia—"she had second thoughts, and...uhh..."

"And what?"

"I don't know." He took his glasses off and rubbed the lenses with the edge of his shirt. "She's evil. You know that?"

"What do you mean?"

He put his glasses back on. Karen was looking at him like he was cat vomit that she had to clean up, and something snapped in Terrance. "Maybe you're too much of an empty-headed bimbo to notice, but there are dark, evil forces out there. Shannon sided with them. And that's kind of an issue."

The disgusted look faded into something much more unreadable, but then it returned. "You're a real prick, you know that? Waving around your little faerie sword doesn't make you some special warrior, fighting evil."

"I am well aware of that," he said, not hiding his exasperation. "I am no warrior. I am just a computer programmer. Nothing more."

Karen studied Terrance's face, her expression neutral. "You should probably tell Shannon this and end it."

Terrance nodded.

Karen stood there for a few more seconds, looking like she was about to say something else, but finally turned quietly and left.

Terrance took out his phone and stared at it for a while. He really didn't think he was up to talking to Shannon, so instead he typed out a text. A breakup by text was pretty low, but so was murder, so Terrance didn't think he should feel too bad about it. He typed out, *You win. I tossed the sword. Now leave me alone.* After a little hesitation, he hit the Send button.

He headed back to his cubicle, though he was feeling too drained to work. Still, getting lost in his work seemed like the only possible escape from the pain he was feeling. He found Pendergrass standing by his desk.

"I was looking for you," he said. "It's stopped working completely."

"What?"

Pendergrass looked panicked. "The main algorithm is busted. I'm pretty sure it's now just returning negative one to everything. Did you deploy any changes to it recently?"

"No...I've been gone the last day or so."

"Well, look into it now. I was about to try to figure it out myself."

Terrance sighed and sat down at his desk. "We really need to replace that garbage. That code is nearly indecipherable. Who wrote it?"

Pendergrass shrugged. "I don't know. All I know is it was written a long time ago, probably before many coding standards were settled. We're talking back when C code was a novelty. The stuff is ancient."

"'Ancient' is the word for it." He brought up the file. "I'll see what I can see."

"Okay, tell me as soon as you figure it out." Pendergrass headed off.

Terrance dove once more into the mishmash of oddly named variables and unhelpful comments. Once again, it was extremely difficult to follow the flow of the logic, but he ran the algorithm in his test setup and soon found the problem. For some reason, there was a branch the code would go down based only on some odd math against the date. After exploring it for a while, he realized it had only started going down this particular path that day. And it was easy to see why it was breaking, because the code down that path was garbage.

One part of the code jumped out at him. There was a comment reading, "as you wait, it consumes," followed by the line:

td = dest < home;

He had no idea what any of those variables were supposed to mean or what they did for the program. The thought jumped into his head that "td" were his initials, and he stared at the line a while longer. He remembered how the Infinite said things were hidden in ancient texts, and Pendergrass had declared this code to be ancient. Could this be a message for him? If so, who put it there?

He shook the thought from his head; he had determined that he was done with this sort of thing, and there was no reason to stumble down the path to more tragedy. Instead, he did what seemed the sensible thing: began to fix the code so that the program never went into the section of nonsense logic.

After Terrance had worked for a while on getting the fix into production, he suddenly felt a chill. "I have an announcement," boomed Darlor's voice. The demon was standing at the end of the room, looking out over the cubicles. "There will be a new empowerment ceremony tomorrow."

Terrance shuddered, thinking of the creature below the building, and of what this ceremony might entail. But this was the challenge, wasn't it? Terrance knew he would see awful things on occasion and there was nothing he could do about it. Because what could he do other than get himself killed trying to fight powers far stronger than himself?

"I hope we can avoid an incident like last time," Darlor added.

He thought of Talia's being delivered to the horrible creature while everyone just stood there and watched. He wondered if that was part of how the Adversary fed off of them. But was it Talia that it would have been feeding off of, or those who stood by and did nothing?

It was a pointless thought, because nothing was the only real option. Maybe he helped a little with Talia that one time, but she was dead now—because that was all that fighting such forces was likely to achieve. There was no winning against immortal soldiers or powers that controlled reality.

Terrance decided the simple solution was to not come in tomorrow. He had already missed a lot of work, but he wasn't yet up for the challenge of being like the others and ignoring the evil. But eventually he would be—he'd have to be. He couldn't stop it, so there was nothing he could do other than learn to tolerate. To deaden his outrage to such things. To be empty of such emotion. To be hollow inside.

"No," Terrance heard himself utter.

"What?" Darlor demanded.

Terrance found himself stepping up from his desk and standing in the cubicle hall to face Darlor. *What am I doing? I threw away my sword; there is no pretending that I can do anything to stop these people.* Rationally, this was pointless, but the memory of Talia crying for help kept echoing in his mind, and he could not repeat the scenario in which he would just stand by and watch. As futile as he knew fighting the Darkness was—as suicidal as it seemed—he knew that he couldn't accept any other option.

Terrance looked at the terrible Darlor and shuddered in fear. But more than that, he was angry. He somehow managed to say in a calm voice, "If I see the unnamed creature from below again, I will kill it." It seemed like a pointless boast when he didn't even have a sword, but it didn't feel like a lie either. Somewhere deep down, he felt that he would destroy that evil thing.

Darlor said nothing immediately; he just glared at Terrance with fierce eyes. Around him, Terrance could see heads popping up from behind cubicle walls to watch the scene unfold. Now a bit of embarrassment was thrown into the mix, but the anger was still what ruled him.

"Let's talk in my office," Darlor finally said.

"Okay." He followed the demon, doing his best to ignore all the eyes watching him. Inside Darlor's cave, he closed the door behind him.

Darlor walked to his throne. "Sit."

"I'm good." Terrance tried to keep his voice firm, but he could feel his heart pounding inside him. He was so defenseless and exposed right now, and he had no idea where this was going.

Darlor stood too, his dark, scaly form much taller and larger than Terrance. "Do you understand the choice you are making?"

You have to back down or you will be killed, yelled a voice inside Terrance. The logic was sound, but he also felt that it was wrong. "I understand enough," he answered Darlor.

Darlor was still now, like a statue—a gargoyle. "You are a good programmer, Mr. Denby."

"Thank you."

"Do you not enjoy that job?"

"I do. I like programming very much."

"Then you should program. If you pursue these other things beyond your concern, then you put it all at risk. You could lose your job and your salary."

Terrance considered that and shuddered a bit. *You are going to lose everything.* "If that happens, it happens."

"You could lose your health insurance."

That made Terrance stop. He hadn't thought about running around fighting evil without health insurance; that seemed like a really bad idea. But he looked at the demon standing there, and knew this was all just to scare him. That's what all this was about: to get him to yield out of fear. And the fear was screaming at him. *Are you suicidal? Do you want to die?* He did not want to die. But the whole idea of submitting to the evil out there felt a lot like dying—and that was the death he was truly scared of. "I'm going to fight whatever evil I see. I'm doing what I must; you do what you must."

Darlor finally moved, a slight nod. "So be it."

The demon leapt at Terrance, plowing into him and smashing them both through the drywall, landing out in the open-air cubicle area. Terrance was dizzy from the impact, but saw Darlor standing over him with enormous leathery wings spread out behind him, making him look five times his normal size. Terrance tried to look around for something to grab as a weapon, but Darlor seized him with one claw and tossed him across the room, where he smashed into a cubicle divider that surprisingly had less give than the office wall.

Terrance could hear a great commotion of people shouting around him. He looked up and saw everyone watching, but no one helping.

Terrance reached for a nearby chair, but Darlor seized him by the arm. "We try to let you serve us without having to constantly remind you how small and pathetic you are," Darlor said.

"Oh, shut up!" Terrance managed to retort as he tried to pull away Darlor's claw while hitting him in the face. The demon's skin was like rock.

Darlor's other hand went to Terrance's neck and lifted him into the air. "We offer you everything," Darlor said as he walked forward. Terrance realized he was heading toward a window. "Most are smart enough to accept, because the alternative is to die pathetically and alone."

"You offer nothing I want," Terrance said as he feebly tried to pull Darlor's claw off his neck. Darlor slammed him against the window. It held, but he could feel it cracking against his back.

"Beg for mercy and forgiveness, and perhaps you'll get to see another day," Darlor said, still pressing Terrance against the cracking window. Terrance could see the faces of his coworkers staring, but no one was going to help him. *What did you expect?* asked the rational voice inside him. *How was this going to lead to anything other than you dying pathetically?* But Terrance didn't feel pathetic. Perhaps he could do nothing to fight, and perhaps he was going to die, but he would have a head held high.

"Screw you. You're a lousy boss."

Darlor slammed Terrance into the window again, and this time it shattered. He dangled Terrance over the street ten stories below. "Goodbye, Mr. Den—"

Something metal had lodged itself into Darlor's head. Terrance could feel the demon's grip loosening, so he clung to Darlor's arm tightly as his feet kicked out at the nothingness below him. But Darlor began leaning forward, and Terrance fell from his hand, grabbing onto the window ledge as Darlor's huge form toppled out the window, his useless wings rippling in the wind as he fell to the street below.

Terrance looked up, and there above him in the window, with battle-axe in hand, stood Karen, wild-eyed. She quickly regained her senses, dropped the axe to the floor, and reached through the window to try to pull Terrance up by one arm as his feet unsuccessfully attempted to find a foothold on the wall below him. "Someone help!" No one came. "Lance!" Karen shouted. "Come on!"

"Fine." Lance ran over and grabbed Terrance by the other arm, helping pull him back inside. Terrance miraculously suffered only a few small cuts against the leftover pieces of broken glass, and when he was fully inside and on the floor, he let out a sigh of relief, then picked himself up. The rest of the office still silently stared, and Lance looked at Karen and Terrance with a raised eyebrow. "You know you guys are in big trouble, right?"

"Oh, really? Thanks, Lance!" Karen yelled, picking back up her axe.

"*Everyone* is in big trouble," Terrance told Lance as he dusted himself off. "And some of us are trying to do something about it." He turned to Karen. "When did you get that axe?"

"Not long after you brought in your sword. I found a...gnome village near my house. I got the axe there and I've held on to it for a while, but I just wasn't sure about using it." She looked out the window to where Darlor had fallen. "This doesn't really seem like my sort of thing."

"Well, thanks," Terrance said, catching his breath.

"Where is your sword?" Karen asked.

Terrance looked at the floor. "I sorta chucked it."

Karen groaned. "I'm surrounded by idiots."

"So are you battling evil now, too?" Lance asked.

"I guess." She looked at Terrance. "What do we do now? There are *things* everywhere today."

"We'll meet up with others." Terrance didn't look forward to seeing Vivian, since he'd abandoned her after getting her husband and the others captured, but he didn't know what else to do. It was a heavy pressure, someone else looking to him for answers in these matters. He thought he could tell Karen the truth, which was that he was clueless, but he didn't want to scare her.

Terrance looked around at all the coworkers watching them, and spoke as steadily as he could muster. "As you have probably seen, the forces of evil are out...in force. They're getting harder to ignore, and we are not going to do that anymore. We are going to take them on. Who is with us?"

No one spoke or moved forward.

"Okay then." It had seemed worth a shot. He turned to Karen and Lance. "Let's get going."

Lance hesitated. "I'm not really a part of this."

"Just come on!" Karen shouted. They headed for the elevators and pushed the button for the ground floor.

"Are they going to be down there waiting for us?" Karen asked.

"If they are, we fight them," Terrance assured her.

Karen looked down at her axe. "I have no idea how to even use this thing. And you don't have your sword. And Lance...well, I don't expect Lance to do anything."

"That's good," Lance said.

"The first thing you need to understand," Terrance said, speaking slowly and steadily, "is that our enemies try to appear fearsome, but they are much weaker than they seem, and we are much, much more powerful." That seemed to ease Karen's fears a little, and it helped Terrance's fears as well, even though what he said was only what he hoped to be true, not what he was sure he truly believed.

The elevator stopped.

And then it accelerated downward with at least twice its normal speed. It shot past the ground floor and descended to the unmarked floors below. It finally stopped at the bottom—the sub-subbasement. Terrance tried pounding the ground-floor button and then the others, but none reacted.

The elevator doors parted. Outside stood several hooded figures with eyes shining out from shadowed faces. One hissed, "Offerings for the unnamed thing that resides below."

Lance was crouched in the corner of the elevator. "You're supposed to take the stairs in case of an emergency."

CHAPTER 32

The hooded figures were armed with what looked like old, well-worn swords with uneven edges and cracks. Still, they were far more than Terrance had.

"The ancient creature from below will feast upon your bones," one of the figures said. Terrance could make out little of its face in the shadows, but something didn't seem human about it. "And then you will—"

"Shut up!" Karen screamed, stepping in front of Terrance and brandishing her axe. "Out of my way or I will hack you to pieces!"

"Silence, woman! You have—"

Karen's face went red and she let out a sound somewhere between a roar and a scream as she swung her axe at the nearest cloaked figure, cutting him down. She followed that with another wide swing, hitting two more of them. Terrance was impressed; Karen really seemed to be jumping into the battling-evil thing with much more ease than he had. Still, there were about half a dozen of the armed cultists, and it looked like Karen would soon get overwhelmed. They were all focused on her, though, which gave Terrance an opportunity to dash forward and snatch a sword from one of the fallen cultists. As soon as he had a weapon, two of them turned their attention to him, and he was blocking attacks before he had the chance to deliver any. He dodged around them looking for an opening and soon found himself next to Karen, who was still screaming and swinging wildly. It was then that Terrance realized the cultists had moved between them and the elevators, and were pushing them backward.

Though he really didn't want to, Terrance took a glance behind him. There was the stage, and from the pit in the center emerged long, writhing tentacles like a swarm of anacondas coming for them. "Trouble!" he managed to yell as he turned his attention back in front to block a sword strike. Karen didn't seem to hear, and kept swinging at her attackers until a tentacle wrapped around her arms and chest. She let out a much less fearsome scream as it began to pull her backward.

Frantically, Terrance shoved away the cultist he was parrying with, to give himself a moment to turn his attention to Karen. He ran and swung with all his might at the tentacle that gripped Karen, but the battered sword he held was as dull as it looked and didn't even seem to scratch the rubbery flesh. The mouth of the creature rose out of the pit, an opening filled with sharp teeth, easily large enough to fit them both in at once. And Karen was being slowly pulled toward it. Terrance took a glance at the cultists, but they were now hanging back to watch the show. Seeing the horrible maw loom near, Terrance frantically stabbed at the tentacle, and this resulted in some progress as he actually broke flesh. The grip on Karen loosened, and she squirmed free and grabbed her axe, now screaming fiercely while hacking at the many tentacles. Something grabbed Terrance's leg and he fell over. As he was dragged across the floor, he tried to swing his sword, but another tentacle grabbed his arm. He was headed toward the mouth with nothing to grab on to or brace against. He yelled to Karen for help, but she was overwhelmed by the creature's other appendages. The mouth of the unnamed beast, held aloft by a long, thick neck, rose into the air in anticipation of swallowing Terrance, as thick, mucous-like saliva oozed between its three-inch razor teeth.

Suddenly, the mouth tilted back and let out a horrible, pain-filled shriek that shook the whole room. Near the creature, he glimpsed something white. A horse. With a horn protruding from its head, which was now embedded in the unnamed beast's neck.

A small figure in white jumped into the fray, slashing at the tentacles with a sword in each hand. *Talia.* The tentacles holding Terrance loosened, and he slipped free. The cultists now charged, but Terrance saw Felicia and Donald run past him to meet them, and soon Karen was at their side, wielding her axe. Behind him, Talia was going after the creature's neck, stabbing it repeatedly as its wounded limbs flailed about. Terrance found the battered sword he'd been using and was about to decide who to help when he realized it was all over. The cultists lay dead, and the unnamed beast was now a motionless pile of tentacles. Terrance ran to Talia. "You're alive!"

Talia flicked the blood from her swords and returned them to the sheaths under her cloak. Then she slapped Terrance so hard, it knocked him to the ground. "I don't know what's more likely to destroy us: your cowardice or your lust."

He got back to his feet. "I was just trying to help her. I didn't know things could...end up as they did."

Talia looked at the weapon Terrance was holding. "What happened to your sword?"

"I...threw it away. I..." He wasn't even sure how to finish. "I'm useless, okay? I fought seeing the truth about Shannon, and I tried so many times to ignore the other evil I saw. And even when I did fight, I just...I couldn't do anything. And then after what happened with the faeries, I couldn't face you guys again, especially Vivian and her children..."

Felicia patted him on the back. She had a backpack on and looked like she had just come from school. "It's okay. We'll figure it out."

"We've all had trouble with this," Donald said. He had a suit on sans tie like he had just snuck out of work.

"Everyone is held prisoner," Terrance answered. "The forces of the Darkness now seem to be everywhere. This seems like more than a minor screw-up."

"Your mewling about it certainly isn't helping." Talia turned to Karen and offered her hand. "I'm Talia. You fight with zeal. It is good to have your help."

Karen accepted the handshake. "Karen Hunter. Thanks for coming to save us."

"I knew Terrance worked here, and thus we came to check on him. He may be useless, but each person lost to the evil out there is a great loss despite their apparent lack of worth, and evil is out in full force, as you may have seen." She managed a slight smile for Karen. "At least out of this we found a new fighter, which makes it seem like much less of a waste of time."

"Well, I don't really understand what's going on here," Karen said, "just that some things are evil and I have an axe."

"Well, when you see something that is evil, make sure to smite it with your axe and not take it to your bed." Talia shot a quick glance at Terrance.

"By the way, I'm Donald." He smiled broadly at Karen.

"And I'm Felicia."

Karen looked Felicia over. "Do your parents know you're out fighting evil?"

"I left a note."

"So you know Terrance?" Donald asked.

"Well, we're coworkers. Also, he had been dating my friend...Shannon, who I guess you might kinda know."

Felicia nodded. "Yeah, I met her once, and she seemed nice...though I guess she wasn't."

"She nearly cut me in two when she betrayed us," Talia said.

"How...how are you alive?" Terrance asked.

"My unicorn healed me." She turned to the white horse that stood back from the group. "Here, Cloppers." The unicorn slowly walked up behind Talia. "They have healing powers and are good friends to have."

"And Randolph?" Terrance uttered.

There was a touch of sadness in her face, but it quickly disappeared. "He is gone from this world; that's what death is. Only a small measure of each man exists in this world and is vulnerable, but all that Randolph truly is has gone somewhere beyond us now. As best we understand about death, the Adversary can no longer feed on him, but he and the others who have fallen are still trapped somewhere away from their true selves. And they shall remain that way until the power of the Adversary is destroyed. So if you want to honor the dead, keep fighting."

Karen approached Cloppers and slowly reached up to touch the spiraled horn on its head. The unicorn reared, startling Karen so much she nearly fell over.

"Only maidens may approach a unicorn," Talia told her.

Karen backed away from Cloppers. "Well, that's...judgmental." She took out a cigarette and lit it.

"I don't know if you can smoke here," Felicia said.

Karen puffed her cigarette. "It's an evil, underground lair where we killed everyone; I kind of doubt there are smoking regulations."

"Actually, there's a sign right there." Felicia pointed to the No Smoking sign on the wall.

Karen shrugged. "Who is going to enforce it?"

Talia snatched the cigarette from Karen's mouth, threw it to the ground, and stomped it with her sneaker. "Enough chat; let's get going."

"So...uh...is this all over?" called someone from behind them. It was Lance, carefully stepping over the bodies of the cultists.

"It has but begun," Talia announced. "I know you; you're Terrance's friend and even more useless than he is. Are you ready to fight?"

Lance stared long and hard at the dead mass in the pit. "No...I'm not really a part of this."

"Everyone is a part of this," Talia said. "You either take a stand against evil or you eventually become its servant."

Lance scoffed. "You know, you don't win many friends with that 'you're either for us or against us' rhetoric."

"I don't seek friends; I seek allies."

"So, what now?" Terrance asked.

Talia pointed to a cave that went off the main room. "Come. Follow me. The protection of the faeries is gone, evil feels no need to hide in the dark, and much of our group is held captive. There is much to do for those willing to do it. We must make our plan to fight back."

They all followed her, including Lance, who didn't seem to know what else to do.

Donald dropped back to walk next to Terrance. "Sorry I wasn't there for what happened. I was so tired, I didn't even answer the phone when I got the call. Sometimes I'm not sure how to balance needing to keep a job in the regular world and all of this. I'm not sure I always get my priorities right."

"It's best you weren't there," Terrance said, "or you probably would have just ended up killed or captured."

"Hey, don't blame yourself for that. You had honorable aims with that mission, and we're all just learning here about how we can take on the Darkness. I'm sure Randolph had no regrets."

"Thanks." Terrance now felt mildly less like a complete failure.

"No problem." Donald took his tie out of his pocket and began to put it back on. "So, that Karen...is she seeing anyone?"

CHAPTER 33

They hiked through the caverns for what seemed like miles. Cloppers followed, but hung back a bit since much of the group were not maidens. During the hike, the only light came from sparse torches on the walls. Finally, they heard the sound of water running, and they soon came to a much brighter part of the cave, so bright that it took Terrance's eyes a few moments to adjust. Large windows were carved into the rock wall, through which the sun was shining, but directly in front of the windows flowed water. It fell so evenly that it was like a shimmering windowpane through which they could peer to see the green of a valley below.

They came to a rising staircase, and after ascending for a few minutes, they reached an exit from the caverns. It led out into a shaded jungle, with little sunlight coming through the dense canopy above them. The trees all looked quite old—tall, wide, and covered in moss and vines.

Karen looked around with fascination. "Didn't know we had a jungle near town."

"Didn't feel near," Lance complained.

"Come. We're almost there," Talia said.

"Is this a new hideout?" Terrance asked.

Talia nodded. "Yes. The previous one was destroyed when someone led the enemy there."

Karen caught up to Terrance. "Is she talking about you?"

Terrance sighed. "Yes."

"I thought you were like this warrior with them," Karen said, "but you sound like a screw-up."

"Thanks for that observation." Terrance hurried after Talia.

They soon caught sight of what looked like a building ahead, but as they got closer Terrance realized that it was in fact the largest tree he had ever seen. Its base was as thick as a skyscraper, and it stretched so high beyond the jungle canopy that Terrance couldn't see the top. Dotting the light brown trunk high above the ground were a number of windows. At the base, there was a large, doorless opening leading inside.

"Is this where they make the cookies?" Lance asked.

"It's long abandoned," Donald answered.

"So no cookies? You know, this might be where I part with you guys." Lance looked around the jungle. "How do I get back to town?"

"There is a path that goes east of here." Talia pointed to a dirt path leading into the jungle. "Follow it until you reach the singing crystal garden, then take a right. Keep going that way and eventually you'll reach a bridge over a giant crevice. Head over it but be careful, as wind comes up from deep within the bowels of the earth. Keep going, and you should soon see a rock structure that resembles an eagle. Stand below, and eventually you will come to the Iron Chariot, which will take you to town. It costs a dollar twenty-five if you have cash. If you only have credit or debit, you will have to purchase a card with at least five dollars on it."

Lance nodded along to the directions. "Is the Iron Chariot a bus?"

"It is much more than a bus," Talia said. She thought for a moment and added, "But mainly it's a bus."

"Okey dokey. You guys have fun."

"Are you sure you don't want to help?" Terrance asked. "Important battles are starting, ones that will affect the whole world...and beyond, I guess."

"Yeah, I'm pretty sure," Lance said. "This all seems really dumb." He looked at Karen. "Are you sure you want to be a part of this?"

"Very sure." Karen still gripped her axe. "I want to fight. I can't just stand around anymore."

"All right. See you later." Lance turned to head down the path, Cloppers keeping his distance and watching him warily.

"One more thing," Talia called out. "There are nymphs in the jungle. They will lead you to your death. If you see an attractive woman on your journey, ignore her."

"Ignore attractive women—got it." Lance headed down the path and disappeared into the woods.

"Well, he's probably dead now," Karen said.

"We can't waste our time worrying about the fate of fools." Talia walked toward the tree. "Let's head to the top."

"This tree fort is pretty neat," Felicia said.

"Unless you're afraid of heights," Donald added.

Karen looked around worriedly as they headed into the tree. "I'm afraid of bugs. Seems like a tree would be filled with bugs."

"Heights and bugs are not the main things we have to fear now," Talia said. "Though I do not like spiders."

Inside, the main part of the tree was hollow, with light coming down from somewhere far above, farther than Terrance could see. The walls were bare except for the scattered windows carved in the trunk. There was a big pile of leaves to one side—which seemed kind of weird to have *inside* a tree. And little lights floated about. "Are those lightning bugs?"

"Pixies," Talia answered.

"Do they bite?" Karen asked, keeping a close eye on one floating near her.

"I'm sure they're capable of it."

Cloppers had followed them inside, though he stuck to an area near the tree base, away from the group. Talia led everyone to a wooden box made from large branches tied together, big enough for all of them to stand inside. On its top was a large metal ring. "What's this?" Terrance asked.

"Get inside and you'll see," Talia answered.

They all climbed into the box, and Talia closed its door—which was simply more branches loosely tied together—and fastened it closed on a hook with a small bit of rope. She picked up what looked like a flute hanging from the side of the box, and played a few notes.

A sudden loud screech caused Terrance and Karen to crouch to the ground. Silhouetted against the light above, a large bird descended, almost as large as the box they were in. It seized the metal ring with its talons and lifted the box into the air with a flap of its enormous wings. Soon they were rising high above the ground, dangling in the bird's grip.

Karen slowly lifted herself up to peer out the side. "What does OSHA think of this?"

"We are far beyond the realm of OSHA," Talia answered.

"It's okay," Donald assured Karen. "It seems like the bird has done this thousands of times."

Terrance slowly straightened up from his crouch. "Birds are technically dinosaurs. I don't know why I brought that up...it's just that it's a really big bird, which made me think of it."

Karen rolled her eyes. "Thanks, Terry. That was really useful."

When the ground was no longer in view, the bird set the box down on a wide ledge carved into the inside of the tree. The opening at the top from which the light shone was now much closer, and Terrance could make out blue skies above them until the bird briefly blocked the view as it flew through the opening and disappeared beyond sight.

Talia opened the door of the box. "Vivian will be here in a little bit, and then we'll figure out our next course of action."

"Who is Vivian?" Karen asked.

"We might need to explain some things to Karen, since she's new to this," Donald said.

Talia nodded. "Yes, why don't you and Felicia catch her up? We'll need her axe in the battles to come."

"Battles to come; oh, yay," Karen said, chuckling.

"You said you wanted to fight, and you will get the opportunity," Talia said. "As for me, I was nearly cut in two, fell a great distance, and have been fighting ever since, so I think I'm going to rest a bit and read a book."

"What about me?" Terrance asked.

Talia's eyes darkened. "I don't know, Terrance Denby, what about you? What can you add?"

Terrance thought about it. "I guess nothing."

"Then get on that." Talia headed for a door that led out to the exterior of the tree.

"Talia is just a bit upset because of...everything," Felicia explained. "But we're glad you're okay and with us now."

Terrance sighed. "Yeah, I'm sure I'm a big boon to the whole operation."

"There's a room that's actually got some comfortable furniture." Donald pointed to a wooden door a little further along the ledge. "We'll be in there talking to Karen if you want to join us."

Terrance watched them walk off and contemplated what exactly he was going to do to help. He didn't have a sword—not that he was ever much use with it anyway—and beyond that, all he ever seemed to do was cause more mess for everyone. The more he thought about it, the more he couldn't understand what the remainder of the Infinite had to gain from rescuing him. Talia certainly seemed of two minds about it.

He headed for the door she had exited through. It brought him to a balcony on the outside of the tree, where it was a beautiful, bright day with a clear blue sky. Above him were more large branches as, surprisingly, the tree continued up quite a bit further despite how high the bird had taken them.

Terrance mounted some steps on the balcony that led to a large, thick branch jutting far out from the tree. Talia was sitting at the far end of it, and he approached her. The branch was just wide enough for a person to walk easily along it, but there were no railings. Far below, he could see nothing but the green of the treetops, yet despite the height, he was strangely unafraid. He walked up behind Talia and stared for a moment at the view. Beyond the jungle below were mountains and valleys. And past the mountains...

"Is there something you want?" Talia asked.

"Yes."

"What?"

Terrance tore his eyes away from the view to look at Talia, who sat below him holding a Kindle. "I don't know. What are you reading?"

"Historical romance fiction."

"I didn't know that was a genre."

"This one takes place during the Russian Revolution."

Terrance nodded. "Sounds boring."

"It's not." She stared at him with her doe eyes. "I'll ask once again: is there something you want, Terrance Denby?"

"I...want to say sorry for all the trouble I caused."

Talia set her Kindle down and stood up to face him, her eyes narrowing. "Are you truly sorry? Early on, I warned you that that pretty little thing was going to try to drag you into the emptiness of this world, though little did I know the exact depths she was trying to pull you down into. I suspect you had an inkling of it but pursued her anyway."

"Yeah, I made a big mistake trying to lead two lives...but in the end I was just trying to help her."

Talia laughed. "Oh, well aren't you the big hero? Were your motives really pure, or were you just hoping to have it both ways: to finally follow your conscience and keep your little toy?"

"Hey! She's a person...somewhat. And it wasn't just me; the others thought there was a chance to save her."

"Out of compassion, they humored you. And look how we all paid for it."

"I'd do it again!" Terrance said, his voice rising. "If falling into the Darkness is as horrible as you say, then it was worth a chance to save someone, and I would do it again!"

Talia seethed. "Well, Randolph won't be there the next time, and perhaps your whore will cut deeper on the second try and properly finish me off. But of course, there will be no second time for the faeries. They are gone, and now the forces of the Darkness have overrun us. All the world is crumbling because of that one foolish attempt. I am sure the Adversary is laughing at the result of your showing compassion to one of his minions."

"How was I supposed to know this would all happen?!" Terrance yelled, startling some birds from a nearby branch. "I still don't have the slightest clue what the hell is going on! I don't know why I was thrust into this or what I'm supposed to do!"

"Well, it's not whine and feel sorry for yourself," Talia said in a much angrier but more measured tone. "You are so useless. Where is your sword?"

That deflated him. "I told you. I threw it away. I don't know where it is or how to get it back."

"You are pathetic, Terrance Denby. We need to be warriors greater than imaginable, and you are less than a man. Why are you even here? Why don't you just shuffle back to your pathetic, meaningless existence and live in a little shell of inanity until oblivion comes? You already tossed your sword; why don't you just give up entirely?"

"Because I can't!" Terrance bellowed. "I don't care if I'm useless or if I accomplish nothing; I can't shut my eyes again! I know what's wrong, and I know what's right, and I'm here whether I can do anything about it or not. Maybe in the next battle I'll get hacked apart by some demon, but I'm going to try anyway because I can't stand idly by. I know that is not an option. I don't understand much, but what I do know is that—"

He was cut off by Talia's lips pressing against his own. He stared in shock, but her eyes were closed. It seemed to last a long time, and then she backed away a step. They looked at each other silently for a few moments, and finally Talia sat down and picked up her book. "I would like to rest. I'm going to read."

Terrance didn't say a word. He slowly turned and left, more confused than ever.

CHAPTER 34

Terrance sat alone on a ledge, contemplating his circumstances as he watched the little lights float around the massive interior of the tree. There was so little he could make sense of. All he knew for certain was that he missed his sword.

"Vivian is arriving," Talia announced from the doorway to the balcony. She met his eyes briefly but quickly turned away to go inform the others.

Terrance headed back out to the exterior ledge. He could no longer see the treetops below, as some clouds had moved in around the tall tree, blocking the view. The cloud cover extended out quite some distance, and a ship was floating upon it. As it came closer, he could see that it was Swaggerty's ship, and at the helm was the bear in his red vest. The ship slowed and came to a stop next to a branch. Swaggerty lowered a rope ladder and Vivian climbed down. Swaggerty followed with Vivian's two small children clinging to his back.

"A cloud ship?" Karen asked from behind Terrance. "That's a thing?" The others had come out to watch, as well.

Vivian took her children by the hand and walked toward the group, smiling. "Good to see you all."

She looked genuinely happy to see them, but all Terrance could think of was how he'd been responsible for getting her husband—the children's father—captured, and he was unable to come up with anything to say.

"Hey, it's the stupid-question guy," Swaggerty quipped. "The one who almost got me killed."

Terrance turned red. "S-sorry."

"That's okay." Swaggerty waved a paw. "So how is the evil blonde girlfriend?"

"We broke up."

"Well, buck up. There are plenty of soulless monsters in the sea." Swaggerty turned to Vivian. "I need to get going. It sounds like you people are really getting the hammer dropped on you this time, and I don't want to be anywhere near when it hits."

"Understood. Thanks for the ride," Vivian said.

"Bye, bear!" the children called to Swaggerty in excited voices. He waved at them and sauntered back to his ship.

Vivian approached Karen. "I see we have a new face. I'm Vivian."

Karen shook her hand. "Karen. I know Terrance from work."

"Well, it's good to have you here. We'll need the extra help if you're willing." She looked around at the group. "I'm still waiting to hear word on the others. Krampsky should have some information and will be here soon—he's part of another group of the Infinite."

"And then a rescue mission?" Felicia asked.

Vivian smiled. "Well, of course."

"And these are people Terrance got captured?" Karen asked.

Vivian's smile faded, and she glanced briefly at Terrance. He felt himself shatter under that short gaze. "Um...things happened," Vivian said, "and we'll do our best to rectify them. So anyway, Krampsky will be here soon, and then we'll make a plan." She turned to Terrance. "You want to talk briefly?"

He feared nothing more. "Sure."

"Grace! Daniel! Come on!" she called. They were staring over the edge of one of the branches, but got up and followed their mom. As Terrance walked inside with Vivian, he glanced at Talia, but she didn't meet his eyes.

Vivian led him inside the tree and to another door, which opened into a large interior chamber furnished with a few benches made from stumps, and what looked like a desk at the front of the room, made from a much larger stump (though certainly quite small compared to the tree it resided in). There were a few windows on one wall, through which sunlight shone, somehow emphasizing the empty, ghostlike quality of the room.

After Vivian closed the door, Terrance wanted to speak first but had trouble thinking of what to say. He watched the children run around the room, then he looked again at Vivian and lost it. Tears streamed down his cheeks. "I'm so sorry. I'm a coward...I'm worse than a coward. I not only got your husband captured, I just ran off and...this elf—"

"It's okay." Vivian smiled gently and reached out with one hand to pat him on the shoulder. "It's not your fault."

"It is my fault! I got them all involved to help my girlfriend and—"

"And the forces of the Darkness came at you with all their strength because that was so threatening to them. You scared them, Terrance."

"But they captured your husband and the others and killed Randolph...and they destroyed the crystal palace. And now their evil is everywhere and coming for us, and I had tried to ignore it. To hide! And—"

"And here you are, back and ready to fight. I know this looks bad and you feel guilty, but we're all struggling through this. We all get scared. We all make mistakes. And certainly none of us understands everything." She motioned behind him, and Terrance turned to see Grace and Daniel laughing happily as a glowing pixie kept floating near them, then darting away. "Children see this world better than we do.

They have no preconceived notions, and they approach everything as if it were a great wonder. That's because they see everything for what it truly is. As we become older, we become worldlier, and we close our eyes and no longer notice the wondrous things around us. To truly *see*, we have to be like children. We have to look at things anew. It's from their perspective that we need to understand the world."

Terrance watched the children, but all he could think about was how their father was being held prisoner by the followers of the Darkness and how they and their mother were under a greater threat with the enemy now prowling the streets. And he couldn't even imagine how they could win against that enemy. "You're not scared? You don't fear all the creatures out there and what they could do to your family?"

"What do we fear?" Vivian asked. "We fear losing what we have. You don't know how often I've regretted not taking a picture of certain moments with my children, knowing that once it passes, it's gone forever. They keep growing, and what I have with them now will one day be gone, with only a few fading memories and a handful of photos to remember it by. But I've come to realize the greatest moments are ones that could never be captured with a mere picture, such as the feeling I had cradling them in my arms when they were little babies. Sometimes I'm sad about how that's already gone, but I don't think it is. Things like that change you—somewhere deep, somewhere permanent and beyond this world. Pictures and memories fade, but the greatest things we experience in this world are part of who we truly are, and they last forever.

"What I'm saying is that the greatest things we have can never be taken from us. The worst that those who appear so powerful in this world can do is to end our lives here, but that is very little in the scheme of things, because one day the Adversary's power will fail and we will be reunited with our full selves. So there is little to lose in this fight, and much to gain by defeating the evil that traps so many souls. We have to hold on to what we know is true and continue onward without fear. Do you understand?"

Terrance chuckled ruefully. "I think so, a bit...but at the same time, not at all."

"Well, what led you to this? Why did you take up a sword?"

"It was the faeries. They gave it to me. I don't know why they chose me."

Vivian smiled. "They didn't choose you. They didn't just float by one day and chuck a scabbard at you. You found them."

"Only by accident. There was this squirrel"—Terrance hated that squirrel—"and there was this road I had always driven past, but I decided to check it out one day."

"Yes. You decided to go there, because you were looking for something. What were you looking for?"

"I wasn't looking for anything, I was..." Terrance noticed the view out the window. There again in the distance were mountains. Beyond them...there was something. He knew it. But he didn't know how to get there. "I don't know what I'm looking for. I just know it's...important."

"And you're on the path toward it now. We all are."

Terrance looked down to his hip, where the sword had been. "Except that I threw away my sword."

"You'll find it again."

"The faeries are gone; it's not like they can get me a new one."

"They never gave you the first one. Terrance, you still need to understand how powerful you are. I know it often seems like a hollow assurance, with the whole world trying to make you feel small."

Terrance chuckled. "And Talia. I'm not even sure why she came to rescue me."

Vivian smiled. "You know she's infatuated with you."

Terrance thought of the awkward kiss. "She's...confusing."

"Ever since you spoke up when they were going to feed her to that creature below your office building, she's had a thing for you," Vivian explained. "I think she's expected a lot out of you since then—and I get the sense that you haven't felt that you've been what you believe you should be."

"Even when I had my sword and tried to use it, I was useless. I want to help—I want to fight this fight—I just don't know how I can be of use to anyone."

Vivian looked him in the eyes. "In this world, everyone has an idea of the courageous warrior who fights with great skill and easily slays all foes. To win this fight, that is not the warrior we need. We need someone greater."

Terrance frowned. "I don't know how to be that person."

"I don't believe you."

He could see from her face that she meant it, but that didn't mean much, considering what he was planning to go up against. And every time he looked at her children, he was reminded that he got their father captured and that there was no real assurance things would ever be right for them again. But he had to try to help, and he was determined to do so. He just needed to somehow find that warrior within himself.

And then a thought struck him. "I saw something...in a computer program...an old one. It was a message, and I think it was meant for me."

"What did it say?"

"I'm not sure...it was 'dest less than home,' which doesn't seem to mean anything. Or 'dest under home,' maybe." *The cavern!* "I think I'm supposed to find something in the cavern beneath my apartment. My destiny, maybe." He had a thought about himself with sword in hand, finally the warrior he was supposed to be. "Or maybe it was just some junk code I'm making too much of."

Vivian put her hand on his shoulder. "Go and do this."

"But what about the rescue mission?"

"You'll catch up with us, I'm sure. But if this quest of yours will help you, then you need to go do it now."

"Okay. But I'll be back to help you get your husband."

She smiled. "I know you will, Terrance. I do not doubt that."

Felicia stuck her head into the room. "Krampsky is here."

"Good," Vivian said. "Let's see what he's found out."

They headed back to the exterior balcony of the tree, where a middle-aged man in a police uniform was standing next to a griffin. Karen was closely watching the creature. "Does it bite?"

"And claw," Krampsky said.

"We're finally getting the police involved?" Terrance asked.

Krampsky looked down at his uniform. "Oh. Uh...no. Please know that none of this I'm doing here is in my official capacity as a police officer. I just didn't have time to change after my shift. Anyway, I can't stay long, because the fighting is getting fierce out there. They are not letting up this time; we lost two from our group during a recent assault. I'm not sure where they're going with this. I'm guessing they're hoping we're demoralized after what happened with the crystal palace and that they can beat us into submission."

Talia smiled. "They're quite scared of us."

Krampsky nodded. "That's one way of looking at it. Anyway, we confirmed that your people are being held in the fortress on the mountaintop. And we're hearing that they're planning a public execution."

Terrance finally saw a little bit of worry creep into Vivian's expression. Her children paid no attention, though, giggling and watching what looked like a monkey jump from branch to branch above them.

"Things are changing," Vivian finally said. "It shows that we're getting to them."

"So we plan a rescue?" Felicia asked.

Vivian nodded. "Of course. I think my parents should be able to watch Grace and Daniel, and then we'll get going." She looked at Krampsky. "When we've retrieved the others, we'll help with the fight in the streets."

"I'm not sure how long they'll keep this up," he said. "They're trying to wear us down with constant battle, but they're now so bold about it that many more people are starting to notice. I don't know what their endgame is."

"Theirs is nothing but a path of destruction," Talia declared. "We will help them along."

Vivian looked at the group. "Everyone ready to march into the heart of enemy territory?"

"My schedule is clear this time," Donald said.

"I just need to call my parents again and I should be good," Felicia said.

Talia's hands went to the hilts of her swords. "I am always ready."

"I'm still not really sure what's going on, but I'll help," Karen said.

"I can get to that other thing later," Terrance said. "I'll do what I can to help."

Vivian shook her head. "No, you have a personal quest to do. We won't be heading out right away, so perhaps we'll meet up with you again before it goes down."

"Okay." He had no idea what the quest was going to be like, but he felt certain he would be more use to them after it. If he succeeded. He really didn't have any idea what he was heading into.

"Good luck." Krampsky climbed back onto his griffin. "The forces of evil can't attack us so relentlessly forever; something has to give. But it won't be us." With a flap of its giant wings, the griffin took off.

"You have a quest?" Talia asked.

"Yeah...I think so. Um"—Terrance peered over the edge of the tree—"how does one get down from here?"

"Follow me." They all followed Vivian back into the tree. She led them to an alcove in the wall that appeared to have a pit inside.

Terrance peered down it. He felt a gust of wind blow up from below, but he couldn't see anything. "What do we do here?"

"I want to do it!" Daniel exclaimed and jumped into the pit. Grace giggled and followed him. Terrance looked at Vivian, who just nodded.

He jumped into the pit and began freefalling, just as one would expect to do when falling down a pit so deep you can't see the bottom. He flailed his arms wildly—not that there was anything to grab on to—and he could see lights flashing by, perhaps windows he was falling past. He could only imagine what he looked like from the outside. But as he fell, he felt more and more wind rushing up against him. Eventually, he even felt his fall slow down, until he was actually descending so slowly that he was no longer panicked. That's when he could see a grate below, from which the wind was rushing up. It was slightly slanted, though, and as he neared it, he was pushed out an opening to the side and landed in a pile of leaves, where Daniel and Grace were playing. Terrance looked around and realized he was at the base of the giant tree.

"Again!" Daniel shouted.

"Look!" Grace exclaimed, pointing at Cloppers, who was standing near a wall. The children raced over to see the unicorn.

Terrance climbed out of the pile of leaves as one by one, Vivian, Donald, Felicia, Talia, and Karen landed there.

"Who exactly put this all together?" Karen asked, looking more than a little annoyed as she brushed leaves off.

"Just one of many, many mysteries," Felicia said.

"Mommy! Can we ride the unicorn?" Grace called out. She was standing next to Cloppers, patting his flank.

"He's not a pony at a fair for children to ride for five dollars," Talia said, and then paused. "Then again...I don't see why they can't."

Vivian walked over to Cloppers. "He's friendly, right?" The unicorn reared when she got near.

"You have to be a maiden to approach him," Talia said.

Vivian looked offended. "I'm married."

"He doesn't care," Talia answered.

"He doesn't seem to like you, Mommy," Daniel said.

Vivian rolled her eyes. "Yes, I guess I'm not getting a unicorn ride."

Talia picked up Grace and put her on Cloppers' back, then Daniel. "So, what are we down here for?"

"We're seeing Terrance off," Vivian answered, looking at him. "You might as well get going. We'll be working on our plan for a bit before we head out."

"Okay...I guess I'll see you guys soon...I hope."

"We'll try not to destroy all evil before you meet back up with us," Donald said.

Terrance thought for a moment about what he was potentially taking on, and he felt excited. He remembered how Erica had gotten her bow from her personal quest, and Terrance could only assume some new weapon waited for him to make up for losing his sword. This was his time to finally become a warrior. "I know I need to do this. And then I'll be back, and there won't be any more hesitation from me again."

Vivian paused as she watched her children on Cloppers' back as he trotted around. "Just remember who you are, and everything will work out."

Terrance felt he was still finding out who he was. "I guess I need to get back to my apartment." He turned to Talia. "What were the directions you gave to Lance?"

"Avoid nymphs."

CHAPTER 35

The Iron Chariot seemed pretty indistinguishable from a bus, but it did get Terrance to within a short walking distance of his apartment. As he arrived, the sun was beginning to set. He looked at Lance's apartment above his own and wondered if he should check to make sure he'd gotten back all right, but decided to first relax on his couch for a bit, as it had been a busy day. When he entered his apartment, he found his couch already occupied.

She was in a new black outfit. It looked like a leotard with fishnet stockings, and on her face was a mask that resembled a demonic maw with sharp teeth, covering her mouth and nose. Still, she was quite recognizable by her eyes and the blonde hair tied in a ponytail.

"You look like an evil ninja," Terrance said. A sexy, evil ninja.

"Night Mistress," Shannon answered, still sitting on the couch. The TV was on, showing some guy explaining his paint choices for a room. Apparently Shannon had been watching HGTV while waiting for him. "I got a promotion," she said. "I'm even quicker and stronger now."

"Well, I'm the same speed and same strength." Terrance noticed the sword strapped to her back and wondered what her purpose was here.

She slowly stood up. In her hand was a blue bag from Best Buy. "I got you a gift. I know it must have been pretty hard the way I played you, and I wanted to apologize."

She handed the bag to Terrance, and he opened it. Inside was Legendary Quest. He had almost forgotten about that game, but he *really* wanted to play it.

He left the game in the bag and set it down on the coffee table. "So what exactly are you sorry for? Since you destroyed the faeries' palace, I can see all your friends and minions out everywhere hunting people down. Is that what you're sorry for?"

"I'm sorry that you feel hurt, as you don't quite understand—"

"Oh, I understand perfectly," Terrance said, his tone firm but not angry. "And you understand as well. I know that your trying to leave the Darkness wasn't a complete subterfuge from the beginning. But you got scared. I'm done with the fear, though. I don't care how powerful the forces of the Darkness seem, I will stand against them."

Her eyes showed shock. "I thought you said you were done with all that!"

"I was wrong. I'm not going to stand idly by. And I'm certainly not going to join you."

Her eyes narrowed. "So we're enemies now?"

He glanced at her sheathed sword again. "That's your choice."

She looked him over. "Where is your sword?"

"I...misplaced it."

She chuckled. "So you're really going to take on the Darkness and all its power? Do you have any idea what you're up against?"

"I'm up against evil. And I will fight however I'm able."

Shannon reached up and removed her mask. Underneath, her lips were blood-red. Her expression turned to one of deep concern. She reached out and touched his arm. "Terrance, please don't do this. I...love you."

She was close enough that he could smell the sour-apple scent of her hair. He'd never realized before how artificial it smelled. "And I love you...at least the parts of you left after the Darkness has taken away so much. Do you really want me to be like you? To be hollowed-out inside? To give away everything?"

"That's not what this is! Do you understand how powerful the Darkness is? You can either join them and share in that power, or you can be crushed like you're nothing! There's no choice here; don't you see?"

Terrance nodded. "That's the conclusion I came to. I either have to fight the evil or be a part of it. I also don't see much of a choice there."

Shannon frowned. "So, destruction then?"

She was right; it did seem a rather hopeless battle. But hopeless or not, he was in it. "I don't think they're powerful enough to destroy me."

Shannon gabbed Terrance by his arms and flung him effortlessly on the couch. Then she straddled him, pinning him there. "You're delusional." She moved one hand to his neck. "Do you have any idea how easy it would be for me right now to just—" She stopped and squinted at him carefully. "I smell her."

"Smell?"

"I have enhanced senses...like Wolverine." Her comfort with comic-book references reminded Terrance of why he was so attracted to her. She sniffed the air. "I thought she was dead, but..." She took her hand off Terrance's neck and brought one finger to his lips. And then her face turned so sad that Terrance wanted to reach up and comfort her except for the fact that she had pinned him quite well. "Is that what this is about?" she said.

"No, she just suddenly kissed me recently..."

Shannon tightened her grip on Terrance's shoulder. "I'm prettier. I have a larger chest. I'm quite sure I'm much more fun."

"That's not what this is about. I want to be with you...I really do. But not like this. I've chosen my side in this fight. I wish you hadn't chosen yours."

Shannon slid off of Terrance and sat on the far side of the couch, away from him. "We never finished watching *Farscape* together," she said.

"Well, if you want to know, the two main characters die at the end."

Shannon raised an eyebrow. "What?"

"Crichton and Aeryn are killed in the last episode—like, disintegrated—and it just comes out of nowhere."

"That's stupid."

"It was supposed to be a cliffhanger, but the show was canceled, so it was the last episode."

"And that was it? They're dead?"

"Well, a miniseries was made later," Terrance said. "I assume they were resurrected somehow for that."

"Assume?"

"I never saw it. I was waiting to watch it with you."

They sat there silently for a few seconds, both staring forward instead of at each other. Finally, Shannon stood up and put her mask back on. "When I see you again, I will kill you." Then she walked out of the apartment.

Terrance sat for a while longer, looking at the Best Buy bag on his coffee table. It was tempting to just forget everything for a while and finally play Legendary Quest, but he had a real quest to attend to. He got off the couch, stared for a moment at the door Shannon had walked out of, took a deep breath, and prepared to meet his destiny.

CHAPTER 36

As Terrance descended the ladder from his coat closet, he felt he was in a bit of a rush. Currently, the others were getting ready for the rescue at the fortress, and he wanted to be done with this quest in time to help, since he still felt responsible for their capture. At the same time, he had no idea how long this would take.

He was soon down in the glow of the crystal-lit caves. He walked out to the giant open area with the underground lake. There were numerous other tunnels leading out of the area, and there was also the temple across the lake, so he had no idea where to start looking.

"Hi, Terrance!" called Jenna the mermaid, popping her head out of the water. "Whatcha doing?"

"Oh, um, I'm looking for something down here that's...meant for me. Like a quest I'm supposed to do."

"I can help you find it!" Jenna exclaimed. "Just come in the water with me and I'll lead you to it!"

"You think it's in the water?" Terrance hadn't really planned on swimming, or he would have changed into swim trunks.

"Yeah, there's a lot of stuff down here in the water. I can show you!"

"I don't really want to get wet."

"Come on, you swam in this water the other day; it's really nice."

"Do not listen to her," croaked another voice. Out of the water rose the large, green scaly creature he'd met the other day. "She will lead you to your doom."

Jenna frowned at the creature. "Oh, shut up, Carl!" She looked at Terrance. "He's the one who will doom you! Just look at those teeth; he'll eat you."

It was a convincing argument; the monstrous creature, Carl, did have a huge mouth full of sharp teeth, and looked like he could easily swallow Terrance whole (or render him not whole). Still, Terrance didn't want to jump to conclusions. "Carl, I'm looking for my destiny down here—a quest meant just for me. Do you know anything about that?"

"I have existed many years and know many things. I will show you what I know if you come with me."

"He's just going to eat you if you go in the water," Jenna said. "You should come with me or you're going to really regret it."

"The mermaid—though seemingly sweet—is what you should fear," retorted Carl.

"Can't one of you just tell me where to go?" Terrance asked.

Jenna shook her head. "Not really; I kinda have to show you."

"It is I who must lead the way," Carl insisted.

Terrance grimaced. "I have to just blindly trust one of you? I don't really know either of you."

"You know me," Jenna pouted. "We talked about Aquaman and you agreed he was really cool."

"I didn't agree to that," Terrance blurted out, and quickly regretted it, as it was not an argument he wanted to waste time on again. He looked at the temple across the lake, which was one of the most conspicuous features of the cavern. "What about that temple over there? Should I check that out?"

"No, it is a terrible place," said Carl.

Jenna shook her head as if responding to whether Aquaman should be kicked out of the Justice League. "You don't want to go there. It's filled with ghosts."

"Ghosts are real?" Terrance asked.

"Yep," Jenna said. "Haven't you ever watched *Ghost Hunters*?"

Terrance smiled. "This reminds me of something: the end of the computer game *Myst*. This is a spoiler, but the game is like a million years old now. Anyway, there are two brothers who each keep telling you not to trust the other. Finally, at the end, there is one thing they agree on: don't touch the green book, because it's dangerous. So, guess what you're supposed to do?"

"Stay away from the green book because even they agree on it?" Jenna asked.

"It does seem like a terrible idea to meddle with the green book," Carl said.

"I'm going to that temple," Terrance declared. "I don't know what game you two are playing, but I'm not a part of it." He smiled, feeling proud of how he had figured things out.

"So which of us do you want to take you there?" Jenna asked.

Terrance frowned. "Oh yeah." It was quite a long swim to the temple, so it did look like he'd have to trust one of the two to get him there. He looked at the massive, scaly creature with the sharp teeth, then at the cute, smiling mermaid. "I think I'm going to have to go with the obvious choice, Carl, and have Jenna help me cross. No offense."

"None taken." Carl sank below the water until he was just a giant shadow moving down below.

"You can ride on my back!" Jenna exclaimed, moving near the shore and turning around.

"You can carry me?"

"Oh yeah, no problem. Come on!"

213

Terrance took off his glasses and put them in the hard case in his pocket that he'd thought to bring along for a situation such as this. He also took out his cellphone and set it on a nearby rock. "You think that will be fine here?"

"Yeah, it's not a high-traffic area."

Terrance slowly waded into the water and climbed onto Jenna's naked back, sitting down with his hands on her shoulders. She took off, a little faster than Terrance would have thought she could manage. "You've given people rides like this before?"

"Just short ones, since I never really go anywhere. Such are the ways of the water nymphs."

"Never go anywhere?" Then the last word finally registered in Terrance's head. "You're a nymph?"

She flipped over, sending Terrance into the water. He splashed about frantically as he looked around, seeing that he was halfway between the shore and the temple, and thus a decent distance from either. Then he saw Jenna's face as she floated in front of him. She was still smiling, but there was now something scary about the smile. "I finally have you out here alone." Before Terrance could react, Jenna disappeared below the water and Terrance felt a tug as he was yanked below as well. He hadn't properly held his breath, and was already in a panic as soon as his head dipped beneath the water. He tried to swim away, but Jenna had a tight grip on his left leg and kept pulling him further below. He was soon at the bottom of the lake, Jenna holding his leg tight as he tried to kick away. And in desperation, an odd thought came to mind—perhaps the single oddest thought since Terrance had first gotten his sword: *What would Aquaman do?* Terrance stopped trying to kick away and instead wrenched himself around so he faced Jenna. This change in movement momentarily confused the mermaid, causing her to pull closer to Terrance. Terrance got his free leg down against the lake floor and pushed himself toward Jenna, swinging his fist in a mighty underwater punch that connected to the mermaid's head. She fell back, clutching her face, allowing Terrance to burst up toward the water's surface.

He gasped for air as his head crested the surface. Terrance wasn't familiar enough with Aquaman comics to know if the superhero had ever punched a mermaid in the face, as that didn't sound very heroic even though Terrance was feeling a bit mighty at the moment. He saw the massive Carl floating a few yards away, gazing at him. "Okay, you were right," Terrance told him. "She tried to kill me."

Carl opened his giant mouth full of teeth and charged at Terrance, who had suspected that might happen and therefore already had his hand wrapped around the gun tucked into his waistband holster. He pulled out the Glock and fired at Carl, who cried out before turning and sinking beneath the surface.

Terrance awkwardly swam toward the temple while holding his gun in hand. He didn't think Aquaman ever used a gun—he knew Batman certainly never did—but he wasn't Aquaman or Batman. He was effing Terrance Denby.

Nothing else attacked him, and he soon reached a dock made of stone that stretched out in front of the temple. He pulled himself up out of the water and stood on the dock, looking back over the lake for a second before turning to look at the temple. It stretched high above him, its face ancient and crumbling, the pillars in front of the doorway looking like they might collapse at any moment. From the entrance and the windows he could see, it looked quite dark inside. It really did seem like the sort of place that would be filled with ghosts. Terrance paused for a long while as he considered whether he really wanted to enter it, but then he heard a splash behind him and quickly ran inside.

CHAPTER 37

"You have come, Terrance Denby."

The voice echoed throughout the temple. The place was dark, with a few torches scattered around, though each one seemed to give enough light only to illuminate the pillar it hung from. Terrance put his gun back into the holster tucked under his shirt and tried to brush his clothes smooth—which was rather pointless, since they were soaking wet. "Who are you?"

"I am the one who will test you." The voice seemed to come from everywhere.

"And what do I get if I pass the test?"

"What do you require?"

"I need my sword back...and any other weapon that can help me fight the forces of the Darkness and rescue those I got captured." Terrance thought a little more. "And I want answers."

"Your sword will be returned. You will get what you need to destroy the Darkness and defeat its minions. And you will get the answers to all your questions." There was the sound of stone scraping against stone, and Terrance could see a light ahead, growing bigger as a stone door lifted up. "Let us begin."

He considered asking the tester how dangerous this would be, but he realized that with what the tester had offered him, there was no way he would refuse—or at least that he shouldn't, when people were counting on him. And going forward would probably be easier not knowing. Still, he took one last glance at the exit behind him before proceeding.

He entered what appeared to be a small, empty room, lit a bit more brightly than the entryway, as this room had more torches. A sudden crash made Terrance jump, and he turned to see that the door behind him had slammed shut. It reminded him of The Legend of Zelda when Link would enter a new room in a dungeon and was about to be forced into a battle with a mini-boss.

A section of the floor began sliding away in the center of the room, and from the new hole rose a pedestal. On it, a small white rabbit sat, curiously sniffing the air. Next to the rabbit was a ball-peen hammer.

"Kill the bunny with the hammer," commanded the voice.

Terrance raised an eyebrow. "Wait? What?"

"The hammer. Take it and use it to kill the bunny, to complete this test."

Terrance looked up...not that the direction seemed to matter with the disembodied voice. "Why do you want me to kill a bunny?"

"The reasons are unimportant. I will give you all that you desire, but first the bunny must die by your hand. So pick up the hammer and crush its bunny skull. It is your destiny."

Terrance had assumed the disembodied voice was part of the quest he sought, since it knew his name, but now he was wondering if he should have asked for some form of identification. Still, if this was what it took to help the Infinite, he thought maybe he would have to kill the rabbit. He watched as the rabbit sniffed the air and seemed blissfully unaware of the drama around it. Then he stared at the hammer. He just had to pick it up and...

"Know what?" Terrance said. "This is stupid. I'm not killing a bunny, you weirdo."

The platform with the rabbit and the hammer lowered back down, and the floor closed above it. "You have passed the test of compassion," the voice said. "You may proceed." A stone door across the room now opened.

"Oh, okay. That was...interesting." Terrance headed into the new room. It was another small, empty space lit by torches, and once again the door slammed shut behind Terrance.

"Now, the test of your mind."

Terrance nodded. "Okay. That doesn't sound so bad."

"I will give you a riddle," the voice said. "You will answer it correctly or you will die."

"Die?!" Terrance looked around the empty room to try to see what might kill him. "You'll kill me if I get a riddle wrong? Is there a time limit on this?"

"You have until you die to answer," answered the voice. "Here is the riddle..." As he spoke, the words of the riddle were burned into the wall to Terrance's left.

I swing the axe triumphantly,
Fist in the air,
Only to be made the fool.
I pick a flower not for my love,
But for whom I hate the most.

Terrance stared at the words for a few seconds. "Can I at least get a category?"

"The category is: Things You Must Answer So You Will Not Die."

"You're enjoying this, aren't you?" Terrance yelled. He then tried to concentrate, because he was worried about being killed at any moment, and answering the riddle seemed like the only way out of it. And the whole reason he was here was that he believed the Infinite's claims about his own power in this world, so answering a riddle should be nothing.

He considered the part about an axe, but of all the people he could think of who wielded an axe, nothing seemed to fit the rest, not even vaguely. Then he concentrated on the last part about a flower, trying to think of when one might pick a flower for someone one hates. *Maybe if it was poison*, he thought, but still nothing fell into place. He tried to think of what other purposes one might have for this flower-picking scenario, but he couldn't think of any.

"You must answer, or you die."

"That's not helpful!" Terrance shouted up at the voice. He was shivering from his soaked clothes, so he moved near a torch, hoping it might dry him off and help him focus his mind. He stared for a moment at the flame. *A flower for one I hate...*

Terrance smiled as it all clicked into place. "I know the answer. You are Mario, from the original Super Mario Bros. game."

"Is that your final answer?"

This made Terrance hesitate, but he felt time was short if he wanted to be of any help to the others. "Yes, I mean, he has his fist in the air when he jumps to get the axe that's past Bowser, and then he's made a fool because the princess is in another castle. And the flower he picks for his enemies is the fire flower that lets him shoot fireballs. It all seems to fit. So"—Terrance took a deep breath—"final answer."

There was silence. It seemed to last an eternity, during which Terrance once again tried to imagine what could kill him in this seemingly empty room. Finally, the voice spoke. "I would also have accepted Luigi. You may proceed."

The door across from Terrance slowly slid open. Cautiously, he entered the next torch-lit room, which was much larger than the first two. He was on a raised area over a pit, and overhead was a domed ceiling with light shining down through its center, onto the pit. In the pit stood a massive figure with rippling muscles and the head of a bull.

"You will fight the Minotaur," the voice announced.

Terrance stared at the beast. It had to be at least nine feet tall, and in its hand was some sort of mace so large that Terrance doubted he would even be able to pick it up. "Well...I don't have my sword." He reached for his holster. "I do have—"

"No guns," said the voice. "You may use only the weapon I provide to you." Another torch lit up near Terrance, revealing a long wooden stick below it. "Here is a bo staff. You strike with the end of it. Either end works."

"Thanks for the bo staff fighting instruction," Terrance said through gritted teeth, as he picked up the stick and looked at the massive Minotaur. "That creature is going to smash me to pieces with his metal club thingy."

"Flanged mace," the voice told him.

"Yeah, with that." Terrance looked at the bo staff in his hands. The only experience he'd had with one was a brief period when he was younger of pretending to be Darth Maul. "And if I don't fight him?"

"Then you fail the test," the voice answered. "And those whom you know as the Infinite—both the captured ones and those going to rescue them—will die."

"You can see the future?"

"I can see the truth no matter what time it resides in."

Terrance looked again at the Minotaur, which stood silently staring back at him. "And if the Minotaur kills me?"

"Then they also die. If you wish for them to live, you must fight and win."

"And I *can* win this, right?"

"There is a possibility."

Terrance twirled the bo nervously. "Like how big?"

"You don't want to know."

"How do I know that anything you're telling me is true?"

"If you think me false, then leave. Maybe I'm lying and everyone will end up okay."

But the thing was, Terrance didn't think the voice was lying. For some reason, he knew he had to do this if he wanted to help the Infinite. Before he let himself debate it any further, he jumped into the pit.

He instantly regretted it. The Minotaur looked much larger and much fiercer up close. Still, Terrance tried to calm himself. "I don't really get what the big deal is about Minotaurs, anyway," he said, trying to keep a steady voice. "What do you have...like, bull powers?"

The Minotaur snorted and charged. Terrance fled. There wasn't much room to run around the pit, though, and the Minotaur had much longer legs. *You have to fight!* he told himself. *The only way to win is to fight.* So he pushed away the fear for a moment and stood his ground, swinging the bo as the Minotaur came near.

The Minotaur swung back with his mace (the flanged one), and the force of the blow shattered the staff and knocked Terrance to the ground. The beast stood over Terrance and reared back for the finishing blow. All Terrance had time to do was put up his arms to shield himself and wait for the end.

But the end didn't come. Terrance peeked through his arms, and the Minotaur was gone.

"You have passed the test of courage and sacrifice. You have passed all the tests, Terrance Denby. You are worthy."

Panting, Terrance got to his feet. "I'm done?"

A door opened on one side of the pit. "You are done with the tests. Now receive your reward."

Terrance entered the doorway and found a stairway leading down. There was another doorway at the bottom of the stairs that led out to a lit platform surrounded by darkness. Terrance could see neither walls nor a ceiling—just dark all around, except for the platform. What it was lit by, he could not tell. On the platform was a stone table, and on the table, a scroll. Beyond the platform, Terrance could sense something moving in the darkness—something massive. He could hear a faint sound above, of two people discussing which house to buy. "Is that my TV?"

"I often hear you in your apartment," said the voice, now clearly coming from whatever massive creature waited in the darkness before Terrance. "I have tried many times to summon you."

"You're the thing that pounds on my floor when I make noise."

"I have come to this little universe to rest, and sometimes your noise disturbs me...but that is not the matter here. You have completed the quest, and now your destiny awaits."

Terrance walked over to the table. He was hoping for something more than a scroll, but still he was quite curious about what answers were inside it. He slowly and carefully unfurled it—not certain how old it was—and read the words inside.

FEAR IS YOUR DIRECTION.

Terrance stared at the words for a few seconds. "Is this it?"

"It's a prophecy for you," the voice answered.

Terrance rolled up the scroll and set it back on the table. He took a deep breath. "Why did I waste my time on this quest when I could have just gone to a Chinese restaurant and gotten a FORTUNE COOKIE?!"

"You seem mad. Was this not what you were expecting?"

"Yes, this was not what I was expecting!" Terrance yelled. "I need a weapon, not some trite little phrase! Can you at least get me my sword back?"

"It's your sword; you're its keeper. Only you control it."

"So how do I get it back?"

"You decide that."

Terrance wanted to overturn the stone table with the scroll on it, but it looked very heavy. "Please. I've been trying to be a hero; I've been trying to fight the evil. But I'm useless out there. I need help."

"That is the problem: you've been *trying*. You need to *do*."

Terrance wanted to scream. "Now you're just paraphrasing Yoda! Why won't you help me? Didn't I pass your tests?"

"Yes...but they were kind of stupid tests."

Terrance couldn't really argue with that.

"Anyway, we're done here. Do you want to take the scroll, in case you need to read it again?"

"I think I memorized it." Terrance sighed.

"Okay. Well, I am going back to sleep. Yours is a nice quiet little universe to hide in...but I guess not so much for you. Keep the words of your prophecy in mind. And go on your way, defeat evil, remember that the power is inside you, believe in yourself, yadda yadda."

"I don't need a pep talk!" Terrance yelled. "You said before the first test that you'd give me answers, at least. So, what exactly is the Adversary? How do we defeat him? Am I really some sort of infinite being?"

"I said you would get answers. I did not say when or from whom."

Terrance seethed quietly for a few moments. "Here's what I'm going to do now: I'm going to take up tap dancing and practice it every day."

"If you do, I will complain to your landlord."

Terrance shuddered. "Don't do that."

CHAPTER 38

There was a ladder leading out of the pit, and the doors between the rooms were all open, so Terrance quickly made his way back outside the temple to the giant, crystal-lit cavern. He saw a small boat with oars at the stone dock, which he rowed back to shore. After he got out of the boat, he heard a splash behind him. He turned and saw Jenna sticking her head out of the water, a big shiner on her left eye.

"You gave me a black eye," she said, frowning.

His first instinct was to apologize, as she was so pathetic-looking, but he stopped himself. "You tried to drown me. You got off easy."

"And I think you really hurt Carl. Do you have a permit to carry around a gun like that?"

Terrance felt a small pang of fear. "I...uh...don't have to show you that. Again, you tried to kill me. What was that all about?"

"Oh, it was nothing." Jenna waved her hand dismissively. "It's just what we water nymphs do. We try to seduce men using our feminine wiles, to trick them into the water so we can kill them. To be more progressive, we now sometimes try to do it with women too...but not as successfully. Not to be homophobic, but it kind of makes me uncomfortable to seduce and kill a woman."

Terrance stared at her in disbelief. "And why do you do this?"

"I already told you: because I'm a water nymph. The others nymphs say I'm not that good at the seducing because I spend too much time reading comic books, but it really seems to me that most of it is just not having a shirt on."

"Oh, you like comic books," he said, laughing. "Who is your favorite superhero?"

Jenna thought for a moment. "Power Girl."

Terrance grimaced. "Really? Out of curiosity, how do you read comic books?"

"I have a waterproof tablet, and I read them digitally."

Terrance picked up his cellphone from the rock where he'd left it. "And you have money to buy them?"

"No, I just use credit card fraud," Jenna explained cheerily.

"Have you ever thought about not murdering people and not committing credit card fraud?"

Jenna thought about it for a moment. "Nope. Hey, so how'd your quest go?"

"It was...pointless."

Jenna frowned. "I'm sorry. Well, do you want to come in the water again? It's nice and warm, and I won't try drowning you this time."

"No. Goodbye, Jenna."

"See you around!" the mermaid called as Terrance walked away.

"Probably not," Terrance answered. He made his way back to the long ladder and up to his apartment, where he changed into dry clothes and plopped down on the couch, trying to think of what to do next. He had been so certain this quest would finally make him a warrior—that he would get some new weapon and be what he knew he should be in the fight against evil. But he was still empty-handed. He would now give anything to at least get his sword back. He tried to remember when he first got the sword. He'd always thought the faeries had given it to him, but he didn't recall any of them carrying it. It was just there on the ground after he talked to them. Did he make it appear?

Terrance closed his eyes and envisioned the sword lying in front of him. When he opened his eyes, all he saw was the blue bag with the video game from Shannon.

"Trying to use the Force, mate?"

Startled, Terrance turned to see Beauregard standing next to the couch. "You wouldn't be able to help me get my sword back, would you?"

The elf hopped onto the couch. "Nope, not really in my wheelhouse. So you went on a big quest? Did the giant entity that lives below end up being any help?"

From Beauregard's little smile, Terrance could tell he already knew the answer. "I received a prophecy: 'Fear is your direction.'"

"And what do you fear right now?" Beauregard asked.

"Pretty much everything."

The elf patted him on the back. "Then you have a lot of directions to choose from."

Terrance took a deep breath. "Am I really an infinite being with great power to fight evil?"

"You look more like a schlub on a couch. You know, I told you not to get involved in all this. But no one listens to me. Like when I showed your friends the underground passage to the fortress on the mountain—I told them it wasn't going to end well for them, but they didn't listen."

"You know where they are?" Vivian had seemed confident that Terrance would just find them after his quest, but he wasn't sure how. He was about to try texting Talia, but then realized he'd never gotten her phone number.

"I know lots of things," Beauregard said. "I just kind of hover around watching, observing. And somehow people get a sinister vibe from me."

"You're like a squirrel."

"Exactly."

Terrance stood up. "Can you take me to them?"

"That's not a good idea. You don't have a weapon, and even if you did...well, come on. How do you expect to be of any help to them?"

"I don't know. I at least want to tell them that I tried, and to see if there is something I can do. Maybe I can just carry things, but I'm going."

Beauregard hopped off the couch. "If you want, I can go tell them you completed your quest, but that you're still weaponless and useless and will just get in their way."

"I'm not abandoning them again. And I'm not abandoning this fight; I will not ignore the evil out there. I might not be able to do much, but I'm not doing nothing. You know what I'm afraid of? Giving up. I guess that gives me some direction."

Beauregard laughed. "You people are such gluttons for punishment. You can't even comprehend the danger you're about to wander into."

"I haven't been able to comprehend a lot of things lately." It would be lying for Terrance to say he wasn't terrified, but he knew it was right to at least try to help the Infinite. And with nothing else making much sense, he'd stick to what little he knew. "Whose side are you on, anyway? All you ever seem to do is try to convince me to give up. Is that reverse psychology?"

"Could be regular psychology."

Terrance studied Beauregard for a moment. "I'm not going to get straight answers out of you, am I?"

"Only to questions you'd rather not be answered."

Terrance rolled his eyes. "So will you please take me to Vivian and the others?"

"Well, since you said the magic word, follow me." Beauregard led him back down the ladder to the caverns below Terrance's apartment. He took a different tunnel than the one that led to the lake, and soon it began to darken as no more crystals were visible in the walls. Just when there was nearly no light left, Terrance saw a minecart before them.

"Am I getting in that?"

Beauregard nodded. "Yep. Only way you'll catch up with your friends. Ever ride a minecart before?"

Terrance climbed into the rusty metal cart. "Like in *The Temple of Doom*? No."

"Well, this won't be as scary as that, because you won't be able to see anything." Beauregard walked over and pulled a lever, and the cart started to click and clack down the track, a little uneasily at first but soon picking up speed. Almost immediately, Terrance was plunged into pitch darkness. The cart was shaking fiercely, and he felt he must be traveling at a tremendous speed, but he could see nothing around him to judge how fast he was going. Except for an occasional pair of shining eyes.

Terrance ducked further down into the cart, to get out of view of the eyes. Eventually, he felt the cart change speed, and he peeked out to see light ahead. The cart was about to careen into a wooden barrier, and he let out a yell, but it bumped against the barrier with only a slight jolt and came to a stop. Terrance peeked further up out of the cart and saw Vivian on the other side of the barrier, holding a torch.

"Wow, you do everything spazzy, don't you?" Karen asked. She was standing behind Vivian along with Felicia, Donald, and Talia.

"How did the quest go?" Vivian asked.

Terrance climbed out of the cart as everyone looked at him expectantly (well, Talia just looked at him with her typical stoic, slightly disdainful gaze). "I completed it, I guess," Terrance told them. "All I really got out of it was a...prophecy."

"Did that help?" Vivian inquired.

Terrance shrugged, although "no" seemed like a more honest answer.

"Still haven't gotten your sword back?" Talia asked.

"No."

"I'm sure you'll figure things out soon," Donald said.

"Yeah, you completed a quest by yourself," Felicia said. "That has to mean something."

Terrance walked over to join them. "I hope so."

"Anyway, we'll be there soon," Vivian said. "Just help how you can, and I'm sure you'll do well."

She and the others seemed sincere, but he couldn't help but feel like he was the "special" kid whose self-esteem they were trying to improve. They continued their march through the dark caves, Vivian leading the way with her torch. Talia stayed at the rear and touched Terrance's shoulder, slowing him so that they dropped a bit behind the others and could talk privately. "I just wanted to clarify about the kiss," Talia whispered. "I'm not trying to have sex with you or anything."

Terrance chuckled. "I know; women can't control themselves around me because I have such animal magnetism."

"You really don't."

Terrance's smile disappeared. "So what did you want to clarify about the kiss?"

"Just that I didn't want to have sex with you. I'm not that kind of girl."

"The kind who has sex?"

"Relationships between people are not something to take lightly," Talia said. "Lust makes you see people more as objects than as the beings they really are. It's another thing in this world that pulls you into it and puts blinders on you, preventing you from seeing what truly *is*. Plus our relationships with other people define much of who we are—not just here but for our true selves beyond this world. So one must be quite careful with one's relationships."

Terrance sighed. "I already broke up with Shannon—and did it a second time in person before my quest—if that's what you're getting at. She said she's going to kill me when she sees me again."

"I wasn't talking about you," Talia snapped. "Not everything is about you. And it's not unlikely that we'll see Shannon soon, so I hope you're prepared to fight her."

"Oh, yeah. Super prepared. Have I shown you my invisible sword?"

Talia glared at him. "What is your problem? I'm getting really tired of your attitude. Everyone else is cheery, knowing they are in a worthwhile fight against evil and that we will win, while you do nothing but mope and brood."

Terrance grimaced. "You're not cheery."

"I'm...cheery on the inside."

"Well, I'm having a little trouble with the cheer, because as hard as I try at this, I don't seem to get anywhere. I know it's my own fault that I threw away my sword, but I was never any good with it anyway. I don't know what I'm doing wrong; I went through this whole quest thing hoping that it would lead to my finally becoming a warrior or whatever it is we need, but all I got was a useless little phrase on a scroll and then was told, 'Do or do not; there is no try.'"

Talia nodded. "That is your problem: you're *trying*."

"What's that supposed to mean? You're the one who keeps pushing me to be more."

"To *be* more, not try to be." Talia thought for a moment. "Maybe I did wrong by you; you didn't seem to get the message. You told me you fought a vampire while unarmed."

"Yeah, he laid me down with one blow."

"Why did you fight him?"

"He was about to bite some woman, so I felt I had to do something, but I didn't have any ability to fight him."

"And what happened to the woman?" Talia asked.

"Well, while the vampire smacked me, she snapped out of her trance and got away."

"And later, you fought that demon to save those kids."

Terrance sighed. "I had my sword that time, but it was swatted out of my hand before I even had a chance to swing it. I only survived because you saved me."

"The kids got away because you intervened," Talia said. "And in the food court, you helped me fight that Hollow One."

"Yes, she had superpowers, and I'm not even good at using a sword against a regular person."

"Yet you jumped right in, and we won that battle—a good part of that because you distracted her and tripped her up. And Karen told me how you took on a demon in your office."

"Yeah, my boss." Terrance shook his head. "I don't even know what I was thinking there. I didn't have my sword and knew I had no chance against him."

"Yet you stood up to him," Talia said.

"Well…yeah…but I would have been dead if not for Karen."

"Yes, she told me how your fight inspired her to action. And today, did you not take on a quest by yourself, not knowing the danger?"

"It was pretty stupid," Terrance said. "Though once again, it was demonstrated that I don't know what I'm doing. I had to fight a giant Minotaur, and I barely lasted a second against it."

"You thought you'd do better?"

"Well, I had hoped…but no, I didn't really see how I could defeat it."

"So why did you fight it even if you thought you couldn't win?"

"The tester told me that you guys would be doomed if I didn't finish the quest," Terrance said. "It didn't seem like I had a choice."

"You had a choice. And you chose to face nearly certain death to help others."

"And was easily defeated. I was just lucky the Minotaur didn't actually kill me as part of the test."

Talia shook her head. "I don't know how you're not getting this. Remember when you saved me?"

Terrance furrowed his brow. "When did I save you?"

"When we first met. When they were going to feed me to that thing under your office building."

"I didn't save you. You broke free and saved yourself."

She hesitated for a moment. "You know, their goal isn't to kill us in this world—at least not until they break us first. They can only feed off of us if we do not fight back. Their forces got me at a bad time, and what you saw, I believe, was their idea of a final straw to break me. They wanted me to plead and cry for help in a room full of people while no one paid attention—to show me how fruitless resisting them was just before that creature tore me apart. But it didn't work." A tear slid down Talia's cheek. "Someone spoke up. And that was enough to remind me what I am and that the forces of the Darkness are never as powerful as they seem. When others just watched as evil raged before them, you had the courage to act. And that saved me."

Her face was very serious, as usual, but he detected something else in her expression: admiration. "I just did what it seemed like someone should do," Terrance said.

"As you have done many other times, with good results. That is my point. You are trying to be a hero, but you have no reason to *try*. You just need to be what you already are." She hesitated, then added, "Well, maybe that plus just a little bit more." She pulled back her cloak and removed the sword and sheath from her right hip. "Here. Take this."

"I couldn't."

"I have two. Just take it and stop worrying about your sword. You have the power to fight evil; just understand that."

He took the sword and attached the sheath to his belt. He felt a little odd, wearing a girl's sword, but it certainly made him feel better to have a weapon for taking on what lay ahead.

"There, you smiled," Talia said, stoic as usual. "That's the right attitude."

"Hey, what are you two doing back there in the dark?" Karen called out.

They had let the others and Vivian's single torch get quite a way ahead of them, so they ran to catch up. "Just making sure Terrance is prepared," Talia said.

"Good, because we're about there," Vivian said, pointing ahead of them down the tunnel toward an eerie red glow.

They moved forward, and soon emerged from the cave into a large cavern, where heat sweltered about them. The path was now a rock bridge, and on either side was a drop of about a hundred feet, into glowing red lava. Terrance watched as something large emerged from the lava and quickly dived back into it with a small splash. "Well, that's ominous."

"We're venturing into the heart of evil in this sliver of reality," Talia said. "You can't even fathom the horrors that await us here."

Karen looked a bit worried. Donald noticed this and said, "Let's not go overboard; we're going to be okay."

"I said they are hard to fathom," Talia answered. "I didn't say we couldn't defeat them."

"But everyone certainly be on your guard now," Vivian said as they all continued to move slowly across the stone bridge over the lava.

There was a noise. A ringing. Terrance pulled out his phone and saw that it was Pendergrass. "Oh. It's work." He answered, just as he thought he probably should have sent it to voicemail. "Hello?"

"Hey, Terrance, where did you go?" Pendergrass asked.

"Well, after Karen and I slew Darlor, I assumed we were fired."

"Oh, well I don't know about that. That's an HR matter, and they haven't contacted me. I really need you to work on that legacy algorithm code."

"Okay. Yeah. Well, right now I'm in the middle of something. Have you noticed how the forces of the Darkness are hunting people down?"

"Um...I've seen something of that. Why?"

"They might be after me, too, which could make it hard to get to the office."

"Then telecommute. You should be able to do everything remotely."

"Okay, I'll do that," Terrance said. "I'll get in touch with you tomorrow."

"Sounds good. Bye."

Terrance hung up and looked around at the group, fumbling to get his phone back into his pocket. "Sorry about that. It was work. I guess I still have to go in tomorrow...if I survive this."

"We'll be fine," Vivian assured him.

"I still have my job?" Karen asked.

"I guess—apparently there isn't actually any rule against slaying a demon," Terrance said. "But I'd talk to your supervisor."

"So, we good to go?" Felicia asked, looking ready to burst. "I want to find these things that we can't fathom that took everyone, and punch them in the face."

Vivian smiled and led them forward to the end of the stone bridge. Her smile looked genuine, yet Terrance detected some hidden worry there. As they got to the other side of the bridge, they entered a new stone-lined tunnel, which was dead silent—somehow *more* than silent, like the ominous quiet just before a storm hits. Terrance may not have lost his job, but he was not very confident that he would be back at work tomorrow.

CHAPTER 39

Following directions Beauregard had given them, they moved some stones to give themselves just enough space to crawl through the tunnel wall into what looked like a storage closet. Inside were old-looking shackles, rusty knives, a disturbingly worn-looking axe, a vacuum cleaner, and a copy of Monopoly with a box so worn that it was barely holding together.

The closet was pretty cramped when all six of them had climbed in. "So I guess we've snuck into the fortress," Terrance said. "Now what?"

"Make sure your phone is on vibrate," Donald answered.

"It is...now."

Vivian opened the door a crack and peered out. "The coast is clear." She pushed the door the rest of the way open and led everyone out into a dimly lit hallway with more stone walls.

"So how will we find the dungeon?" Karen asked.

Felicia pointed to a You Are Here type of map hanging on a nearby wall. It showed that the dungeon was on the same floor and just a little further down the hallway. Vivian led the way as the group carefully crept along, keeping a lookout in all directions. Eventually they came to a huge, open area with a ceiling at least three stories high and barred prison cells lining the walls. It didn't have a solid floor, though—only a rope bridge stretching from one end of the dungeon to the other. Judging by the glow coming from beneath the bridge, Terrance assumed more lava lay below. A pair of cavefish stood near the entrance but hadn't noticed the group hanging back in the shadows of the hallway.

"Quickly and quietly," Vivian whispered.

Talia and Donald snuck up on the two guards and slew them both before they could sound an alarm. "I got the keys," Talia announced, holding aloft a key ring after yanking it off of one of the dead cavefish.

"But where are they?" Donald asked, looking around.

Terrance and the rest crept into the dungeon. There were hundreds of cells lining the walls—some high up above them—but they all looked empty.

"Over here!"

They turned to see Curtis calling to them from a cell at the far end of the dungeon. In the cells next to him were Joyce, Travis, and Erica.

"Let's be quick about this," Vivian said as she led the way across the rope bridge. It was solid enough but still swayed a bit much for Terrance's taste, especially when he looked down at the lava below and the things moving inside it. Still, they crossed the bridge with no problem, and Talia moved quickly to unlock the cells.

Curtis immediately ran to embrace Vivian. "We were wondering when you would show up." He looked at Terrance. "And you're alive! Last we saw, you were falling off the ship."

"Yeah, I don't really understand the physics there," Terrance said. "But somehow I didn't splat."

"They had us scheduled for execution today," Joyce said, "and I'm the surgeon on call tomorrow. So that wasn't going to work."

Erica spotted Karen. "Hi, I guess you're new. I'm Erica."

Karen introduced herself and shook Erica's hand. "I'm a friend of Terrance's...and Shannon's."

Erica nodded. "Ah, well, Shannon can be very nice...some of the time. Anyway, thanks for coming to rescue us."

"It was nothing," Karen said, and it really had been. This had seemed far too easy to Terrance, but with the combination of the secret passage and the forces of the Darkness being engaged elsewhere, he thought that maybe that was all it was.

"I'm really sorry about all of this...and about Randolph," Terrance told the group.

"It's not your fault, bro," Travis said. "You're just trying to do what's right, like the rest of us...and sometimes it's harder than we think. I'm sure Randolph is doing well wherever he is now. He'll just be waiting on us to finally bring the fight to the Adversary."

"Are you all okay?" Felicia asked. "What did they do to you?"

"Just the usual nonsense of trying to convince us that we're doomed," Joyce said. "If you get good at ignoring their threats, it becomes white noise and is actually kind of relaxing."

"Now let's find our weapons. They should be nearby," Curtis said, heading back over the bridge with the rest following. He was near the other end when a figure emerged from the shadows.

"Stop right there." It was Shannon in her new ninja outfit, with her sword held out, touching the rope supports of the bridge. "Or you all die right now."

"Shannon?" Karen exclaimed. "Why are you wearing a mask? It's not doing a good job concealing your identity, so I don't see the point."

"It's just cool-looking." With her free hand, Shannon touched the demonic gaping maw of the mask that concealed her nose and mouth. "What are you doing with these idiots?"

"I'm fighting evil," Karen said. "And I guess you're evil. Plus, you look really stupid in your new outfit."

"No, I don't," Shannon retorted, and Terrance had to agree: she did look pretty cool. Shannon tapped the rope with her sword. "But you're going to look really stupid clutching that axe as you fall into lava."

"Come on, Shannon!" Terrance pleaded loudly, stuck near the back of the group. "You don't want to kill us!"

"No, I want to kill *you*," Shannon yelled. "The rest will just be *with* you."

"Not an amicable breakup, huh?" Donald said.

"It's still not too late," Curtis told her.

Shannon laughed. "Oh, what the hell do you know? Hey, Karen, please explain to me what it is that you all are hoping to accomplish."

Karen hesitated. "Well...I'm kinda new at this. I don't really get the big picture yet."

"None of these imbeciles know what they're doing!" Shannon shouted. "We're trying to keep order, and you people ruin everything and force us to attack you. Yet you still can't even begin to understand the power you're messing with!"

"Well, sure," Joyce said, laughing. "Only someone backed by a force of immense power could threaten to cut a rope."

Shannon frowned. "Yes, try to act like this is just a joke." Behind her, more enemies emerged—Hollow Ones and cavefish. Despina appeared, holding two small figures close to her: Grace and Daniel. Vivian and Curtis gasped.

Despina smiled wickedly. "Any bravado left?"

"Mommy!" Grace cried. "This woman is scaring us!"

"It's going to be okay," Vivian said in a calm voice as if merely reassuring her about a spider. "This is just silly adult stuff." She looked at Despina. "What happened to my parents, who were watching them?"

Despina laughed. "The rules are changing. You can't keep anyone safe."

Terrance was horrified. He had to do something, but there was little he could do, stuck near the back of the rope bridge. "This is what you want to be a part of, Shannon?"

"This is all there is!" she shouted back.

"So do you surrender, concerned parents?" Despina cooed.

"Why?" Curtis growled. "Because you are threatening our children? You and all the Darkness out there threaten our children every single day! This is why we fight, and we will never back down!"

"All that's changed is that you're now more direct," Vivian said, her tone more subdued yet somehow more threatening than Curtis's. "It just shows how desperate you are. How much you fear us. And I assure you, your fear is well-placed."

Despina sighed. "Well, you're quite fearsome, stupidly marching right into our trap. Now we get to execute you in front of these wireless video cameras, which are connected to the worldwide internet. We're going to be...um...flowing the video—"

"Live streaming," Shannon corrected her.

"Live streaming the video," Despina continued, "so everyone around the world will see on their computer monitors what happens to people like you."

"We knew this was a trap," Vivian said. "That's why we always had other plans."

"We had other plans?" Terrance whispered to Talia.

"Oh, yes, sorry," she said. "I guess we came up with them while you were out questing, and never told you."

There were sounds coming from outside. Explosions. Shouting. Despina looked around in confusion. "What's going on?"

"We know that when the forces of the Darkness act the strongest, that is when you are the weakest," Vivian said. "So our plan was never simply to free the others and flee. Our plan was to fight—as it is the plan of the other Infinite. You've increased your attacks on us to try to get us to cower, but instead we are all here and ready to crush you, ready to march through those gates that your fortress protects."

There was fear on Despina's face, and she backed away, still clutching the children. "You fools. You don't know what you're doing." She turned to Shannon. "Cut the rope."

Shannon made one last bit of eye contact with Terrance, and then swung her sword, severing one of the rope supports. The bridge lurched to one side, and instinctively Terrance moved backward toward the stable ground behind him. He turned to see Joyce make a dive off the bridge onto the ground, and he tried to follow as the other support began to snap. He jumped the ledge and landed right at the edge as the bridge gave way beneath him. He scrambled for something to grab on to as he began to slip off, but Joyce grabbed his arm and helped pull him to safety. Terrance spun around to see the rest of his friends clinging to the bridge as it dangled over the lava.

"Gonna be one of those days," Joyce said. "Now let's just help—"

As Terrance began to stand up, he saw movement behind Joyce. "Look out!" he cried as Joyce turned to receive an axe blow to her abdomen. She fell back into Terrance, who helped her to the ground as Chet stood back watching and chuckling softly. Terrance frantically tried to find a spot to apply pressure to Joyce's wound, but there was blood everywhere.

Joyce grabbed his wrist. "You're taking this way too seriously." She smiled, and then went still.

Chet readied his axe. "Now I just need to cut a few more ropes, and you can watch the rest of your friends fall and burn."

The captured children, his friends dangling over lava behind him, Joyce's dead body—it was hard not to take seriously. In fact, it was overwhelming. But out of all the emotions boiling inside Terrance, one won out: anger. And he had someone he was quite ready to take that anger out on. He stood and drew his borrowed sword, yelling as he charged at Chet. Chet surprised him with a backhand, knocking him to the ground.

"Pathetic," Chet chuckled. "By the way, Shannon is very sad about how things ended with you." He faced the end of the rope bridge and raised his axe. "Sad and looking for comfort."

Terrance stumbled back to his feet as Chet's axe fell. He swung his sword at the axe head with all his might, and the clash of the weapons knocked him back, but the path of the axe was deflected enough that it struck the ground, missing the rope by less than an inch.

With a quick glance down, Terrance could see that the others were still uneasily climbing up the dangling bridge. He looked back at Chet, who towered over him with the giant axe, poised to strike. He was speaking again, some sort of mocking, but Terrance wasn't listening. He was concentrating on one thing: he was going to kill Chet.

Terrance ran at him, and Chet swung his axe. Terrance ducked under the arc of the blade and swung his sword at Chet in response, but Chet somehow positioned the metal axe handle so that it blocked the blow. He shoved Terrance with the axe handle, knocking him back to the ground, then swung at him again, but Terrance rolled out of the way and the axe blade embedded itself into the stone. Terrance saw his chance and sprung to his feet, swinging his sword as hard as he could at Chet's head. And it connected...with a useless clang.

Chet laughed as he freed his axe from the stone floor and stood up straight. "How am I to withstand the power of the Infinite?" His laughing was interrupted when he had to quickly block a blow from Talia. Terrance glanced back to see Donald scrambling up, as well.

"There's a battle outside," Chet said as he backed away. "I'll see you out there." He headed behind the cells and disappeared.

Terrance looked at Joyce lying dead on the ground, then at the sword in his hand. "I couldn't even pierce his armor. I don't get it. I can't even—"

He was interrupted by Talia's smacking him across the cheek. "Stop whining. You kept him from cutting the bridge. Good job."

Terrance and Donald went to the dangling bridge and helped the others climb up. They were soon all safely on the ground, looking uneasily at the corpse of Joyce.

"They're going to kill us, aren't they?" Karen asked, cradling her axe.

"They can only harm us in this world, nothing more," Curtis said. "But they can never defeat us. Not when we fight."

It sounded like a fierce battle outside, with shouts and explosions. "We need to join the fight," Vivian said. "We need to"—her confident facade cracked, and tears welled in her eyes—"rescue Grace and Daniel."

Curtis rushed to her and held her tight. "We will."

"This is the day the forces of the Darkness will know defeat," Felicia said.

Talia bent down and gently closed Joyce's eyelids. "Evil knows defeat every day on its march toward destruction." She stood up and drew her sword. "But today they no longer get to hide from that fact."

CHAPTER 40

They quickly found an exit on their side of the dungeon behind the cells.

"We need to find our weapons," Erica said.

"They're never far," Curtis replied. They were soon in a hallway, and there was one door to their left. Curtis opened it, and inside was an armory filled with swords and maces, all black in color with jagged edges, basically screaming, "Hey! Look at me! I'm a weapon of evil!" But there was also a chest, which Curtis proceeded to open. "And here they are." He handed swords back to Travis and Erica, along with Erica's bow.

"So I'm the only one with an axe?" Karen asked.

"That just means you're special," Felicia said.

Terrance peered into the chest. "My sword wouldn't happen to be there, would it?"

"You lost your sword?" Curtis asked.

"Um...yeah. I'm borrowing one of Talia's."

"Well..." Curtis patted him on the back. "I'm sure it will turn up."

Terrance peered into the chest. "What about"—he hesitated—"Joyce's sword?"

Curtis had a melancholy smile. "It's not there."

They headed back into the hallway, up some stairs, then down another hallway until they came to the entrance of the fortress. There, the large, wooden front doors were open, revealing the scene outside. Everywhere there was fighting, as men and women clashed with opponents in black armor. But for each fighter that appeared to be one of the Infinite, there seemed to be five of the enemy. In the dark, cloudy sky, Terrance could see the silhouettes of many chimeras and a few griffins flying about. Every so often he saw fireballs stream by, and he assumed they didn't come from his side.

"Well, this is exciting," Travis said, keeping close to Erica.

"We find Grace and Daniel and get them back," Vivian said. "Then we head for the gate and what lies beyond."

They charged out into the field. Terrance glanced behind them at the fortress, beyond which he could see giant stone gates, closed and impenetrable-looking. He wasn't quite sure he wanted to know what lay beyond them.

Their group soon clashed with a dozen cavefish. Terrance mainly stood out of the way, while the others handled them deftly, even Karen easily felling a couple with swings of her axe. But Terrance soon spotted a golden, nearly naked figure standing in a field nearby. "There's Despina!" he yelled.

They ran toward her. She stood in an open area, alone except for Grace and Daniel, whom she held close. "You've made a big mistake, demon," Curtis growled.

As the group neared, black smoke enveloped them. When it faded away, they were surrounded on all sides by cavefish and Hollow Ones.

Despina laughed. "You people really enjoy charging into traps. I hope we're filming everything so the world can watch it on the...um...computer stream. You know what I mean, the uh..."

With a guttural scream, Vivian charged Despina, who was forced to dodge away and let go of the children. The surrounding enemy descended on the group, and fighting erupted all around Terrance. Ready to help, he charged the nearest target—a Hollow One—but his enemy strongly parried the blow, sending Terrance off-balance. Just as the Hollow One was about to counter, another blade cut through its armor.

"We need to get them out of here!" Curtis shouted as the Hollow One burnt away. Grace and Daniel huddled against his legs, obviously scared.

Terrance nodded to Curtis, but Curtis immediately had to turn away to handle another attacking enemy. Terrance grabbed Grace by the hand, and she held on to her brother with her other hand, and seeing an opening in the fray, Terrance urged, "Come on," as gently as he could while still making himself heard over shouts and clashes of metal. He began to lead the children away, but soon a cavefish attacked, so Terrance blocked with the sword in his right hand while still holding on to Grace with his left. He tried to attack back but swung too wide. The cavefish reared back to stab, but an arrow in its forehead jerked its head back. Terrance didn't have time to spot Erica in order to thank her, and put all his effort into getting the kids out of the melee. Somehow they made it out of the clashing forces without further incident, and he spotted a cave at the edge of the battlefield that could be reached by steps made of rocks.

"We're almost there," he reassured the children, frequently glancing back over his shoulder to see if anyone was following them and to make sure Grace still had Daniel. They climbed the rock steps and entered a spacious cave, its interior lit by an eerie yellow glow that Terrance figured was from lava in some unseen precipice. He started to wonder whether going into a cave around here was a smart idea, not knowing what kind of things might be lurking inside.

"Mommy and Daddy are fighting the bad people?" Grace asked.

Terrance nodded. "Yeah...they should be here soon."

Daniel was nearly in tears. "It's scary here."

"Well, there's nothing to worry about. I'm one of the good guys, and I'm here to protect you."

"Oh, are you?" someone laughed.

Terrance looked up. It was Lacey in her dark demon armor, standing just inside the cave entrance.

Vicky strode up beside her, smiling wickedly and twirling her sword. "I believe we made some threat about tearing you apart if you broke Shannon's heart."

"And she's quite upset," Lacey said. "I think she'll move on, though. You, on the other hand, are not leaving this cave."

Terrance pushed the children behind him and pointed his sword at Lacey. His heart was racing, but he tried to slow his breathing. "Don't act like you care for Shannon. I saw how scared you were when you thought we were going to save her. And I assure you, you have good reason to fear me."

Elissa and Amber entered the cave, brandishing their weapons. Amber smirked. "I know there is a big battle going on outside, but let's take our time with this."

Terrance held his sword as steady as he could and managed a smile. "You think you brought enough to take me on?"

"Little dearies," Lacey said in an overly sweet voice to Grace and Daniel, "you might want to close your eyes. It's about to get R-rated for gore and violence."

"Why are you wearing that?" Grace asked.

"I'm a warrior fighting to protect the world from crazy nutjobs," Lacey explained. "You can be one too when you grow up."

"You look like a bad person," Daniel said.

"Well, I'm not. We're the people keeping this world together and making sure it doesn't fall into destruction and chaos."

"Then why do you look so evil?" Grace asked.

Lacey sighed. "You're a stupid kid, so you're not going to understand." She looked at Terrance. "Now, Terrance, prepare to die."

"Why don't you two go sit behind that rock over there," Terrance said, pointing to a large rock behind them. The kids did as he said, and Terrance turned to face his four enemies, pointing his sword tip at Lacey's eyes. He took a deep breath. "I warn you: I'm very good at this."

She giggled. "Oh, the big hero. Going to slay all the bad people. It'll be an epic battle, I'm sure. We'll probably—"

Terrance charged her, thinking surprise might be his only chance to get even one of them. Lacey took a single step back, and Terrance's swing hit nothing but air. He swung so hard, though, that the sword flew from his hand and clanged against the cave wall.

Lacey and her friends erupted in laughter. "Oh wow," Lacey said, walking up and patting the now-unarmed Terrance on the shoulder. "Do you need a mulligan on that swing there, champ? I really don't get how you deluded fools think—"

Terrance silenced her with a head-butt. He had never head-butted anyone before—not on purpose, anyway—and he instantly regretted it. He doubted that he'd hurt her more than he'd hurt himself as he stumbled back, dazed. Out of the corner of his eye, he could see Amber charging him. He ducked down, but lost his balance and tumbled into her legs, tripping her. He scrambled on all fours for his sword, grabbing it and swinging it around just in time to block a blow from Elissa.

"Mommy!" Daniel yelled excitedly.

They all turned to see Vivian entering the cave with a glare that could melt steel.

Lacey giggled. "Oh no! The mama bear is angry! She's gonna give us all a whuppin'."

"Stay away from my children," Vivian growled.

"But we're saving them," Elissa said. "Saving them from silly people like you who—"

Vivian charged, swinging her sword. Elissa tried to block, but her sword shattered and Vivian sliced right through her. Vicky attacked next, but Vivian parried her blow and cut cleanly through Vicky's helmet and head. With that, both Elissa and Vicky were gone in a blue fire.

Terrance jumped to his feet, and with Amber's back to him, he charged for the kill. She spun around, but Terrance continued with his stab, impaling Amber through the torso. Somehow, she still managed to wallop him with her gauntleted left hand, sending Terrance stumbling backward and spitting blood. She struck at Terrance with her sword and he tried dodging away, but the blade cut into his arm, the pain making him yelp and fall back to the ground.

Amber stood over Terrance, his sword embedded just below her ribs. He'd thought there was supposed to be some sort of vulnerable spot on the Hollow Ones near where he'd struck her, but he now realized he probably should have had someone clarify exactly where that spot was. As he crawled on his back away from Amber, he glanced behind her to see Vivian fall as she fought Lacey. Vivian wasn't going to save him; it was up to him to save her.

Amber reared her weapon back for the killing blow, but he leapt to his feet, grabbing the sword that was still stuck in her torso and yanking it upward. It sliced straight through her chest and she instantly burnt away to nothing. Terrance had no time to savor the victory, as Lacey was pressing an attack on Vivian, so he ran toward Lacey and attempted to strike a blow. She met his blade with hers, knocking him back a little. She looked from Terrance to Vivian, who stood holding one hand over a bloody thigh wound but didn't look any less determined. "Oh, take the stupid kids," Lacey sighed. "You're all going to die here anyway." She ran out of the cave.

Vivian stumbled past Terrance toward Grace and Daniel, who were still standing by the rock Terrance had sent them to. She hugged them and asked if they were okay.

"Those bad ladies were trying to hurt you and Mr. Terrance," Daniel cried.

Vivian hugged them tighter. "Yes, but they're gone now, so you don't have to worry."

Terrance looked at the wound on his left arm. It was shallow and bleeding only a little, so he decided to ignore it for now. Of more concern was the scene outside. The cave entrance offered a pretty good vantage point of the battlefield in front of the fortress, the whole scene lit brightly by a full moon. There was fighting everywhere, yet Terrance could mainly see only the forces of the Darkness.

"Thanks for your help," Vivian said, limping up next to him.

He smiled. "Just doing what I can."

"That's all any of us can do."

Terrance continued to peer out at the battlefield but was able to spot only a few people from his side. Fireballs flew through the air, and everywhere were screams and the clash of steel. "It doesn't look good out there."

Vivian nodded grimly. "It never does."

Terrance knew Shannon was out there, too. That made him apprehensive, when it seemed he should have been scared enough simply by the threat of death.

"It's scary here," Daniel cried, hugging Vivian's unwounded leg.

"Why are there all these bad people trying to hurt everyone?" Grace asked softly.

Vivian knelt down to address her children. "People can be silly sometimes, and they can forget what's right and what's wrong, but don't you worry about that. Instead, look at all the good people who have come to stop them. No matter how scary things get, there will always be good people who will help. So you don't have to worry or be afraid, because you're never alone. There will always be good to fight the bad, and the good ones will never give up. Okay?"

The kids nodded, and she hugged them again. "Where's Daddy?" Grace asked.

"He's out there fighting the bad people," Vivian explained. "We'll see him soon."

Daniel suddenly gasped, staring out at the field. Terrance followed his gaze to see the battlefield darken further. Blocking the sky was the dark, gigantic form of Malcus. He roared, a terrible scream that made Terrance want to hide and cower, but instead he was frozen in place by fear. Dark flames shot from Malcus's mouth, burning a section of the battlefield until nothing—until no one—was left there.

Terrance turned to Vivian, who could no longer hide her fear about her husband's being out there, exposed. He glanced down at Grace, but she didn't look worried. Instead, she looked up at him expectantly. "Are you going to go fight the dragon?"

Terrance turned back to Malcus and found that he couldn't take his eyes off the terrifying creature as his whole being filled with dread. It took him a moment to realize that someone had spoken to him. "Excuse me?"

"You're one of the good guys," Grace said. "So aren't you going to go slay that dragon?"

Daniel's eyes were fixed on him, too, the small child's fear fading. Terrance turned his gaze back to the creature that was so fearsome, he barely had the bravery to look directly at it, then back at the two children looking to him with so much hope. Terrance took a deep breath and said the only thing that made any sense: "Of course."

CHAPTER 41

Fear is your direction.

"Are you sure about this?" Vivian asked incredulously.

Terrance was not sure. In fact, he was absolutely terrified. He was so scared of Malcus that he wasn't sure he could gain enough control of his legs to move in the creature's direction, let alone slay him. And yet, he knew what he had to do. "If we're going to get to that gate, someone needs to bring down that dragon."

Vivian watched as Malcus hovered over the far end of the battlefield, near the fortress. "Do you have any idea how you'll do it?"

"Not yet," Terrance admitted. "But I once fixed a piece of code written in Fortran...and I didn't even know Fortran. It was scary and intimidating, but sometimes you just have to jump in there and figure things out." Putting it in coding terms made it seem slightly less daunting to Terrance, though intellectually he knew it was not an applicable analogy.

"Just...be careful," Vivian said, not hiding her worry at all anymore.

Terrance nodded, and through a great force of will, commanded his legs to carry him through the cave exit.

"Bye, Mr. Terrance!" Grace called to him as he left. "Good luck."

Terrance took one glance back at the children and gave them his best imitation of a confident smile, then set his eyes back on the doom ahead of him.

He ran as quickly as it seemed safe to do while holding a drawn sword (he assumed the scissors rule applied), trying to stay away from the battles raging around him. He tried to look for anyone he knew, and for a moment he thought he saw Talia's white cloak, but he saw mostly people he was unfamiliar with, men and women in normal everyday clothes, wielding swords and other weapons against demons and dark soldiers. He saw a number of those people fall to the enemy as he ran past, and he wondered about Karen out there in the midst of such carnage, having joined the fight only earlier that day. Of course, she seemed to take to the fighting much better than Terrance ever did.

He dodged past a few more battles, then saw a lanky demon ahead. It was at least eight feet tall, its limbs thin and spindly, with giant claws on each hand. A man lay dead at its feet, and it locked its red eyes on Terrance as it began to charge toward him, baring its maw of sharp teeth. "Oh, crap!" Terrance exclaimed as he swung his sword wildly to try to keep the thing back. The creature let out a terrible shriek, and a sword point suddenly appeared, sticking through its abdomen. The sword point was then withdrawn, and the thing turned to confront Curtis, who quickly stabbed it again. The demon collapsed to the ground.

"My kids?" Curtis asked.

Terrance kept a lookout on all sides, feeling exposed on the battlefield. "They're with Vivian—they're fine. She's lying low with them in a cave. How's the fight going?"

"We're barely holding our own; we won't last out here forever. We need to keep pressing toward the gate." Curtis pointed in that direction, but now the view of the gate was blocked by the giant Malcus, who stood guarding it. He sat on the ground, his massive wings folded around him, and he was almost like another fortress guarding the gate—not as large as the first but much more intimidating. "Apparently, we'll need to get through *that* thing somehow."

"Well...uh...that's what I was going to do. I was going to...slay that dragon."

Curtis looked more than a little unsure. "How do you plan on doing that?"

"Probably something involving this sword here." He pointed to the sword he had borrowed from Talia.

"It seems a bit suicidal to take that thing on without a plan."

"Yes, it does *seem* suicidal." Terrance stared at Malcus and was once again filled with overwhelming terror. "But it's what I'm doing. Someone needs to take it down, and I don't think we have time to write up a formal strategy."

Terrance noticed some movement further down the mountain. It was like a dark wave, but it was slowly moving uphill. He squinted, and could soon make out some detail in the moonlight: it was an army of soldiers—thousands and thousands of them. Terrance's heart sank. "They aren't coming to help us, are they?"

Curtis looked worried but still managed a slight smile. "There goes retreating as an option. We have to get to the gate, and soon." He looked back at Malcus. "If you say you think you can take the dragon down, then do it now. I never like to say something is impossible, but I don't think we'll last long once the Darkness's reinforcements get here."

Terrance looked at the army headed their way and then at the giant dragon, and wasn't sure which he feared more. No, he was pretty sure it was the giant, demonic, fire-breathing dragon. "Can you help me with this?"

Curtis continued staring at Malcus. "I can't even bring myself to get near that thing. Perhaps this is your fight, Terrance, if you honestly believe you can do something about that beast." Curtis turned to survey the battle around him. "We're already outnumbered here and we'll need to hold until Malcus is defeated. I'll handle that fight, and you do what you need to."

Terrance took one last uneasy look at the wave of soldiers steadily climbing up the mountainside, then turned his gaze to Malcus and the gate. "What lies beyond the gate?"

"Something that they very much want to guard," Curtis said, then ran from Terrance to clash with some cavefish charging toward them.

Terrance couldn't shake the feeling that this whole battle was doomed from the start, and that he had picked the most doomed part of it. He knew that it was the fear talking, though, and he commanded his legs to keep taking him toward Malcus, who got larger and larger as Terrance approached. As he ran, he could see more of the Infinite falling to the enemy on the battlefield. They had claimed to be beings of limitless power, but they looked weak and vulnerable compared to the armored enemy, and they were soon to be hopelessly outnumbered by the army heading up the mountain. And Terrance certainly did not feel powerful himself. But as he looked at Malcus in terror, there was also boiling inside him the notion that this thing must be destroyed.

The area around Malcus was clear, as it seemed that everyone, the Infinite and enemy alike, preferred to keep their distance from the terrible creature. As Terrance approached, he couldn't help but feel like a mouse holding a pin, trying to slay an elephant. Malcus observed the battle in front of him with its eight eyes, and Terrance realized that the dragon didn't even see him—he was too small to be of any notice. He crept closer until he was underneath Malcus's raised head, leaving him at little risk of being spotted. The part of Malcus nearest Terrance was its right front leg, which was covered in scales that looked like jagged chunks of obsidian, and the nails on the claw were each almost as big as Terrance. He looked up, and the rest of the body seemed to be covered in the same scales, with no soft spot to be found.

Slowly, Terrance reached with his sword toward one of the toes, to test exactly how strong the scales were. He poked one, but it felt like tapping a rock.

A warm breeze suddenly hit Terrance from above. His head shot up to see eight huge eyes staring down at him. Malcus's face split open, and the snake-like tongue hissed.

Terrance bolted. He could hear the thunder of Malcus's steps behind him, but it was only a short way to the fortress, and though Terrance had seen Malcus's fire burn through stone, he hoped the dragon wouldn't burn down his own fortress.

There was an open door ahead and Terrance dove through it, rolling as he hit the ground, the sword clattering to his side.

"Well if it isn't the mighty Ance."

Terrance looked up to see Shannon standing over him. He was in a large entryway, in which a stone chandelier hung from a high ceiling, glowing as though it contained lava. He scrambled to his feet and picked up his sword, but was careful not to hold it in too threatening a manner. "Hey."

Shannon's sword was still in its sheath. "Were you trying to fight Malcus?"

"Yeah, sorta."

She threw her hands in the air. "Are you insane?"

Terrance answered honestly. "Maybe."

Shannon scowled. "Do you people have any idea what you're even trying to accomplish here?"

"We're going to get through that gate you're guarding."

"And do what?"

"Um...I dunno. What's past the gate?"

Shannon rolled her eyes. "Things beyond the concern of your little minds. Well, it's no matter; reinforcements will soon be here and this will all be over, and you all will have accomplished nothing other than your own deaths." Shannon drew her sword. "And I will kill you personally."

"Really?"

Shannon nodded. "Yep."

Terrance readied his sword. "I don't want to have to hurt you."

Shannon sighed. "You can't, you idiot. Even if by some miracle you defeat me, I'll just come back. That's one of the many reasons this is pointless and you're all destined to lose."

"Your side seems very intent on making us give up," Terrance said. "But don't you see? We never will. We're not scared of you no matter what you throw at us. And that is why the Darkness is destined to lose. You didn't pick the more powerful side, Shannon. You picked the losers."

Shannon frowned, then raised her empty left hand. An invisible force smashed into Terrance, sending him backward and slamming him into a wall. Shannon's hand began to glow with a dark flame. Terrance ran for cover behind a pillar as fireballs flew toward him, singeing his clothes with near misses and exploding against the wall behind him.

"Come on, Ance!" Shannon yelled, walking toward the pillar he was hiding behind. "Show me a fight! You're supposed to be so much more powerful than us, and I'm waiting to be impressed."

Terrance looked toward the exit of the fortress, and could see something large moving out there. As he listened to Shannon's footsteps coming closer, he remembered what Talia had told him: *You just need to be what you are.* So he decided on the most 'Terrance' response to this situation. He ran.

There was a nearby stairway, and he headed for it as fast as he could as more fireballs flew his way, barely missing him. It was a curved stairway, so he was soon out of Shannon's view, but he could hear her cursing and running after him. Once again, Terrance wondered how he was helping anyone accomplish anything. This wasn't even high-quality running-away, because he knew that going up meant that eventually he was going to hit a dead end. And sure enough, the stairs soon ended, so he ran into a hallway and into the first room he saw. He dashed through the room, then finally hit the end of the line: a balcony overlooking the battlefield. He could hear Shannon close behind as he frantically searched for somewhere else to go. That's when he saw that just below him, Malcus was spewing dark flames at a nearby fight, indiscriminately incinerating forces from both sides. In the distance, Terrance could see the army still marching up the hill, ready to bring a quick end to the Infinite.

Shannon strode toward him, sword in one hand as the other glowed with a blackish-blue flame. She was frowning. "You want to give me a fight, at least?"

"Actually, I really don't have time for this. We'll talk later." Terrance raised his sword, and before he could think it through any further, he jumped off the balcony, down toward Malcus.

CHAPTER 42

Terrance's intention was to use the momentum of his fall to drive his blade into Malcus. However, it turned out to be quite difficult to aim a sword while falling through the air. He slammed into the dragon's back, his sword point glancing off the jagged scales.

Malcus lurched upward, and Terrance wrapped his left arm around one of the many spikes on Malcus's back while barely clinging to his sword with his right hand. Up, up into the night sky Malcus flew, toward the brightly shining full moon. Terrance didn't even want to look behind him to see how far down the battlefield now was. It was just him alone in the sky clinging to a stone-scaled dragon larger than a whale.

This was a really, really bad idea.

Malcus leveled out, and Terrance was no longer dangling from the dragon's back but could now get to his feet—though he wasn't sure how smart that would be, since the dragon could change course at any moment. And he couldn't even begin to imagine how he was supposed to harm Malcus from his current position anyway. Down below, he caught a glimpse of the massive movement of troops up the mountain toward the battlefield. Whatever Terrance was going to do, he had to figure it out soon.

Looking around, he saw movement out of the corner of his eye, and turned just in time to block a sword blow.

"Nice dragon-slaying, genius!" Shannon shouted at him over the wind rippling past. "What's your plan now?"

Very uneasily, Terrance took a few steps back, away from Shannon. "I was going to find its weak point and hit it for massive damage."

Shannon moved toward him. "This isn't a video game, you twit."

Terrance knelt down a little so he could hold on to one of the dragon's spikes for support while pointing his sword at Shannon. "No, this is you fighting on behalf of a super-evil demon dragon. Is nothing really clicking here, saying to you, 'Maybe I shouldn't be doing this'?"

"Says the guy who chose to leap with a tiny sword onto an invincible dragon!" Shannon was seething. "You didn't have to do any of this! You didn't have to make this your fight! We could have been happy together!"

Terrance shook his head. "No! There is no happiness down the path you chose! There is no happy ending where you just stand by and watch evil happen and do nothing to fight it!"

"We'll see how this ends!" Shannon leapt at him, swinging her sword. Terrance blocked it, but the blow was so strong, it knocked him off balance. He grabbed another of Malcus's spikes to keep from tumbling off. Shannon swung at him again, but this time he dodged and her sword clanged against one of Malcus's spikes like it had hit a metal pole. Terrance tried to counter, but Shannon kicked him, sending him onto his back. She swung down at him, but he got his sword up in time and their blades clashed together.

Shannon pressed her blade against his, teeth clenched and blonde hair flowing in the wind. Even when about to kill him, she was gorgeous. "Got any tricks up your sleeve, champ?" she growled. "Any green shells you've been holding on to?"

Terrance caught a glimpse of something moving near them. He turned a little to see a griffin fly past Malcus, and then something white tumbled into Shannon, knocking her over. Talia reached a hand down to Terrance and helped pull him to his feet. "I saw you jump on the dragon and thought maybe you would need some help."

"Good assumption."

Shannon was clinging to a spike, barely having kept herself from going over the edge. "You!" She screamed at Talia, then turned her glare to Terrance. "This is really who you left me for?"

"I told you, it's not like that," Terrance pleaded.

"We kissed only once," Talia said. "I thought it was a very good kiss, though."

Terrance turned to Talia. "That's not...that's not helpful right now."

"You're no longer leading him around by his lust," Talia told Shannon. "He's broken free of your wiles, you evil slut."

"That is *really* not helpful," Terrance growled at Talia.

With eyes full of fury, Shannon screamed and charged at Talia, who adeptly dodged and knocked Shannon away. She turned to Terrance and quickly shouted, "I'll handle her; you slay the dragon!" She returned to her fight with Shannon.

Yeah, just go ahead and slay the giant, invincible dragon we're standing on, Terrance thought as he looked around at Malcus. He could hear blades clanging together behind him, but he tried to concentrate on finding a vulnerable spot on the dragon. He tried stabbing between two scales, but the blade was deflected without even leaving a mark. So he moved forward, toward Malcus's head—a place he'd rather not go near, but he figured it was more likely to have a soft spot, since the creature's eyes couldn't be stone.

Malcus dove down, and Terrance held on tightly as his feet lifted up and dangled in the air. He glanced behind and saw Talia and Shannon in a similar situation near Malcus's back, each hanging on for dear life with one arm and swinging her sword at her opponent with the other. Malcus let out a roar, and Terrance turned to see the dragon's dark flames being spewed down on the battlefield before it lurched back upward.

Terrance had to hold on just as tightly again, his feet now dangling below him. He heard a scream, and looked over his shoulder to see Talia clutch a wound on her arm as her sword tumbled away. Shannon stabbed at her, but Talia let go of one spike to drop down and grab another one nearby; she missed and fell to Malcus's tail, grabbing a hold there. Shannon was ready to pursue the unarmed Talia for the kill, so Terrance let go and tried to slide down Malcus's back toward Shannon. It was not a clear path, and he ended up smacking into several spikes before becoming wedged between two of them. Shannon slid down toward Talia, and Terrance, now stuck, took the only option that appeared to remain and tossed the sword. It spun through the air and looked like it was about to strike Shannon, but she dodged to the side. Instead, it flew right to Talia, who reached up and grabbed it by the hilt, the sword now back to its true owner.

Malcus leveled out its flight and, after getting a foothold, Talia lunged, her sword piercing Shannon through the abdomen. Stuck together, they tumbled off the side of the dragon.

Terrance was now alone and swordless on the beast, but, wedged tightly between two spikes and thus with little risk of falling, he considered laying down his head and taking a nap to try to forget all of this. But the people below were counting on him, and though Terrance couldn't fathom what he was supposed to do, giving up was not an option. He pushed and freed himself from the spikes. Somehow, he would take this dragon down.

He ran up Malcus's back, then carefully made his way along the dragon's long neck until he was on its massive head, which was the size of an SUV. He climbed over the top until he saw Malcus's dark, spider-like eyes, which looked like maroon dinner plates. Now he just needed something to hit it with, and that's when he remembered. Terrance reached into his waistband and pulled out his Glock. Somehow, he had completely forgotten it during this whole battle, but for some reason it felt as useless bringing a gun to a battle of good and evil as bringing a knife to a gunfight. Plus, he was certain he really needed a permit to be carrying it this far from his home. Still, it was all he had, so he pointed it at the nearest eye and fired at point-blank range.

There was an ear-splitting scream, and then the sky darkened above Terrance. He looked up to see one of Malcus's giant paws coming down at him. He tried to dodge out of the way but had little room to move, and one of the claws snagged his shirt. Terrance was lifted up and flung into the air like a bug, his gun flying out of his hand.

The world was spinning. Judging by the quick glimpses Terrance caught of the dots moving around on the land below, he was thousands of feet in the air. Despite that, as he heard Malcus roaring below him, preparing for another attack, all he could concentrate on was somehow stopping that beast. It seemed impossible to think of how to accomplish such a feat, but as he hurtled out of control into the night sky, he realized how ridiculous the situation was. He was Terrance Denby, a programmer who specialized in web applications. And he was thousands of feet in the air fighting a giant monster while a battle between good and evil raged on the ground. He laughed a little, because it was so ridiculous. Logically, Terrance knew he was about to die, but he didn't let his mind dwell there because as Joyce had told him, that would be taking things way too seriously. Instead, he focused on something he was much more certain about: he was going to kill this stupid little dragon.

The upward momentum from Malcus's fling finally came to an end, and for the briefest moment, Terrance hung completely still in the air. Above him flickered the stars of the night sky, tiny lights of distant, unimaginable worlds. Suddenly, he saw something hurtling toward him. And almost as if he expected it, he reached out to receive his sword. He quickly unsheathed it as he began to fall back to earth head-first. Directly below him was Malcus, hovering over the battlefield, breathing fire. Terrance pointed the sword straight out ahead of himself and straightened his body so that he could plummet down onto the dragon like a missile. The wind tearing at his eyes made it hard to see, but Malcus was a very large target. He was moving with incredible speed, and his last thought before impact was that this was going to really, really hurt.

The sword point jammed into Malcus's head, cutting straight through scale and skull, as Terrance's body slammed into Malcus's neck. It was like getting hit by a truck. Terrance was dizzy and could barely tell what was happening, but he could feel Malcus lurch away. He held as tightly as he could to the sword, but it pulled free of the dragon's head. The last sight he saw as he fell to the ground was the giant beast flapping its wings wildly as it smashed through the fortress before crashing into and shattering the giant stone gate.

CHAPTER 43

Claws snapped around Terrance's torso before he could hit the ground. "Hold on!" yelled a voice that sounded like Talia's. Terrance was then roughly set down, tumbling a bit and finally losing his grip on his sword before coming to a stop. He looked up to see a griffin flying away. Terrance was now sore all over and a part of him wanted to stay lying down, but there was still much clamor surrounding him, and he knew couldn't just lie there while a battle raged and a massive army approached. Plus, it was finally time to see what lay beyond the gate. He got to his feet and saw the enormous, dark form of Malcus, lying motionless where the gate had been.

"Ain't so big, are ya!" Terrance shouted at Malcus. But Malcus still was quite big, though he was also quite dead. Terrance turned to the fortress and watched as the last bit of it tumbled over, no longer able to support its own structure after the damage it had received.

"Amidala!" came a cry from behind him.

Terrance turned to see Shannon standing there, staring worriedly at the crumbled fortress. He looked again at the giant pile of rubble and then back at Shannon. "I'm sure she's okay," he told her, but didn't really sell it.

Now her eyes locked on him, her face tense with rage. "What did you do?"

"Well...um...you said Malcus was invincible, but I guess not so much."

She roared and leapt onto Terrance, pinning him to the ground, then slapping his face over and over while shouting, "You stupid idiot! You mindless little—"

She was knocked off of Terrance by Talia, who wrestled her to the ground. Shannon grabbed Talia's hair and pulled, screaming incoherently the whole time.

Talia tried to turn away, slapping back at Shannon's face. Terrance ran over and pulled the two apart, realizing that stopping two people from fighting on a battlefield may have really been missing the point. He could see tears in Shannon's eyes as she staggered to her feet, then quickly turned and ran away.

"Man, this has been a really messy breakup." Terrance looked around the battlefield. The fighting was continuing, but now the Infinite were pressing toward the gate. And then he turned to see that the approaching army was almost upon them.

"She brought it on herself by aligning with the forces trying to destroy us," Talia said. "Have you seen my swords?"

Terrance shrugged. "No, but I found mine." He pointed to his sword lying nearby on the ground.

"Finally," Talia uttered before running off.

"We'd better get to the gate!" Terrance called out to her as he bent down to retrieve his sword. He briefly wondered what had happened to his gun, but he figured it was probably lost forever. Anyway, he didn't feel he had any use for it now that he had his sword back. Well, unless he were attacked by a mugger. Terrance smiled a little as he grasped his sword again, but as he got back to his feet, Chet was standing before him.

"You will have no victory, little man," Chet uttered. "Slaying Malcus accomplishes nothing, and there isn't anything beyond that gate that will save you fools."

"I guess we'll see about that."

"You will see nothing. You will simply watch as everything you treasure—"

Terrance sighed. "I get it; you're a huge douche. You don't have to keep reiterating it." Terrance's entire body ached and he really did not want a fight, but he also was not feeling the least bit scared of Chet. "Just shut up and swing your silly little axe."

Chet stood silently for a moment, then roared and charged. Terrance met the attack with a swing of his own, and Chet's axe blade flew off its handle. Chet was briefly startled, then spun around and ran away.

"Yeah! That's right!" Terrance shouted. "Run, you little twerp!" Terrance turned and saw that the army was now only a few yards away from him and charging. "Oh, crap."

These enemy forces appeared human but were well-armored, with skull-shaped helmets. Terrance chose the running option once again, but it did not turn out well, as he almost immediately tripped on a rock and fell. One of the soldiers was soon standing over him, pointing a sword down at Terrance's head. "Terr?"

It took a moment for Terrance to place the voice. "Lance?"

"You know this guy?" asked a female soldier standing next to Lance.

"Yeah, he's a coworker," Lance said. "Hey, Terrance, this is Carmen. I met her on the charge up the hill."

"Hey." Carmen waved at him with her hand that wasn't holding a jagged sword. "So isn't this weird...whatever is going on here?"

"What are you doing here, Lance?" Terrance shouted.

"Oh, well, these people were going around saying that there was big trouble up on this mountain and the whole world was threatened and they would make us into invincible warriors to fight back."

"It was a little confusing," Carmen said, "but everyone seemed to be going along. This is all kind of new, though; I mean, I'm an aerobics instructor. I've never even held a sword."

"Dammit, Lance!" Terrance yelled as he slowly pushed himself up off the ground. "Talia said if you didn't join us, you'd end up against us."

"Yeah, I guess she did. I didn't really take her seriously."

Terrance shrugged. "I guess I thought it was just bluster at the time, too."

"Who is Talia?" Carmen asked, then leaned close to Lance and said more quietly, "Are we supposed to stab this guy?"

Terrance was now surrounded by enemy soldiers. "Well...I kind of have to go," he said, but they didn't move.

Talia suddenly came bowling through the circle of soldiers, knocking a few of them over. She swung her two swords around menacingly, and the others backed off.

"I found my swords," Talia said.

"That's good; we should run."

"Agreed."

Terrance and Talia dashed away toward the dead Malcus and the remains of the stone gate, with the enemy soldiers in hot pursuit. Ahead, a group of cavefish tried to block their way, but Talia quickly stabbed two of them while Terrance cut down another.

"I think I'm getting better at this!" Terrance called out to Talia as they ran.

"Pat yourself on the back later!" Talia yelled back.

They were soon at the gate, and between Malcus's massive carcass and pieces of the giant stone gate, there was only enough space for a single person to fit through at a time. Terrance let Talia go first, then took one last glance back at the soldiers charging them before heading in after her to confront whatever lay beyond.

CHAPTER 44

A few dozen of the Infinite were standing before Terrance. The first he recognized was Krampsky, in his now-torn police uniform. They were in some sort of dark valley, with stone walls stretching far up above them. "Anyone else coming?" Krampsky asked.

Talia turned to face the small entrance they'd just come through, with her swords drawn. "I doubt it. That army was right behind us."

"The army was just regular people," Terrance said, facing the entrance as well, assuming that attackers would emerge at any moment. "It's like they just assembled everyone off the street to come after us."

Krampsky nodded. "They must have been desperate to stop us. Let's find out why."

It didn't seem like the enemy was coming through the gate, so Terrance turned back to the group to find his friends. He spotted Curtis standing with Karen, Donald, Felicia, and Travis. "I found my sword and slew Malcus," Terrance informed Curtis.

Curtis smiled. "Sorry I doubted you for even a moment. You've found yourself, I think."

Terrance looked around. "Where are Vivian and the kids?"

"She texted me; they're hiding in a cave," Curtis said. "I think they'll be okay for now."

"Did you see Erica?" Travis asked Terrance and Talia with desperation. "I lost track of her on the battlefield."

"I'm sorry...no," Terrance answered, now feeling guilty for bragging of his triumph.

"She's strong," Talia assured him. "She'll be okay."

"We can't go back," Curtis said. "The best way to help everybody is to move forward and put an end to all of this."

"Then let's do it," Travis urged. "Let's do it now." He took one last glance back at the entrance.

"Everyone ready?" Krampsky called out.

There was a collective shout in response, and the group marched forward, weapons drawn.

"So what's happening now?" Karen asked, holding her axe carefully.

"No idea," Donald answered. "We're in new territory."

"Quite literally," Felicia said, looking up at the sky. Terrance had noticed the sky as well; it wasn't a normal night sky, seeming to have thousands more stars than usual. Colorful nebulas were brightly visible, and there were even some planets, including gas giants that hovered nearby, much larger than the moon ever was. "Where do you think we are?" Terrance asked.

"Someplace they very much don't want us to be," Curtis answered.

They continued through the valley until the gate was far behind. Eventually, in the distance they could see a thin tower that was so tall, it seemed to never end but to simply disappear into the night sky. As they got nearer, they exited the valley and entered an enormous clearing. It was surrounded by steep cliffs, but cut into the cliffs were what appeared to be hundreds more pathways like the one they had just emerged from.

"I hope someone took note of the one we came out of," Donald said.

Everyone paused for a moment to wonder at the sight, but soon began moving again toward the obvious destination: the tower. It was light-colored, as though made of marble, and it was actually quite wide at the base, not as thin as they'd thought—just impossibly tall. A golden door was visible just ahead, so Krampsky led the way, then opened it.

As they headed inside the tower, it was immediately very familiar to Terrance. And there on a throne at the other end of the room sat the Caretaker.

"So you're here," he said, wearing another golden mask of an impassive face. "What now?"

Krampsky pointed his sword at the Caretaker. "You leave our world, and you take your evil with you."

The Caretaker floated off his throne and down toward them, chuckling softly. "Or what?"

"Or we destroy you," Krampsky answered.

The Caretaker was silent a moment. "Okay, I choose destruction. Go ahead and destroy me; I'm terribly curious to discover how you plan to accomplish that."

There was silence. As Terrance had suspected, no one did have an idea of how to destroy the Caretaker. Finally, Talia cried out and charged, stabbing the Caretaker with both swords. All that accomplished was to cause his robe to rustle, as there was nothing solid to stab.

"I believe I have already explained my noncorporeal existence to most of you," the Caretaker said, "so this is a rather useless battle. You cannot remove me—which is good, because there is no world without me. As I've explained many times, everything collapses without my intervention."

"Surely you can tell by now that we're not interested in the lies you feed us," Curtis answered. "We want to be free of you, and we will not stop fighting until that happens. We will not just sit still and perish."

The Caretaker laughed. "Then I guess you'll perish by more active means. Weren't there more of you when this started? What do you think happened to your dead?"

The Infinite were silent for a moment. Finally, Krampsky spoke up. "We do not know for sure, but—"

"Yes, you do know," the Caretaker interrupted, anger in his voice. "They're gone. Forever. You know this in your hearts despite whatever nonsense you've bought into. If you only had my perspective and could see the destruction left in the wake of the entities you know as faeries. Whole worlds destroyed. After we rid your realm of those creatures, I thought perhaps we could bring your world back to order in a peaceful way."

"You mean by your forces attacking us constantly to try to cow us into submission?" Curtis asked bitterly.

"Yes, it doesn't seem that peaceful to you," the Caretaker said. A hint of malice seeped into his voice. "But believe me, there are much, much harsher ways of dealing with you."

"Bring your worst!" Talia shouted. "You are less than nothing to us, and we don't fear your power."

The Caretaker chuckled. "It will not be me who shall deal with you now. That you are here means I have failed. So another comes."

Terrance tried to imagine whom this might be, and he could see from the expressions of the others that this was new information to them, as well. Karen looked particularly confused. "Aren't you the so-called Adversary guy behind all of this?" she asked.

The Caretaker floated toward her. "I'm guessing you all think that. By the way, we haven't met yet, Karen Hunter. I am the Caretaker of your world and of countless others. I'm sure that on your way in here, you saw the other pathways to my tower. Each one of those leads to another universe that I am in charge of. But in the scheme of things, I am what I believe is called middle management in your world."

"If you're not in charge," Krampsky said, "then bring us to whoever is. Bring us to the one behind this all, and we'll deal with him."

The Caretaker laughed. "You have no idea what you're asking. This is like a bacterium demanding an audience with the president. That which you ignorantly call the Adversary is a being completely beyond you—so far above you that you could scream your feeble words up at him and they would never reach his hearing. I know that you imagine this evil entity plotting machinations against you and feeding off of your 'infinite selves' or whatever lunacy you've settled on, but the one in charge of this all is no more aware of your world than a man who owns a beach house is aware of each grain of sand on his property."

The Caretaker floated back a bit from the group. "Or I should say, he *was* not aware. Victory is yours, people. You have his attention. He is coming. And when he arrives and finishes with you, I assure you that despite all your bravado, you will finally have no more will left to fight." The Caretaker floated back to his throne. "We are done here. You can show yourselves out. If you wish to meet your adversary, simply take the pathway straight ahead and return to your realm. My forces will stand down now; you won't have to worry about them. No, they certainly are not what you should be worrying about."

They all stared silently at the Caretaker.

"Or stay here and keep pointlessly trying to stab me," the Caretaker added. "I have nothing but time."

"All right," Krampsky said, "if the Adversary is coming to our world, we will go meet him." He led the way back out of the tower.

"Should we have left him there?" asked a woman whom Terrance didn't know. She wore an apron and looked as though she'd come to the battle after a shift at a supermarket. "It seems like we should have done more to try to destroy him."

"He has no real power over us and is not worth worrying about," Curtis answered. "Let's finally confront the true evil behind this."

"And then what?" Karen asked. "What do we know about him?"

"Well, obviously not much," Donald said with a rueful laugh. "Most of us thought the Caretaker *was* him."

"He did say that the forces of the Darkness were going to stand down," Felicia said. "Maybe we can find who we're missing when we get out there." She looked pointedly at Travis and Curtis.

"Hopefully, she's waiting out there," Travis said, managing an unconvincing smile.

Karen looked worried. "But what do you think this Adversary is going to do to us?"

There was no answer, and Terrance figured everyone was as clueless about this as he was. The threat was not to kill them but to rob them of their will to fight, and he shuddered at all the things he could imagine that meant.

"We may not know exactly what lies ahead," Curtis said, "but we know we'll be fine. He can't do anything of lasting significance to us, no matter how much power he pretends to have."

"They are all kind of a broken record with that power-beyond-our-comprehension stuff," Terrance commented.

"Okay, we will resist him, but then what?" Karen asked. "Can we defeat him?"

"We *are* defeating him," Talia answered. "That's why he'll be coming to put on some big show to try to scare us away from the fight. But we can't be defeated, because our power is unending. He, on the other hand, no matter how large and powerful he seems, is a finite being. If he must use his power to try to crush us, then he is that much more weakened. And we will keep fighting until we force his hand again. As long as we continue this battle no matter what, he will one day have no power left, and will finally be defeated."

Karen looked somewhat assured. "And how long will that take?"

Talia shrugged. "It will take as long as it takes. The important thing to remember is to always keep fighting. We lose only if we decide to lose. If we never give up, then our victory is assured."

They reached the gate and the motionless, spiky corpse of Malcus, and carefully made their way through one by one. Back outside the crumbled fortress, the forces of the Darkness were still milling about but no longer looked ready to attack. In front of them stood Despina, who stared at the Infinite angrily as they emerged from the rubble. "Find what you were looking for?" she asked in a mocking tone.

"We were looking for the Adversary," Krampsky said, "and he is coming here."

"Yes," Despina said, her anger fading into what looked more like fear. "I can tell."

It was then that Terrance noticed that something was a bit wrong with the world. All the stars in the sky twinkled rapidly as if in a panic, the full moon began to take on a reddish hue, and there was a slight shudder in the earth as if it were having trouble holding itself together. There was a sense of doom in the air, almost weighing Terrance down under its enormity.

"You've destroyed everything," Despina continued. "I guess you call that victory, but you will soon know fear and suffering like you have never—"

"Daddy!"

Curtis's kids broke through the straggling forces of the Darkness and ran toward their father. Behind them were Vivian and others of the Infinite who hadn't made it to the gate. They all ignored Despina and went to each other.

"Erica?" Travis called out, searching desperately through the crowd.

"Here!" Erica answered, hobbling near the back of the group, clutching her arm. Travis ran to her and held her tight. "Ow," she gasped. "Sorry, I got surrounded, so I ended up surrendering, since this new army that came isn't exactly a kill-happy group. Actually, I met a girl in the army who works at this vintage clothing store I hadn't heard of. I might want to check it out if"—she stared up at the sky—"if the world isn't ending or something."

Curtis finished hugging his children, then embraced his wife. She smiled at him but didn't hide well the worry in her face. "What happened in there?"

"The Caretaker was not the Adversary," Curtis answered, "but the Adversary is now coming to crush us...or something."

Vivian took a deep breath and looked up, as if the sky might fall on them at any moment. "Almost hoping for a little bit of a break from all this."

"Can we get ice cream?" Grace asked, apparently not picking up on any of the doom.

Vivian tore her gaze away from the sky and smiled at her children. "I don't see any reason why not."

"Can I get two scoops?" Daniel asked.

"You can't eat two whole scoops," Curtis said in a teasing tone.

"I can!"

"I guess we'll see." He turned to address the rest of the Infinite. "We will see you all...later, I guess."

"Hard to know what the future brings," Krampsky answered. "But we will meet up again one day, of that I am sure. Good fighting."

"Same to you all." Curtis headed off with his family, and most of the remaining Infinite began to depart.

"I'd better get home," Felicia said. "I have a paper due tomorrow."

"Will there be a tomorrow?" Karen asked.

Felicia shrugged. "If there is, and I don't have the paper, I'll get a zero. I'll see you guys later." She took another glance at the ominous sky. "In this world or another."

"Good luck with the paper," Terrance said as she headed off.

"So how long will it take for the Adversary to get here?" Erica asked.

"No idea." Travis said. "I think he wants us to have time to properly dread his arrival, or something."

Erica laughed. "Yeah, that sounds about right." Her smile faded a bit as she looked at the sky again.

"Hey, uh, Karen," Donald said, looking nervous, but not because of the doom enveloping them, "you want to maybe get a bite to eat?"

Karen eyed him suspiciously. "Is this one of those 'The world is going to end, so we might as well—'"

"No. No! Just food...if you don't have plans." He looked at the others. "You guys can come, too."

"Food sounds good," Erica said.

"I'm in," Travis added.

Talia shrugged. "I'm not that hungry."

Terrance glanced at Talia. "I guess I'm not really, either, but you guys have fun."

Donald, Karen, Travis, and Erica headed off together as one of the soldiers of the Darkness approached. Lance.

"Who's that with Karen?" he asked Terrance.

"Does it really matter?"

Lance gazed up at the sky. "So what's happening? It kind of feels like the world is ending."

"The Adversary is coming for those who oppose him," Talia said. "So you'll probably be fine."

Carmen came up behind Lance with her helmet off, looking scared. "Do your friends know what's going on? No one seems to know what's going on."

"It looks like the world is ending," Lance told her.

Carmen's eyes grew wide.

"You probably shouldn't be alone during this," Lance told her. "Hey, why don't we go get some drinks?" He put his arm around her, and they walked off.

"Your friend is not a good person," Talia said.

Terrance grimaced. "Who is?"

"Well, some try harder at it, at least."

Terrance looked at Talia. There was just a bit of worry creeping into her normal resolve. "So...what are your plans?"

Talia stared back at him with suspicion. "I'm not going to have sex with you because everyone thinks the world is ending, if that's what you're thinking."

Terrance sighed. "Know what? I have this video game at my apartment I've been really wanting to play. Might be a good time for that."

Talia almost frowned. "You want to be alone?"

Terrance shook his head. "No."

"I don't like video games."

"Of course you don't." It felt like the shaking in the ground was growing heavier. He looked up at the stars, and they weren't only blinking rapidly but now seemed to be swaying. "Want to walk? Let's at least get away from the dead dragon and demon soldiers and whatnot."

"Okay. Let's walk."

They had made it only a short distance away when a familiar voice called out, "What are you two up to?"

It was Shannon, her face a mix of bitterness and worry. A few yards behind her stood Lacey and Chet. Terrance regarded them cautiously, then turned to Shannon. "Just walking to clear our heads. The Adversary is coming and is going to crush us or some nonsense."

"Not nonsense," Shannon said. "You have no idea what's going to happen to you."

"And what does it matter to you?" Talia asked. She motioned to the people behind Shannon. "You chose your side. Nothing to worry about for you; perhaps the

Adversary will bring you a nice present wrapped in a pretty bow for your loyalty. But when you open it, you'll find the box empty—same as all his other promises."

Shannon stared angrily at Talia, but again Terrance noticed a little more in her expression. "Are you scared?" he asked.

"Of course I'm scared!" Shannon shouted. "You fools broke the world! We have no idea what's happening now! This affects everyone, not just you. And we don't know what the approach of the ruler of the Darkness will bring."

"We stand against him, that's what," Terrance said. "You can, too."

Shannon laughed, though there was no mirth in it. "Oh yes, I'll switch to the side against the all-powerful entity just in time to be one of those in the path of its wrath!"

"It would show him we don't fear him," Terrance said.

Shannon frowned. "The fear is all over your face." For a moment, it looked like she had something more to say, but she turned and headed back to her chosen company.

Terrance and Talia continued on their walk, taking a faded path that led down the mountain. Talia turned to him. "You do look scared."

"I'm guessing that has something to do with how I feel really scared." Terrance took his glasses out of the hard case in his pocket to get a better look at the sky. It was no longer black but a sort of purple, while the stars shone even brighter as they flickered. Terrance could also feel that the trembling of the earth had increased. "I never quite had the confidence in this that you do, that we're some sort of powerful beings who can't be defeated."

"And yet here you are, ready to oppose the Darkness and all that controls it."

"Yeah...well...I guess I just want to believe it can be defeated."

She took his hand in hers. "It can. You know that. We all do. Somewhere deep inside the *real* us that doesn't reside only in this world."

Terrance smiled at her, but he could see fear in her, as well. As they moved further along the mountain, away from the fortress, the land looked less barren and foreboding. There were grass and trees bathed in a blue light from the odd sky. Terrance saw a big rock and sat on it, and Talia took a seat next to him. He stared up at the red moon and could almost swear that it was revolving. "He's going to be here soon," Terrance said. "I can feel it."

"Quite soon," another voice answered. "So I am out of here."

Terrance turned to see Beauregard standing next to him. "Out of here to where?"

"I believe you saw the pathways to other realms," Beauregard answered. "I have many choices of worlds that are not about to be destroyed. You know, I told you people this would happen, but no one ever listens to me."

"We're not about to be destroyed," Talia insisted.

"Fine. Ignore the obvious. Luckily, I'm used to traveling to other realms, so it won't affect me."

"What are in these other realms?" Terrance asked.

"That's not a simple question," Beauregard said. "We're talking radically different universes. Places beyond your comprehension."

Terrance rolled his eyes. "Yes, I know; everything is beyond my comprehension." He thought for a moment. "Are there others like us fighting against the evil in those realms?"

Beauregard snorted. "Oh yes, but none yet with this rousing level of success. Have fun dealing with the Adversary in person."

Talia's interest was piqued, as well. "Can you get in contact with them? Maybe we can join forces."

"This isn't like some sci-fi alternate-universe thing," Beauregard said, "where it's just like here but everyone is wearing cowboy hats. They are places that differ from this one in ways your brain wouldn't even be able to process. Entirely different constants rule their physical laws...if they even have physics."

"Well, it's hard to accept that there are others opposing the Adversary and we can't do anything together," Terrance said. He thought for a second. "Can we...at least send them a message?"

"What you mean is, can *I* deliver them a message," Beauregard said. "I'm not your errand boy."

Terrance looked him right in the eyes. "Please. If you can move between realms, you need to help."

He laughed again. "Need? You think I want the Adversary's wrath? Still...I guess a single message won't hurt."

Terrance turned to Talia. "What should we tell them?"

"I'd recommend, 'Don't oppose the Adversary, or you'll get destroyed like us,'" Beauregard said.

Talia ignored the elf. "We need to tell them what we've learned so far. What we know about the power of the enemy, the Caretaker, the—"

"Whoa whoa whoa," Beauregard interrupted. "You need to keep it simple. And I mean really, really simple. Again, we're talking radically different universes here. You give me too much, it will get lost in translation. The best I can pass on would be a single simple statement."

"One statement?" Talia exclaimed. "What knowledge can we pass with that?"

Terrance considered it. He had defeated a giant dragon and finally come into his own against the forces of the Darkness, but he wasn't overwhelmed by any great sense of accomplishment. Instead, he just felt comfortable, like this was what he should be doing. "Tell them that...that they have to understand what they truly are. They have to remember that they are more than what they seem."

Beauregard was silent a moment. Finally, he nodded. "I can work with that. I'll get it to who needs it. Have fun with the end of the world, you two." And the little elf walked off, disappearing into some nearby brush.

Terrance and Talia sat silently, nothing left to say as the earth continued to shake beneath them and the sky shuddered above. He could feel her gripping his hand tighter, and he squeezed back.

And then it arrived. The sky turned red and the stars disappeared. All before them was pulsating red, with blackness at the center. It took a while for Terrance to understand what he was seeing, but soon it became obvious. It was an eye—a single eye so large it filled the entire view of the sky. He could tell there was more to the creature, but it was so enormous that the rest of it was beyond their sight. As the eye stared down on them, Terrance was filled with such an oppressive dread that he had to fight to not collapse to the ground. He looked over at Talia, and tears were streaming down her face. She turned to him and briefly regained some composure. She nodded, and he nodded back. Then, hand in hand, they stood up, facing the creature immense beyond anything they could even attempt to imagine. Terrance drew his sword and pointed it at the Adversary. With great force of will, he uttered, "Bring it!"

And the world shattered beneath them.

EPILOGUE

An ear-piercing noise jolted Terrance out of unconsciousness, leaving him disoriented and confused.

"No bad noise." A hand weakly slapped Terrance on the face. "Stop bad noise."

He pulled himself from the bed and turned off the alarm clock. He looked at Shannon, who still lay there, her head buried in a pillow. "You need to get up, too, you know."

She grunted and reached out with one hand, blindly waving it in the air in an attempt to slap Terrance again.

Terrance headed to the kitchen and fumbled with the coffeepot, then plopped down on the couch and stared at the turned-off TV. Something was bothering him, but he had trouble putting his finger on it.

Shannon came in and sat down beside him, dressed only in panties and his Legend of Zelda T-shirt. "What's wrong, Ance?"

"Nothing...just had a weird dream last night." He leaned back. "I was a warrior or something, fighting evil."

"Ooh. Sounds like a neat dream. Was I in it? Did you have to rescue me?" She frowned. "You'd better not have rescued some other woman."

"You were in it. But you were actually like...a demon warrior fighting on the side of evil."

"What? Is that some crack about my being in law school?"

"No, it was"—Terrance thought for a moment; it seemed like there were some important details from the dream that he was forgetting—"just a dream."

"Well, I don't like it. If you have any more dreams, you make sure I am a good guy in them and am awesome." She shook her fist at him. "Or I will wallop you. I will punch you so hard, you will spit out blood and teeth and you will forever after be deformed and ugly."

"You're taking this a bit too far," Terrance said.

She stuck out her tongue at him, and he smiled at her. He didn't know what he was worrying about. Everything was fine. Great, even.

* * *

Terrance actually got out the door early. He wasn't sure why; he just had a constant feeling that he was after something. Something *important*. Nothing he could put his finger on, though. He listened to a rock station as he drove to work, and a news break mentioned a woman who had been shot while holding her baby. The woman had died, though the baby was fine but motherless. It was the sort of violence Terrance was used to hearing about every day and that usually rolled off him like water off a duck's back, but this time a sadness suddenly gripped him. There was so much violence and hate that he heard about constantly, but now that he thought about how numb he was to it, it made him a bit disturbed.

The news ended and music started playing, and Terrance went back to focusing on his drive. But when he got to the small, forested area he passed through every day, he slowed as he neared that unmarked road that he had always seen but didn't know where it went. He was extra curious about it today for some reason, and since he was early, he went ahead and turned onto it. The tree-lined road twisted further into the woods, going on for several yards until it stopped at a small clearing of dirt. Terrance parked his car and got out. Ahead were a few more trees, and through them he could see the back of a large building. Running the map of the area through his head, he figured it was a Home Depot. So, there was the mystery of that road; nothing special about it.

He noticed movement on a nearby tree trunk. A tiny ladybug scuttled up the bark to purposes unknown, though it seemed quite intent in its actions. Terrance then spotted a mushroom growing near the base of the tree. It was a perfectly sculpted little white umbrella. It was something so simple, yet Terrance realized how unbelievably complex it was, as well. It arose out of the ground in the shade of a tree, somehow feeding and tending itself and taking on its perfect shape with no knowledge or help.

Near the mushroom, ants scurried about, each working independently yet all with a similar goal. They were a whole community working together, and like the mushroom, they had simply arisen out of the ground. A long time ago, there were no such things as ants, and somehow they came to be as they were now—fully formed creatures, each working toward a purpose.

Terrance looked up at the trees towering above him, green leaves rustling in the wind. These enormous things had each started as a tiny seed, yet somehow had grown to their enormous size using nothing more than the material they found in the soil and the air and the rain that fell from the sky. It seemed almost absurd to him that this was possible.

Terrance shook the thoughts from his head. These were all ordinary things, things that he saw all the time and never paid much attention to. The only absurd thing was the strange, sudden interest he had in them. He went back to his car and headed to work.

* * *

At work, Terrance trudged to the break room and filled his mug with coffee. Karen walked in with her usual frown. He met her eyes, and for a brief time they stared at each other. There was some thought just out of Terrance's grasp that he knew was sitting in his mind, but he couldn't fathom what it was. He turned away from Karen before things got awkward, and left wordlessly as she went to the fridge.

He paused at the aisle to his cubicle to sip his coffee, taking a moment to look at the window at the far end and the light shining through it—light that had just finished traveling millions of miles in its journey from its source. He headed to his chair, moved his mouse to wake his computer, entered his password, and opened a browser. On the home screen were some news highlights, including a mention of some new slaughter over in Africa. It was the kind of news story Terrance usually never gave a second thought to, but this time he stared for a moment at the image of a crying child standing in a war-torn area. *What is wrong with the world?*

Terrance shook the thought from his head and minimized the browser. The background of his desktop was of some rural landscape—or, to be more precise, a series of small colored squares creating an approximation of a rural landscape. His screen was made up of millions of these little squares being constantly redrawn sixty times a second at the command of the processors inside the computer. It was only a hundred years or so ago that humans were just figuring out how to use electricity to light a room, and now it was dancing around at their command, calculating math equations and playing cat videos for people all across the world.

"You're staring at your computer screen like a weirdo."

Terrance turned to see Lance standing at the cubicle entrance. "Just having a weird day."

"Problems in bed?"

Terrance shook his head. "No. Why do you always go there?"

"You just seem like the sort of guy who would have problems in bed."

"Thanks, Lance. This is a good talk. But no, everything is good." Terrance moved around his mouse pointer as if to prove to himself there was nothing special about it—nothing worth contemplating. "Everything is great."

* * *

At lunch, nothing seemed appealing to Terrance, so he left the office building and wandered around downtown. A long time ago, this area was dirt and grass, and now structures made from stone and steel and glass blocked the sky. To someone a hundred years ago, these sights would be amazing beyond belief, but now these buildings were commonplace. Boring.

He looked straight up at the blue dome above him. It was a beautiful day, with a few clouds drifting in the sky. The clouds were the size of mountains, yet they floated effortlessly through the air. Peeking out from behind one of the clouds was the sun—an immense inferno so hot that even though it was millions of miles away, Terrance could feel its heat. It was so bright that it lit up the entire world.

A car horn honked, and Terrance looked down to see two cars stuck at an intersection and a driver yelling profanities. Eventually, one car screeched off in rage. It was a common display of anger—not even directed at him—and yet he felt bothered for some reason.

Terrance walked to a nearby vendor to get a hot dog and a Mountain Dew. He looked around for a place to sit and eat, and there was a bench nearby on which sat a young woman in a gray suit, eating a salad. He sat on the side of the bench furthest away from her and began to eat his hot dog. He glanced again at the woman; she had large, doe-like eyes that were intently gazing at something in front of her. He followed her gaze to a squirrel that sat in a small tree, apparently staring back.

"I never trusted squirrels," Terrance said.

The woman slowly turned to look at him. "Do I know you?"

"Uh...no. Sorry." He took a bite of his hot dog.

"I didn't mean I was offended by your talking to me. It's just a woman alone has to be careful of men approaching her. But you don't look like a rapist."

Terrance chuckled. "Thanks. That means a lot."

"I just meant it doesn't look like you're someone who could easily overpower women."

"Less thanks, I guess."

She cocked her head a bit, studying Terrance. "Maybe I've seen you around here."

"Well, I work around here. I'm a programmer. My name is Terrance."

"I work around here too. I'm a CPA." She hesitated. "Talia." She looked back at the squirrel.

That seemed to be the end of the conversation, so Terrance went back to eating and watching the squirrel. It just sat there, sniffing the air.

"Why are we here?"

Terrance turned to the woman. "Huh?"

She was still looking ahead at the squirrel. "That was it. There was no more to the question."

"Then, I guess my answer would be: I don't know. Maybe there is no reason. Maybe we just are."

She nodded. "It doesn't feel like that, though, does it?"

"Sometimes"—Terrance thought for a second—"it feels like we're in a dream...but every so often our mind wakes up and we realize it's a dream." Terrance grimaced. "I am rambling. I must seem like a weirdo."

"Yes. Somewhat." Talia stared at him. "Are you hitting on me?"

"No, I...have a girlfriend. I don't know what I'm doing. I'm having a weird day."

"And what is a normal day?" Talia closed her salad container and stood up. "See you around, Terrance." She walked away as the squirrel scampered down the tree.

* * *

Terrance made his way back to his cubicle. Before entering, he stopped to look at the cubicle walls. They were made of some sort of fabric that was held together by a frame of hard metal that was somehow made into the perfect shape. It was then lined with plastic—a moldable material that was extremely common, yet Terrance had no idea how it was made. This cubicle wall represented years—millennia—of humankind's knowledge about manufacturing, culminating in these simple barriers that people never usually paid any notice.

"You're being weird again," Lance whispered, walking up behind Terrance.

"Yeah, it's just..." Terrance went into his cubicle and sat down, trying to bring words to his thoughts. "You ever think about how amazing our existence is?"

Lance sipped his coffee. "What do you mean?"

"Just...everything. It's like so much of the world we're just used to and walk by without ever really looking at it, but pretty much everything around us is just amazing when you really stop and see it." He now felt like this important idea was hanging nearby, almost in his grasp. "And there are awful things, too...things we're used to ignoring as well...and...and...well, I don't know. It feels like I need to do something, yet I'm just here, not doing anything."

Lance nodded thoughtfully as he took another sip of coffee. "Are you smoking something? I never thought you were cool enough to do drugs."

Terrance slouched in his chair. "Just having a really weird day."

"You're a really weird guy. But if you want my advice, don't freak out about normal everyday stuff, because that would make you insane."

Terrance nodded and Lance continued on his way. Terrance stared at his computer screen, trying again to put his thoughts together. Everything was normal...same as the day before and the day before that, and he had never felt like this in the past. Maybe it was the dream he'd had that morning, he thought, but most of the details of that were quite faded, and he could recall almost none of it, other than a *feeling*. A feeling of purpose.

Terrance went over things logically in his mind: he had a job he liked and a great girlfriend. There was no big thing missing from his life—certainly nothing he could comprehend and put into words. Whatever was happening to him today, it was just an odd feeling that would pass—he was certain of that.

He brought up the code he was working on. Once again he pored through it to try to understand the old legacy code. It was filled with cryptically named variables and unused functions—a complete mess to try to understand and debug. But diving into it certainly took his mind off things. Code all followed a certain logic—though this code seemed to be trying its best not to. Still, he knew that if he scrutinized it closely enough, it could be understood. Code could always be understood—the mystery could always be solved. It was nice that way.

Trying to follow the logic of the code, Terrance eventually found what he was almost certain was an unreachable section of the program. He wondered what it was for, but it was as indecipherable as the rest of the code. Some of the variable names almost looked like the programmer had just mashed the keyboard. It was more than a page full of complicated-looking junk, but scrolling through it, Terrance finally spotted one comment:

TODO: remember who you are.

Terrance's right hand went to his hip, reaching for something that wasn't there—but something that he knew should be. All the while, he kept staring at the simple bit of text on the screen, filled with a strange but absolute certainty that this message was meant for him.

ACKNOWLEDGEMENTS

First off, I'd like to thank my wife, the lovely and talented SarahK, for all her support and ideas. I would get nowhere without her. I'd like to thank all the beta readers, including my sister, Sarah E. Fleming, Charlie Hodges, Steve Horth, HCG, Kevin Edwards, Seth Morris, and Mark Sizer. And thanks to all the readers of my blog, IMAO, who have encouraged and helped my writing.

Thank you to Rachel Lucas for editing the novel and for the ideas she contributed. I'd also like to thank Steven King, as I read his book On Writing before starting on this, and while I didn't quite follow his writing method completely, I think trying some of his approach added to the novel. And thanks to Adam Bellow, David Bernstein, Elena Vega, and the rest of Liberty Island for first getting this novel out there to everyone.

Thank you to my parents, who have always encouraged me and helped shape who I am. Also thank you to my in-laws, who have always supported me, with a special thanks to Patrick O'Neall, who was very encouraging when he read my first novel but has sadly since passed away. I'd also like to thank my kids, even though they get in the way of my writing more than anything, but are still an inspiration.

And finally, thank you to God, who always makes sure life is a grand adventure as long as we take the time to see the world as it is.

ABOUT FRANK J. FLEMING

Frank J. Fleming is a novelist and a scripted creator for *The Daily Wire*. He has also written satire books, wrote approximately 666 articles for *The Babylon Bee*, and wrote columns for *The New York Post*, *USA Today*, and *The Washington Times*. Frank is a Carnegie Mellon University graduate and used to be a really good electrical and software engineer back when he was inclined to have a more useful occupation than writing. He lives in Austin with his wife and four kids and is a really cool dude.

Subscribe to his Substack at FrankJFleming.com to get writing updates, short stories, and other fun content.

www.ingramcontent.com/pod-product-compliance
Lightning Source LLC
Chambersburg PA
CBHW071129200626
46817CB00018B/2508